Clash of Empires

THE MALLORY SAGA
Book 1

Paul Bennett

1

Dedicated to the memories of:

Jonas Segal – teacher extraordinaire – Cass Technical High School, Detroit, Michigan
Milton Covensky – history professor – Wayne State University
Jack Bennett – my father, a gentle man who loved to talk about history with his son.

Printed in the United States of America
First Printing, 2016
Hoover Books
mallorysaga@gmail.com

Acknowledgments

In the beginning, there was curiosity. This led to a search for more Roman-era historical fiction, a search that led to the novel Marius Mules 1, by S.J.A. Turney. After finishing the third volume, I overcame my reluctance, and opened a Twitter account for the express purpose of contacting Mr. Turney. Since that initial encounter, I have formed electron-based friendships with a bevy of authors, reviewers, and fellow travelers from around the world. In addition to a bounty of excellent books, I gained from them the confidence to take on blank page and let loose the Muse inside, resulting in this - my first novel. I owe a big thanks to the following (and I'm sure I'll forget someone): Simon James Atkinson Turney, Gordon Doherty, Debby Foulkes, Prue Batten, Hannah Methwell, Rob Hagar Bayliss, Robert Southworth, Glynnie, Kate Quinn, Stephanie Dray, Stephen A. McKay, Matthew Harffy, Anna Belfrage, R.S. Gompertz and all of those who may find a hint of themselves in the parentheses.

Regarding whatever innate talent I may have, I must give a big thank you to my ninth grade English teacher at Jackson Junior High School in Detroit, Michigan. Mrs. Winkler managed to coax, and at times coerce, my imagination – she taught me how to read a book, and also how to write. I wrote my very first fiction in her class. It was a science fiction account of some elephant-like aliens who helped mankind survive some sort of predicament. I don't remember much but, one detail remains with me; probably because it exhibits the wit and humor I try to employ in my writing. The ending to the elephant/alien story revealed, 'and they worked for peanuts.'

I developed, early on, the habit of not liking to change the first version of whatever it was I was writing – whether that was a letter, a school paper or exam, or some piece of creative authoring. Somewhere during the process of writing Clash, I realized that I was not a good enough editor, and I would have to suffer the indignity of someone who was good enough to, and was capable of, critiquing, changing, and cajoling me into making Clash even better. Thank you, Marguerite Walker II, for doing those things, even though there were times, after reading your comments/advice that I blurted out words you don't read in the Bible.

While it was my Muse who inspired the words, fueled on coffee and the likes of Within Temptation and Loreena McKennitt coming through my headphones, it was a group of old friends from Detroit who undertook the mission to encourage this oft-discouraged writer. They read what I wrote, and actually liked it. So, Chuck, Ralph and Debby, thanks for keeping me on track.

TABLE OF CONTENTS

Chapter List

Prologue

June 15, 1749 – November 30, 1749

The governor of New France, the Marquis de la Galissoniere, appointed the former garrison commander at Crown Point and Detroit (Pierre-Joseph Celeron de Blainville) to mount an expedition into the disputed territory of Ohio. Celeron's goals were twofold. His first, to plant engraved lead plates bearing the French monarch's crest, and claim the area for King Louis XIV of France. However, no one, including Celeron, believed that the lead plates would keep the British from trying to claim the land for themselves.

The second purpose was removal of any Englishmen he encountered, and to make it easier to convince the Indians to ally with France. With a force of 213 men, he could easily send any English trapping party on their way out of the disputed area - but that size of force was not enough to convince the many Indians drawn to the English to switch to the French.

The French reached the Miami village at Pickawillany of La Demoiselle, well known to the British as Old Briton, Even after ordering Old Briton to leave the area and to cease doing business with the English traders, Celeron realized the futility of the situation. That evening, sharing a glass of wine with Captain Henri LeBlanc (his second in command) before retiring for the night, Celeron exclaimed, "I do not understand the stubborn behavior of these Indians. Why they continue to cling to the English does not make any sense! The English do not have the will to enforce their ridiculous claims in this territory."

May 28, 1754

The Virginia colony dispatched a party of Virginia Militia to investigate French activity around the Fort Duquesne area (modern day Pittsburgh, Pennsylvania), led by Lieutenant Colonel George Washington. He learned from Seneca Chief Tanaghrisson that thirty-five French troops were camped in a nearby ravine. Washington decided to investigate; while his troops surrounded the unguarded camp, a shot was fired. The plan to talk to the French quickly became an inadvertent but deadly ambush. This 'shot heard round the world' resulted in a massacre that saw French commander Jumonville dead, along with 10 of his troops. Many of the original two hundred were captured; however, at least one French soldier escaped, and made his way back to Fort Duquesne to report the incident. Washington, knowing that a reprisal was coming, returned to his base camp to strengthen the recently constructed Fort Necessity. On the third of July, six hundred French – accompanied by one hundred Indian allies – began their assault against Washington and his 293 men. The truce soon called led to Fort Necessity's surrender to the French the next day.

While war between England and France was not officially declared for another two years, these shots began the world war, the real first world war if you will, which engaged the governments and people of most of Europe, eastern Canada, and the British colonies in America. Britain eventually won, gaining Canada and the promising Ohio frontier, but its victory was not cheap. The British government soon determined to levy the American colonies, to help pay the costs of the war.

The cries of 'no taxation without representation' and 'give me liberty or give me death' were responses to this decision, which fed the flames of rebellion, leading to the birth of the country twenty years later on July 4, 1776.

Spring of 1749

Thomas Mallory was born in 1709, the third of five sons of Angus and Moire Mallory. As the family farm was not large enough to divide among the boys, in 1730 Thomas – always seeking adventure – and his 18 year old bride Abigail left their small village in County Kilkenny, Bennettsbridge, Ireland, bound for the Massachusetts colony to seek a new beginning,

In 1744, they moved to Rivertown, Pennsylvania, just west of Philadelphia. Thomas joined the militia in 1745, and served active duty in King George's War. That service rekindled his desire to be something other than a farmer. In 1750 the Mallory family (including Thomas and Abigail, sons Daniel and Liam, and daughter Elizabeth), and their friends Joseph and Henry Clarke and Pierre Baptist, uprooted from Rivertown, Pennsylvania and crossed the Susquehanna River and the Allegheny Mountains, to their new home in the French-controlled frontier.

Chapter 1

A Journey Contemplated 1749 – Autumn

Thomas Mallory stopped chopping, and wiped the sweat from his brow. "Saints preserve us," he sighed, "it'll take more wood than this to see us through the winter." He swept his glance over the small leasehold farm his family worked. His wife, Abigail, removed the freshly baked bread from the outdoor oven, and went into the cabin to begin cooking supper. Daniel, his eldest son, harvested the last squash and pumpkin from the nearby field, while daughter Elizabeth spread feed for the ducks and chickens. Liam, the youngest, was away hunting. "Aye, and what about the spring? What will they think about my plans for the spring?"

Thomas never did much like farming, but it seemed to be the best way to feed his family. He leased a small plot from a member of Philadelphia's merchant aristocracy. It was not the life he had envisioned for himself or his family. For fifteen years he toiled, knowing he'd never make a decent profit. Nonetheless, he saved every spare farthing so that, at last, they could move west and begin a new life.

A few years back, Thomas joined the militia for a brief time to take part in King George's War. He met William Trent, an adventurous woodsman and officer in the Virginia militia. After that conflict concluded, Trent intended to return to Virginia. He stopped by the farm, looking for a place to bed down for a few nights. He regaled them with his stories of the frontier, about his trip down the Ohio River, and the opportunities waiting for men with vision and courage. "This is only the beginning," said William, "but I plan on opening a trading post along the Allegheny River. If I'm any judge of events, it won't be long before the frontier will be teeming with them that's looking to make their fortune. Hunters and trappers first, then settlers. Once things are settled there, it will be back to the Ohio River to start another trading post."

Thomas' time with the militia, coupled with Trent's ideas of the frontier, planted seeds of adventure and profit. William wrote to Thomas a few months later, asking him to be his business partner; Thomas quietly accepted. He kept the decision to himself; the time to tell the family would come soon enough. He needed to convince Abigail that the move would be more than worth the risks involved, as the British, French, and various tribes of Indians (some of whom sided with the British, others with the French) disputed who would control the area.

****

As Liam followed the movement of the deer, he realized that he was never so at peace as when he was in the woods. For as long as he could remember, he made the most of every opportunity to be outside, both marveling at nature and studying it. Indeed, he had come to know the area around his home very well; he hid now on a small mound, overgrown with brush. He knew from experience that the deer used the trail below to travel to a small creek for water. He also knew that he would be too far away for an effective shot with his favorite weapon, the bow, so he had his musket. The deer was now broadside to Liam, the hindquarters obscured by tree branches, but the front shoulder was in the open. Liam fired; the shot hit and knocked the deer down, but it was soon back on its feet, staggering away. Liam resisted rising and following the deer right away. He knew that that would only cause the deer to panic even more, causing it to run – it would be farther away once it finally succumbed to the wound, and Liam was sure the shot was fatal. 'That got at least one lung, maybe both,' he said to himself, as he rose just enough to keep an eye on the deer. The wounded deer was still walking, but quickly losing blood and becoming weaker.

Liam, satisfied that it would not be going too much farther, sat back down to wait for a few more minutes, giving him time to think and daydream. As usual, he thought about Indians, and how they used nature to survive. He was most in awe of Indians and their way of life, though he had encountered them only fleetingly. Not many Indians lived near his family's farm along the Schuylkill River, near Philadelphia. The last of them, the Delaware tribes, had been pushed farther west by the encroaching white settlers. He learned about native tribes from a former Black Robe, a priest who had lived with his Order in the village of Teatontaloga near the white settlement of Albany.

Pierre Baptiste was now the Rivertown village apothecary, having learned from the Mohawk about the various herbs and plants that they used for assorted ailments. He was also an amateur naturalist; he agreed to teach Liam about the Mohawk – including their language – in exchange for Liam gathering up and bringing him herbs and any other interesting plants and critters he could find. Liam peered over the brush in time to see the deer collapse to the forest floor. He slowly got up and stretched his cramped legs. When he reached where the deer had fallen, he noticed the pink froth that had been seeping out of the deer's mouth and nose. 'Yep, got the lungs,' he said to himself. Liam then field dressed the deer, removing the unwanted innards, and placing the heart, liver and kidneys in a pouch. He used a long strip of rawhide to wind around the torso, keeping it closed as he hoisted the carcass up onto his shoulders. Using the legs as handles, he began the short but laborious trek back home.

"Pa?" called Daniel as he gazed off to the woodland that bordered the tilled soil. "Here comes Liam, looks like we'll be havin' venison for supper."

"Aye, that it does," replied Thomas. "He may not help out much here, but I am glad he's such a fine hunter."

Liam strode toward the farm with the fine, young, white-tailed buck draped across his brawny shoulders. Thomas and Daniel helped Liam hoist the carcass up, and tie it to an overhanging branch of the tree that Liam used for skinning his prey. "Only took one shot to bring him down, got him right behind the front shoulder and got him in the lungs," Liam said as he began the skinning process.

"When you've finished the butchering, head over to the Clarke's and invite them for supper tonight," said Thomas. "Things aren't going so well since Joseph's wife died, and this will help. Besides, I have big news to share, and I'd like them to be a part of it."

"Sure, Pa, can I ask Pierre to join us? He's in need of a good meal as well, and it's him that taught me to shoot."

Shrugging his shoulders and smiling, Thomas replied, "Don't see why not. Least we can do to repay him for teaching you to shoot so well. Besides, I was going to suggest you bring him along. My news may interest him."

Liam finished the butchering, hanging some of the venison in the smokehouse and bringing the rest to Abigail. "Here you are, Ma. We're having company for dinner tonight. I'm just leaving to fetch Pierre and the Clarkes. Pa says he has some news to tell everyone. Wonder what it is?"

"Your Pa can be secretive, but I'm pretty sure it has something to do with that letter that he got the other day. He doesn't know I saw it delivered, and he's been muttering to himself about it ever since. Ask Daniel to bring me another bucket of water, I need to make more stew if our guests want to eat."

After relaying his mother's request to Daniel, Liam rode their draft horse to deliver the message. Pierre was in the village, so he stopped first there first. It was only a couple of miles to the Clarke's cabin on the other side of the village. "Liam, my young friend, what brings you out of the woods and into civilization today? Is there an emergency at the farm?" inquired Pierre, washing his hands and arms in the outside basin, cleaning off the guts and blood of a dead young fox he found and had been dissecting.

"No emergency, unless that's what you call a dinner invite," replied Liam, "Pa has something he wants to tell us, and asks if you can come to dinner. I'm off to ask the Clarkes the same."

Pierre nodded, saying, "I'll head over as soon as I get cleaned up."

****

The Clarke cabin was situated on land that was, for all intents and purposes, a peninsula, as the river at that point formed an upside down U. The landlord, a wealthy Virginia aristocrat, had supplied the village with the material to build a small mill, and a forge for blacksmith work. It was on this land that Joseph set up both. Liam arrived to find Joseph repairing a wagon wheel, the sound of hammer on anvil echoing off the dense forest across the river. His son, Henry, was cleaning a raccoon hide with the fur still attached – a difficult task, his mother had taken care of these sorts of things. Martha Clarke had been a very industrious woman with many talents. Sorely missed by her husband and son, Martha had contracted a fever the year before. She died, despite the ministrations of her family and Pierre.

Joseph saw Liam first. He dropped the hammer after one last clang, wiped the sweat from his face, and walked over to the cabin. "Well, howdy there, young Mallory," said Joseph as he extended his hand in greeting. "What brings you to our bend in the river?"

Liam slid off his horse and, accepting a cup of cool water from Henry, said, "My Pa asks if you and Henry would come by tonight for dinner. Got me a fine buck today and Pa has something he wants to talk about."

"Can't say no to some fresh venison and fine company," answered Joseph. "Besides, it will save me from having to eat the less than savory stew that we two cook up. By the crowning glory of the Holy Trinity, I surely do miss my wife. I'll have Henry hitch up our wagon. While he's doing that, I'll grab a couple jugs of ale to add to the festivities."

Rather than ride home on the broad, saddleless work horse, Liam hitched him next to the Clarkes' horse, and climbed into the back of the wagon. "What's that you're working on, Henry?"

Henry tossed the raccoon hide to Liam. "Trying to stretch this out for a winter hat. Thought it would be a nice present for Elizabeth. If I trap a couple more of these critters, I can make her some mittens as well."

Tossing the hide back to Henry, Liam said laughingly, "I'm sure she'll be pleased. Just the other day, she said to me that she hoped handsome Henry would make her a raccoon cap and mittens."

It was no secret that Henry was in love with Liza, and had been since they were old enough to talk. Liza was fifteen now. She'd grown into a very beautiful woman; while she wasn't exactly leading Henry on, she did occasionally drop hints that other boys in the village were desirable, when she felt that Henry was complacent about their relationship.

The rest of the trip to the Mallory farm, the three planned a hunting trip for the first snowfall. They arrived to see that Pierre had helped Liza set up a spit of venison over the outdoor fire pit. Thomas and Daniel were arranging some roughhewn stools, for sitting on while they enjoyed one of the last warm September evenings. Soon, it would turn bitterly cold and snowy – at least, it seemed so; the woolly caterpillars had a thicker coat than usual. As if on cue, a flock of geese passed overhead, their arrow head formation pointed south.

As they clambered down from the wagon, Liza turned toward them and said with a mischievous grin, "Welcome, Mr. Clarke. I see handsome Henry has accompanied you. I thought he may have left the village, as he has not been by to see me in at least two weeks." Leaving Henry trying to sputter a reply, the men sat and passed the ale jug, chuckling at Henry's discomposure. Liza returned to the cabin to help her mother, but only for a few minutes. Soon she was standing in the doorway listening to the men talk, but with her gaze firmly upon Henry.

****

Thomas, eager to learn more about Pierre, asked him how he came to Rivertown. While Thomas liked him well enough, he was concerned about Pierre being French, and was anxious to find out if that would be a complication in the future. Pierre gazed into each one's eyes, and gauged that the time was right for telling the whole story. He began.

"When I was a growing boy in the south of France, my parents took me traveling with them. My father was a trade merchant. He did very well by it, and took us on some of his expeditions to Spain and North Africa. I invariably found a way to lose myself in nearby towns and villages while my father and older brother were busy with customers; my mother was too involved dealing with my two younger sisters to notice my absence

"I have always been a curious sort, fascinated by other peoples' cultures – how they lived, what they believed, and their languages. One day, I found my way to a small enclave of Moors just outside of Cadiz, Spain. While I sat by the well listening to the women, an old man sat next to me. Speaking in French, he said he was Hasam, the leader of this group of Muslims — a very much diminished people in both number and influence, since most of the Moors and the Jews had been driven from Spain over the course of the last few hundred years. I spent the next four days with him, learning much of his religion and the history of his people. I also learned their language; in fact, I have a God-given talent when it comes to languages. I can speak Arabic,

Spanish, German, Latin, Huron, Mohawk, and of course French and English. I do not say this as a boast; it is just the way of things. Some men are born warriors, some are born to be kings, I was born to learn, to absorb knowledge like a sponge in water.

"Naturally, I was raised as a Catholic, and was as devout to the Church as any thirteen year old boy could be. I must admit, however, that when sitting around the various village wells, I wasn't just listening to the women talk, if you know what I mean," he said with a mischievous wink of an eye and a sly smirk, "so to learn another's view of God was an eye-opening experience.

"Hasam told me, too, of the Jewish religion. Even after pondering through the years what he taught me, it still astounds me that the God of the Catholics, the God of the Muslims, and the God of the Jews are the same God – yet through blindness and a lust for power, each of these religions claim God as their own, to the utter damnation of the souls of the others."

Pierre paused telling his story to take a sip or two of his ale. He was silent for a few moments, and stared off into the distance. Finally, with a shake of his head and another sip of ale, he resumed his tale. "You must forgive me if I drift off now and then. Telling my tale brings back memories, and I like to savor them while they last. As I was saying, I had learned quite a bit from Hasam, and that has stayed with me. Still, and despite my doubts about the nature of God, when the time came to decide my future, I chose to become a Jesuit monk, a Black Robe as we came to be known to the natives here.

"My training in France was a mixed blessing. I enjoyed the solitude, and the chance to read books I had not had access to. I was eventually assigned to the established mission with the Mohawk. My superiors saw this as a just reward for my somewhat lax attention to the daily rituals. They were more than happy with my ability to translate and copy text, but finally came to the conclusion that I would be better off somewhere else, so to the New World I sailed.

"The priest in charge of the mission, Father Colon, didn't have the time to track a wayward monk while trying to keep the Mohawk tribe from splitting up. Seems that the godly Black Robes had succeeded in converting many to Christianity, but they took that success too far, haranguing those who refused to believe - with the promise of hell awaiting. I did not want to be caught up in that rancorous dispute, so I spent much of my time learning the language, and talking to the older Mohawks about their spiritual beliefs. My fellow Black Robes were aware of my unorthodox ecclesiastical thoughts, as I often engaged them in debate. A couple of them, enraged at my attitude, began to spy on me — looking for a way to renounce me to Father Colon."

****

Abigail appeared from the cabin, and announced that the stew was ready. With Pierre's promise to continue his story later, they headed to a meal of fresh venison and a bean stew. Joseph told his son, "Henry, bring along that jug. Eating and talking are thirsty work."

"Right, Pa," Henry answered. Like his father, Henry was tall and wiry, and both were endowed with an adventurous spirit. When Martha died, Joseph gave up on farming, and became the village jack-of-all-trades: part-time blacksmith, part-time miller and part-time butcher. Henry followed in his father's footsteps, though he spent as much time as he could roaming the countryside with Liam, hunting or gathering specimens for Pierre. As he grabbed the jug, Henry told Liam, "Pierre sure has led an interestin' life. I hope I get to have some adventures. Not likely to happen while living here, though."

"That's for sure," replied Liam. "The more I listen to Pierre, the more I wanna get away from here. He's never told me much about his past, only that he was no longer a Black Robe. I think tonight we may hear the whole of it."

"I swear, Liam, this is the best venison I have ever eaten," said Thomas as he sliced off another hunk. "That raises a question in my mind. I wonder if the deer taste this good farther west. Now, the reason for this question is that I received a letter a few days ago from William Trent. When he was with us last year, he hinted at needing a partner for his trading post out by Fort Duquesne. Well, he has asked me to be that partner, and after mulling it over, I've decided it is time for us to move west to the frontier. I know it will be hard, and I know there will be dangers, but I also know that I cannot remain a farmer forever. We have enough saved to pay off the landlord, and to procure what we need for the move."

Abigail was a strong woman, physically and mentally. She knew that no amount of argument was going to dissuade her husband, and was actually surprised that it took so long for something like this to happen. In addition to his recent muttering, the clues to Thomas' longing, subtle as they were, were evident for quite some time.

One way she saw his dream was how he handled their sons. Daniel was the oldest, and at nineteen years of age was more attuned to the land, more of a farmer, than his father. Daniel never faltered in his duties around the farm; indeed, he took on more than his share of the toil. On the other hand, Liam was never much help, other than to feed the livestock, or to help with the harvest. Abigail would often complain to Thomas about Liam and his lack of help, and Thomas would chide Liam — for a few days, he would pitch in more vigorously, but only for a few days. Thomas, being of much the same mind as Liam, would often feel a little envious of Liam and his freedom to explore.

Elizabeth, however, did concern her mother a little, as she was more prone to daydreaming and would often do her chores haphazardly. This was somewhat surprising to Abigail. She knew that Liza was smarter than what she let on; she just needed to learn to focus on the here and now, not some fanciful future that would never be.

"Well, husband, I do not know why it took you so long to arrive at this decision. I have known ever since William filled your head with dreams of a different life, one that doesn't involve tilling the soil." At this little jab, everyone chuckled.

"Have you had any news from Trent regarding the French and their Indian allies?" asked Pierre. "They can't be expected to just let an English trading post thrive in their territory."

"He did write that things were certainly in some turmoil between the English and French, but he has found a spot on one of the feeder creeks to the Allegheny that is well secluded and defensible. He plans to keep things slow trading-wise until the situation improves, but he is sure that it will. I get the sense from him that he knows more than he is letting on regarding the future of the area. So, yes, there will be an element of danger involved, but so far, the French have left him alone." Thomas put down his fork, and gazed at the faces of his family and friends. Liam was smiling from ear to ear; Daniel, on the other hand, seemed more apprehensive.

Joseph glanced at Henry, raised his eyebrow, shrugged his shoulders, and said, "The boy and me have nothing keeping us here, might you want a little company on this venture?"

"I was about to put it to you," replied Thomas. "I would welcome most keenly your company and your help. What about you, Pierre? Is there anything or anyone keeping you here, or would you be willing to join this crew?"

"Perhaps it would be best if I finished my tale before I answer. You may not want me along after hearing the rest of the story," replied Pierre with a sly grin on his face. "One thing you must understand. I did not join the Church or the Jesuits in order to serve God. No, I did it as it was the best way to get an education, to learn and to think. This may help to explain my disinterest in the rituals and vows required of me. I did enough to keep from being thrown out while in training, but was always being watched and judged.

"As I said earlier, I was being spied on, so I began to exercise caution. I assumed more responsibility for the daily tasks laid before me, even to the point of saying Mass on occasion. This lasted for a couple of months, until some visitors arrived from the Oneida. One of their important warriors, Mendoah, came to talk to the Mohawk chief Donehogawa about recent incursions into the Oneida's territory by a Shawnee band led by a ruthless brave, Chogan. Mendoah's daughter was with him, the most beautiful woman I had ever seen. Her name was Suitana, and she had come along in order to spend time with Onatah, a Mohawk woman gifted in healing. I came to know Suitana, as I was also a student of Onatah. During our time with Onatah, we took many walks in the woods and fields, gathering plants, goose down, and whatever other materials Onatah said were good medicine. On occasion, our hands touched as we reached for the same plant or bit of bark, and each time we let our hands linger together a little longer, until we were both sure that we each desired the other. I have said that my vows were not the most important thing to me, especially the vow of chastity. Indeed, I was not the first Black Robe to run afoul of that prohibition, including the two priests who were intent on destroying me. Mendoah, along with Donehogawa — my best friend among the Mohawk — and a handful of Mohawk braves left the village to deal with the Shawnee. It was then that my Jesuit brothers made their move against me. Suitana and I met at a beautiful spot on Schoharie Creek for our lovemaking, a place canopied by elm trees and under the flowing leaves of willows. Usually, we were careful not to be followed, but on this day I was expected to say Mass, though I had not been advised of that. When one of the other priests saw me heading away from the village, he followed me. Seeing our intentions, he raced back to the village to tell Father Colon. When the good Father and my Brothers arrived, I was asleep in Suitana's arms.

"I am always shocked when whites bitterly complain about the savagery of the Indians when, after all, we whites are just as cruel if not more so. I was beaten with club, fist, and booted feet to cries of 'blasphemer, spawn of Satan, fornicator.' Unconscious, I was dragged from that lovely spot into the creek, and left for dead. They dared not touch Suitana, out of fear — and rightly so. Mendoah would have killed them without hesitation if they had. As for me, I was now an outcast, for as you can readily tell I did not die that day.

"When Suitana returned to the village, she told Onatah that I was near death. Onatah gathered up her medicine pouch and made her way to the creek, where I was barely breathing. She was able to pull me from the water, where she then began tending my many wounds. I was unable to move from that spot for two weeks, while they continued to nurse me back to health.

"When I was finally strong enough, I said a tearful goodbye to Suitana and Onatah, gathered up the supplies they brought, and headed away from the village with no real destination. I worked my way south, stopping at the few farms and villages I happened upon to work for food and a place to stay until I was ready to move on. I arrived in Rivertown; when I learned that the village needed a doctor, I decided to stay to render what help I could. I am, however, ready to move on, and will join you if you will have me."

With that said, Thomas took one last gulp of his ale, wiped his mouth on his sleeve, and said, "That settles it, then. I think you'll all agree that the time to leave will be in the spring. We can use the coming winter to prepare. We need to stock up; we need to bring practically everything we're gonna need out there. Let's go back outside, and enjoy a relaxing evening one last time before we get too busy."

They all did as Thomas suggested, and soon the sounds of laughter and light-hearted banter filled the night. No one noticed, at least not outwardly, that Liza and Henry had snuck off to the other side of the cabin. When she was sure they were out of sight, Liza grabbed Henry and pulled him to her. Kissing him softly, their lips finally parted. She asked, "When are you going to marry me, Henry?"

"In two years, Liza, you know your Pa said you couldn't marry until you turn seventeen," replied Henry as he stroked her hair and gazed longingly into her eyes. "This is hard on me, too, you know, but now at least we'll be together more often. We better get back to the others before they start talking about us."

"Oh, my handsome Henry," Liza replied with a big grin, "they've been talking about us for years."

That night, as Abigail brushed her hair, she turned toward Thomas as he climbed into their bed. He looked up at her, noticing the frown on her face. "What's on yer mind, Abby?" he asked.

Putting down the brush, she sat on the edge of the bed and took Thomas' hand. "You know, dear husband, that I would never disagree with you in front of the children, and I'm not really disagreeing now. But, I am concerned about the dangers involved. The journey itself will be hard, and we don't know what we will face from the Indians."

"I've given that a lot of thought," he replied. "We left our home in Ireland to find a way to establish a home and future for our children. This farm is a stepping stone to reaching that goal. I see this chance to make it happen, and I can't let it pass us by. This trading post will grow, and we will grow with it; the children will have their future. I know that it will be difficult, but the experience will prove to be quite an education. We'll be as prepared as we can be for the trip, of that you can be sure."

"You ease my mind, husband, but I'm sure you'll understand if every so often I mutter a prayer to Saint Christopher for safety and strength," she said as she slid under the blanket and pulled Thomas to her. "I am blessed to have such a family and I would see them safe. We will do that together, wherever we are."

****

"I suppose you're happier than a hog in slop," Daniel said to Liam, as he sat on his cot repairing a hole in his breeches.

Liam grinned at his older. "What, because of the chance to explore new territory, to have a life of adventure? Well, I'd be a fool if I wasn't happy. Not all of us are cut out for farming, or being settled in one place."

"You know what happens to that hog? It gets slaughtered," replied Daniel. "Be sure to put out that candle afore you fall asleep, little brother."

"Aw, you worry too much," Liam replied, "good night, older brother."

Daniel mulled over the events of the evening, trying not to feel disappointed at the prospect of uprooting and starting over. The farm was just beginning to become what he envisioned; with hard work and help from the others, it would someday be profitable. But he had to admit to himself that what the farm was now was due mostly to his efforts. His Pa and Liam certainly provided labor, but not the zeal Daniel possessed. Despite his attempts to bring them round, he could not penetrate their restless spirits. Perhaps, he thought, this new beginning will provide the chance for him to realize his dream; yes, perhaps. In the meantime, he would put forth the effort required to prepare for the journey.

****

Overriding any anticipation or excitement about her Pa's announcement was the plain fact that Liza was going to be seeing and spending a lot of time with her handsome Henry. She had known for quite a while that he was the one, despite the teasing she gave him and his haphazard approach to making time to see her. At times, she was jealous of Liam, as Henry seemed to spend more time with him than with her, but then there were the times when Henry was just so sweet. Besides, he was the handsomest boy in the area, standing just a shade under six feet tall with broad shoulders and an unruly mop of brown hair that hung to his shoulders when not tied in a tail. His face was like that of one of the old Greek gods that Pierre told her about; the only marring feature was a scar under his chin from a hunting accident, and even that added a rugged cast to his look. Yes, she thought as she finally gave way to the yawning and laid down; this was going to be the best of journeys.

Chapter 2

The Move

The weather was tempestuous that winter. Heavy snowfalls and bitterly cold temperatures made for hard work preparing for the move. The village was especially quiet, as everyone stayed indoors as much as possible. Even in these frigid conditions, though, some still moved about; after all, business and daily life don't stop for the weather. Thomas and Joseph enjoyed a pint of ale at the village inn, while they discussed the progress of the preparations. Suddenly hit with an icy blast, Thomas proclaimed, "Aye! Sarding, hell, would you be closing that door, stranger, afore you turn us all into blue-skins?" as he pulled his hat down further over his ears. The stranger stood in the entrance, letting his eyes adjust from the brightness outdoors to the darker atmosphere of the inn — not thinking that he was also letting in the frigid air.

His look one of embarrassment and disbelief, the stranger closed the door and walked to Thomas. "I beg your pardon, I just wasn't thinking. Cold air must have frozen my brain. Phil Burke is my name, from Philadelphia," he said, extending his hand in greeting. The owner of a fleet of three ships and a lumber mill, Phil Burke was a moderately successful businessman. As he neared forty years old, he was troubled that the sedentary nature of a business office made him a little portly. Tired of the lack of physical activity, and despite the frigid conditions, he made a rare – for him – trip to Rivertown to purchase a load of lumber. After stabling his wagon and team, he stopped in the village inn for warmth, and a room and meal.

"Thomas Mallory, and Joseph Clarke, at your service. Please join us, won't you?" Thomas asked. He caught the innkeeper's eye and motioned for another tankard of ale. "What in the name of all the saints in Ireland are you doing wandering the streets of this frozen village. when you could be basking in the warmth of a fine home in Philadelphia?"

Joseph reached across the table and shook Phil's hand. "Phil Burke, eh? Might you be the owner of the lumber mill? I have done business with you, if you are he."

"I am, and that's partly the reason I am here. There's a supply of lumber I need to pick up, though I wish I had sent one of my drivers instead. I cannot remember when I have felt so cold. Excuse the vulgarity, but I believe my arse is frozen shut, and my bollocks are stuck together and frozen to my right thigh. Joseph Clarke, you say? Now that my brain is working again, I recall hearing from one of my teamsters that you are preparing to move to the frontier, to run a trading post.

"Well, now, this is most fortuitous. The other reason I subjected myself to this arse-shutting trip was to have a chat with you. I have been mulling over expanding into the fur trade, and this may just be the opportunity I've waited for. I would very much like to accompany you to this trading post, so I can get a firsthand glimpse of the potential for profit." Phil paused for a moment to take a drink, taking a glance at Thomas and Joseph. He thought he saw a look of doubt on their faces.

"You may not know it to look at me now, but twenty years ago I was lean and fit, and I can assure you I will not be a burden. I'll leave you to discuss it, but let me sweeten the pot a little. Part of my lumber business is building freight wagons. I will supply this expedition with any wagons we need. I can also supply the horses; I have a strong business relationship with the gentleman who breeds and raises the finest draft horses and mules in the colonies. So, you gentlemen talk it over. I will be staying here at the inn for at least three days, unless of course another blizzard arrives, in which case I may be here until June."

Smiling, Phil rose from the table to arrange his lodging. Thomas took a long pull from the tankard of ale, belched noisily, and turned to Joseph. "Well, now, that was interesting, and that's a fact. I am inclined to take him up on his offer. That solves the wagon problem. I didn't fancy trusting the ones built here. It is a rugged ride ahead of us, and the sturdier the wagons and horses are, the better."

"I agree about the wagons. I just hope he is sturdy enough," replied Joseph.

Thomas turned to look at Phil. "Aye, he is a bit soft, but then again he made it here from Philadelphia without freezing to death. Methinks he's made of sterner stuff than what his appearance belies."

****

Pierre stopped at the inn for a pint, and to speak with Thomas and Joseph. They relayed the news about Phil Burke joining the group, and his offer of as many wagons as they needed. This was good news; Pierre loathed the idea of leaving any of his equipment or books behind. Later, at his small cabin in town, Pierre packed all of his medicinal stock of herbs and plants, as well as assorted medical tools he'd acquired through the years.

****

Two days later, Phil Burke returned to Philadelphia, laden with lumber and anxious anticipation for the coming spring. In addition to tending to the needs of his regular customers, the plan for an early May departure meant he would be very busy in preparations, including arranging for six wagons to be built; acquiring horses and mules to pull them; and hiring drivers to get the wagons to Rivertown. Phil felt sure his accountant would be up to the task of handling things while he was away, though he would update his Last Will and Testament just in case. "'Tis only prudent," Phil sighed as he pulled the wagon into his corral. "After all, this ain't no church picnic I'm attending."

Trent planned to lead them on a route that crossed the Susquehanna at Wright's Ferry. There, they would turn north until they reached the Juniata River floodplain, and follow it west to meet the Allegheny Mountains. That's when things would be challenging for both drivers and animals; after meandering through wooded valleys, they would climb more than 2,500 feet, to mountainous elevations that might still have vestigial winter snow on the peaks. The entire trip would take almost a month, if they didn't run into any major problems. The caravan would consist of six wagons, each pulled by four mules. Thomas, Joseph, Daniel, Henry, Phil, and Stump Nose Emerson would be driving. Trent and Liam would scout and hunt for the entire party. The remainder of the livestock — eight draft horses, six spare mules, and two milk cows — were the responsibility of Henry and another of Trent's cronies, Rob Carter.

There were two additions to the group: Jack Tomlinson (in the employ of Phil Burke) would help with the driving and the care of the mules. The other newcomer was a timid, 18 year old apprentice brewer, Timothy Edward Winslow. Trent wanted to have a brewer at the post, to supply the group with ale – and, later, to open a tavern for trappers to wind down with a pint or two.

Timothy was a third generation brewer from Salem, Massachusetts. He'd left home to ply his trade in Philadelphia. There, he met Trent, who convinced him that this move was a great opportunity. This would be his first experience in the wild. He had no real sense of what might come, but carried within him a fear and dread of Indians and their legendary savagery, ideas planted in his mind by the tales of those who frequented his father's Salem tavern.

****

Phil arrived with the mules, and the packed and ready wagons. Two mornings later, the dawn excited the senses. The sun rose through a cloudbank, its diffused light reaching out in every direction to illuminate an otherwise clear blue sky. Robins and cardinals welcomed the warm day with song, which seemed to add to the buoyant mood of the travelers. Henry and Liza walked back to the farmhouse from their final visit to their special spot in the woods. They arrived just as Thomas cried out, "Hee-yaw!" and cracked his whip over the backs of the mules pulling the lead wagon. So began the trek to the frontier. Henry hurried to his wagon. Helping Liza up to the seat, he endured some good-natured ribbing from Pierre and Phil – they were almost left behind.

The first leg of the journey went as smoothly as was expected, while men and mules got used to working together. They reached Wright's Ferry on the third day, with enough time to cross with half of the wagons. They continued on to find a good spot for a day's rest. The remaining wagons crossed the next morning, and made their way to join the others. That night, all enjoyed a feast, as Liam brought in two turkeys and three rabbits for dinner. Phil and Stump Nose played their fiddles, and everyone danced and sang, while keeping in mind the arduous days to come. Thomas took a burning brand from the fire, and relit his pipe. "How many days 'til we reach the Alleghenies?" he asked Trent.

"Three, maybe four, days. For the most part, there is a trail of sorts, wide enough for the wagons – probably an old game trail, used by the Delaware and Shawnee a few years back. Since it is still early spring, there will be some marshy areas; we need to be careful going through those, don't wanna get bogged down in any of 'em. Once we start climbing, though, I 'spect we will still have snow up high. Glad we have extra mules and those farm horses; we may need 'em."

Daniel joined them at the fire after having checked on his mule team; one of them seemed to be limping slightly, the result of a kick to the shin by another mule. "To me, the more important question concerns Stump Nose. How did he ever get the nose to match that name?"

"Hey Emerson," called Trent, "come and regale us with the tale of your name."

Stump Nose Emerson sat down by the fire. He was the son of a sailor, but had not acquired his father's love of the sea, opting instead to become a fur trapper and trader. He tossed back the last of his ale, took a deep breath, and began: "It happened, must be going on twenty five years now. Lordy, how time does fly. I was trapping beaver and hunting bear up on the Mohawk one winter, not too far from a Mohawk village. They let me be, seems they liked the bear pelts I would trade them. Anyways, one day I'm pulling out my last trap; had me a nice beaver in it. Before I could release the trap, I saw two black bear cubs heading towards me. All of a sudden, out of the woods comes charging this huge she-bear. I had time to get off one shot, but as I fired, I slipped on the damned beaver tail and missed the bear. I had no time to reload, so I took off a-running, knowing my only chance was to reach the Mohawk village. I screamed my head off to get someone's attention, hoping they had a loaded musket. Luckily, I weren't that far from the village. Well, I'm pumping my legs like I never done before, occasionally glancing back to see the bear gaining on me. Finally, I reached a cornfield at the edge of the village. I turned my head one more time, and saw I had little time left before the bear was upon me. Before I could face forward again, I tripped over an old cornstalk, and landed face first, smack dab into a tree stump. I screamed something horrible, as the blood poured out of my nose. It must have smeared my face something awful. The bear heard my scream, and saw, I guess, my new face - and took off the other way. I made my way to the village on wobbly legs, and a kindly Mohawk healer got the blood to stop, but could do nothing with my smashed nose. Unfortunately, there were a couple of other traders in the village. Once they dubbed me Stump Nose – well, it kinda stuck."

"Yeah, well, I am sorry to have been responsible fer spreading that around," laughed Rob Carter, "but how could I not? Besides, you weren't too pretty to look at, anyway. Now, you have an excuse fer being ugly."

Henry choked on the swallow of ale he had just taken, prompting Thomas to laughingly pound him on the back. When Henry regained his composure, Thomas said, "I swear that is the funniest nickname story I ever heard tell, and I believe it is a good way to end the evening. We have an early start in the morning, and I would take it kindly if there were no lingering after effects."

****

The Juniata River, winding east from the Allegheny Mountains to the Susquehanna River, traversed a varied landscape Flat pockets of woodland were interspersed with marsh and meadow. Spring wildflowers were just beginning to show. Some were picked daily by Liza and Abigail as they walked beside the wagons, to add a touch of home to the nightly meals – the women quickly learned that walking was much more comfortable than sitting in a wagon, where every bump was a shock to the spine. During stretches of flat and straight driving, Pierre joined them, pointing out the different plants and herbs along the way. Liza was especially drawn to these impromptu tutoring sessions, and found she wanted to know more about how to tend wounds and treat sickness. It also kindled an idea that had been in the back of her mind since the trip began. The more she thought about the possible need for the group to defend themselves, the more she was convinced that she should learn to shoot. She was determined to voice that request to Henry.

There were times, however, when Liza sat with Henry, and endured the jarring and pounding. During one of those times, Henry lost his concentration. His mules wandered a bit off of the path, and became mired up to the front axle in a low-lying bog of clover and skunk cabbage. They were knee deep in oozing mud, but contentedly munched away on a patch of cowslip. Pierre and Stump Nose watched what happened from their trailing wagons. They brought their teams to a halt, and ran to Henry's wagon. "How in the world did this happen?" asked Pierre. "No, don't tell me, let me guess. Something to do with youthful hankering, perhaps? Well, don't just sit there, you two, get down and unhitch the mules. We'll have to pull this out backwards."

Stump Nose headed to the rear, returning with Rob and four of the horses. They hitched them up and tied them to the back of the wagon; in a few minutes (with help from Henry and Liza pushing from the front), the wagon came free with a jerk that caught Henry off guard – and pulled him face first into the skunk cabbage plants where the wheel had been. Stump Nose burst out laughing, hands slapping down on his knees, "Haw, haw, haw, that ought to cool off his youthful desire, I swear it should."

The river was just less than a hundred feet from the wagon trail, so Henry ran to take a quick plunge in the icy cold water to remove some of the muck and mire from his face and hair. Meanwhile, Rob and Pierre hitched the mules back to the wagon. They were soon on the way once more, just slightly behind the three lead wagons. When they reached the stopping point for the night, Thomas and Joseph went to talk with Henry and Liza. But, seeing how dejected Liza looked, and how miserable Henry looked and smelled, they abandoned their carefully planned speeches. All they said was, "Don't let it happen again."

****

The third day traveling along the Juniata River was more inclement. It started with an early morning fog that refused to burn off, and gradually turned to a steady rain – soaking everyone, and turning what trail there was into a slippery morass of mud. Trent and Liam returned from their scouting, and called a halt for the day. "No use going any further today," Trent said, "we're in the foothills now. We'll rest tomorrow, to dry out and get ready for the climb. Check all the harnesses and wheels; make sure they're ready to take the extra strain."

"How's it look up ahead?" Thomas asked Trent later, as they tried to keep their dinner out of the rain.

"Tough to see the peaks in this weather, but the few glimpses I got weren't good. Looks like we still have snow up high. We should be fine, but we need to be wary of slides, especially with this rain."

****

They left the Juniata behind on the second day of their trek through the mountains, and veered south, to take advantage of the many valleys and passes that would lead them west. The mountains topped out at around 2,500 feet here; while snow remained on some of them, the weather had turned warm – even in the higher elevations. Trent and Liam rode a couple miles ahead, looking for a good spot to camp. Timothy had joined them today, feeling quite different than when he was with the wagons. Out here in the silence, he imagined a tomahawk-wielding Indian behind every tree or boulder. Liam tried to reassure him, but it was hard for Timothy to control his skittishness.

As they came over the top of a rise, Trent motioned for them to stop and be quiet. Timothy, fear etched on his face, pulled his musket from his shoulder, and readied to fire. Trent grabbed the barrel, and gently pushed it down. "Easy, there, Timothy, lad. No need for muskets today. We're about to meet up with an old friend of mine, Old Briton, chief of the Delaware."

Liam took one look at the advancing throng, and realized that this was no mere hunting party. This was a whole village on the move, but, why? Old Briton and his tribe had settled in the same area for years – what would force them to leave? "The French, them and their Shawnee allies. Has to be the reason," said Trent as if he were reading Liam's mind. "Let's see if we can do some trading, maybe hire a guide to see us through the mountains."

Trent and Liam found Old Briton. While the three spoke, a group of warriors and young boys surrounded Timothy, all jostling for a better look at this young white woodsman. Suddenly, one of the boys reached for the musket. Timothy grabbed at it, and caught the trigger. The musket was still in the cocked position – he squeezed the trigger, and a shot rang out. His startled horse reared, throwing Timothy into the crowd. Luckily, the fired musket ball hit nothing but earth. Two of the warriors screamed at Timothy as he began to stand, but calm was quickly restored once Old Briton and Trent determined the nature of the event, and defused the situation. Old Briton agreed to accompany them back to the wagons, where they would have a feast and do some trading.

The scene back at the wagons was chaotic and noisy. A boulder-filled avalanche had knocked one of the wagons onto its side, half burying the mule team in the process. Pierre and Abigail were tending to the driver, Jack Tomlinson, who suffered a nasty bump to his head. Pierre also pulled Jack's left shoulder back into place – it separated when he hit the ground. Daniel, Joseph, and Henry frantically dug out the mules, while Thomas worked to unhitch them from the wagon. Liam, Trent, and a few Delaware warriors were able to push the wagon back on its wheels. "We'll need a fresh team," said Thomas. "The three mules that survived are a bit too skittish right now, and I want to push on for a bit, and get away from here. No tellin' if there's another slide about to happen."

That night, despite the physically draining activity of the day, the travelers held a feast in honor of Old Briton and his people. The weary travelers ate roasted haunches of venison, bear, and one unfortunate mule. The old chief, with sadness in his eyes, told how the French had finally – after many years – forced Old Briton to leave Pickawillany Village. They hoped to find a suitable site along the Juniata – game was still plentiful there, and the English colonists held sway over the territory. After a little haggling, Old Briton traded the services of one of his braves, Noshi, as a guide for the wagon train. In return, Trent gave the Delaware some new axes, a cooking pot, and a mule. All agreed that tomorrow would be a day of rest and repair, and then the final push through the mountains.

****

Noshi led them through steep-sided canyons, following the course of the Little Juniata as it swung to the southwest toward the final gap ahead. They had traveled for sixteen days, and were looking forward to the relatively flat last leg of the trip. When they emerged from Shawnee Gap, Noshi pointed them north. "He says that there is a creek a day or so ahead, that we will be able to follow most of the way west," Trent explained to the group at supper that night. "Once we reach that point, we're only five days from the post. We'll be hidden from view, for the most part, while we're in the creek valley. Once we head for higher ground, we'll need to be more alert for French patrols, or bands of Shawnee."

The creek valley proved to be a godsend in terms of terrain; for a few miles, at least, the wagons had flat ground to roll on. It also provided some protection from prying eyes; once they left the valley, they found evidence of a recent campsite. From that point on, Trent and Liam scouted ahead a few miles. They saw and heard nothing of concern. On their twenty second day, the wagon train came to its last obstacle, the Kisakismetas River. According to Liam, it could be forded about two miles upriver from their position. Just one more night of fitful sleep under a wagon. Tomorrow, they would arrive at their new home.

Chapter 3

A Wedding and a Departure

The trading post was situated on a peninsula in a bend of the Kiskiminetas River. When they arrived two months earlier, the only building was the store. A canoe landing sat right outside the rear door of the store. Since then, the post began to take shape. Thomas and Abigail enjoyed living space separate from the bunkhouse, which was large enough to accommodate twenty or so workers or traders spending a day or two in civilized company and comfort. The rest of the post included a large vegetable and herb garden, a brew house for Timothy, a stable and corral, an outhouse, and Phil's tent.

His was no ordinary tent – it more resembled Caesar's campaign tent, complete with ceiling-to-floor curtains that portioned off the space into three distinct rooms. The front room was furnished with a large wooden desk, and a couple of comfortable chairs. The bedroom contained a four-poster bed and matching nightstand. The third room held the woodstove and a small kitchen area. Phil had little idea how to pitch this particular tent; with the help of Stump Nose and Rob Carter, the tent was eventually ready in five hours – requiring many tankards of ale, and a dictionary's worth of profanity. Naturally, Phil took quite a bit of ribbing for his comfy living arrangements. While taking it all in a good-natured manner, he did explain, "I don't have them fancy things solely for my comfort, although that is a factor. No, the real reason I choose my tent over the bunkhouse is my health. The odors that issue forth from a dozen or so not too clean bodies are not meant to be inhaled."

Daily routines became established as the days passed. Liam, Daniel, and Henry spent most of their time hunting, often singly. They also used this time to scout the area for any signs of outsider activity. Abigail and Liza kept the kitchen going, and always had a pot of soup or stew simmering. Liza also helped Pierre in the garden, and learned useful tidbits from Pierre about the medicinal uses of different plants. When Daniel wasn't hunting, he helped Liza and Pierre, finding, by his farming intuition, the right spot for the garden. A handful of topsoil held near his nose, he breathed in the fertility of this plot of land, and determined that this is where his farm would be. Thomas and Joseph oversaw the store, and whatever construction or repair work might be required. Timothy turned out to be not only a brewer of exceptional quality ale, but also a fair baker. He kept the post supplied with bread, and the occasional pie or cake.

Stump Nose and Rob Carter, after leaving for a few days to set traps further up the Allegheny returned to help with the livestock.

Near Fort Duquesne, Jacques Ouellette (an irascible Frenchman, known as Jimmy Two Birds) operated a larger trading post. Though French, Ouellette was loyal only to himself and his pursuit of profit. In addition to this trading depot, he owned a tavern-inn-brothel in Fort Duquesne, and was rumored to supply the French militia with muskets and lead for shot. To keep their smaller post supplied with the goods needed for survival and for trading, Pierre and Rob Carter (who also spoke French) often drove two wagons the distance to Two Birds' depot.

Trent was usually away from the Mallory post, scouting out new locations for future trading posts. Having met him a few years back, he made arrangements to buy all his supplies from Two Birds –too well known to the French authorities, Trent made a point to stay away from the fort. Trent also paid Two Birds to buy his silence as to the location of Trent's post. Two Birds thought that Trent was mad, or at least a poor businessman, to have offered the bribe, but was content to take the unanticipated financial gain without the twinge of a doubting conscience. Trent didn't care what Two Birds thought – his concern was keeping the French out of his business, and he didn't mean the trading business. Trent recognized early on that there would be conflict between the French and British — who would reap the rewards of ruling North America? He also recognized that the fur trappers could be a good source of information – information that could be useful to the colonial military. For Trent, that meant to one man in particular, George Washington.

Phil and his driver, Jack Tomlinson, spent as much time as they could with the trappers who came to trade, who told them about of the fur business. While most of these trappers did nothing more than take in their surroundings a little more carefully, they also reported any movement by the French or their Indian allies. The more adventuresome among them entered Shawnee camps as traders and friends to the French, a foolhardy but effective way to gauge the mood of the Shawnee. By and large, the trappers brought back the same information. The French were cracking down on any British within what they deemed their private domain, while the Shawnee were making noise about raiding those settlers who came too close to their villages. As Rob Carter put it: "It's as if the whole countryside is a tinderbox, ready to flare up. All that it's waitin' on is for someone to strike the flint to the kindling."

Despite the mood in the territory, things were going well at what was now known as the Mallory-Clarke Trading Emporium. Trapping and hunting was the best anyone had seen over the last year and a half, which was music to Phil's ears. He now owned the transport end of the business, and had two routes for his wagons, one going to Albany and the other to Philadelphia.

Love was also reaching new heights, as Liza turned eighteen and dropped not so subtle hints to Handsome Henry that it was time to marry. Henry always came up with an excuse, including waiting until the time was right. The arrival of trapper Stan McNeil (also a Methodist minister, known as Old White Collar because of the collar he kept in his saddle bag, just in case his preaching duties were needed), left no doubt in Liza's mind that the time was right. On a warm September afternoon, Handsome Henry and Liza wed.

****

The wedding was as grand an affair as possible, considering the remoteness of the post. Liza had ordered material for her dress and veil from Jimmy Two Birds months in advance. Abigail gave Liza her grandmother's ring, while Henry wore his father's ring. Everyone pitched in to decorate the post, and to dig additional fire pits for roasting of venison, pigs, turkeys, and a huge cauldron of rabbit and vegetable stew. Timothy outdid himself, both in baking and in the quantity and quality of the ale he provided. Jimmy Two Birds arrived with three barrels of French wine to add to the festivities. McNeil, having sampled the ale and the wine beforehand, preached the Biblical story of the wedding in Cana. He claimed that even Jesus would have been hard pressed to outdo the beverages on hand.

The happy newlyweds were feted by an unruly but pleasant group of trappers, hunters, woodsmen, and a few Mohawk. Music filled the night sky, as no less than three fiddles, two guitars, a harmonica or two, and Joseph (surprising all with a fine tenor voice) contributed to the merriment. As the party gained momentum and hilarity, so too the party goers' comments became less inhibited. Good-natured barbs about the wedding night could be heard from every corner of the grounds. Henry, feeling giddy, noticed that he was out of ale. Without thinking, he demanded of his new bride, "Woman! Bring me another tankard of ale."

"Whoowee, would you listen to the mouth on that man? Handsome Henry, unless your legs are broken, you can darn well get your own drink!" responded Liza. "Of course, if you're already too drunk to do that, then you may be useless to me later." This brought about a tremendous gust of laughter from everyone, including Henry, now red-faced from embarrassment as well as alcohol.

Phil announced that the couple could use his tent for the next few nights, or at least until their new cabin was ready to use; he would sleep in the bunkhouse. That set off a flurry of comments. "Why, Phil, my old friend," replied Stump Nose, "you're going to give up that comfort and all, and dwell with the unclean? How will you survive?"

Phil, staggering a bit as he made his way back to the campfire from an ale keg, said, "My plan is a simple one. I'm going to hold my breath all night." At this point, Phil released a tremendously loud and especially smelly fart. Rob Carter, who sat next to Phil – and downwind as well – almost fell off the log seat. "Damnation. If you add any more of that to the air, we're all gonna die in the bunkhouse tonight."

****

The morning air had a definite chill to it; the frosty grass crunched underfoot as Liam made his way up the slope in front of the trading post. He hunted alone this morning; Henry couldn't drag himself out of his warm cabin or out of the arms of his insistent wife, and Daniel was with Pierre, returning any day after getting supplies from Jimmy Two Birds. Not that Liam minded. He used these times to hone his skills as a tracker, focusing his whole being on the hunt without any distractions. While tracking a wild turkey, he heard a rustling of leaves behind him. He dropped to the ground, and crawled behind two large oak trees. As the Mohawk brave crested the small rise and came into view, Liam pulled an arrow from his quiver, drew back his bow, and took aim. Donehogawa froze when he saw the movement up ahead, and heard the unmistakable sound of a bowstring being drawn tight. The warrior held out his hand, palm facing forward in a gesture of peace, and spoke in English. "Put bow down, little white man. Mohawk not hurt you."

Liam stood his ground, smiled, and replied in perfect Mohawk. "Tell your braves to put theirs down, and I will." Donehogawa, startled by this unexpected response, complied. Soon, six Mohawk braves appeared, their weapons no longer at the ready. His fingers and arms began to tire from the strain and tension, so Liam lowered his bow, but kept the arrow nocked.

"I am Donehogawa of the Bear Clan, war chief of the Mohawk. Our village lays many sleeps to the east. We are returning there, after joining our Mingo friends for a raid upon the Shawnee. Who are you, and how is it you speak our language?"

"I have heard of you, Donehogawa, from the man who taught me your tongue. My name is Liam Mallory. I learned of the Mohawk from my friend, Pierre Baptist. He is with my family, at our trading post on the Kiskiminetas River." Donehogawa sat, and beckoned Liam to do the same, while the other braves gathered wood for a fire. One of them, Degandawidah, strode off to hunt game for their dinner.

"The Black Robe is with Trent? It would be good to see him again after so many years. I knew him when he was still a Black Robe. I was not in the village the day that he was betrayed and beaten. If I had been there, he would have not been so badly used. He would have been asked to leave the village, but as a friend, not as an outcast. The Black Robes would have insisted on it, as he broke their rules. They have had too much influence in Mohawk affairs . That he is still alive shows he is blessed by the Great Spirit. How is it that I have been to Trent's, and have not seen you before?"

Liam was more relaxed now, and in a state of more than a little awe as he faced this powerful and well-known Mohawk chief. "My family has only been there for a few months. We moved there to be partners with Trent. I was hunting for the post, and was close to shooting a turkey when you arrived."

"You hunt with bow and arrow, while most white men use the musket. Did Pierre teach you that as well? You are an interesting young man, Liam Mallory. You would fit in well in a Mohawk village. Come with us, and live with the Mohawk, if only for a little while. We can learn much from each other."

Liam was surprised by the request, and at the same time felt excited at the prospect of fulfilling a lifelong dream. He replied, "That would please me, but I need to get word to my family before I could do that."

"I will send one of my braves back to the trading post with the news. He will talk with Pierre. We will tell them that you are coming for a visit, and that you are free to return at any time. You may choose to stay. I see in your heart that you are Mohawk. It is fourteen sleeps to reach our village, and we need take no more time than that. I have much news from our Mohawk brothers living near the big water Gichigami, where also live our enemies – the French and the Ojibway."

****

So it was that Liam joined the Mohawk band, who made haste to their main village northeast of the town of Albany. During this time, they did very little hunting, living mostly on pemmican – dried venison and cranberry – and whatever berries were available, such as strawberries, blueberries and Concord grapes. Five days into their journey, Liam rose earlier than the rest, and hunted before the day's march began. The braves were dismayed by his disappearance that morning, as Liam had left the camp without rousing any of them from their sleep. When told of Liam's absence, Donehogawa said, "We cannot take the time to look for him. Perhaps I was mistaken thinking he could live among us." They were surprised a few hours later when the group walked to a ridge, and found Liam – who waited for them with a butchered white-tail buck which lasted them until their arrival at the village. This did much to strengthen Donehogawa's belief in Liam, and quelled some of the disquiet in the hearts of the others.

Donehogawa introduced Liam to the tribe in the village longhouse the night after they arrived. He named him Otetiani, which means "he comes prepared". While most of the tribe welcomed him, some among the younger braves looked down on the newcomer. One young brave, Wahta, refused to call Otetiani by name; instead, he called him English, or white boy, attempting to disgrace the newcomer. Otetiani found it difficult, but managed to keep his composure when faced with these taunts of disrespect. He knew that he would eventually have to prove himself. He only hoped it would not be in the form of a fight, as he knew he was no match for Wahta, whose name meant Maple tree – for good reason, as he stood several inches over six feet, and was as broad-shouldered as a tree trunk.

Otetiani's chance came a few weeks after arriving. Early one morning, one of the women returned to from tending a field near the woods, saying she heard a flock of wild turkeys.. A hunting party formed, with Wahta as the leader. Otetiani gained permission from Donehogawa to join the hunt, much to the displeasure of Wahta. "White boy can come, but he stays at the back, so I don't have to look at him." With Wahta in the lead, the hunters jogged out of camp and into the woods. They slowed to a walk when they heard the turkeys, in a grove of trees situated on the top of a rise just ahead of them.

As they began to climb, Wahta suddenly stopped. He heard, and then saw, a rattlesnake just a few feet to his right. The snake was agitated, and coiled. If Wahta made any move, it would strike. Otetiani saw it, too. Pulling an arrow from his quiver, he took quick aim and let it fly. The arrow caught the rattler in the head, severing it before coming to rest in the trunk of a maple, the head pinned against the bark. Wahta, with a look of surprise and relief, turned and said, "Otetiani, you are now and forever my brother: Snake Slayer." He retrieved the arrow (the snake's head still attached) and placed it in his quiver. Gesturing to Otetiani to join him in the lead, Wahta resumed the hunt. They brought down three wild fowl, the last one by Otetiani as he caught it in flight, his shot slicing between two trees no more than a foot apart. 'Oh, niiawenhátie (what's going on)?" exclaimed Wahta as he clapped Otetiani on the back, laughing. "I think Snake Slayer is just showing off now. He is Mohawk."

That night, most of the tribe gathered in the longhouse. Wahta retold the story of the hunt, complete with descriptions of his own fear when confronted by the rattler. When he finished, he pulled the arrowhead out of a pouch at his side. After earlier removing the shaft of the arrow, he had made a necklace out of shell beads strung on a deer-hide thong; the arrow-snake head hung down the middle. He walked to Otetiani and placed it around his neck, saying, "This is Snake Slayer. This is my brother."

Orenda watched and listened as her father Donehogawa explained to Otetiani the history of the Iroquois Nation, and the part the Mohawk played in this confederation of tribes. The Mohawk were the easternmost tribe of the confederation, and so protected the front gate. They defended their territory from any encroachment, especially from their bitter enemies – the Algonquin-speaking people, and the Huron tribe. The Huron, though not the force they once were, had always been a particular thorn in their sides, frequently raiding Mohawk villages.

In order to maintain the preeminence of the Iroquois Confederacy, the Mohawk nation needed to align itself with the whites – first the Dutch, and then the British. These partnerships meant that they were better armed than their enemies, and enabled the Mohawks to become the foremost native power in an area stretching from the east coast to the upper Great Lakes. Donehogawa also taught Otetiani many of the spiritual ways of the Mohawk, while his wife and his daughter (Onatah and Orenda) taught him the daily life of a Mohawk. They spent hours refining his language, and their use of plants for food and medicine. Even though Liam/Otetiani was particularly drawn to the warrior ethos, he recognized early on that it was to his great advantage to learn all that he could from these two formidable Mohawk women. It wasn't necessarily his plan to fall in love, but the daughter of Donehogawa soon held his heart.

****

Otetiani, Wahta, and three other braves sat around the campfire after a long hunting day . They traveled all the way to the shoreline of the large Lake Ontario; the day neared its end with the western horizon seemingly on fire as the setting sun reflected off the few clouds in a panorama of red, orange, pink and blue over the lake. Slabs of venison roasted on spits over the fire, while the men busied themselves cleaning the many deer and beaver hides acquired during the hunt. They had been away from the village for two weeks, during which time Wahta noticed that Otetiani became increasingly quiet.

"What is in your heart, Snake Slayer, my brother?" asked Wahta, "You have barely said two words all day. Does my brother long for his own people?"

Otetiani looked up from the beaver pelt he was scraping and said, "I am sorry for my silence. My heart does indeed have a longing, but not for my white family. I do miss them, of course, but I am very happy being with my Mohawk family. No, my brother, my heart is full of the sight of Orenda. It is she who has quieted my mouth. This has me concerned, as I have never felt this way before, and I do not know that she feels the same about me."

Wahta and the others erupted into thunderous laughter, nodding their heads and pointing at Otetiani with huge grins on their faces. "Snake Slayer," said Wahta after he caught his breath, "we have been wondering when you would admit to the cause of your heart sickness. We have known for many days that you desire Donehogawa's daughter. Do not concern yourself with this. I have seen how Orenda looks at you. Almost the whole village has seen this, including our chief, her father. Speak to him when we return to the village, but, for now, it is better that you take your mind away from that which you can do nothing about, and tell us more of the ways of the whites."

****

Three days later, the hunters approached their village when Wahta held up his hand to silence the idle banter. "I see too much smoke for the fires coming from the village," he said, "something is wrong." The rest of them, now aware of what Wahta saw, dropped the travois piled high with hides, pelts, and meat, and rushed to his side. "I hear shouts and screams. Our enemies must be attacking." Without a moment's delay, the five hunters – now warriors – ran the rest of the way, only pausing when they reached the forest's edge.

A band of Shawnee were raiding the village; one group herded captive women and children toward the river to their canoes, while the others were engaged in holding off Donehogawa and the warriors who fought to defend the camp. Among the captives was Orenda, who struggled mightily against the Shawnee brave attempting to put a noose around her neck. "Go to Donehogawa," Wahta directed the three braves, "Snake Slayer and I will attack the Shawnees taking the captives to the river."

The Shawnee had surprised the Mohawk; Donehogawa valiantly led the defense, but the surprise was so complete that the raiders were able to gather captive women and children who had been working in the fields. Donehogawa, despite having taken an arrow in his right leg, rallied his warriors and pushed the Shawnee back. The arrival of the three extra warriors was enough to send the Shawnee retreating to their canoes and those holding the captives. Wahta and Otetiani raced to the river, Otetiani loosing arrow after arrow. He took down two Shawnee, while Wahta barreled into them, striking heads and shoulders with his tomahawk. The Shawnee brave who was leading the tethered-together captive group turned in time to see him coming, and dropped the rope to reach for his tomahawk. Orenda, now free from the Shawnee's grasp, took advantage of the situation, and kicked the distracted warrior in the groin. Gasping for breath, he backhanded her across the face, not knowing that it would be his last act, as an arrow from the bow of Otetiani pierced his throat.

Chogan (the leader of the Shawnee raiding party) was a much-feared warrior, but he knew he could not win against Wahta and Otetiani. Leaving the captives, he ran to his canoe and grabbed his war lance. Wahta twisted to the side, so that Chogan's throw did not hit his chest with full force; instead, the glancing blow created a long bleeding gash in his side. When Chogan and the rest of the remaining Shawnee hurriedly dragged their canoes into the river and paddled away, Otetiani stopped his charge to tend to his fallen friend, while Orenda led the rest of the captives to safety behind him. Otetiani drew goose down from his pouch, and Orenda bent to help stuff it into Wahta's wound. They helped him rise and gingerly walk back to the village.

Onatah knelt at her husband's side, while another brave pulled the arrow from Donehogawa's leg. The arrow had ripped through the large muscle in his thigh, but had missed the artery. Onatah applied goose down to the wound to stop the bleeding, while she made a poultice of dried curly dock and cattail root to set on the puncture, securing it with a strip of deer hide. Two other braves required attention, but one was beyond any help as his skull had been crushed by a tomahawk blow. While Orenda and her mother tended the wounded, Donehogawa saw to the disposal of the Shawnee dead. Otetiani stayed with his friend, who was ministered to in the village longhouse by Orenda. When she finished bandaging Wahta's torn side, Otetiani reached out and lifted her face to look at her bruised and swelling cheek. As their eyes met, she took his hand tenderly and kissed it, saying, "You are Mohawk. You are my love." With tears in his eyes, Otetiani could only reply, "And you are mine."

They were married in the village longhouse two weeks later. In the tradition of the Mohawk, Onatah sat by the side of her daughter; since Otetiani's mother was not present, Wahta's mother was honored to sit with him. Orenda held a wedding basket containing bits of material and clothing. This symbolized her promise to her husband and any future children they may have, that she will mend and clean their clothing. Otetiani also held a wedding basket; it contained the wedding cake made of white corn and strawberries, meaning he will for the rest of his life provide the food for her and their children. Donehogawa stood and addressed those in the longhouse.

"We are here to see my daughter wed to a man who I am proud to know. I am honored by his bravery in battle and by his skills as a hunter. I am honored by his devotion to the Mohawk way. I am honored to begin this ceremony with our prayer to our Mother Earth."

Donehogawa then raised his hands to the sky, and prayed. "I speak for the people, who give greetings, love and thanksgiving to our Mother Earth, then to the waters of the world; to the fish life; to the food, corn, beans, and squash, and all the garden food; to the berries, and their leader, the strawberry; to the trees that are the forests of the world; to the animals, big and small, and to their leader, the deer. To the medicines that heal our sicknesses, growing in the mountains, the fields, the river's edge, and in the forests; to the grasses of the world that provide food for the animal life; to the birds, who greet our eldest brother the Sun with beautiful songs to bring satisfaction and enjoyment to us, the humans; to the Eagle, who is the leader of all bird life, we greet and thank you for your gifts.

"To the four winds who bring warmth and coolness; the changing of the four seasons for the people; to our grandfather, the Thunder, for renewing the lakes, the rivers and quenching our thirst. We, your human relatives, give you our greetings and thanks — to our eldest brother, the Sun, for the light and the warmth for all that grows and allows our children to live; to our grandmother, the Moon, for the birth of our children; to the Stars, for the morning dew and for their great beauty during the night; to the four sacred Sky Dweller beings who protect and guide us, as the Creator instructed them; to the ultimate, our Creator, who provided all that is necessary for our life, and asks only that we be grateful. We ask you, our Creator, now, that power and guidance be given to the people and this young couple, who start a life together as you intended. Our Creator, your people are of one mind and we send you our love, greetings, and thankfulness. The Creator made Earth. From the Earth, man was made. Man became lonely, so woman was made to be a companion. The Creator put them together to populate his world. His wish is carried on. Welcome to everyone here."

****

Life continued in the village; each day had its tasks and chores, though Otetiani and Orenda often went through the motions, as they performed them while learning to live together. Later in his life, Otetiani often said that this time brought the most peace he had ever known. His usual restless spirit calmed in the sun of Orenda's love and devotion. They lay in each other's arms long after the dawn had broken, and endured much good natured ribbing from the others in the village. One morning, before dawn, Otetiani, after rising from their sleeping pallet, bent down and gently kissed Orenda on the forehead. She stirred and opened her eyes, "Where is my husband going? I am getting cold without you next to me." She flung the bear skin blanket off of her body, and with a mischievous grin said, "Come back, before I freeze."

"Beautiful one," Otetiani replied as he knelt before her, ran his hands over her breasts, and kissed her lips. "I miss the times when I hunted alone. It is time for me to start living up to the promise that I would provide for you. It snowed last night; that will make my task even easier, and I will return to warm you before you know it." He pulled on an elk hide jacket, grabbed his bow, and left the longhouse after blowing a kiss to his smiling wife as he pulled the door closed.

The air was crisp and very cold. The fallen snow was dry and light; even though several inches now lie upon the ground, walking was not a hindrance. Otetiani left the village to follow the frozen creek into the woods. The sun began to peek through the low level clouds in the eastern sky, and revealed a clear blue horizon in the west. Otetiani always found great pleasure in the contrast between the dark green pine trees and the deep blue of the sky; today the sight was enhanced by the addition of several inches of dry snow lying on the uppermost pine boughs. Snow rose from the branches at the touch of a breeze, and blew smoke-like into the frigid air. Otetiani smiled at the sight, remembering when a wet clump of snow fell from an evergreen and landed on his brother Daniel while he was sleeping. Yes, he missed these times of solitude –yet, it seemed that maybe not as much as before.

As he continued deeper into the woods, he saw the tracks of an animal that he had only rarely seen. He had learned – from his father, and from Pierre, and most recently from Donehogawa – that while never very plentiful (because of the deep woods and lack of grazing), buffalo still roamed in the area. He followed the trail, until it opened up to reveal a small meadow where a grazing buffalo cow used her massive head to clear the snow away from the grass hidden beneath. Otetiani dropped to his knees, and crawled to a mound topped with the trunk of a tree that had fallen long ago. He breathed deeply as he pulled back the bow string and took aim. The buffalo looked up from her grazing and shook her mane. Otetiani, to his surprise, could not release the arrow; frozen to the spot, all he could do was watch and listen as she pawed the ground, and gave out a short grunt. Two calves emerged from behind a copse of oak trees to join their mother. The cow gave another grunt, and the three moved into the shelter of the trees. Before she disappeared, she stopped, turned to look at Otetiani, and nodded her head up and down. Otetiani was surprised that he was able to move again, but he remained transfixed to the spot and it seemed to him that he heard a voice coming from the direction of the buffalo saying to him, "Well done, now we are brothers."

****

When Otetiani finished telling her about his encounter with the buffalo, Orenda said, "That is a powerful vision. You must tell my father. He is wise in these matters."

Donehogawa sat by the fire in his longhouse when Orenda and Otetiani came to him. His wounded leg was healing nicely, though he would always have a slight limp. He looked up from the new pipe he was carving, and said, "My children, I am glad to see you. Come sit by me and tell me, how is married life?" The two blushed slightly as they sat beside their chief. Otetiani then told Donehogawa of his confrontation with the buffalo. When he finished, Donehogawa remained silent for a few moments. .

"It is indeed a rare thing to see buffalo in this area. When I was a boy, my grandfather told me his grandfather's stories about the many buffalo that once lived here. I have seen the great migration road he told me about, made by the passing of vast buffalo herds near the Ohio and into Cantuckee, the hunting ground of the Shawnee and Cherokee. To see one here and for it to have spoken is strong medicine, my son. I cannot remember the last Mohawk to have the buffalo as his spirit animal, but this cannot be anything other than that. The Great Spirit has marked your spirit in this manner; of that there can be no doubt."

****

Despite the weather – the winter had been long, cold and snowy –the hunting had been good, and the tribe fared well. Spring was in the offing; the slightly warmer weather saw, the snows began to melt, crocus and fiddlehead ferns began to appear, and the creek was no longer frozen. Otetiani and Wahta were returning from a very good hunt, both of them struggling somewhat with the weight of the elk Otetiani brought down with one shot through the heart. Having strung the gutted carcass onto a long oak branch, the pole bounced on their shoulders as they walked. Otetiani released his end of the burden, and drank the icy water.

Otetiani was eager to learn more about his new family and people, which added to the good impression he made, both with his skills as a hunter and his willingness to teach some of the younger braves. However, when they arrived at camp, the usual crowd of women and young boys was not there to greet them. For once, the rest of the village was more interested in something other than the two returning hunters. They laid the elk down, and headed toward the excited villagers gathered around another returning group of braves.

The tall black man with them looked rather confused, as the villagers gaped up at him while listening to the brave telling how they rescued him. Looking over the crowd, he saw to his surprise what appeared to be a white man carrying an elk into camp. He waited as the white man approached, and with a wave of his hand yelled to Otetiani. "I certainly hope you speak English. I've not had time to master the Mohawk language yet."

****

So it was that a runaway slave named Rufus was adopted into the Mohawk family, and received the name Teeyeehogrow: man with a double life. From the start, Rufus gave his all in adapting, and learning how to be a Mohawk. Otetiani assisted greatly; he spent many hours with Teeyeehogrow teaching him the language and how to hunt and track. Teeyeehogrow learned quickly, and soon could communicate with other members of the village. Although he became a regular at Donehogawa's side (to glean the history and spiritual lessons from so great a chief), he cherished most the time he spent hunting with Otetiani and Wahta .

****

Having risen before dawn, the three tracked an elk as it wandered deeper into the woods. The elk stopped suddenly, and then sprinted away – evidently spooked by something or someone. It was then that the three hunters smelled and then saw the spiral of smoke rising from a clearing near the creek at the bottom of the hill they were standing on. Wahta whispered, "We should see who it is, but until we know, we should remain hidden." They crept down the hillside so quietly that the early morning birdsong was not disturbed. Dropping to their knees, they crawled the last few feet to the edge of the woods. They could see the Shawnee warriors gathered around the fire for breakfast. Movement from the far side of the camp drew their attention, as a captive woman was being led to the creek to get water. "Come," whispered Wahta, "we must tell Donehogawa. Those Shawnee are the ones who raided our village. Chogan is with them."

Within minutes of hearing the news, Donehogawa was leading a band of warriors to the Shawnee encampment. Wahta led, Otetiani and Teeyeehogrow at his side. The Shawnee were taking turns beating an Abnaki brave they had captured, and took no notice of the Mohawk warriors running silently down the hill toward them. Chogan emerged from his teepee, rearranged his blackbird headpiece, and then dragged the captive woman out so she could watch her man being tortured. An arrow from the bow of Otetiani found its mark, and a Shawnee brave fell to the ground. Another brave tomahawked the Abnaki, then turned to face the charging Wahta. Wahta ducked under the swinging tomahawk and brought his lance up, striking his foe in the belly. As he withdrew the barbed point, a coil of intestines came with it. Wahta flinched slightly so as to avoid the slippery guts and the instant odor of a pierced bowel. The Shawnee fell to his knees, and clutched at his escaping innards to no avail –the blow from Wahta's tomahawk killed him instantly.

Other skirmishes meant that three more Shawnee were dead. Chogan released his hold on the woman, and came face to face with Teeyeehogrow. Chogan was by far the better fighter, but Teeyeehogrow was a worthy opponent based on his size alone. Teeyeehogrow feinted with the lance he held in his right hand, while he readied his strike with the tomahawk in his left. Chogan, whose quickness caught Teeyeehogrow by surprise, grabbed the lance and pulled, bringing Teeyeehogrow into the arc of Chogan's descending tomahawk. Instinct alone saved Teeyeehogrow from the full force of the blow, as he rammed his shoulder into Chogan's chest. The tomahawk missed his head but its momentum took it along Teeyeehogrow's back, leaving a deep cut from shoulder blade to above his hip. Screaming in pain, he shoved Chogan away and fell to his knees. Chogan, seeing Wahta and Otetiani run to help their fallen friend, knew once again that he was no match for the two of them. Bellowing in anger, he turned and escaped to the safety of the woods, vowing revenge on the two Mohawk warriors.

****

The Abnaki woman knelt by her dead husband, and sang her lamentation, while Otetiani busily staunched the blood flow from Teeyeehogrow's back. She moved to Otetiani, pointed to herself, and said, "Kateri." She then pushed him out of the way and continued to bandage Teeyeehogrow's wound. He flashed a big smile at her, despite the pain. When she finished, she helped him stand; from that point until they reached the village, she never left his side. Donehogawa explained to him that Kateri now belonged to him because he had rescued her from Chogan. Teeyeehogrow as a former slave did not want to own any person; he did the only thing remaining to do, and so Kateri became his wife.

****

Liam had lived with the Mohawk for nearly two years when Jack Tomlinson arrived in the village, with a wagon full of bearskins, deer hides, and beaver pelts bound for Albany. Timothy Winslow accompanied him. Having finally succumbed to his fears, Winslow left the frontier outpost for a more civilized existence. Jack passed along the news that Abigail was with child. Because of the risks due to her age, she wanted Liam to come home before the baby was born in five months. As Donehogawa had planned a trip to that area, a party of Liam, Orenda, and the warriors Dadgayadoh, Deganawidah, and Wahta left the village two days later to make the journey to Trent's outpost. The journey of 450 miles would take two weeks to complete without hardship. For the first week, Otetiani was content to ride along with Orenda. Often, they lagged behind the others, lost in each other's company. Orenda noticed a change, though, in Otetiani as they neared the trading post. He seemed distant, far away in thought; at times, he rode off alone. During one of those times when he rode ahead of the group, Orenda sought out her father, to ask him if he knew what was troubling her husband.

Donehogawa looked at his daughter, saw the concern in her eyes, and said, "Orenda, my daughter, Otetiani is troubled by the buffalo spirit and he is confused as he comes closer to his white family. The buffalo is a powerful guide, but it is makes one yearn to be free to wander our earth mother, as the buffalo does. It is also a hard thing for Otetiani, now that he has embraced the Mohawk life, to face his former life. My daughter, it is for you to ease his troubled spirit. I think it is time to tell him of the child you carry. Do not look at me like I can look in the heart of a woman to see what is there. I learned of the child from your mother."

Orenda smiled at her father, and replied, "I should have known that mother would tell you. I am glad I spoke to you. I feel that you have opened my eyes. Yes, it is time to tell Otetiani about his coming child."

Otetiani was riding ahead of the group, needing the time alone to sort through his mind's confusion. The thought that puzzled him the most was whether he was Otetiani or Liam, but the buffalo dream also played upon his mind, giving rise to his normal restlessness of spirit. Glancing back to find Orenda brought some measure of comfort, but he still struggled. He noticed that she was riding with her father, and thought he saw sadness on her face.

They made camp by a small stream. Otetiani sat with his back to a willow tree that overlooked a small waterfall and dozed, the buffalo dream having invaded his sleep. The nearly full moon was all the light that Orenda needed as she walked to her husband. He awoke at the touch of her hand upon his shoulder.

"Wake up, my love," Orenda whispered in his ear, "I have something to tell you."

Otetiani opened his eyes, cupped his hand over the curve of her cheek, and said, "My beautiful one, I have not been myself lately. My spirit is restless, my mind confused. I have seen sadness in your eyes, and I am sorry that I am the cause for this – but I am torn about our future."

"Oh, my husband," Orenda replied as she took his hand in hers, "I know that you are troubled, and that the buffalo dream is strong, but know this. I will be by your side through whatever path you choose, and so will the child I bear."

Tears flowed down Otetiani's face. As he stood, for the first time he noticed the swell of Orenda's belly. "We have a child coming?" he asked. He took her in his arms. "We will raise this child as a Mohawk." They walked back to the campfire and settled down for the night. Soon Orenda was asleep, her head on Otetiani's shoulder. Otetiani, his mind playing back what he had learned, felt more peaceful than he had in a long time. Instead of the buffalo dream, he fell asleep to a vision of a Mohawk village and children playing.

Chapter 4

The Raids

Thomas couldn't stay still; he alternated sitting on a stump by the fire pit, and nervously pacing around the circle of fire. Daniel and Otetiani looked at each other, and smiled at their usually stoic father's unease. Within the cabin, Abigail accepted a sip of cool water from the now noticeably pregnant Orenda while resting from the last contraction. Liza wiped the sweat from her mother's forehead, saying, "One more push, and I think we'll have that new baby." Abigail thinly smiled at her daughter. "I hope so. I am running out of energy. Maybe 42 years is too old to have a child. It was certainly easier when you were born." She caught her breath sharply, exclaiming, "Oh, dear Lord, it is time."

Orenda watched from the foot of the bed; after a few seconds, she said, "I can see the baby's head. One big push, Abigail, and we have a new life to celebrate." Liza helped her mother out of the bed and to the birthing stool they had borrowed from the Cranes. Orenda knelt in front and smoothed out the blanket that was placed under the stool. Abigail, her face once again covered in sweat, her hands pressing down on the arm rests, knuckles whitened from the pressure, with her remaining strength yelled and pushed hard. A moment later Orenda eased the squalling newborn down to the waiting blanket. Liza picked up the child and swaddled her in the blanket while Orenda replaced it with an old linen sheet to catch and wrap the placenta. "It's a girl, Mama!" cried Liza, as she placed the little one on the bed and gently wiped her face removing the mucous from the tiny nostrils. Abigail felt one more contraction and soon they heard the plop of the afterbirth hitting the sheet.

Orenda helped Abigail stand, moving the birthing stool aside while she guided her the few steps to the bed. Liza handed the baby to her weary, yet smiling mother. Abigail took one look at the tiny face, and said, "It is only by God's grace that she arrived safely." The baby finally stilled her cries as her mother, after checking the tiny hands and feet, placed her nipple in her daughter's mouth; the whimpering replaced by the sound of gentle sucking. "Tell your father that his new daughter, Grace, is waiting to meet him."

Liza came out of the cabin grinning from ear to ear, "Come in, Pa. Grace, your youngest, is waiting to see you." Thomas tapped out his pipe. Wanting to look his best, he ran his fingers through his hair, and straightened his shirt. His sons followed him into the cabin as Thomas entered.

Sated for the time being Grace let go of the teat as her father and brothers came in. "Say hello to your daughter, dear husband," Abigail said. Thomas lifted the child, tears in his eyes. "I am not a God-fearing man, but at times like these I can be. Grace is a most wondrous gift and I thank God for her safe arrival, and for the health of my beloved wife." He kissed the child on the forehead and handed her back to Abigail. "Now, it is time for a little celebration, I think. Otetiani, Daniel, get those ale casks out. I feel a mighty thirst coming on."

****

The trading post took on a party atmosphere, with plenty of singing, laughter, and dancing. The traders who were there joined in the festivities, two of them producing fiddles. With Phil Burke playing a banjo, Irish jigs and reels soon filled the night air.

From the top of the hill overlooking the post, hidden by the cover of the woods, two Shawnee braves watched the proceedings below. "It is time to teach these English a lesson," Huritt said. "Our French brothers would be very happy for this place to be destroyed. Let's attack tonight. The English are in no position to defend."

Chogan smiled at his friend. "That is what I would like to do – but, look again, Huritt. The white man called Snake Slayer is alert. His bow is ever at his side, and the other Mohawks with him also watch. No, we cannot attack tonight. We have more warriors coming in two days. That is when we will attack, and destroy this place." They turned, and jogged back into the woods, to their camp three miles away.

Two days later, hangovers now forgotten, Otetiani, Daniel, Joseph, and Henry left the post to hunt, while Trent, Donehogawa, Dadgayadoh, Deganawidah, and Wahta left on a separate mission. They were anxious to get firsthand information after a trader arrived that morning, bringing news of a Shawnee party heading south out of Fort Duquesne. Pierre and Liza canoed across the river, to a meadow teeming with the plants Pierre used for their healing properties. With the news that there may be a Shawnee party in the area, both Pierre and Liza took their muskets. In the back of the main building, Orenda rocked Grace to sleep while her own child moved within her. Nearby, Abigail took a well-deserved nap in the back room she shared with Thomas, who was in the front talking to two traders - Rob Carter and Stump Nose Emerson - about their load of furs brought yesterday. Phil Burke examined the furs stored under the canvas canopy of a freight wagons. He picked up a beaver pelt and exclaimed under his breath, "I cannot believe the quality. I'm sure as I can be that I've come to the right place at the right time."

Chogan, certain that he had accounted for everyone, turned to the seven warriors with him and said, "Remember, I want the white woman and her child alive. Kill the rest," he added with a hint of disgust, "but leave the Mohawk woman to me." Silently, the two Huron and six Shawnee jogged down the hill, the rising sun behind them making them almost invisible as well. The two Huron headed to the southern end of the encampment, in order to keep watch on Pierre across the river. Three of the Shawnee raced to the front door of the main building, while Chogan, Huritt, and the other Shawnee veered off to the side door. Unnoticed and forgotten, Phil glanced out of the wagon just in time to see the raiding party entering the building. Climbing over the pile of furs, he exited the rear of the wagon and ran to his tent to get his musket.

Rob Carter and Stump Nose Emerson turned when they heard the door flung open behind them. Rob managed to get off a pistol shot and mortally wounded one of the attackers, but died when another's arrow pierced his throat. The third Shawnee, armed with an old musket, fired from the doorway, hitting the side of Thomas' head with a grazing shot. He fell backwards from the blow, slamming into the wall behind and falling unconscious and out of sight behind the counter. Stump Nose - trying to climb over the counter - was felled by a tomahawk to the back of the head. Pulling him back and dropping him to the floor, the Shawnee warrior scalped Stump Nose while the other Shawnee did the same to Rob. Hoisting their trophies in the air, they raced back out of the cabin, their shrill victory cries reaching Pierre and Liza.

Chogan burst through the door of the Mallory's living quarters, Huritt and the third warrior at his heels. Huritt went to Orenda to take Grace from her, but she kicked out and up, catching Huritt in the genitals. He slapped her twice with an open hand, took the baby and, grimacing, headed for the door. Abigail was yanked from her bed, a rope looped around her neck, and led outside. Chogan, malice etched on his face, grabbed Orenda by the hair and dragged her out of the door. Setting her up against a tree, he tied her to it so that she stood facing him. He pulled his knife and cut away her buckskin dress, her extended belly thrusting forward. One of the warriors, watching from across the yard, yelled out, "Chogan! No! Leave the woman. She is the daughter of Donehogawa, and wife to Snake Slayer. They will not rest until they hunt you down." Growling with disdain, Chogan answered, "I am not afraid of an old man. As for Snake Slayer, I say let him come. He will die slowly, as I roast him and then piss on his ashes."

Phil emerged from his tent, his musket loaded in time to see a Shawnee leading Abigail out of the cabin and across the yard, heading for the far hill. He dropped to one knee, raised, aimed, and fired the musket hitting the warrior above the groin, the ball boring through his liver. He fell to the ground dying, but hung on to the rope causing Abigail to fall as well. It was then that Phil saw what was happening at the tree. With no time to reload, he got up and charged toward Chogan, brandishing his musket like a club. Huritt had raced toward the hillside upon hearing the shot that took down his fellow attacker. He now stopped, and - placing the baby on the ground - drew his bow to loose an arrow, hitting Phil in the shin just before Phil could swing his club. Phil toppled to the ground, clutching at the arrow protruding from his leg. Chogan reached down and pulled Phil up by the hair to cut away his scalp pulling it away with a resounding plop. Phil had never known that pain that intense could possibly exist; it was a mercy that it knocked him unconscious.

Stuffing the blood-dripping scalp in a pouch at his waist, Chogan returned his attention to Orenda. Using his knife, he sliced her open from breast to crotch and stepped back as coils of intestines and the contents of her womb spilled out. Her voice wavering yet defiant, Orenda told him, "Otetiani will find you, Chogan." Infuriated by this second reminder of a revenge-seeking enemy, Chogan drew the blade across her throat. He then walked over to Abigail as she lay on the ground, and took the rope from a now-dead would be captor. "Get up, white woman, and keep up with us, or you and your baby will die," he snarled. He pulled her to her feet, and headed up the hill.

****

Trent's group moved at a fast clip back the way they had just come. About an hour earlier, they came upon the empty Shawnee camp. They found the tracks of the Shawnee, as they were taking a more circuitous route to the post to stay out of the view of Trent and the Mohawks with him. It was a good three hours back to the trading post, even at the pace they were keeping. They all knew that was not near fast enough.

Chogan headed toward a new camp, where they would spend one night before making their way to Fort Duquesne to sell the captives to the French. He was hoping to get there in three days, but he knew that despite the threats, they could only move as fast as the white woman was able.

Pierre had just finished bandaging the wound on an impatient Thomas' head; he headed to check on Phil when came running into the yard. Trent took in the sight of the brutalized Orenda, as Liza placed the fetus on Orenda's maimed body so that - even in death - she could hold her baby. William Trent was a hardened veteran of many skirmishes and the like with

Indians over the course of his career - first as an officer in the Virginia Militia, and now as a frontiersman - but this was too much; he was soon vomiting. Pierre came to him with a cup of water, and told him, "They've taken Abigail and the baby. Rob Carter and Stump Nose are dead; Thomas has a minor head wound and a nasty bump on the back of it. Phil Burke is dying; Chogan scalped him alive."

"Chogan has gone too far, too bloody far," Trent replied angrily. He took a sip of water to rinse out the taste of bile. "Did Otetiani say how long they were going to stay out? We need to get on Chogan's trail soon if we're going to catch him."

"He hoped to be back tomorrow, but would come in today if they were lucky on the hunt. Thomas is anxious to get going, but he needs a day; we can't move Burke, he's in too much pain to be jostled about. Plus, there's the question of what do we do with Liza? She can't stay here," answered Pierre, as he watched Liza doing what she could to attend to Orenda's body.

"I will send Wahta to bring them in; we can make our plans when they arrive. In the meantime, we can prepare the dead and begin the burying."

Trent left to talk to Wahta, while Pierre approached Liza. "Why don't you go sit with Phil? I don't think he'll last much longer; I will finish up with Orenda."

Phil moaned as Liza wiped his face with a cool wet cloth, being careful not to touch the jagged hole that reached from the top of his forehead to the back of his head and from ear to ear. Liza could not imagine more horrible wounds than those Chogan had inflicted on Phil and Orenda. Gasping in pain, Phil opened his eyes and tried to smile. "All I wanted was the fur," his voice weakened by pain and loss of blood. The pain even affecting his memory, "You tell that Henry to marry you quick before I recover and steal you away, and tell Otetiani to get that bastard Chogan." With that Phil stiffened in a spasm of pain, and once again fell unconscious.

It was getting on late afternoon, the sun peering out from beneath a cloud as it sank toward the horizon. Otetiani, Daniel, Henry, and Joseph did have a good day's hunt, and were returning to the post with a yearling doe and three rabbits when Wahta reached them. Henry was in the lead, and saw Wahta first. "Ho, there Wahta. You come to help us carry back our kill?" said a grinning Henry. However, Otetiani noticed the look of distress on Wahta's face. He stopped in his tracks, and dropped the deer he carried over his shoulders.

"What is it, Wahta? Why are you here?" asked Otetiani.

Wahta walked over to Otetiani and placed his hands on Otetiani's shoulders, saying, "Snake Slayer, my brother, the Shawnee and Huron have raided the trading post. Chogan is their leader." Here, Wahta's voice failed him as he looked into Otetiani's eyes, seeing the usual brightness begin to fade. With a deep breath and bowed head, he forced himself to continue.

"They have taken your mother and the little one captive; your father has been wounded, but will live. Carter and Stump Nose are dead, the fat white man Burke will soon die. Pierre and Liza were across the river, and are safe." Wahta paused. He raised his head; looking Otetiani in the eyes, he said, with a mixture of sadness and hatred, "Chogan killed Orenda and the unborn child."

All of the warmth of the day seemed to disappear, replaced by a chill that overtook Otetiani, who grabbed Wahta by the arms in order to keep from falling. He tried to hold back, but soon was sobbing, crying out, "Orenda, my beautiful one."

Wahta shook Otetiani gently to get his attention. "My brother, you must hide your grief for a little while. We must get back. Trent and the others are leaving at first light to trail the killers."

The thought of revenge snapped Otetiani out of his sobbing distress. "Let us go. I will feast on Chogan's heart!"

They reached the post just as Trent, Pierre, and Donehogawa finished burying Orenda, thinking it wise to spare him the sight of the savagely maimed corpse. Deganawidah, Dadgayadoh, and Liza had gently placed Phil on a litter, and were slowly moving him to the Mallory's bed in the cabin where he could be the most comfortable. When the hunting party appeared, Liza immediately ran to Henry to stand crying into his shoulder. The others walked over to Trent, taking in the somber scene of a massacre. The two dead Shawnee were lying next to where the common grave would be dug. Carter and Emerson were laid out in front of the cabin, to be buried separately.

Flies buzzed incessantly around the pools of blood and tissue where Phil and Orenda had been assaulted. Otetiani sat down next to Donehogawa, at the foot of Orenda's grave. Neither spoke while Donehogawa placed a bowl of burning tobacco at his feet, and pulled the smoke over his face and head, silently commending his daughter to the Great Spirit. Completing his ritual, Donehogawa spoke to Otetiani. "Otetiani, my son, we have lost much this day, but now she is in the care of the Great Spirit. Come, we have much to discuss with Trent and the others, then we must eat and rest."

Otetiani looked at his Mohawk father, his eyes filled with hatred. His voice filled with cruelty. "I will rest, honored father, after I have eaten Chogan's heart. Leave me now." Seeing the grim determination on his face, Donehogawa left Otetiani by the grave and joined the others.

Except for Wahta, who sat close to Otetiani, everyone else gathered around the cook fire. Food had been prepared by Liza and Henry, and now they all settled back to make their plans. Thomas - finally able to move about without feeling dizzy - joined them, adamant that they all pursue the marauders. Trent, however, felt that there was more to this raid than just the usual Shawnee desire to take captives. "I think Chogan was spurred on by the French. This may be a move on their part to gain control of more of the Allegheny River. Colonel Washington needs to be told of this. He is now on his way to this area, with a company of militia to keep a closer eye on Fort Duquesne." He stopped, realizing that he needed to explain how he knew about Washington.

"I was once a captain in the Virginia Militia serving with the colonel. He decided that he needed someone on the frontier to supply him with information. I volunteered to build this trading post, to use as a base for gathering the information. A few of the traders are also employed by the colonel, so you can see how useful this place was."

****

Wahta could see the canoes as they came ashore behind the main cabin. He ran to take a closer look, his tomahawk at the ready. He relaxed when he saw that it was a band of Mingo, and that Half King Tanaghrisson led them. The Mingo were an ally of the British, and Half King was a known hater of the French. As a boy, he had been captured by the French and sold into slavery. His contempt for them had not diminished with time. He held no great love for any white man, and only barely tolerated the British.

With an air of superiority and an arrogant stride, Tanaghrisson walked past Wahta without greeting or even recognition. He approached the camp fire. Waving off Trent, he spoke to Donehogawa in Mohawk. "Honored brother. I have grave news. The French have sent an ambush party to destroy that pitiful fort of the young white colonel over in Great Meadow. We have come to attack the French. You must join us!"

Donehogawa was somewhat taken aback by this overstepping of authority, as he was a Mohawk war chief whereas Tanaghrisson was only the leader of a mixed village of Cayuga and Seneca hotheads. He did not have the power to make decisions of this importance. Donehogawa knew that he needed to reestablish the proper hierarchy, to bring Tanaghrisson down a notch - but he also knew that events were happening much too quickly for a full council meeting of the Iroquois to determine a course of action.

"Tanaghrisson, half king of the Mingo, sit and eat. We will talk with our white friends about this." He turned back to the others and relayed the news Tanaghrisson had brought. "It is clear to me that we must find these French troops, and see if they are planning to do what Tanaghrisson says. It is also clear to me that I must return to my village, to bring them the news of our beloved Orenda's death, and to begin preparations for possible war. What say you, Trent?"

Trent relit his pipe, and smoked for a moment before he spoke. "This is the way I see it at present. Colonel Washington must be told of the French troops, who must be found, and a determination made whether their intentions are peaceful or otherwise. Chogan must also be found, and made to pay for his actions. We have adequate numbers to split into two groups, but we also have a severely injured and dying comrade who cannot be moved. We cannot leave him here alone."

Trent took another puff on his pipe, the smoke trailing back over his head. He was beginning to feel the effects of little sleep the last two days, and found himself having to roll his shoulders and stretch his back to relieve the tension and weariness. "Our best course of action, I think, is for the Mallory men, Pierre, Wahta, and Degandawidah to deal with Chogan. The Clarkes and Liza will stay with Burke until his passing." He paused for a second to look at Joseph and Henry. "I suggest that once Burke is dead, you follow us up the Kiskiminetas, and join Colonel Washington at Great Meadow. I will go to Washington with Tanaghrisson. Donehogawa and Dadagoyadoh will head down the Allegheny to Mahoning Creek, which will take them to their village."

All present nodded in agreement. The rest of the discussion centered on supplies, and reviewing the route the Clarkes would take to Great Meadow. Once finished, they prepared for rest, as the next few days promised little of that. Even Wahta dozed off, despite his determination to stay awake with his brother, Snake Slayer.

****

Pierre had been staying with Phil Burke. Just before dawn, he, emerged from the cabin carrying Phil, who died during the night without regaining consciousness.

The sun rose through a line of gray clouds, and reflected off a larger band of ominous rain clouds coming in from the west. Daniel and Pierre completed Phil's burial, and joined Thomas and Degandawidah for a hurried breakfast. Wahta brought food to Otetiani, who picked at it listlessly. Now that there was no reason to remain at the post, Henry and Liza would travel with the Mallory family. Liza refused to be parted from Henry, and was most vocal in her appeal to help rescue her mother and sister. That she was a decent shot with a musket was the tipping point in her favor. Donehogawa and Dadgayadoh had the longest trip to make. They left just as soon as it was light enough to see the river, their canoe gliding with the current of the

Kiskiminetas as it hurried to meet the larger Allegheny. Donehogawa took one last glance back at his daughter's grave, and watched Otetiani kiss the mound one last time before joining his companions.

Trent, Joseph Clarke, Tanaghrisson, and the rest of the Mingo loaded up their canoes and set out upstream on the Kiskiminetas. They would follow the river to the point closest to Great Meadow, and make the rest of the journey overland. It would take two days to reach Fort Necessity.

****

Abigail, driven by the need to protect her child, kept pace most of the time, even though it seemed as if every muscle in her body screamed in agony. Just five days after having given birth, her strength was not what it usually was, but her focus on staying alive for her baby drove her forward. Those times when she started to flounder, a stern reminder from one of the Shawnee would get her going again. When Chogan thrust the water bucket at her, he said to her, "One more walk, then we sell you to French."

Otetiani once again led the way, winding through the forest to follow the trail of Chogan and his band. This was the third morning of the chase - the distance between them was closing. They passed the first two campsites, and had a good idea of the distance to the third one - the one they would be at tonight. The first day out from the post had been a wet one, which added to the misery Thomas felt, his head pounding with every step. The pennyroyal tea that Pierre made for him each time they stopped helped for a while, but never lasted until the next stop. Now, they were traveling in sunny but humid conditions. Liza, with occasional encouragement from Henry, kept pace, but stayed back with Thomas if he fell behind.

They followed the tracks of the Shawnee-Huron raiding party, which led them to a small clearing by a creek surrounded by hills on three sides. The two Mohawk warriors with them, Wahta and Degandawidah, spotted the lone sentinel, and broke off from the rest of the group to deal with him. Kesegowiase was deep in thought about the raid on the trading post. He was confused as to how the Great Spirit felt about the torture they applied to the Mohawk woman and her unborn child. This behavior seemed to be at odds with how he understood the Great Spirit. These were his last thoughts as a hand clamped down on his mouth and a knife slid through his ribs and into his heart.

Silently, Otetiani, Daniel, Thomas, and Pierre crept through the underbrush and leaf litter, until they reached the top of the hill overlooking the Shawnee-Huron campsite 30 feet below. Henry and Liza remained at the base of the hill, in order both to protect Liza and to act as reinforcements, should the need arise. Pierre signaled them all to stay down, and keep quiet while he walked into the camp, hoping to forestall any violence (though he knew that was not likely). The Shawnee and Huron warriors were preparing their evening meal. Abigail was forced to carry water from the nearby stream. The baby was curled up on the ground near the fire, tiny moans coming from her sleeping form. Chogan, the leader of the raiding party, stood and pulled his tomahawk from his belt when he saw Pierre appear from the woods.

"What do you want here? I know you, Black Robe. You are the beaten one," snarled Chogan.

"I know you, too, Chogan. Are you still chattering away like that blackbird you wear in your hair? I have come to ask you to release the white woman and baby. They will only slow you down, and the British will be looking for you."

"Your British are nowhere near here, but my brothers the French are, and they will pay for these whites. Go now, before I change my mind and kill them instead."

Chogan then picked up the baby and made a threatening motion with his tomahawk. Abigail - having not understood the conversation - threw the water bucket at Chogan, screaming, "Leave my baby alone!" She charged him, holding nothing in her bare hands. Chogan turned and took the brunt of the wooden bucket on the back of his shoulder. He turned again, bringing the sharpened blade down on Abigail's head and killing her instantly. As she hit the ground, Otetiani drew back his bow and let fly an arrow that hit Chogan in the leg. Thomas, maddened by what just happened, ran down the hill, pulling his knife and tomahawk. Otetiani took aim with his bow and took another shot at Chogan. Chogan saw his enemy draw back and loose another arrow and knowing of Otetiani's skill reacted quickly. Using his only defense, he picked up the oaken bucket to use as a shield, so that the arrow did not hit his face.

Daniel, Wahta, and Degandawidah fired their flintlocks, killing one of the Huron and wounding the other Huron and the Shawnee. Chogan saw the madness in Thomas' eyes as he ran towards him. Once more, he swung his tomahawk and the baby was dead at his feet. He then stood, an arrow projecting out both sides of his right leg, and prepared to meet the charge of the enraged white man. A shot rang out from Huritt's musket, hitting Thomas in the chest and dropping him to the ground. Chogan limped over to Thomas and grabbed him by the hair, intending to scalp his enemy, but Thomas brought his knife up and into the groin of Chogan. As Chogan fell, Thomas' one last effort swung his tomahawk to catch Chogan in the neck, a mortal blow severing his jugular. With all of his companions either dead or wounded, Huritt sped across the creek and ran for the safety of the trees.

Pierre, stunned by the rapidly declining situation, rushed over to Abigail, but he could tell there was no helping her or the poor baby. Pulling Thomas away from the still gushing wound that killed Chogan, he started to plug the wound in his chest with goose down. Thomas reached up and took Pierre's hand. With great effort, he told Pierre, 'Tis no use, my friend. Bury me with my wife and child, and take care of the rest of my family."

"It will be done," replied Pierre, as Thomas took his last gasping breath.

Henry and Liza came over the hill and down into the camp. For the second time in three days, they gazed upon the bloodied ground of battle. For the second time in three days, they stared at the bodies of friends or loved ones. Liza, a look of disbelief crossing her face, sat down next to Daniel. "All of them are gone?"

"Yes, little sister," replied Daniel as he hugged her, "they are gone, but at least Pa killed that monster," pointing to Chogan's bloody corpse.

The shock of what had happened began to replace the adrenaline-laced battle fury as Daniel, Liza, and Otetiani joined Pierre by their parents' and sister's bodies. Daniel wept softly, saying, "It wasn't supposed to be like this. Oh, God, it wasn't supposed to be like this." He then helped Pierre and Liza straighten out the bodies and begin to clean them for burial.

Otetiani, on the other hand, stood near his parents for a moment without making a sound. He noticed the two wounded Shawnee lying on the ground under the watchful eyes of Degandawidah. Dropping his bow, he grabbed his father's tomahawk and walked toward the prisoners.

"Otetiani!" cried Pierre, "That will not bring your parents back, nor will it be right."

"They deserve to die. They deserve to die slowly," replied Otetiani, a ferocity in his voice that Pierre had never heard before.

"Yes, my young friend, perhaps they do, but are you one to make that judgment of another? Your father killed Chogan; it was he who needed killing today. It was Chogan who killed Orenda and your child as well. He has paid with his life."

"I know in my heart that what you say is right, but my blood still boils with hate." Turning to the two wounded Shawnee, Otetiani told them, "You are very lucky Pierre is here today. If we meet again in battle, know this: I will tear out your hearts while they still beat, and leave them for the crows and coyotes." As he walked away, he looked at Pierre and said, "Look to their wounds, Pierre, but don't be gentle."

****

They completed the painful task of burying their parents and their infant sister during a persistent drizzle, which dampened their spirits even further. The dead Shawnee and Huron were buried in a common grave, including the Shawnee prisoner who did not survive a belly wound. The remaining prisoner suffered through Pierre none to gently setting the broken bone in his lower right leg without uttering a sound. After he finished, Pierre tossed him a tree limb and told him to make himself a crutch.

The exception to the common grave was Chogan. Otetiani would not be swayed to allow it. Instead, he took the bloodied corpse down to the creek and after removing the heart, rolled the body into the water. He then threw the heart into the woods, "for the crows and coyotes," Otetiani said softly to himself. He returned to the camp and, rolling himself up in his blanket, lay near the fire. He fell immediately into a dreamless sleep.

The Shawnee Huritt, having doubled back after his flight from the camp, watched from the cover of a large oak as Otetiani of the Mohawk desecrated the body of Chogan, his lifelong friend and brother. When Otetiani returned to camp, Huritt crept to the creek and carried away his brother, vowing a painful death for Otetiani.

Daniel sat by his family's grave. He stared off into the twilight, sobbing occasionally, his shoulders rising and falling with each cry. Pierre came to sit next to him, putting his arms around Daniel's shoulders and cradling him like a small child. "Why?" sobbed Daniel, "Why?"

Pierre pulled back a little to look into Daniel's eyes. "That's a question we all ask at least once in our lives, and is one for which I know not the answer. What I do know is that we must always cherish the memory of those who go before us, and not let the circumstances turn us to hate. I am more afraid of Otetiani in that regard than of you, Daniel. You are strong, and will be stronger. Come, let us see what we can do about food, and then get some sleep. Plenty of time to decide what to do tomorrow, the promise of a new day as Otetiani would say."

Daniel slept fitfully through the night and finally gave up trying, standing to shake off the chill of the early morning. The sky was just beginning to brighten in the east, but it did nothing to stem the remorse eating away at him. The grim results at the post; now, his parents and baby sister were dead; and, so too seemed the future Thomas Mallory envisioned.

He took a deep breath of the crisp morning air. As he exhaled, he felt the thoughts that would keep him down replaced by a steel resolve. "Plans to be a farmer will have to wait," he muttered. "For now, it is the way of woodcraft and war." He knew he would never be as good as Liam or even Henry, but he knew enough, and was learning daily. As was Liza, he reflected for a moment, she has become quite a good shot; better than me, he chuckled. The chuckle faded away quickly, and was replaced with a grim determined look. "I am going to war," he exclaimed to the heavens. "But I vow to finish what my father started."

Liza heard Daniel's cry; she sat up to see his upraised fists shaking at the sky. The hawk soared over the trees at the top of the ridge, and the stark reality of her situation hit her. Her men, including her husband, would be going to war. Her darling Henry would be going into danger, but what would become of her? Surely they won't allow her to go with them. One thing she did know; just as she heard Daniel's vow, she too, determined that when the time was right, they would rebuild.

Since the morning came in clear and cool, the fire was rekindled to take away the chill from the bones and muscles that had been on the trail and under stress for many days. They decided their next move nearly without debate, once Otetiani abandoned the notion of tracking the rest of the Shawnee-Huron war party. Degandawidah and Wahta would take the Shawnee prisoner to their village, and let Donehogawa decide his fate. Otetiani knew that Donehogawa – whose daughter and unborn grandchild were brutally murdered – would try to fairly judge him. Daniel, Otetiani, Henry, Liza, and Pierre would use this day for resting, and for repairing tears in their breeches and boots from the furious chase of the last few days. Tomorrow, they would track and join the force Colonel Washington was leading. They all felt that conflict was now inevitable, and their skills as woodsmen and fighters would be needed.

Chapter 5

Fort Necessity

Trent finished the last leg of the trek by late afternoon. He entered Fort Necessity alone, and approached Washington. "Mr. Trent, I was not expecting to see you here," said Washington, "you have news for me?"

"Yes sir, Colonel. A combined group of Shawnee and Huron attacked the trading post. It seems their aims were to capture the white women and kill everyone else. Mallory's wife and baby were taken; his other daughter wasn't in the compound at the time of the attack. They brutally murdered the Mohawk woman, Orenda. You may recall that she was the wife of Otetiani Mallory, an adopted Mohawk. Among the dead are two of my agents, Rob Carter and Stump Nose Emerson. "

"Do we need to send out a rescue party, or is that already taken care of?" asked Washington.

"The rescue is being attempted by the Mallory men and a couple of Mohawks. That is only one piece of information, however. Tanaghrisson and a band of Mingo came with news of a contingent of French troops heading here. He is keeping an eye on them from his camp a couple miles away. If we leave soon, we can be there in a few hours."

"Tanaghrisson? He's a bit of a hothead, isn't he?"

"He is that. A haughtier, more self-important man is hard to imagine. When he came to the trading post, he completely ignored everyone except Donehogawa, the Mohawk war chief. He was disrespectful, even though Donehogawa is his superior in the Iroquois Nation.. It was interesting to witness Donehogawa basically telling Tanaghrisson to sit down and be quiet."

"Well, let us hope he doesn't start anything before we get there. I'll issue the orders. We can be ready to leave just after sundown; perhaps we can surprise the French at dawn. At any rate, we need to find out what they are up to. Why don't you go get a few hours rest? You look exhausted."

"Thanks, Colonel, I could certainly use some sleep," Trent replied as he turned to walk away.

"Oh, say, Trent, you're familiar with the Mohawk, can you tell me who that is?" asked Washington, pointing to a tall black man with the contingent of Mohawk scouts.

"That is Teeyeehogrow. He was adopted by the Mohawk a couple years back, and has become one of their best warriors. My guess is that he's a runaway slave, but that's none of my business," replied Trent while trying to stifle a yawn.

"I see. He is a fearsome looking specimen, I'll say that. He also looks very familiar. Do me a favor, and ask him to come to my tent in half an hour. Because it is my business, I believe I need to sort this out."

"Yes sir, Colonel. If nothing else, you'll be amazed by his knowledge," said Trent.

****

Colonel George Washington looked up from his camp desk as the tall, lean Negro entered his tent. He dressed as the Mohawk warrior he was. Teeyeehogrow had been his name since he became an adopted member of the Mohawk. "You wanted to see me, Colonel, sir?" Teeyeehogrow said

"Yes, please, come in, have a seat. You may not remember, but we have met before, Rufus, isn't it? Your master came to my place in Virginia for a visit a couple of years ago, and you were with him. So imagine my surprise to find you as part of my Mohawk scouting contingent. I am most curious to know how that came about."

Teeyeehogrow, somewhat startled to be recognized as an escaped slave, gave a few seconds' thought to bolting back out of the tent, but knew that he would not get past the guards at the entrance. He sat down warily, his skin covered in a thin layer of bear fat shimmering in the candlelight. "Yes, Rufus was my slave name. I am now known as Teeyeehogrow. It's a long story, but if the Colonel wishes to hear it, I will oblige."

"How could I not wish it, pray you, continue."

"I was sold as a young boy to work your friend's tobacco fields outside of Baltimore on Chesapeake Bay. My master is, as you know, a kindly gentleman. One day, he noticed me solving a problem for the slave foreman. He took me from the fields, and gave me a proper education. After a few years, my job became teacher to the slave children. When my master's children grew to an age where they needed a tutor, he gave me the task of teaching them and the slave children, an enormous responsibility requiring a tremendous amount of trust on my master's part. It was a wonderful experience, and I truly loved doing it, but I desired more than anything to be free – to not belong to anyone, to do what I chose to do.

"I was sent to Baltimore to pick up some needed material for the slave school I had started. When this opportunity presented itself, I ran. One thing I should mention, as it is important to know that I did not abandon my charges completely. I made sure there would be someone to take my place before I could leave. One of the other children, now a young woman, has taken the reins, so to speak, and the teaching continues."

"One moment, please, Rufus. Guard! Bring me a wine cask and two goblets from the quartermaster tent. Thank you.

"I know how thirsty one becomes in the telling of a tale. I am fascinated, and you haven't gotten to the exciting parts yet, I warrant. It could not have been an easy journey. Ahh, here is the wine. Now we can continue and be refreshed at the same time." Washington filled two goblets, and handed one to Teeyeehogrow.

"Thank you. It has been a while since I have had a taste of good wine." Teeyeehogrow sipped, and nodded in appreciation. "This is exquisite, Colonel — from France, I believe."

"Exquisite, and quite expensive, I might add. I import it from France, as you surmised. I don't think I will be getting any more from there for a while. Tensions are running pretty high, not only here on the frontier, but in Canada and Europe as well. I'm not usually a pessimist, but I don't know how war can be avoided. Anyway, let's enjoy the wine, and please continue with your tale."

"I didn't go to Baltimore. Instead, I boarded a ship and headed up the coast to Boston. It was easy to convince the ship's captain that I was on business for my master, given that I had a letter stating so. Of course, it originally had Baltimore as my destination, but with a little manipulation on my part, I changed it to Boston. I gathered enough supplies to last a week or so, and headed off in a northwesterly direction, hoping to find my way to the Albany area. For some reason I can't explain, I felt drawn there; I felt like my true home was in the land of the Iroquois.

"I took the better part of six weeks, hiking through dense woods, fragrant meadows, and endless hills. Along, of course, were the pantheon of traveler's miseries – drenching rain, howling wind, hordes of flies and mosquitos, and blistered feet. I foraged for berries and the like, occasionally taking corn from a farmer's field, and I hunted small game with a bow I acquired in Boston.

"I had avoided being seen since leaving Boston, until – while tracking a rabbit – I came upon two farmers, out doing some hunting of their own. They yelled at me to stay put, but I had no intention to do that, and took off in the other direction, heading for a fast-running stream just ahead. The farmers took shots at me, one ball thudding into a tree just to the right of me, the other scudding harmlessly in the dirt behind me. The stream was running high from heavy rains the past week, but I had no choice. I jumped in, and let the current take me away. I managed to get a look behind me, to see the farmers at the stream's edge, arguing. I guess they decided that I was a fool, and they would find me downstream, drowned, for they turned back."

Teeyeehogrow paused, and drained his goblet. His rapt attention interrupted, a startled Washington rose and refilled Teeyeehogrow's cup. "Without a doubt this is one of the more exciting tales I've ever heard," Washington said as he sat down, his hands folded on the desk. "Pray, continue."

Teeyeehogrow took another sip, and continued. "I let the water take me for a few minutes, and then I heard the louder sound of a large rapid – or worse – ahead. I grabbed an overhead tangle of an uprooted tree hanging in the water on the far bank. With no little effort, I pulled myself ashore, soaked, sore, and without supplies – but safe for the time being. I made my way up the hill and slipped into the woods, following the ridge as it meandered alongside the river until I was too tired and hungry to go any further. I coiled into a restless sleep.

"I awoke to find that I was surrounded by six seated Mohawks, which I later learned was a hunting party. Trying not to show my fear, I sat up and unsheathed my knife. The brave nearest me reached behind him, and then offered me a piece of dried venison from his pouch. In reasonably good English, he told me to eat, and to come with them, as there was a party of whites from the nearest settlement on my trail. I found myself in the position of being able to choose my destiny for one of the very few times in my life. That is how I came to be here as Teeyeehogrow of the Mohawk." He set his goblet on the desk.

"I have been with the Mohawk for close to two years now, and am respected among my warrior brothers. I have a wife, a captive Abenaki; she, too, has adjusted to her new tribe and family. We have a good life, and I would not surrender that life easily."

Washington opened a drawer in his desk, and withdrew the sheet of paper he handed to Teeyeehogrow. He looked at Teeyeehogrow, saying, "Ordinarily, in a case like this, I would be forced into a position of turning you in, but I like to think of myself as a fair and reasonable man. Besides, there are extenuating circumstances in this case, as you will see by the document I just handed you. I will give you a moment to look it over."

While Teeyeehogrow read, Washington sat back with a smile on his face, watching for Teeyeehogrow's reaction with a sly smile "How did you come to have this most welcome news? For once, I am at a loss for words," Teeyeehogrow said, his smile reaching ear to ear.

Washington handed the goblet back to Teeyeehogrow. "Let me be the first to congratulate you on your freedom," he replied, standing to shake Teeyeehogrow's hand. "I happened to stop by your old master's place on the way to this campaign. He was very distraught at your absence, and was much afraid of what would happen if you were caught. As I was getting ready to depart, he handed me that letter, and asked that I keep an eye out and an ear open for news of you. He had an idea you would be heading to the frontier, so I agreed, never thinking that we would cross paths. What do you think the odds of that happening are? Do you believe in fate, Teeyeehogrow? Perhaps we'll have some time to discuss the nature of the universe later, but for now I have much work to do. All that letter needs is for you to fill in your slave name, and I will make it official. Your prior master, Simon, did not know what to put down for your new last name, so he left that for you."

Taking a quill pen from the Colonel, Teeyeehogrow filled in the space with his full name. "I think it only fitting that I honor my old master. I shall be known as Rufus Atkinson-Turney, though I think my Mohawk family will still see me as Teeyeehogrow, which in Mohawk means man with a double life."

****

Trent awoke to the staccato sound of the night rain hitting the tent's roof. He shook the cobwebs from his sleep-deprived mind, and ventured out to find Colonel Washington leading his troops to the French encampment. The detachment of forty men marched toward the woods, where at least they would be less rain-soaked. The weather made the night even darker; without even a little starlight available, the going was slow. Although it took longer to reach the camp of Tanaghrisson than Washington had planned, they reached it before daylight. Trent introduced Tanaghrisson to Washington, a meeting that did not sit well with the colonel, as Tanaghrisson adopted a superior air over this young white officer.

Washington told Tanaghrisson that his intent was to speak with the French – Tanaghrisson first responded by exclaiming, "I came here to kill the French, not to talk with the dogs!" Washington made his intentions even more clear, and Tanaghrisson promised to abide by the wishes of the white commander. Satisfied that he had made his point to the Mingo leader, Washington bade Tanaghrisson to lead the way to the French camp.

The rain had stopped by the time of their undetected arrival. The Mingo crept around the small ravine, and took up a position on the side opposite Washington's militia. While Washington gave last minute instructions to his men, a shot rang out. As the smoke from the barrel of his just-fired musket swirled away, Tanaghrisson let out a scream of victory. The Mingo fired more shots; Washington's militia, thinking that the fight was underway, shot down into the completely surprised French troops. By the time Trent and Washington gained control of the chaos, ten French troops were dead and 25 were prisoners — including the badly wounded French commander, Jumonville.

"Who fired that first shot?" asked a furious Washington. "There will be hell to pay for this bloody fiasco."

"It had to be one of the Mingo. That was their war cry I heard after the shot was fired," replied Trent. "I'm guessing it was Tanaghrisson. I'll go and see if I can get an answer from him."

Washington ran his hands through his hair, nodded, and said, "Yes, perhaps it should be you that talks to him. I'm going to see Jumonville, and try to get some answers from him." Washington headed to the tent where the wounded Jumonville lay. When he entered the tent, he found the rear wall slit open, and Jumonville dead from what appeared to be a tomahawk blow to his head. A few minutes later Trent returned with the news that Tanaghrisson and his Mingo had slipped away, and were nowhere to be found.

"I did learn that at least one of the French troops escaped, and is no doubt headed to Fort Duquesne. It won't be long before they send out a larger force to retaliate," Trent said. "We had better return to Necessity, and prepare for an attack. I also found out from one of the prisoners that the commander at Duquesne is Jumonville's half-brother. I don't think he'll be in the mood for a parley."

"Damnation!" uttered Washington as he pulled the blanket over Jumonville's battered head. "Blasted barbarian has put us in a precarious position. If the French send out a large enough force, we will not be able to hold them off for long. I know the men are tired, but we need to get back quickly. I'll send Teeyeehogrow out to scout when we've returned to the fort. He'll give us ample warning of the size of the force, and when we can expect them."

****

Daniel and the others were not very impressed by Fort Necessity . They had travelled for three days since their raid on the Shawnee, and only one day after a minor skirmish with a Shawnee scouting party. Daniel's left arm was bandaged from a wound sustained during that brief encounter. "Looks more like Fort Doubtful," remarked Daniel. They marched across the large meadow that surrounded the fort, coming to a halt at one of the defensive trenches Washington had ordered dug.

Standing inside the circular palisade, Trent saw the group, and rushed out to meet them. The first thing he noticed was that neither Thomas nor Abigail was with them; by the look on the others' faces, he knew they were dead. He also saw the cold hatred on Otetiani's face, a look that was unlike any he had seen on this usually happy and carefree young man. "Come, let's get you settled in the fort," said Trent, "we can talk later. Colonel Washington will want to hear what happened. I fear we all have bad news to relate."

The fort was really little more than a circle of vertical logs surrounding a hastily-built cabin. Used to store provisions and ammunition, it also served as Washington's office. The troops bivouacked in tents outside of the palisade. A few shooting platforms were constructed on the inside of the wall; slots allowed them to fire from and on the defensive ditches still being dug outside the walls — these would give the defenders a somewhat protected vantage point to fire their muskets. The two gates were situated opposite each other, the rear one not much more than a hole in the wall. Trent and Daniel entered the cabin, to find Washington poring over his report about the unfortunate battle.

"Ahh, Mr. Mallory, come in. Trent gave me the details of the raid on the Trading Post when he arrived. If you would, please sit. Tell me, were you successful in tracking down the fiends?" Daniel sat down and told Washington of the events since the raid.

Washington's voice faltered for a second. "My good man, I am so sorry about your loss. Life is uncertain enough, how much more so in this frontier tinderbox? We've most assuredly found that out in the last few days. I fear that things will be getting even hotter in the near future." Washington held up his report. "I also fear that this report, when it reaches London, will start fires in Europe as well. What are your plans? If there's anything I can do to help, be assured that I will."

"Colonel, I thank you for your kind words," Daniel replied. "We have talked it over, and with your permission, we would like to sign on as scouts until such time that we can safely get my sister out of here. Pierre Baptist, who asks if he could be useful as an interpreter, would also like to lend a hand with the medical needs of the fort."

"Does this offer of scouting include your brother Otetiani? Trent tells me that he has changed since the horrible deaths of his wife and child."

"Well, Colonel, I think he already made his choice. He left the fort with Teeyeehogrow and your Mohawk scouting party."

Washington stood up and extended his hand out to Daniel. "I accept your offer, and that of Mr. Baptist. I am sorely lacking in the French language, and I'm sure my surgeon can use the help. You and the rest of your party can rest for a few days. We will determine our next move when Teeyeehogrow returns."

"Thank you, Colonel," replied Daniel as he stood and shook Washington's hand, "we'll be ready when you need us." He left the cabin and into a bright, sunny day, a sharp contrast to how his depleted soul felt.

The scouting party retraced the route back to the ambush site, knowing that the French would be sending out a reconnaissance party. Otetiani, Teeyeehogrow, and the three braves with them were hidden above the ravine, in a forest of oak, maple, and pine. It was a typical early summer day, morning warm sunshine surrendered to a buildup of threatening clouds late in the afternoon. The chirping of wood thrush and warblers filled the air, accompanied by the rustling of squirrels and chipmunks. Ordinarily, Otetiani found these peaceful sounds soothing, but not today — quite possibly, he would never again feel that peace. He could not escape the thoughts of the cruel slaughter of his family, and the birdsong only reminded him that he would never hear Orenda's voice again. Otetiani did not smile even when a blue jay alighted on a branch above one of the braves, lifted his tail, and dropped his waste on a Mohawk shoulder. The others started to chuckle, but were brought up short by Otetiani's malevolent glare .

When the first Shawnee brave came into view, Otetiani gasped and reached for his bow. Teeyeehogrow grabbed his arm, and stopped him from taking an arrow from his quiver. Shaking his head, Teeyeehogrow said, "No, Otetiani. There are too many for us to fight."

Otetiani responded, "That Shawnee was the one who escaped our raid on their camp. He was part of the raid on the trading post."

"His name is Huritt," responded Teeyeehogrow. "He will be just as anxious to kill you. Chogan was his brother. Come, we must slip away before they know we are here."

****

For the next three weeks, the troops spent their days digging defensive trenches. Regular patrols checked on the French positions. Toward the end of June, the garrison strength increased as a contingent of one hundred soldiers from the South Carolina militia arrived, bringing the number of effectives at Fort Necessity to nearly four hundred men. On the first of July, Teeyeehogrow returned from patrol to report that the French force numbered about six hundred men.

"Colonel, there is more to report," said a downcast Teeyeehogrow. "The French have a band of Mohawk with them."

Washington, showing his surprise and quick realization, replied, "How can that be? The Mohawk are allies with us. Oh, I see it now. They have convinced the Jesuit converts to join them."

"It's worse than that, Colonel. My Mohawk brothers and I cannot fight against fellow Mohawk, no matter their religious persuasion. I am afraid that we will have to leave this place before they arrive, as these converted Mohawk will not have the same reservations about fighting us. Their priests have poisoned their minds against us. I am also afraid for Otetiani and the rest of his party. If you are defeated, the Shawnee with the French will seek vengeance against them. They must leave with us."

"I see," replied Washington. "Can you wait until tomorrow? I would ask that you carry a letter to General Braddock, advising him of the situation. He is currently building an invasion force at Fort Cumberland, but I suspect it will be quite a few months before he is ready."

"Certainly, Colonel, the French won't be here for two days. I am saddened by this. I had hoped to fight by your side, and to continue our talks on the nature of the universe. I love my life as a Mohawk, but sorely miss having conversations of a more educated kind. Perhaps the future will grant us the time that the present does not."

"I believe we will have that time again. Our fates are intertwined in some way, of that I am sure. I will have the letter ready for you by tomorrow night."

****

The French and their Indian allies arrived, their numbers more than twice than Washington's troops. Through steady rain, the two forces exchanged fire. Both suffered casualties, though the British lost more men than the French. Looking out from one of the few raised platforms at the forces arrayed against the fort, Washington knew that they could not hold. He turned as his second in command climbed up to the platform. "Well, Captain Mackay, it appears we are outnumbered, and outgunned. I do not see any way of holding this position, and my conscience will not permit me to order my men to do so at all costs. Let us hope the French commander is of the same mind, and offers us terms."

"Aye, Colonel," replied Mackay, "and let's hope they can restrain their allies from falling on us while we are defenseless."

The next morning, the French commander Captain Louis Coulon de Villers called for his adjutant, Lieutenant Charles LeFurge. "Arrange for a flag of truce, and assemble an honor guard. I wish to speak with the British commander, and hope he is a reasonable man." LeFurge saluted, but barely concealed his disagreement with his commander as he left the tent. LeFurge had no appetite for a peaceful settlement of this conflict. He wanted nothing more than to destroy the British.

LeFurge's hatred of them was bred into him. From the time he could talk and understand, his father and uncles instilled in him their version of English perfidy against the

French throughout history. These persistent reminders gave birth to an intense desire to play a part in any venture that would see the downfall of Britain. However, as he was from a family that traced their military history back to Charlemagne, he followed orders, and now found himself riding out with his captain to meet with his enemy.

When the sentry announced that the French wanted to parley, Washington hastily put on his best uniform while his honor guard formed at the gate. As the two parties drew more closely together, Washington caught the malevolent stare coming at him from one of the French officers. Washington remarked to Captain Mackay, "That young lieutenant over there doesn't appear to be very happy. Well, time to see what they have to say." Washington then rode out alone to meet the French commander, his horse standing between the two honor guards.

"Thank you for coming to meet with me, Colonel," began de Villers. "I am Captain de Villers, commander of Fort Duquesne. I wish to avoid any more bloodshed. I hope you can see the senselessness of continuing this siege."

"My compliments, Captain," replied Washington, "that is most thoughtful of you. What terms are you offering, and can you guarantee that your native allies will abide by those terms?"

"Despite the loss of my brother Jumonville, and because I deem you to be innocent in his death, I am prepared to be generous. Your officers and men are free to leave with their weapons; however, your cannon and store of ammunition will remain. One of my Huron scouts who was at the battle has reported that my brother was shot by a Mingo brave. "

"You are most generous, Captain. I accept. Please know that I am deeply sorry for the killing of your brother. The Mingo who shot him was Tanaghrisson. I had hoped to confront him, but he and his band slipped away before I had the chance."

"That is unfortunate, but it will serve to allay your concern about my allies. I will dispatch the Shawnee to hunt down this band of Mingo. You need not worry about my Mohawk contingent, as I will tell their priests to restrain them. They will listen to the Black Robes, I am sure.

"However, there are two other items. The Black Robes noticed a man standing on the wall yesterday; they believe he is Pierre Baptist. They would like him delivered to them for questioning regarding some irregularities, shall we say, during his time with the Mohawk as a Black Robe himself. And, I am informed by my Shawnee scouts that you also harbor the fugitive Mallory brothers, who we believe are spies. I must insist that they be handed over. I hope these conditions are not too much of an indisposition concerning your surrender. "

"What you propose is acceptable, except for Baptist. As far as he is concerned, I have no authority over him, and cannot order his arrest. I will speak to him, but if he does not turn himself over voluntarily, then I'm afraid there is nothing I can do. Regarding the Mallory brothers, I am conducting my own investigation into their activities. If I find any truth to your allegation, I will compel them to surrender to you. Surely, my good Captain, you will not undo your generous proposal based on the words of civilians, Black Robes or no.

"No, Colonel, I will not. The priests will be made to see reason in the matter of Baptist, but I must insist that the Mallory brothers be turned over to me. I will have the surrender document prepared. Shall we meet at dawn tomorrow?"

Washington, taken aback at the Frenchman's comments about Daniel and Otetiani, hid his feelings and replied, "My thanks, Captain de Villers, I will await you at the gate at dawn."

Washington and de Villers saluted each other, and returned to their respective honor guards. As Washington approached Captain McKay, he said, "The terms are most agreeable, but the Mallory party must leave tonight with Teeyeehogrow. It seems that the Jesuits among the Mohawk are harboring a grudge against Mr. Baptist, and the French want to arrest the Mallory brothers. I will not be an accomplice to any type of religious inquisition, nor will I ever abandon my operatives – and I still have need of their services."

Captain de Villers was reviewing the surrender document he had just written when Lieutenant LeFurge approached his tent. "Permission to enter?" asked LeFurge, as he saluted in his usual crisp manner. Captain de Villers looked up from his camp desk, returned the salute, and beckoned LeFurge to enter.

"May I speak freely, sir?"

"Of course, Lieutenant, within reason."

"Sir, I believe that the terms of this surrender are far too lenient. The English should be made to surrender their weapons, and the officers held accountable for the murder of your brother. Furthermore, our sentries are reporting movement, and the sounds of horses coming from the rear gate of the fort. Because of the rain and fog, they cannot determine who is escaping, but it can only be that renegade Black Robe, Baptist, and the other survivors of the Shawnee raid on Trent's outpost. They need to be apprehended, as that was the original intent of the raid."

de Villers stood, came around the desk, and put his hands on the young lieutenant's shoulders. "I thought I was dealing with a gentleman of honor, but it appears that Colonel Washington is good at portraying one, while lying to cover his true nature. The weather is so disagreeable that pursuit is useless, at least until dawn. I still intend to send Huritt and his contingent of Shawnee and Huron after Tanaghrisson. You, Lieutenant, will lead a mounted patrol to seek out and capture that nest of spies and renegades. I want them alive, Lieutenant.

Go and prepare your troops. I have to change some of the wording in this document. We'll see how Washington reacts to being called a murderer."

****

Otetiani awoke to the sounds of thunder, and of Liza preparing their breakfast. That he had slept surprised him; it was the first time for almost three days. During their short stay at the fort, Daniel told Otetiani what he saw across the river, and how Orenda died. The image of Orenda tied to that tree haunted his dream, as did the sound of her screams as she cried out for him. Daniel and Henry were already awake, and making ready to begin today's trek to Donehogawa's camp on Mahoning Creek.

Teeyeehogrow and Pierre rose before dawn to backtrack, to see if anyone was in pursuit. They stood on a hilltop about two miles from camp, looking down at a troop of French about a mile distant preparing to break camp. "Best to warn the others, and hasten our pace," said Pierre.

Teeyeehogrow nodded in agreement, and replied, "We don't know for sure they are after us, though I suspect they are. There's little chance they won't find our tracks." They returned to their tethered mounts, soothing the trembling horses as a blast of thunder and flash of lightning pierced the early morning quiet.

Another sudden clap of thunder brought a pelting rain that soaked them to the bones as they made their way back to camp. "The beckoning call of the rising sun," spoke Pierre, "the breath of promise on the early morning breeze. Dawn is God's blessing to man and beast, though it seems to be an off day for the almighty. I suppose even God enjoys a bit of variety."

Teeyeehogrow slapped Pierre on the back, and chuckled, "More likely he's mighty agitated about something."

"My friend, you are quite probably truer to the mark," replied Pierre.

With the news that the French were probably tracking them, Otetiani and Daniel took a position a few miles behind the others as they rode, keeping a watchful eye on their pursuers. By mid-morning, the storm had blown eastward. The sun's heat began the drying out process; steam rose from the horses' flanks, and the ground was enveloped in a swirling mist. Birdsong replaced the staccato rhythm of the rain.

On the third day after leaving Fort Necessity, Teeyeehogrow and Pierre led them toward the Mohawk camp on Mahoning Creek, while Daniel took up a position to the rear. They were pretty sure they could reach it by nightfall, if they pushed their mounts a little harder. As they crested a hill, they found themselves looking down at the creek, but could not see the Mohawk camp, and were not sure which direction they should take once they crossed the Mahoning.

The sound of hoof beats from behind had them reaching for their weapons, but as Daniel came into view, they relaxed and dismounted. He came to a halt, the suddenness of his stopping sending up a spray of dirt and leaves. "We've got trouble," he started, "the French have split their pursuit. Now, half of them are heading down to the creek to keep us from crossing, while the rest drive us into it. Liam and I will hold them back for as long as we can, but you need to make haste across the water." Teeyeehogrow motioned with his hand to point to a group of French already getting into position for the ambush at the water's edge.

****

Lieutenant LeFurge directed the six men with him to take their positions behind a scattering of boulders and fallen trees. "We have them now," he murmured to himself as he slid his saber in and out of its scabbard, willing himself to quell his nervousness about his first real taste of battle. There was no way he was going to obey his orders to the letter. "No one fires until I give the command," he ordered. "Shoot to kill, but spare the woman – she'll make a fine gift to our Shawnee friends."

****

Wahta and Deganawidah were returning to the Mohawk encampment from a hunting trip when they noticed the French across the creek, setting up for what appeared to be an ambush. They stopped among the trees above the creek, laid down the deer they carried, and crept to the creek bank to see if they could help the French targets. The sounds of gunfire from the hill in the distance drew their attention, but they could not identify those involved.

****

"We can't take on both groups, there are too many," said Teeyeehogrow. "Pierre, go get Daniel and Otetiani. We'll meet the group behind us from here. We'll have the advantage of being uphill with enough cover to protect us. Liza, I know you're a good shot, but – for now – I need you to reload our muskets. We have two extras, so we should be able to keep up a continual fire. No doubt, Otetiani will use his bow as well as his musket."

Otetiani, Daniel, and Pierre returned, taking up positions behind the trees just as the first of the French horses charged up the slope. They dismounted quickly as Otetiani let an arrow fly; it struck one of the horses in the shoulder, which reared and threw its rider. Daniel and the others then let fly with musket fire, taking down two in their first volley. The remaining three returned fire, but Otetiani and the rest were too well sheltered for any clean hits. When the French troops reloaded and stood to fire, another volley wounded two more. Laying his musket down and holding his palms outward, the lone remaining Frenchman helped his wounded comrades onto their horses, and retreated the way they came.

"Looks as though we won't have to worry about that group," said Daniel. "How do we deal with those in the rocks below?"

From a distance, Wahta now recognized Otetiani. He drew back his bow and released an arrow, striking one of the surprised French in the back, the force of the arrow causing him to stumble and fall into the creek. Wahta shouted, "Snake-slayer, my brother, let us meet our foes together." At the sound of his voice, and seeing one of his troopers floating away, LeFurge turned to see two Mohawk braves shooting from across the creek. He barely had time to duck as an arrow whizzed by his ear.

Taking advantage of the changing situation, Otetiani, Daniel, Henry, Liza, and Teeyeehogrow charged their horses down the hill, muskets at the ready and firing into the rocks. There wasn't much chance of hitting anyone while riding, but it kept the French pinned down as they took fire from front and rear. Thirty yards from the French, Otetiani and the others veered to the right and plunged into the creek, while Wahta and Deganawidah kept up their fire, killing one more of the French and wounding LeFurge. Once his friends were safely across, Wahta stopped shooting, and headed up to meet them in the trees.

With a smile almost as broad as his shoulders, Wahta embraced Otetiani. "It does my heart good to see you again, brother."

Otetiani replied, "Not as much good as to mine to see you. We were in some trouble, and the outcome would have most likely been different without your timely involvement. How far is it to Donehogawa's camp? I fear our horses are sorely tired, as are we."

"We will be there before the sun sets. We will feast on venison, and talk late into the night," replied Wahta.

****

His right thigh bandaged, Lieutenant LeFurge was in pain. He seethed at the thought that, in his first battle engagement, he was so thoroughly routed — and wounded on top of it. All that, and he didn't even fire his musket once, so complete was the surprise attack from across the creek. His smoldering loathing of the English now raged into a hateful inferno, and the need for revenge — especially as he believed his loss occurred because of these uncultured backwoodsmen, and that bastard Colonel Washington who allowed them to leave the fort.

Chapter 6

Braddock Takes Command

The warmth of the weather and their surroundings did much to help keep the hurting at bay for Daniel and Liza. They spent a good deal of time talking about their parents - remembering the good times, the love they felt growing up, the zeal their father felt for the frontier, and their hope to rebuild the trading post. Henry and Pierre stayed out of these conversations for the most part, other than to chime in with remembrances of their own. Liam, however, fell deeper into a malaise fed by the almost nightly dreams of Orenda and their unborn child. He shunned the company of anyone other than Wahta and Teeyeehogrow, and spent most of his time away from the camp - sometimes alone, sometimes with his two friends. Donehogawa did what he could for his adopted son, but not even he could penetrate the wall Liam built – to keep others out, and his hatred smoldering within.

Donehogawa wanted to be back to his village on the Mohawk River before the coming of the snow, and had announced that they would leave this temporary camp after they harvested their crops. This meant that Daniel and the rest had only a few weeks to decide their course of action. They could, of course, go with the Mohawk, but Liza had already repeatedly made known that she was looking forward to sleeping on a bed, rather than on the ground or a bearskin.

Of them all, Liam was the most undecided, until just a week before Donehogawa broke camp. Two days earlier, he went out by himself, and fell asleep against the trunk of a tall white pine in the middle of a meadow. At least, he thought he had been asleep; afterward, he wasn't sure if what he saw came to him in a dream or not. The meadow before him suddenly shimmered in the sunlight, and the sound of distant thunder filled his ears. He blinked his eyes. Before him stood a wounded buffalo, a Shawnee lance sticking out of her side. Her blood flowed freely, a pool of it gathering at her feet swarmed over by flies. She pawed the ground vigorously. Shaking her massive head and shoulders, she loosened the lance until it fell to the ground, followed by her unborn calf. When Liam looked from the calf to the buffalo's face, for a fleeting second he saw the pained expression of Orenda.

The thundering in his ears got louder and louder. The buffalo stamped her feet on the lance, snapping it in two. She looked at Liam, and then back over her shoulder. The thunder of thousands of buffalo stampeding across the meadow was deafening. It seemed to Liam to take hours for the herd to pass. The wounded buffalo was the last to move off into the west. As she gradually flickered out of his vision, Liam heard her voice, "Follow the herd, and find your peace."

****

That same day, Trent and Joseph Clarke arrived in the Mohawk camp, with news and a request from Washington. Trent approached Daniel, Henry, and Liam as they sat around a campfire. "I was hoping to find you here," Trent said. "General Braddock is gathering an army for a campaign against French-held forts out to the west. Mr. Washington is acting as an unofficial advisor, and would very much like to hire your services as scouts. In fact, he wants you, Daniel, and Liam as commanders." He looked skeptically at Liam, sitting with his head slumped over his knees, and added, "That is, if Liam is able. I've known Liam for quite a while now, and have noticed a change in him since the raid. If I see it, then you can be sure others are aware, and will be concerned that his troubled state of mind could render him ineffective."

"You need not be concerned about me," remarked Liam, lifting his head up to stare at Trent with haggard eyes. "My enemies need to be concerned, not you or Mr. Washington."

Trent stood and cleared his throat. "Yes, well, that is indeed reassuring. Joseph and I are off to Philadelphia. The general needs wagons and teamsters for his army. They are coming from as far away as Richmond and Boston. Two hundred wagons to be exact. It'll be a miracle if half that many survive the terrain we have to cross."

Henry walked with Trent to see his father, who was talking to Liza. "Liam will be fine," he told Trent. "Once he starts focusing on the tasks of command, he'll be just fine. Besides," he chuckled, "he'll have me and Daniel to keep him on the straight and narrow."

****

General Braddock's headquarters was a hive of activity, as was the camp surrounding both the headquarters and the temporary village of traders, taverns, and whores. Everyone helped prepare to pack up for the long march to the western frontier to confront the French at Fort Duquesne - a march of over one hundred miles, through dense woods and over the Allegheny Mountains. Teamsters busily loaded the many wagons needed for an expedition this size, their loud voices and coarse language filling the air around the makeshift warehouses. The blacksmiths' anvils rang with the sound of metal on metal, as they prepared shoes for the draft horses and cavalry mounts. Drovers herded the large oxen to the staging area, where they would be hitched to the heavy cannon needed for the expected siege at Fort Duquesne.

Colonel Gordon Doherty strode to Braddock's command post, brushing from his uniform the dust stirred up by the bovine giants. It was time to apprise the general of the state of readiness of his regular army troops. "Well, Sergeant Mulhern, I hope the general is in a good mood, though I suspect he won't be after my report."

Sergeant Glyn Mulhern glanced up from the troop roster he was reviewing. "Aye, Major, Sir ... I mean, Colonel. I'll wager a large whiskey he won't be liking it at all, especially your assessment of the irregulars. I hear tell that our noble general doesn't think too highly of the army of peasants – them being the general's words, not mine, mind you."

Major Gordon Doherty was assigned to Braddock's command after a successful career with the Scottish Highlanders. Promoted to Colonel, he trained the new recruits in this rapidly growing army. Sergeant Glyn Mulhern had served with the colonel for the last six years, and was his right hand man in this effort.

Colonel Doherty had not been in General Braddock's presence other than a perfunctory meeting upon his arrival two weeks earlier, and had yet to form an opinion of his commanding officer. In the meantime, he had talked to other officers on the general's staff, gleaning what he could about the man who was leading this army. Their opinions ranged from extreme confidence to caution – the latter mainly due to Braddock's condescending attitude toward the French and their Native allies.

Doherty did privately appreciate that General Braddock had retained Colonel Washington as an unofficial advisor, as Doherty was impressed with Washington's knowledge of the area around their intended destination. The Colonel was also likeable and easygoing in demeanor, having little of the haughtiness that most officers displayed - particularly toward the irregular militia force and scouts.

The two soldiers guarding General Braddock's command post snapped to attention as Colonel Doherty approached. "Colonel Doherty to see the General, " he said as he returned their salute.

"You may go right in, Colonel," replied one of the guards, "the General is expecting you, Sir."

The command post – a small two room cabin – had been borrowed from a farmer. General Braddock used the back room as his private quarters, and the front room as his office. Doherty opened the door, to be greeted with the haze of wood smoke emanating from a poorly-ventilated fireplace. "Colonel Doherty, reporting as ordered, Sir," he said, while standing at attention and saluting.

"Yes, yes, my good colonel. Come in and take a seat. We need to keep this short; there's just too much to attend to these days," replied Braddock as he added another signed order to the large pile to his right. The pile to his left - although dwindling – remained a few pages taller than the finished pile. He placed his quill pen in the inkpot, put his hands together on the front of the desk, and asked, "So, tell me, Colonel. How are my fine troops shaping up? We need to get on the move soon, so I pray they will be ready."

Doherty placed his hat on the corner of the desk. Before sitting, he moved the chair so he could see the General's face rather than a pile of paper. "Well, sir," answered Doherty, "the 44th regiment, comprising mostly veterans, is in excellent shape. The 48th, however, is mainly new recruits, who are not as advanced as I would like at this stage. It's a pity I didn't arrive here three months ago.

"The militia was a surprise to me. I couldn't imagine an irregular troop being this efficient, almost professional in their manner. The scouts, as well, appear to be most capable. I went out with them for three days, and am impressed with their leaders, Liam and Daniel Mallory. Extraordinary woodsmen; could almost make you believe they could track a flea."

"Ah, yes, the peasants," sighed Braddock, "I suppose they will be useful in some regard, mainly, I think, keeping the wagons moving over the many obstacles I'm sure we'll encounter, though certainly not as frontline troops. No, no, no, I don't think they'll be needed for that. Not against the French and the savage rabble we'll be up against. The 44th and 48th will be more than adequate when it comes to the battle itself. The scouts will certainly be of far more use than the actual militia, but I'm sure you see the sense in that. Don't you agree, Colonel? Of course you do.

"Now, as to the 48th; train them up as best you can. I will need garrison troops for a couple of posts we will leave along the way. We can use those troops of the 48th that aren't up to battle-readiness for that. That will be all for now, Colonel. I'll have an officer staff meeting within a few days to discuss commands and deployment. I expect you to be there. Oh, yes, if you see Colonel Washington, please ask him to come see me. My orderly can't seem to locate him."

"Yes, sir, General," replied Doherty as he rose from his chair. "I believe that Colonel Washington has gone hunting with that Mohawk warrior, Teeyeehogrow, but he is due back before sunset. I will pass the word that he is to report to you upon his return. Good evening, Sir." Doherty saluted and walked back out into the fading sunlight.

Shading his eyes, Doherty spotted Sergeant Mulhern talking to Daniel Mallory. Catching the sergeant's attention, he walked over to him. "Sergeant, had you made that wager, you would be one large whiskey richer."

****

After their initial meeting at Fort Necessity, the friendship between Colonel Washington and the adopted Mohawk Teeyeehogrow grew. They spent many an hour talking late into the night around the campfire with Liam, Daniel, and Pierre. When there were just the two of them, it was not unusual for them to hunt together, as they did today.

As the camp had been occupied for a while, hunting was meager in the near vicinity; all they managed to bring down was one turkey. They sat on the bank of a small stream, cleaning the turkey carcass remains from their hands and knives. "Mighty slim pickings; hope we don't get laughed out of camp." As he scooped a handful of water onto his head, Washington continued, "Maybe if we hadn't been talking so much, we wouldn't be so sparsely encumbered."

Teeyeehogrow laughed, and replied, "Nothing like being upwind and loud when on a hunt. I've found that coming back in a similar fashion makes for an angry wife and squalling children, but our time together is growing short. Once General Braddock has us on the move, I'm afraid we will be much too busy. I surely hope that you can influence him in regard to the use of scouts. I fear he does not understand what he's heading for."

"The General is admittedly wary of the local forces at his disposal, but at least I was able to talk him into accepting eight of the Mingo scouts sent to us. I will continue my efforts, but am afraid that we have reached the point where the General will view my persistent advice with more than just stubbornness," replied Washington. "I don't want to antagonize him such that he discards me altogether - after all, I'm here only as an unofficial advisor."

Teeyeehogrow stood, picked up the turkey, and stuffed it into a linen bag. "By the way, Colonel," he asked, "why is it you are here unofficially? I would have thought an official posting makes perfect sense, given your experience."

Washington unfolded his long legs, and sighed as he stood. "My experience does not include understanding the French. In the surrender treaty at Fort Necessity, the French commander used the word *assassine* to describe the death of Jumonville, implying that I had him killed rather than the truth - he was a victim of that unfortunate encounter, a battle casualty. My superiors in London took the language of the treaty to heart, and felt it proper to discipline me. Being innocent of the charge, and more than a little angry with London, I resigned my commission. It is my good fortune that General Braddock took my side in the dispute, and offered me this chance - not only to assist him, but also to have a chance to redeem my reputation."

****

At the camp, Liam and Daniel inspected a batch of new militia recruits. With the General allowing them to use only eight of the fifteen Mingo scouts sent by Chief Scarouady - who replaced Tanaghrisson after he died - they needed to bolster the ranks. While Liam questioned a recruit, Daniel found himself gazing at Timothy Winslow. He nudged Liam, and shouted, "Private Winslow! Front and center, if you please."

Liam stiffened, his face set in a hard grimace. "We are not interested in a chicken-hearted bastard who will bolt at the sight of his own shadow," growled Liam.

"I agree," said Daniel, "but let's hear what he has to say."

"All right, change our minds, Private Winslow," replied Liam.

"Well, sirs, this is the way of it. I was well settled in Albany, with a new brewery and tavern, when I heard tell about what happened at Trent's. Oh, Liam, I am so sorry for your loss of Orenda," said Winslow, his voice cracking.

"Thank you, Timothy," answered Liam. "Carry on with your story, Private."

"Yes, sir," responded Winslow. "Once I heard, I turned the tavern over to my partner, and enlisted in the militia. I've grown quite a bit in the last few months, and with the help of a friend, I have learned not to jump at my shadow. I have also become a decent shot. In fact, we enlisted together. He was one of the hunters who kept the butchers in town supplied with fresh game, and he taught me how to shoot and track. I know I am asking a lot, but it would ease my soul if I could join your scout troop. I feel I owe it to them that died that terrible day."

"That's all well and good, private," said Liam, "but good intentions aren't enough. Our task will require skill and daring, and you have proven in the past to have neither. Now, you expect us to believe you have learned these skills. I always liked you, Timothy, but that is not enough to sway my judgment."

Winslow made to protest, but a voice behind him, from the ranks of the recruits, cut him short. "I say he is good enough," spoke a tall, thin man dressed in buckskin. He had the look of a hunter, his eyes seeming to pierce their target, and long legs that spoke of swiftness of stride.

"Just who might you be, Private?" asked Daniel.

"Marcus Octavius Winningham, at your service, sir," he replied with a salute and a smile, "named in honor of Marcus Antonius and Octavian Caesar. Two of the noblest Romans to ever antagonize one another. You see, my folks were right fond of the ancient Romans. My sisters are named Julia Antonia and Livia Messalina. My brother has to explain Brutus Cicero when introduced."

"That is quite a fondness," responded Daniel, "but we're still not convinced of Timothy's abilities - though I think I would take a chance with you, Private Winningham. You are not unknown to us; we have heard of you from various sources employed by Major Trent in the Albany area, and you are most welcome to join us."

"I thank you kindly, but unless Timothy is allowed to join, I'm afraid you will have to do without me as well," answered Winningham.

Daniel looked at Liam and sighed. "Troops dismissed. We will let you know of our decisions shortly." As the recruits headed toward where the militia was bivouacked, Liam and Daniel made for the stables. Neither spoke as they saddled their horses. They rode out of camp, to discuss their options without its clamor to disturb them. The brothers rode at a leisurely pace for about an hour. Reaching a copse of oak trees around which the early blooming daffodils and crocuses rose to meet the sunlight, they dismounted and hobbled their mounts, letting them graze on new shoots of grass.

"I don't see how we can pass up the chance to have someone as good as Private Winningham," said Daniel as he took a drink from his water skin. "I've heard it said that he moves quieter than a shadow, and that he can shoot and reload on the run. Course we both know how skittish Timothy was during our time together at the trading post. Could it be that he has changed, as he says? I suppose we could order Winningham to volunteer, but I get the feeling that he would bolt for parts unknown, if he had a mind to."

"Agreed," replied Liam, "he has us over a barrel, it seems. I'm not happy with it; there is much at stake, and we cannot afford to make any errors about the men we choose. Well, Pierre would say that sometimes you just have to go with what life bestows upon you, and we don't have much time to decide. Damnation! We'll have to take Timothy, but the first time he flinches at the wind rustling some leaves, or in any other way jeopardizes our mission, I swear I will send him back."

"Don't worry, brother," answered Daniel, "I think between myself and Private Winningham, we'll be able to keep an eye on our good brewer-turned-woodsman. Who knows? Perhaps he'll surprise all of us. Pierre also says that God moves in mysterious ways; this could one of those times when the Almighty decides to have a little fun."

Liam chuckled at that, which caught Daniel a bit by surprise, as Liam was not given to mirth since the trading post raid. That feeling was lost almost immediately, though, as Liam spat angrily. "Bloody hell, the Almighty can kiss my arse. Was what happened at the post his idea of fun?"

****

Joseph Clarke returned from Philadelphia, sent there by General Braddock to purchase wagons and hire teamsters to drive them for the expedition - a godsend to the men who had worked for Phil Burke, as the business had fallen on hard times with his death. Clarke wiped the sweat from his brow as he clambered down from his wagon. The teamsters with him included Jack Tomlinson, and a young man with the look of an adventurer – the keen-eyed, broad-shouldered and extremely confident young Daniel Boone. "Come along, Boone, I would like you to meet some friends of mine," said Joseph. "I have a feeling you will get along famously with them."

They left the wagons in the capable hands of Tomlinson, to wander the camp in search of the Mallory brothers. They found them at the edge of the sprawling camp, in conversation with Teeyeehogrow and Washington who had just returned from their hunt.

"Liam, Daniel, I hope I'm not interrupting, but I would like you to meet Daniel Boone, a teamster we hired for the expedition. He may be a wagon driver now, but he has the desire – and I think the ability – to explore the frontier once we drive the French out," said Joseph.

"Nothing that can't wait," replied Daniel as he held out his hand. "Welcome to our adventure, Mr. Boone. It's always a pleasure to meet someone of a like mind and ambition."

Boone took his hand and shook it vigorously, saying, "Tain't had the chance to do much exploring yet. But I expect to do some after this wagon job is done. I hear tell of bountiful game, and a land that just beckons to be seen in the Ohio country. Course, I'm in the presence of men much more experienced than me, and am truly glad to meet you. Joseph here has told me much and more of you, and your brother, Liam." Boone then extended his hand to Liam, who shook it wordlessly and then walked away to his tent.

"I apologize for my brother's rudeness," replied Daniel. "He's changed a lot since his wife was killed. He used to be pleasant to be around; now, he's surly most of the time, and hard to get along with. I wouldn't take it personal."

"Joseph told me about that, too," answered Boone. "What a horrible time you both went through, yet you seem to have weathered it."

"I have my moments, believe you me," said Daniel. "Guess that just shows how different we are. Well, let's go to my tent and talk some more over a mug of ale about this land of plenty that beckons you."

The next morning, , Captain Trent joined the other officers — Colonels Doherty, Dunbar, Gage, and Washington – in General Braddock's office, to talk among themselves while they waited for him to emerge from his back-room private quarters. They saluted as he entered, to begin the officers' orders for the upcoming campaign. He bade them sit with a wave of his hand.

"Gentlemen, let us begin. First off, I want to let you know that I have the full backing of my London superiors for an extensive campaign. It will involve the troops under your command, and also those under Colonel William Johnson and Governor William Shirley of Massachusetts. Colonel Johnson will undertake the capture of Fort Saint Frederic on Lake Champlain, while Governor Shirley - with the newly raised 50th and 51st regiments - will attack and destroy Fort Niagara on Lake Ontario.

"Our particular targets are Forts Duquesne, Machault, Le Boeuf, and Presque Isle. The disposition of our troops, both regular and militia, is as follows. Colonel Gage will command the 44th regiment, and Colonel Doherty the 48th. Colonel Dunbar will have charge of the baggage train and artillery.

"Now, as to our ability to reach the forks of Ohio River, I have dispatched an engineering company to build a road through the hundred miles of woods and hills we will traverse. For their protection, I sent along a company of riflemen taken from Gage's 44th. The order of our march will be as follows: the 44th in the lead, with the 48th behind them. The baggage train will trail behind with the militia. Bringing up the rear will be the non-military personnel, the bakers, cooks, sutlers and the like, though I want the blacksmiths and farriers with the baggage train at all times.

"The other, shall we say, camp followers, will come along at best possible speed. I will not slow down for laundry women and whores. We leave in two days' time on the 29th. Gentlemen, I cannot stress enough the importance of this mission. London wants the French driven out, and, by God, that is what we will do. I know that we should not underestimate our foe, nor should we overestimate them. It is my sincere belief that a British soldier is worth at least ten of the French, and perhaps twenty of their native allies. That is all for now. Go prepare your troops and wagons for departure; I will brook no delay. You are dismissed." As the officers stood to leave, General Braddock spoke. "Ah, Mr. Trent and Mr. Washington, would you be so kind as to remain for a moment longer?"

Trent and Washington sat back down. General Braddock, his hands folded in front of him and the hint of a smile on his face, said, "Now as to your responsibilities. Captain Trent, you will, of course, lead the militia and scouts. I pray that they will not disappoint, or cause any delays along the march. I have the utmost confidence in the regular army and its tradition of British professionalism. I have less confidence in the irregulars; I do not intend to rely on them for our success.

"That is not to say that the militia, in particular the scouting parties, will be a total hindrance. I understand from your reports that we have a good group of scouts and guides, but I cannot count on them for anything more than getting us to the battle. I will leave the fighting to the professionals under Gage and Doherty. That is all for now gentlemen, dismissed."

Captain Trent and Washington left the general's tent headed over to the scouts camp, both of them in some amazement over Braddock's dismissal of their worth. "I fear that the General will be in for a dreadful surprise, if he does not listen to reason," said Trent.

"He is so entrenched in the idea of the glorious European style of battle. All we can do is provide him with the best information," replied Washington. "For my part, I will continue to try and change his mind, though I have little hope of success. To use his words, 'Savages may indeed be a formidable enemy to your raw American militia; but it is impossible they should make any impression upon the King's regular troops.' I pray our scouts and militia force will be up to the task, even with this lack of support from the commanding general. I also hope that we can keep Liam from confronting the General, after we tell him of this slight to his abilities."

Colonel Doherty met Sergeant Mulhern outside the General's headquarters with a shake of his head. "The time for drill is over, Sergeant. We leave in two days. I hope the bog-trotting bastards under our command are up to the task. We will be in the shit if they are not."

Henry gazed lovingly at Liza while she mended a tear in his breeches. Cleaning his musket, he did not look forward to the conversation he needed to begin. "Daniel came by a few minutes ago," he started, "he said we would be breaking camp in two days for the march to Fort Duquesne. I wish you would reconsider coming along. This is not going to be a pleasant journey for any of us, let alone a woman with child."

"I know that, husband, but I will not be left behind," replied Liza as she tied off the end of the stitch she had sewn. "I have, as you are well aware, been through unpleasant trips, and have proven myself to be strong enough to endure the hardships."

"But, you weren't expecting our child on those trips," Henry replied, his voice growing more agitated.

"Oh, my handsome Henry, I am not that far along. We will have completed this mission long before it is my time to deliver," said Liza. "I will not hear another word on the subject. I am coming along, and that is all there is to it."

Henry felt that it was at least his duty to try to convince her to stay behind. Deep down, he was glad his wife was so stubborn on the subject, though he dared not let her know.

Chapter 7

Battle of the Monongahela

The morning was clear and warm, a harbinger of the coming summer. The scouting party left the camp an hour before dawn; they expected to rendezvous with the road building crew some fifteen miles away. The scouts were led this morning by Liam; General Braddock wanted Trent to consult with Washington about the terrain ahead. Daniel, Henry, Timothy Winslow, Teeyeehogrow and three of his Mohawk warriors, and Markus Winningham made up the rest of the party. They moved quietly down the trail, blazed over what was once a path used by the native tribes.

It was adequate for moving men and animals. But, Liam remarked to Daniel that night as they made camp, "I doubt the General will be moving as fast as he expects. The wagons are going to have a rough time of it, having to skirt all those boulders and tree trunks along the way."

"Right," responded Daniel, "and we haven't even reached the hilly portion of the trail. That'll slow 'em down even more. I doubt we will have any contact with the French for a few more days yet, but let's set a watch anyway. Two men for three hour intervals ought to be fine for now."

"Good idea," replied Liam. "Put Timothy and Markus out for the first watch. May as well test our Tim sooner rather than later."

Colonel Gage's 44th Regiment marched out in smart style to the cheers of the civilians and the drums and fifes of the regimental band, followed by Colonel Doherty's 48th and their contingent of Scottish bagpipes adding to the festive air. General Braddock and his command staff came next, followed by the lumbering oxen and mules pulling the supply wagons. The drovers, and their herd of cattle and spare horses and mules, trailed behind, leaving the camp followers to deal with the swirling dust and piles of dung left in the wake of this vast train of men and beasts stretched over more than two miles.

The plan was to make ten miles the first day; although the terrain was mostly flat, the road narrowed in spots, slowing down the wagons and artillery. When Braddock halted the group, they had only travelled three miles, a result that did not please the General. That evening, he called a staff meeting, and gave the order for teams of men, mules and oxen to remove the tree trunks and boulders left by the engineers, hoping to speed things along. In the meantime, the rest of his command would stay in camp for an extra day.

Liza and her father-in-law, Joseph, sat in the wagon that held the blacksmithing tools, spare wagon wheels, axles, kegs of horseshoeing nails, and the material to make the shoes. As they moved slowly down the trail, her mind drifted to that awful day of the raid on the trading post; not for the first time, she worried about the baby growing inside her. Joseph did what he could to keep the conversation lighthearted, but he could tell that Liza was lost in her own thoughts. He particularly noticed the way she repeatedly checked her musket.

Pierre rode on horseback next to the wagon, keeping his promise to Henry to keep an eye on Liza during the trip. He, too, often thought back to that day, and his helplessness as his friends were slaughtered across the river. . Nonetheless, he was determined not to show any of this sadness or worry to Liza, using his gift of storytelling to keep her mind occupied as best he could.

Joseph had clambered on and off the wagon multiple times in the course of the march, to lead the oxen through the maze of obstacles. He remarked to Pierre, "I will be much surprised if we reach our destination before Christmas."

Pierre, having tied his horse to the back of the wagon to help Joseph, wiped the sweat from his brow, nodded, and remarked, "I know that the General was informed of the condition of this so-called road. Liam sent Henry back with a report not long after they started out, but the good General is a bit hard of hearing when someone tells him something he does not want to hear, and dismissed both Henry and the report. Let us hope for the sake of the rest of the march that General Braddock becomes a little more sensible."

Joseph shook his head and pulled on the lead rope attached to the oxen, straining to get them moving. "I wonder what the engineers who are responsible for improving this track were thinking, telling the General that it was sufficiently improved."

"Ahh, well," replied Pierre, "as to that, the officer in charge of the road crew has been with Braddock for years, and is well adapted to the General's ways."

****

The militia detachment found itself relegated to the demanding task of pushing and pulling wagons and cannon over hills, and through the tight spots that remained despite the efforts to clear the blockages in the road. Much to Braddock's dismay, the column could not make more than three or four miles a day, due to the terrain and the resulting increased need for repairs. Wagon wheels and axles did not react kindly to the constant pounding produced by ruts and scraping along the sides of rocks and trees. Then, to compound matters, it began to rain – a steady downpour for two days that turned the track into a slippery and rut-creating morass.

"Lord a'mighty, but if this ain't the muddiest I've ever been," remarked Boone, "I may never get clean again." On the seventh day of the march, everyone involved with the movement and repair of the wagons was bone tired and mud-caked from head to toe, and still faced the first of many river crossings in the next leg of the march. The Casselman River was neither very wide nor very deep, but it was fast moving, and strewn with rocks and fallen timber. It would take the better part of the marching day to get all of the wagons across and up the slope on the northern side. When General Braddock became aware of yet another delay in what was becoming a much longer trek than he either imagined or would tolerate, he stormed into his command tent, and yelled at his orderly to get his officers together on the double.

"Gentlemen, I am sorely vexed at the speed at which we progress," Braddock raged through clenched teeth. "I have had enough of these delays and breakdowns. I realize we cannot change the ground or the weather, but we can change our tactics. Starting tomorrow, Colonel Gage will take half of his 44th and half of Colonel Doherty's 48th, the most experienced halves if you please, along with two supply wagons. Two cannon will accompany him, with enough militia for protection and for the brute force needed to keep those wagons and cannon moving. They will make best possible speed to the Monongahela River. Colonel Doherty will take command of the remaining troops of the 44th and 48th, and proceed at a normal marching pace. That should leave him in a position to assist Colonel Gage in the event he makes contact with the enemy, or to assist the baggage train if the enemy attacks it.

"The rest of this army and its baggage will follow along at this snail's pace. My staff and I will accompany Colonel Gage. I realize that this strategy goes against the old adage of the folly of splitting one's forces, but I believe that in this case we can dispense with that old adage. After all, gentlemen, we are only up against savages, and the inept frontier force the French have at Fort Duquesne. We could without doubt prevail even if our force were split into four pieces! That is all for now, you are dismissed. Captain Trent and Mr. Washington, please stay, I would have a word with you about our scouts."

While the rest of the officer corps hurried out of the general's tent, Trent and Washington remained seated. They exchanged looks, but said nothing — waiting for what they suspected were orders they would not like. "What I require from your scouts, gentlemen" began General Braddock, "is that they find me the best possible fords over the Youghiogheny and Monongahela rivers. I deem this more important than the search for the enemy. The French commander by this time knows the size of our force, and will not be inclined to leave his fortification to meet us in open battle. That would be the height of foolishness on his part. No, he will wait for us behind his walls; walls that we will batter down with our cannon. I doubt our troops will actually see much action, as I expect the French to surrender the fort to us once we have them cut off, breech their walls and destroy their gate. Any questions?"

Washington masked the confusion and disbelief on his face with great effort, and responded, "General, I understand the need for the best places to ford the rivers, but do you think it wise to assume the French or their native allies will not attempt some sort of engagement, especially when we are crossing those rivers and are at our most vulnerable? I have spoken with Captain Trent, who knows this area better than anyone, and he assures me that there are numerous places where ambushes can be set up."

"Mr. Washington," chided General Braddock with a dismissive wave of his hand, "even if there are, I do not countenance the use of this type of ungallant warfare, even by the French; it is not an honorable way to do battle, and I will hear no more about it."

When Colonel Dunbar approached Joseph to pick the two drivers who would accompany Gage's forward advance, two names immediately entered his thoughts. "Boone, Tomlinson," Joseph bellowed as he made his way to their supply wagons, "you two just volunteered to go with the lead group." Both Boone and Tomlinson then rearranged the loads in their wagons, to include just what Gage would need at the front: ammunition, food and water, medical supplies. When Boone was satisfied with his cargo, he climbed into the driver's seat.

Pierre approached him and asked, "Mind if I join you, Mr. Boone? I've just had a talk with Mr. Washington, and he gave me the impression that Colonel Gage might need more than just his regimental surgeon in the coming days."

"Tie your mare to the back of the wagon and climb aboard," replied Boone, "I welcome the company. Ole Jack Tomlinson is a fine teamster, no doubt about that, but he ain't much of a talker." Jack looked up from checking the harness straps on his mules, and grunted in reply. "See what I mean?" said Boone. "Now I hear tell, Mr. Baptist that you're a right smart fella. Maybe you can learn me a few things on the trail. While you're at the back of the wagon, reach in and bring out my musket. If what you say is true about Colonel Gage needin' more than his surgeon, then I might be needin' my musket close by rather than not."

The scouting party also split into two groups; Teeyeehogrow took his Mohawks and four of the Mingo, and set out to the Youghiogheny to find a usable ford. Liam, Daniel, and the rest headed toward Fort Necessity, to learn either that there was a French garrison in residence, or that it had been abandoned intact.

"Never thought I'd be looking to getting back into that sorry excuse for a fort," chuckled Henry, as he and the others peered through the trees at what remained standing of the stockade walls. As they warily approached the fort, Liam sent Timothy and Markus ahead to make for the gate. Timothy entered and found no one. Markus signaled to Liam that the fort was empty; the rest of the party made their way inside.

"Tim, Markus," called Liam, "Head back to Colonel Gage, and tell him what we've found here."

Daniel looked first at Liam, and then at Tim and Markus. "Grab a couple horses from Colonel Gage, so you will get back to us quickly. I know how much you'll miss us." Smiling, Daniel patted Tim on the back, and watched as the pair set off at a quick lope down the road.

Turning to Liam, the smile now replaced with a look of anger, Daniel said, "Don't you think you've gone far enough with Tim? You are running him ragged with all the extra duties you assign him."

Liam moved closer to Daniel, and replied in a hushed yet angry tone. "My wife and baby died that day. Our parents and baby sister died because of that day. Our friends died that day. That coward survived that day, because he ran."

Liam made to walk away, but Daniel stayed him with an outstretched arm. "He lives with that fact every day, brother. He is doing what he can to atone, if he even really needs to. It's not that he ran; he was gone months before that day. It's time for you treat him as the man he is, not the boy he was." Liam shook off his brother's arm, and with a grunt walked away. He would not admit that his brother was right.

Colonel Gage sat sideways in his saddle, watching his troops file by him, as they labored in the heat to climb the steep hillside. Despite having split from the slower baggage train, the lead column was still struggling to make five miles a day, and required a day to rest every four or five days. He knew that the ford at the Monongahela was close by, and looked forward to a day to relax a little.

The scouts had turned up nothing in the way of evidence of enemy camps or movement. It appeared that General Braddock's assessment of the French was correct, though Gage also knew that they were still at least three days from the fort — anything could still happen. He didn't share his commander's disdain of the irregulars, and trusted Liam and Daniel to provide him with good information. He slid off his horse and handed the reins to his nearby groom; with a smile, he joined his infantry to march the last mile to the ford.

The early morning serenity of a camp that had not yet bustled into life was broken by the shouts of the lookouts, as the scouting party rushed into the camp.

Seeing Colonel Gage step out of his tent, Daniel trotted over. Between breaths, he said, "Colonel, sir, we found a large force of French and their native allies, heading toward the high ground across the river. If they get there, it'll be hell crossing that river."

Turning to his aide, Gage said, "Get two platoons up and ready to go in five minutes. The scouts will lead them to high ground." Looking around, the colonel asked Daniel, "Where is your brother, Mr. Mallory? I don't see him with the other scouts."

"He was right behind the rest of us when we were crossing a little creek, "replied Daniel. "After that, I don't rightly know. Tim Winslow is also missing. I will take Teeyeehogrow and his braves back the way we came. Henry can lead your troops."

****

Liam silently cursed himself, not for being the last to leave but for waiting so long to do it; perhaps too long, he thought, when he heard the footfall and thrashing tree branches behind him. He came to a boulder-strewn creek too wide to jump across, so he plunged in, the water rising to his waist. Struggling with the current and the need to keep his bow dry, he didn't notice the two submerged rocks until he stepped on one. His foot slipped off its side and became wedged between them, twisting his ankle. The pain struck him sharply, and knocked him face-first into the water. As he came up for air, he saw a brave leaping into the water, a knife in one hand and tomahawk in the other. He tried to find something, anything on the creek bed he could use as a weapon, but could only muster a handful of sandy gravel. He rose quickly, ready to throw, when he heard the sound of a musket firing. He watched his attacker collapse and float away with the current, immediately followed by the butt end of a musket knocking another brave unconscious. Timothy reached down to grab Liam, but Liam pointed to his foot, and said, "Ankle's stuck."

Timothy moved the rocks apart and pulled Liam out of the creek. "I'm gonna have to carry you for a bit, leastways into those trees up yonder. Then, I'll take a look at your ankle while we wait for Daniel to find us." With Liam clinging to his shoulders, Timothy grabbed Liam's legs and hoisted him onto his back. It took a while to reach the trees; every step Timothy took jarred Liam's ankle. Setting Liam down, Timothy headed out to find wood suitable for a splint. Liam sat propped up against a tree, bow in hand and quiver next to him. Timothy returned, and placed the wood on either side of Liam's leg; using the shoulder strap from his musket, he wrapped the leg and splints.

"Just what were you doing so far from the rest of the group?" asked Liam, "not that I'm complaining, mind you. You saved my life, Timothy Winslow. You have my thanks and my respect."

Timothy smiled, and replied, "You'd have done the same for me, despite how you felt about me. Now, why was I there? I had been running with Markus, when I looked behind and couldn't see you. I motioned for Markus to keep going, and I lagged back. When I got to the creek, I saw you in the water, and the other two. I shot one bastard, and clouted the other one. What tribe were they from? I didn't recognize them."

"Ojibway," answered Liam, "they come from the land of the big lakes west of here. I heard that they had partnered up with the Potawatomi and Ottawa, and joined the French. What with the Shawnee included, that makes for a considerable force coming at us. Sure hope Daniel is prompt."

****

Henry led the two platoons hurrying after him. Markus and the Mingo had fanned out to either side. The advance reached the slope. As they began to climb to the heights, they were met with a hail of arrows, lances, and musket fire. Half of one platoon was downed; the others managed to get off one volley before they were overrun.

This was not the type of fight the British regulars were prepared for. The Indians came with their tomahawks swinging, and using their scalp knives on the victims. Henry, downed with an arrow in his hip, was able to snap off the shaft and stand. After shooting one foe, he turned and followed those of the British who had managed to break through, and were running for their lives back to the camp. Pursuit was sporadic, as there were many trophies to be claimed among the dead and dying soldiers.

Meanwhile, Colonel Gage readied the rest of his troops, but the narrowness of the road and the thickness of the woods prohibited a standard military formation. He issued the order for one of the cannon to fire, not against the enemy but as a signal to General Braddock and Colonel Doherty that he had engaged the French.

General Braddock, having spent the night with Colonel Doherty's command, was finishing up a cup of tea when he heard sporadic musket fire up ahead, and then the roar of cannon.

He called for his horse, and said to Colonel Doherty, "Bring your troops up as quickly as possible. I'll send word as to the situation shortly. I'll take Mr. Washington and Mr. Trent with me. This could be the day of our triumph, Colonel. Let us show the French the mettle of the British soldier." Washington and Trent mounted, and followed the general as he headed to the sound of the guns.

Liam stood when he saw Daniel and Teeyeehogrow emerge from the trees. Grimacing at the pain that shot up his leg, he hobbled over to his brother. "Best we get away from here; get to the road, and find out just what the hell is going on. I heard a cannon and it sounds like a fierce fight over by the bluff."

Daniel gave a sigh of relief on finding his brother, but after watching his painful limp, said, "You'll never make it on that ankle. Climb aboard, brother. I'll carry you as far as I can." As they made their way back to the road, and the supposed safety of the British troops, they were met by the survivors of the fight at the bluff. Many of them had discarded their muskets, and anything else that would slow them down, such was their terror after seeing what happened to their fallen comrades. Colonel Doherty stood in front of his ranks when the retreating troops reached him.

Needing to prevent the panicking soldiers from affecting the rest of the army, Doherty stood in his saddle and bellowed to his men, "Stand fast, you bog trotting whoresons. I will shoot anyone who turns tail. We will meet the enemy right here, and send him to perdition."

Liam slid off of Daniel's back and sat down next to Boone's wagon to wait for Pierre, already soaked in the blood of the wounded. He went over to Teeyeehogrow. "First, go find Henry and the others, and have them meet us here. Then, find Captain Trent, and ask if he has any orders for us." Teeyeehogrow headed immediately over to where Gage's troops were struggling to maintain their position, but were steadily being pushed back. He found Henry, and directed him to the rendezvous, and then trotted off to find Captain Trent.

****

Lieutenant Charles LeFurge was finally experiencing the adrenaline-laced euphoria of battle lust. After firing his musket and his two pistols, he was now in the midst of his enemy — the British — carving his way through them with his saber. Fascinated by the scalping performed by his Indian allies, in his reverie, he wondered what it would be like. He was soon startled back to reality, as a musket ball smacked into the tree next to him. Seeing the unfortunate shooter struggling to reload, he charged, his sword slicing through the air, striking his opponent where his neck and shoulder met and almost taking his head off. Blood from the severed artery covered LeFurge's arm and face. Wiping his eyes, he noticed Washington, and gave a savage cry. LaFurge picked up the musket of his fallen foe, quickly loaded it, and took aim. Muttering to himself, "Die, you British bastard," he pulled the trigger.

Teeyeehogrow, running toward Washington and Trent, noticed a French soldier taking aim on Washington. With a tremendous leap, he stretched out and shoved Washington to the ground. The musket ball caught Teeyeehogrow under his armpit and into his heart. He collapsed on top of Washington, who grasped his fatally wounded friend in his arms. Boone and Trent gently removed Teeyeehogrow's body, and laid him on the ground. Washington, somewhat dazed from his head having hit the ground, barely noticed Boone at his side, firing his musket point blank into the head of a charging, sword-swinging French lieutenant. LeFurge was dead before he hit the ground, the top of his head blown off as if he had been scalped.

Colonel Gage galloped over to General Braddock, on the ground, after having a second horse shot out from underneath him. The General scrambled up, declaring he was all right and that he needed another horse. "Colonel Gage, how much longer can you hold here? I've received word that Doherty is set up nicely just a couple miles to our rear."

"We can hold for the time being," replied Gage, "but if they turn our right flank, we may have a panic on our hands." Braddock climbed into the saddle of his third horse and rode to the front of Gage's troops. Seeing the mass of screaming warriors coming toward them, he turned his horse so that he faced his troops – and saw the fear in their eyes.

He wanted to say something stirring, to inspire them, to give them courage. He pulled his sword out of its scabbard, raised it to the sky, and began to speak — but no words came out, only a cry of pain as a musket ball hit his back under the shoulder, puncturing a lung. He slumped against the neck of his horse, as Gage came and took the reins to quickly guide him away from the onslaught.

Boone and Pierre had removed enough of the cargo in Boone's wagon to place Teeyeehogrow's body inside. When Gage came, they took Braddock down from his horse and placed him in the wagon. Pierre climbed in to do what he could to make the General comfortable, though he knew from the pink froth oozing from the General's mouth that the wound was fatal. Boone then headed the wagon back down the road, passing through Colonel Doherty's troops.

Despite the efforts of Gage and Washington to keep the front rank in check, fear took greater hold with every passing minute. The soldiers had been subjected to horrors they had never imagined, as they watched their companions fall to tomahawk blows while trying in vain to reload their muskets – and then the screams of the unfortunate being scalped. Finally, the chaos born of terror took hold. This time, there was no stopping the fleeing troops; they continued to fly past the still-orderly formation of Doherty's command. When the last of them had made it, Doherty gave the command for the front rank to fire, followed by the second, and then third rank. Those three volleys cut a swath of death and dying through the oncoming French, punctuated by a shot by Sargent Mulhern that cut down a Potawatomi chief and halted the French advance.

Washington, Gage, Trent, and the scouts made their way around the enemy after gathering what stragglers they encountered. They caught up with Colonel Doherty on the way back to Fort Necessity. Doherty had sent word on ahead to the baggage train to wait there, and to prepare for a possible attack. Colonel Dunbar dispatched his militia into the woods surrounding the fort, to act as a warning and first line of defense. He then placed his cannon on the road, knowing that using them in the woods would be fruitless.

Wagons lined up, end to end, as a barricade behind which the rest of the troops waited. Colonels Gage and Doherty arranged their men on either flank. The wounded were tended to inside the fort itself. General Braddock was placed on a pallet of straw covered with a blanket, his breathing labored and shallow. The arrow was removed from Henry's hip, while Liam's ankle was wrapped such that he could stand and walk.

All through the night, they waited, but the only movement was of more stragglers making their way to the safety of the camp. In the morning, Colonel Dunbar — who was now in command — called a staff meeting for the surviving officers. They decided that it was safe enough to begin the long trek back to Cumberland, though not before sending Daniel and company to see if they could find the enemy anywhere near. They also decided that they needed to make better time on the march back to Fort Cumberland, so it was that they burned 150 of the wagons along with the supplies they carried.

Daniel and his scouting party returned two days later. They had followed the French and their allies. On the first day after the battle, they finished the scalping and looting of the many dead, and the drinking of two hundred gallons of captured rum. The enemy then headed to Fort Duquesne. The second day saw the majority of the French's allies from Detroit and Michilimackinac leaving for their homes, having gathered their trophies and captives. When Daniel returned, he reported to Colonel Dunbar that Fort Duquesne was vastly undermanned. Dunbar, however, did not intend to order his troops to head west again. The number of available men was dwindling by the day, as many of the militia – unable to face that terror again – simply vanished during the night to head to their homes. "Here's what I don't understand," said Daniel later that day to Washington and Trent, "we clearly outnumbered the French even, with the number of allies they had with them. How could we have been so utterly defeated?"

"It's not always a matter of numbers or even weapons that determines the victor," replied Washington. "If the enemy has the means to frighten its opponent, then the larger forces can be defeated simply by losing their will and their courage. Clearly, that is what happened to our troops, especially the regulars. You cannot fight a frontier battle with European tactics and maneuvers. It is most unfortunate that General Braddock learned that too late. Go, and get some rest. We will be leaving tomorrow morning, after we bury the General."

Chapter 8

Aftermath – Many Trails

They buried General Braddock in the road near Fort Necessity, the tramping of the army and the wagons erasing all trace of the spot in an attempt to protect his body from being dug up and desecrated. Colonel Doherty approached Washington as they rode away from the gravesite. "Mr. Washington, a word, if I may? Colonel Gage has told me of your courage under fire, and of your efforts to rally the troops. For that, I commend you. I am interested in your thoughts about what happened. I must confess that I am much troubled and chagrined at the actions of what I thought were well trained regiments. I watched as our tactics were effective only toward the end of the battle, but by then our foe was more interested in scalping our dead than pursuit."

"I tell you, Colonel Doherty," replied Washington, "if ever I have the honor to lead an army in this kind of engagement, I will not fall prey to the conceit exhibited by the late general. We must fight in recognition of the terrain, and not spurn the tactics of our enemy. I would have an army of woodsmen and hunters, not the narrow-minded 'stand and volley ranks' that London provides."

"For what it is worth, Mr. Washington, I agree with you. I will use what little influence I have with the powers in London to convince them of the wisdom of just that sort of approach in the future. I fear, though, that the wine-bibbing bastards who have never seen a battlefield – let alone a wilderness – will be hard pressed to change their opinions."

"My dear Colonel Doherty, thank you for your kind words and encouragement. I have two or three casks of some excellent French wine waiting for me in Cumberland; I would be pleased to have your company. I had hoped to open them in triumph, but now I'm afraid it will be in remembrance and sorrow."

For the next three weeks, they retraced their steps; three weeks of the helpless wounded being painfully jolted with every rut and bump in the road. Liam and Henry were fortunate, in that they were able to leave the wagon in a couple of days. Liam rode horseback, but Henry had to content himself with walking – his backside still too tender for the saddle.

Each day of the march saw more of the wounded succumb to death, and each night saw a few desertions among the healthy. The final tally was indeed grim. Of the thirteen hundred in the lead column, four hundred fifty six soldiers were killed outright; another four hundred twenty two were wounded. The eighty-six commissioned officers lost twenty-six, with thirty-seven more wounded.

Washington, Gage, Doherty and the other high ranking officers engaged in lengthy discussions about the conduct of the regular troops, and the combat tactics that had failed so miserably against a foe which was, in numbers at least, vastly inferior. Washington – who discovered four bullet holes in his coat, sustained while trying to rally the panic-stricken men – was especially incensed; the manner and the death of Teeyeehogrow only added to his outrage.

A thick, swirling, penetrating mist dogged their steps, as the weary and demoralized army limped back into Fort Cumberland. For two days, it had soaked everyone and everything. Both men still limped from their injuries; Liam's ankle had sprouted a many-colored bruise that ran halfway up his calf. While Henry was mending well, he suffered the good natured taunts of his friends about the new hole in his arse.

By the time they finally reached the fort, Daniel Boone was thoroughly disgusted with being a teamster, and swore he would never again do it. The call of the frontier was strong before he joined the ill-fated expedition, and became even stronger with every passing mile. Though he was sure of himself and his ability to survive in the wild, and against hostile enemies, he was thrilled to find in Liam a partner to join him.

The frustration Liam felt about the British Army's stubborn disregard for the irregular troops and scouts, coupled with his disgust at the way they lost the fight, pushed him to the decision to leave as soon as he could. He also needed to distance himself from friends and family, in the hope he could lessen the turmoil in his mind. To where, or with whom, he had not decided – until the night that he overheard Boone talking about the buffalo sign he had seen a few days before the battle, and his plans to take the Ohio to the Indian hunting ground of Cantuckee. The next day, Liam rode alongside Boone, and asked him about his plans.

"Yes sir," said Boone, with a grimace and a sigh as the wagon bounced over another rut causing the wounded men in the wagon to moan, "saw me the trail of four or five buffalo coupla' days before the battle. They had rubbed off some fur on the trees, and were headed west. I kinda' took that as a sign that it's time for me to shake off civilization, and head for parts unknown. I yearn for the challenge of me agin' the wilderness. Guess I wanna see if I can stand up to ol' Mother Nature, and them that call that land their home and hunting ground."

"I heard tell from the hunters and trappers at Trent's," replied Liam, "that it is a land teeming with game, though the Shawnee and Cherokee see that land as theirs, and don't take kindly to trespassers."

Boone looked at Liam as if to see into his heart, and said, "'Tis true that they are mighty protective of it, and even though they are longtime enemies they tolerate each other in the hunting ground – but woe to any white man caught there."

"I reckon I can make my way undetected," answered Liam.

"I reckon you can," chuckled Boone.

"You do realize that if we make it out of there with our hair intact," Liam said, "there will be others who will want to follow us; many others, especially if the British take control of the Ohio. We could be the ones that bring the civilization we are so ready to escape."

"In which case, I – for one – will just keep going further west," Boone replied, "maybe, one day, I will lay my eyes on the Mother of Rivers."

And so the seeds of adventure took root in the two intrepid woodsmen. They agreed to set out from Cumberland, as soon as Liam's ankle healed sufficiently to start the long trek. They decided to avoid the headwater of the Ohio, which remained under the watchful eyes of the French at Fort Duquesne; they would strike the river further west. This meant they needed to build a canoe, which Liam had done before when he was with the Mohawk.

****

Henry and Liza sat in front of their temporary lodgings, the one room cabin of the unfortunate officer who fell to an Ojibway arrow. Liza's pregnancy was beginning to show. Henry tried to sort out his conflict about their next steps, as he caressed his wife's belly. He liked being a scout, but knew that his immediate future should be as husband and father. "Daniel asked me to stay with the army, though I think he did that just as a courtesy," Henry said. "I told him I would speak with you first, dear wife."

Liza took his hands into hers. Kissing them, she looked into his eyes, and saw doubt there. "Oh, handsome Henry, I will abide by your decision. But, if I have any means to keep you close, then I will do so. I would that you be father to our coming child."

Henry released her hands, and rose. He smiled down at her. "You need not be concerned. I am of a mind to build a cabin for you and our child. I know that Pierre and my father plan on heading to Albany. I deem that to be an ideal place to start our family life and they can be of great service in raising our cabin."

"I am most pleased, husband, and very happy," she replied, smiling, though in her mind she knew that this would not be their permanent home. She took his hand and led him inside the cabin; with a mischievous grin, she said, "I am also of a mind to be a wife to my handsome Henry."

****

Summer was coming to an end; every day saw more red and yellow in the trees, and flights of geese and ducks heading south. The two riders approaching the camp had the look of many days in the saddle; the dust of the road coated their uniforms, making the red gray. They dismounted when they reached the stable area. "Sergeant," said the officer, "see that these infernal beasts are taken care of, and then find yourself a mug or two of ale to get lost in. I will report to the commanding officer; hopefully, I will join you soon."

Lieutenant Colonel Alun Williams rubbed his backside, shook the dust from his coat, and headed to the camp headquarters. He had been in the saddle for near three weeks, making his way from Lake George, north of Albany, with news of the battle fought there on the ninth of September.

When he was announced, he entered to find a colonial Colonel sitting at the commander's desk. "No disrespect intended, Colonel, but I was hoping to report to General Braddock," said a surprised Williams. "When will he be available?"

Washington looked up at his visitor. "The general, my dear Lieutenant Colonel, is dead. Apparently news of our unfortunate encounter with the French has not reached your ears." He stood and held his hand out. "I am Colonel Washington. I have recently received command of the remnants of that costly endeavor. Please have a seat; you look like a man that could use something other than a horse to sit upon."

"Lieutenant Colonel Alun Williams, at your service, sir," Williams said as he shook Washington's hand and sat on the chair opposite Washington. "Indeed, I was unaware of the situation here. I have come from Colonel William Johnson, to report our successful mission in establishing Fort Edward, and the defeat of the French and their Canadian and Indian allies. Colonel Johnson would like you to send it on to London, so the bastard politicians can claim the victory as their very own." Williams handed over the satchel containing the report, and stood up to leave.

"Thank you, Lieutenant Colonel," replied Washington. "Perhaps you would join me for dinner tonight. We can regale each other with our war stories, though I see your tale ends more happily than mine. In the meantime, see my aide; he will direct you to your quarters." Williams saluted, and headed out – but not to his quarters; first he needed a drink, or perhaps two.

****

Timothy Winslow had never been offered so many drinks as today. The tale of his heroic saving Liam had grown with each telling, and now he was getting drunk on ale – ale that did not measure up to his standards, but after half a dozen tankards of the stuff, the quality didn't matter so much. Seemed like everyone was offering him another; everyone except Liam, who had taken himself to the farthest side of the camp. "Tell us again, Master Winslow," chimed in Markus, who was very drunk as well, "of your victory over the savage horde."

Timothy looked over the top of his mug, smiled, and said, "Methinks the tale has been relived too much already. One could have a notion that I single-handedly took out the entire Ojibway nation." After another sip of ale and a loud belch, he continued, "Oh, my, I have had enough of this horse piss. Did the brewer use a dead cat instead of grain? Come, Markus, if we want to live long enough to take part in anymore scouting, we need to drink something a little more pleasing to the taste, and less damaging to the gut."

They staggered to the door, colliding with Sergeant Mulhern as he entered. "Watch where you're going, you drunken sots!" exclaimed Mulhern.

"Terribly sorry, Sergeant," said Timothy, "Let me extend an invitation to drink a better brew than you'll find in this swill shop. We are on the way to my tent where I have my own brew. I've not much left, but enough to make one forget his troubles."

"Tis a fine offer. Since it looks like you are pretty well scuppered, I'm thinking that I'll be doing most of the drinking of your fine ale," answered Mulhern, who had just drank with Colonel Williams and his sergeant. "Aye, and you can be a'tellin' me about your heroic deeds."

****

Liam had pitched his tent as far away as possible from the rest of the camp. Daniel found him sitting in front of it, fletching a new supply of arrows, his injured ankle propped up on a piece of firewood. He hummed a tavern tune. Liam looked up as Daniel neared, and with a smirk said, "Welcome, brother, to my humble abode. Aside from just wanting to spend time with family, I'm guessing Colonel Washington has sent you to learn my intentions, once I can walk comfortably. Well, don't just stand there; in my tent is a small cask of Timothy's finest and two mugs, we may as well refresh ourselves whilst we talk."

Soon, they were wiping the froth from their mouths and grinning at each other like little kids. "You have the right of it about the colonel," said Daniel. "He is most anxious to know your plans, and frankly so do I. You have to know he esteems you in the highest fashion, and rightly so. No one in this army has your ability to track, hunt, and survive in the wild."

Liam put another arrow in his quiver, took another pull on his ale mug, and replied. "Ever since the day my heart was ripped from my chest, I have been looking for a way to repair the hurt, but still I am haunted in mind and soul. I know not if I will ever find peace, if I take revenge, or if I follow the buffalo vision – but I do know that I need relief from the demands of this army. Tell the colonel that I hold him in high regard, but I will not be staying with the scouts. Boone and I are agreed to go together to the Cantuckee land, down the Ohio River."

Daniel shook his head, and sighed. "Knowing you as well as I do, I will not try to gainsay you. I would only ask that you not keep yourself from us while you're still here. Liza misses you, as does Pierre. Come round once in a while, and let us be together as a family – if only for a little while."

"I promise to do that; I'm just sorry that I cannot be who I was, but if you all can put up with the sulking man I've become, then I will be content."

"That went as I expected," Daniel thought as he walked back to Liza and Henry's cabin. "I had a feeling he would be leaving us." Liam's intentions confirmed Daniel's feeling about Henry and Liza's intended return to the trading post. They talked about when to tell Liam. Liza was for telling him now, but Daniel convinced her that it was too early; Liam was still not in a good enough frame of mind for that news. Now that he was going off with Boone, there was no need to rush the subject.

****

Colonel Washington stepped out of his tent, barely avoiding a cascade of rainwater running down the flap. "Bloody rain; will it ever stop," he muttered to himself, glancing up to the silver-gray sky. April had lived up to its reputation, this being the third day in a row of constant rainfall. Washington, whose aide cleaned his boots nightly, felt a little guilty after taking only a few steps in the thick mud that now covered the camp. It was his habit to walk around the camp after his breakfast, but he skipped the last two days because of the pouring rain; despite the continuing downpour, he was determined to make his rounds today. He was not surprised to see Sergeant Mulhern drilling a squad of recruits, and a smile crossed his face when he heard the sergeant dressing them down. "Aye, you're naught but a bunch of gombeens. If any of you mogs had two brains, he'd be twice as stupid."

Washington continued his walk, having stopped to have a word with his quartermaster. Henry and Liza, along with Joseph Clarke and Pierre, left for Albany a couple of weeks previously. He passed their cabin, now the home of Lieutenant Colonel Williams. Washington, much to his surprise – as he was ordinarily an optimist – was looking forward to Williams leaving, to return to Colonel Johnson. Almost daily, Williams found fault with just about everything, but especially Parliament and the state of his lodgings. As he made his way back to his tent, he saw Daniel, Timothy, and Markus heading out, probably hunting, he thought. He was glad that those three were staying, but he felt keenly the loss of Liam, Henry, and most particularly Teeyeehogrow. Not for the first time, Washington fought back his sorrow.

When he reached his tent, he noticed that the rain had stopped. He took another look at the sky, and saw the sun starting to break through. "Things are looking up," he said to his aide. "Now if those chancers in London ever get off their collective arses, maybe we can start fighting again. Good God, I'm beginning to sound like Williams."

Chapter 9

Stormy Horizons – Spring 1756
London

While news of Braddock's defeat and his death startled an unbelieving London populace, the effect on Parliament set more than the North American colonies alive with the sound of war. Europe and the West Indies quickly became battlegrounds in yet another contest between Great Britain and France, as war was formally declared by both nations on May 8th and 9th. A French force of nearly 50,000 troops – mainly colonial militia – stood ready for an offensive against Canada and the frontier forts. This force nearly tripled the North American French population. .Britain's Secretary of State, William Pitt, received authorization to prosecute the war in any way he saw fit. He intended to keep the French military busy — on the continent, on the Atlantic, and in the West Indies — to keep France from supplying the troops necessary to combat the British in North America. With the addition of military help from its Russian and German allies, and by building up its Navy, Britain prepared to defend and extend its empire.

For Washington and the militia leaders, the unexpected defeat meant more men, equipment, and money. The colonial regiments were primed to be at full strength and well equipped, for the first time in anyone's memory. The regular army regiments were to learn militia-style skirmishing, which meant also learning new ways to load and shoot. They would still adhere to the old-style mass volley, but only when that tactic was practicable.

Colonel Doherty and Sergeant Mulhern were reassigned to Fort William Henry, under the command of Colonel George Munro. Their mounts saddled and ready, they approached the nd tent to take leave of Colonel Washington. "Colonel, Sergeant, I see you're all set to abandon me. How will I ever get these recruits trained properly without you?" joked Washington as he shook their hands. "Have a safe journey. I hope to have the pleasure of your company again in the not too distant future."

"It has been a pleasure serving with you, Colonel. I'm sure you'll have no problems training, just as long as you remember the colorful language employed by the good sergeant here," replied a smiling Doherty as he climbed on the saddle. "Until we meet again, Sir."

The Frontier

Wahta smelled the smoke before he saw it. He knew that it was from more than just a cook fire, and that there was most likely another raided white settlement still smoldering. This would be the third one they had come across in the last two weeks. He wondered how many fly-ridden corpses they would find this time. He raised his hand, signaling to the two other Mohawk with him to stand quiet. Hearing nothing but warblers, thrushes, and chattering squirrels, he motioned toward the smoke and started trotting.

With Braddock's defeat, the British military had more or less abandoned this part of the frontier. Most of the tribes involved with the French at Fort Duquesne returned to their homes. Parties of Ojibway, Potawatomi, and Ottawa now freely roamed on a rampage of death, destruction, and gathering of scalps and captives. Even those tribes that had remained neutral were now swayed to the French side, which emboldened many Delaware and Shawnee warriors. Often, the farms they attacked were so isolated from any other white settlements that there was no hope for them once an attack started. The lucky few who survived soon flooded into towns bearing tales of grief and loss, which raised a hue and cry for protection. Washington, whose regular troops were not yet up to this task, sent reinforcement from the militia and the scouts.

Daniel, Timothy, and Markus had been on patrol for two weeks. They concentrated on the farms and settlements north of Great Meadow and Fort Necessity. Most of the time, they accomplished only the burial of burnt or mutilated bodies of men – infrequently, they found a farm not yet attacked, and encouraged the settlers to be prepared or to leave until the situation improved. Rarely did they find living women or children, who were either taken as captives (to be sold to the French), or were taken back to their villages; they did come upon the bodies of women and children who, deemed to be a hindrance, were dispatched along the trail.

Daniel threaded his way through a tangled mess of vines and scrub brush, until he finally cleared the woods. Today, they were heading to the farm of Jonas Baker, a former member of the Massachusetts militia who later settled along the banks of the Meadow River. He could see Jonas and his three sons working in their fields of corn, beans, and squash. One of the boys noticed the three coming toward them, and hollered a warning to the others. Daniel was not surprised that Baker and his sons had their muskets by their sides while they worked the land, but he was concerned that one of them would start shooting. He kept his musket resting on his shoulder as he advanced, holding out his right hand palm up while shouting, "Jonas Baker. I'm Daniel Mallory. We're a militia patrol; you can lower your weapons."

Baker looked the three strangers over. With a hearty laugh, he said, "God's bollocks, boys, one of them there is Timothy Edward Winslow. I knew his father back in Salem, Massachusetts, and met young Tim again at his tavern in Albany. Spent many an hour there, enjoying the finest beer in the land. Come in, and welcome to my homestead." He told the two younger sons to keep working while he and the eldest, Ethan, took their guests down to the cabin.

His wife, Rebecca, hauled water from their well to a cauldron set over the fire pit. She wiped her hands on her apron, and called out, "Jonas, my husband, who in all of God's glory do you have there?" With a wink and a grin, she added, "If you plan on them staying for supper, you better go out and shoot something."

"Now, now, hold your tongue, woman," he replied, "if you'd a'taken notice, they brought their own vittles, and looks to be enough to share."

Markus raised the canvas bags holding the results of their hunt that morning, saying, "We have two turkeys, three rabbits, and a few geese. That should do us amply."

Jonas then noticed the grin on her face. "Ah, woman, you been having me on."

While Rebecca prepared the rest of dinner, Timothy and Markus butchered the game. Jonas, Daniel, and Ethan sat nearby and talked. Jonas was most eager to hear what news there was, and when might Colonel Washington do more than just send out patrols. "No disrespect intended."

Daniel sympathized with Jonas, but stated his belief that things were likely to get worse, until London responded with more troops and money. "You need to be vigilant, Jonas," continued Daniel, "I noticed that you and your sons had their muskets with them. Be sure to keep that up, and you should have Rebecca near to a weapon at all times as well. I reckon you've been left alone so far because you are prepared, but I imagine that Huritt or some other leader will figure your scalps are worth the risk. Me 'n the others will head out early tomorrow and search out this area for a few more days, but then we need to go back to Cumberland. There'll be another patrol coming round in two or three weeks, I imagine."

The Albany area

Liza stood and gazed upon the first home that was really hers. It took Henry, Joseph, and Pierre two weeks to get it built enough so that they could sleep in it. There was still plenty of work to do on it – a door, and shutters for the windows – but, still, it was the most beautiful cabin she had ever seen and was one she felt would be wonderful for raising the child who seemed to delight in making itself known with frequent kicks and turns. The men were busy pulling stumps and moving small boulders from the field they planned for crops. It would be too late to plant this season, but they were not concerned about a food supply. The area teemed with game, and Norman's Creek – good for trout – ran at the bottom of the hill. They were only about five miles from Albany; Joseph intended to bring them what they needed after his monthly trips to the blacksmith shop he would open there. Pierre had agreed to stay on until after the baby was born, and then planned to go to Donehogawa's village for an extended visit. For now, however, he was straining to pry a boulder out of the ground, while Henry urged their plow horse to pull harder.

In the past, they had heard from survivors of raids, and others seeking protection on their way to Albany, about the dangerous situation on the western frontier. Henry felt they were pretty safe, as they were close to Albany and in proximity to the Mohawk main village to their northeast. But a visit from Wahta, returning from the west on his way back to the village, prompted Henry to take extra precautions. He now kept three loaded muskets, one with him, one for Liza, and an extra one in the cabin. Pierre, too, had his musket by his side wherever he went. They also kept a few buckets of water handy, in case of fire.

Cantuckee

It had been three months since Liam and Boone set out from Washington's camp in Cumberland. They traveled overland until they reached the Ohio River southwest of Fort Duquesne – away from the prying eyes of the French – to look for a spot that showed the promise of good hunting and trapping. The original plan was to build a canoe, but they came across a trapper who was willing to sell his.

They paddled up the Licking River (so known because of the salt lick used by deer and other animals in the area), and guided their canoe onto a beach to unload their supplies. Once their belongings were piled on the beach, they loaded the canoe with rocks to sink it, keeping it hidden under an overhanging trio of birch branches. So far, they had seen no sign of any Shawnee, Cherokee, or any other tribe who would most likely take exception to them in tribal hunting ground.

Hoisting their packs onto their backs, they headed into the woods. During the trip, they developed a healthy respect for each other's abilities and knowledge of the woods –the younger Boone especially admired Liam's considerable experience. It took a few days of Boone's almost constant chatter and questions, but finally Liam at least partially let down the wall that shielded him from emotion, and who succumbed somewhat to the exuberant excitement of his youthful companion and became for the most part an amiable companion

On the hike from the river, there was evidence of plentiful game in the area. They also crossed a couple of feeder creeks that looked promising for trapping beaver and muskrat. All in all, this looked like an ideal location to settle over the winter, and then head back east in the spring, their canoe laden with furs and hides. They set up camp in the middle of a dense stand of oak, maple, and poplar trees. A clearing amid the stand was large enough to serve as their base of operations. They constructed a lean-to shelter of lashed-together log walls, its roof covered with evergreen boughs. The front was open, except for the two sheets of canvas which hung from the roof, secured to the front poles on either side. They could be tied together in the middle to provide some relief from wind and rain,. They dug two fire pits; a large one that would be their main cooking fire, and a smaller one set in front of the lean-to, close enough to provide warmth but far enough so to not set the place on fire.

****

Liam hunted by bow and Boone checked and set traps. They both carried a musket as well, but were hesitant to use them unless necessary. The sound of a gunshot could be an invitation to unwanted visitors. After a successful day of hunting and trapping, they remained in camp for a few days, preparing the hides and furs and , laying them out on drying racks in what sun they could find. They had meat in abundance, more than enough to eat, and would preserve what they could for the winter. After they built a small smokehouse, salt would be collected from the lick back by the river. "I'm thinking we should both go," said Boone while picking his teeth, "we ain't the only ones needing salt for the winter. No tellin' what or who we might find there. If I had my druthers, I'd rather it be a herd of those buffalo you dream about. More likely it'll be a band of hair-hunting Shawnee or Miami."

"Buffalo would be best," Liam said as he yawned, "see you in the morning."

The Frontier

The third day after leaving the Baker farm, Daniel, Timothy, and Markus found a recently used campsite and the tracks of a raiding party heading toward Jonas and his family. They took off at a fast and steady lope, and kept that pace up until they heard gunshots. Daniel raised his hand. He signaled to split up and head quietly to the farm about a half mile distant. Reaching the edge of the woods, they saw six Ottawa braves spreading out to surround the cabin. One of them crouched down, putting together the makings for a fire, while another started wrapping arrowheads with what looked like the remnants of a woman's gingham dress. Keeping low, the three scouts crawled through a corn field until they were within musket range. Daniel and Timothy targeted the two by the fire. Markus crawled a little farther, to take his shot on the brave nearest the cabin. When Markus signaled he was in position, they all counted to three and fired. Daniel's shot hit the brave by the fire in the kidney– knocking him forward, his leg resting on the edge of the fire. The Ottawa whose arrow was now aflame pulled back on his bow when a musket ball entered his back and punctured his heart. Markus' target was luckier; he was moving when the shot hit him, and it only grazed his upper leg leaving a painful and bloody quarter-inch furrow along his thigh.

When Jonas saw the Ottawa braves turn toward the corn field, he knew someone had caught them by surprise, and that their attention was drawn away from the cabin for the moment. "Ethan, Micah, get ready to follow me out of the door. Ethan, you go out to the right, find a target, and shoot. Same for you, Micah, but go left. I'll take the middle. After you've taken your shot, get back in the cabin and reload. Ready! Go!" Jonas pulled open the door, and the three ran out and took their positions. The three remaining Ottawa turned to the new sound from behind them, but could not move fast enough to avoid the volley. Two of them died almost immediately, the third would not last the day.

Daniel, Timothy, and Markus ran to the cabin, but lowered their weapons and relaxed when they saw the result. "Well met, young Mallory," said Jonas, "I think you can report to Colonel Washington that ye earned your pay today." They gathered up the four dead Ottawa, and left them by the wounded one – content to let them lie until the morning, when the wounded one was sure to be dead. Then they would bury them.

Timothy looked at the bodies, and said, "I believe we are missing one. There were six in this party and we only have five bodies."

Markus looked over to his friend and with a shake of his head said, "I only grazed the bastard, and then in all the excitement I just plumb forgot about him, thinking he was too hurt to run. He must have slipped off while we weren't lookin'."

"Couldn't be helped," said Jonas as he came out of the cabin, carrying a cask of ale brewed by none other than Timothy Winslow. "Besides, mebbe he'll be a warning to others about taking on the Baker family. God's bollocks, we taught them a lesson."

The Albany Area

The contractions began shortly after dawn, and were becoming more frequent. Pierre helped her to bed, and made her as comfortable as he could. Henry was more of a hindrance than a help; Pierre finally told him to fetch the midwife. Henry hitched up the wagon and headed to the small farm two miles up Norman's Creek, where the midwife lived. To keep his mind off the goings on at the cabin, Henry thought back to an argument he and Liza were having. She told him about her and Daniel's desire to return to the trading post and start it up again; something about continuing their parent's dream. Henry thought it was pure foolishness given the current situation – and while the French were in control of the area it was downright dangerous. Perhaps the birth of the child would make Liza a bit more reasonable about the subject.

Pierre also expected the arrival of Donehogawa and his wife Onatah –having asked Wahta to deliver his request for help – though now it appeared they would be late for the birth. Joseph was also due any day, anxious to meet his first grandchild.

While Liza progressed through labor, and Pierre waited for help, Huritt slowly approached the cabin from the south, across Norman's Creek. With him were a Shawnee brave and two Abenaki warriors. They were confused by the lack of movement around the farm and the cabin, and three of them wanted to back away being wary of a trap, but Huritt was not turning back. These whites had escaped him too many times.

Henry, returning with the midwife, saw the raiders crossing the creek. He told her to lie down in the wagon bed and don't move. He then grabbed his musket, climbed down from the wagon and began running toward the cabin screaming, "Raid! Pierre, raid!" When he reached the front of the cabin, he stopped, took aim, and shot – hitting one of the Abenaki in the arm and momentarily stopping their advance. Pierre flung open the door so Henry could enter, and handed him a loaded musket.

With the added excitement of an Indian raid, Liza was caught off guard by her next contraction and screamed louder than she had. As well as startling Henry and Pierre, the attackers paused in their advance. Huritt motioned them forward again, and they made their way to some cover behind the well and a water trough. Liza's scream also reached the ears of Wahta, who was traveling with Donehogawa and Onatah. At once, he sprinted ahead, only to stop and hit the ground when he saw a Shawnee pointing a musket his way. The shot went high but the shooter was now vulnerable and he went down after having been hit in the chest from a shot from the cabin. Henry put that musket down, and grabbed Pierre's, who had gone over to be with Liza. Wahta made his way by crawling to the back of the cabin. He peered around the corner and saw Huritt. Ducking back behind the cabin, he yelled out, "Huritt, I am Wahta. It will be a shame that it is not my brother Snake Slayer who kills you today." Huritt was about to reply when he heard the sound of a wagon approaching at a fast clip. He saw it just as it plowed into his two companions as they backed away from the well. Screaming at the top of his lungs, Huritt turned and ran back across the creek, having been thwarted again in getting his revenge.

Henry rushed out, and finally quieted down the team of horses. "What on God's green earth possessed you to charge that wagon like that?" Henry asked the midwife.

"I just couldn't stand by any longer knowing the good lady needed me, so I did what I could."

"Yes ma'am. Can't argue with that," Henry replied chuckling. When the midwife got to Liza, she shooed Pierre away while telling him to have hot water handy. However, he soon returned when Onatah arrived, serving as a translator. It didn't take long for the two women of different languages and cultures to understand one another, and each went about helping to bring a child into the world.

The men were all outside, recounting the day's events, when they heard the baby's first cry. Henry stood without moving, like he had been nailed to the ground. Joseph finally gave him a shove, and Henry walked unsteadily in through the door, and into the life of fatherhood. The baby boy was at rest on Liza's chest, her hands cradling his head. Henry was still in a state of shock, but was roused out of it by Liza asking him for the third time what were they going to name the baby? Henry thought for a moment, remembering Liza's father. Then, he looked across the room to his own father, and said, "His name is Thomas Joseph Clarke."

Cantuckee

Shawnee Chief Pucksinwah bent over the kettle, stirring the last bit of liquid left in this boiled down batch of salt. There were three other kettles in various stages of evaporation, and everyone in the salt-gathering group was so involved in the process that they did not notice the two white men, watching them from atop a hill overlooking the salt spring and lick. Liam and Boone froze when they spotted the Shawnee and slowly stepped back into the protection of the trees. "Damnation," muttered Boone. Liam nodded his head in agreement. They were just about to leave when a familiar voice came from the Shawnee below.

Huritt emerged from the woods, carrying a load of firewood. He shouted something, causing his companions to laugh. He had rejoined Pucksinwah's band after the events on Norman's Creek, his quest for revenge on hold for the time being. Liam's face changed in an instant from a smile to one of rage at the sound of his enemy's voice. He pulled an arrow from his quiver, nocked it and made ready to pull back on his bow. Boone reached over; placing his hand on Liam's bow, he gently forced it down. "Liam," he whispered, "this ain't the time or place to pick a fight. You'll only succeed in getting yourself kilt and scalped, and what's worse, you'll get me kilt and scalped as well. I know the anger, the rage that you carry. Your brother told me most of it, but you also talk when you dream. It's actually pretty entertaining listening to your ramblings, but frightening to boot. For now, though, I think we need to just get moving while we still have our hair."

Liam let Boone lower his arm. For a moment, he stared at his bitter enemy below. At long last, he looked away from Huritt. "Let's go."

****

They waited for three weeks before venturing back to the salt lick, time that they spent preparing their shelter for the coming snow and cold of winter. They planned to leave this camp in early spring before the snow melted entirely, and head back to their submerged canoe hidden in the Licking River. Their pile of furs and hides exceeded what they had anticipated; they would have to build another canoe to handle the load. and build sleds to carry their goods to the river. The remaining decisions were the route, and which trading post. Boone was of a mind to go back the same way they came, leaving the Ohio before they reached Fort Duquesne. "The problem with that," replied Liam when the discussion came up again, "is finding somewhere to purchase pack horses or mules. No, the way I see it is to go straight to Fort Duquesne. We keep ourselves hooded, and we should be fine. Not much chance of being recognized anyway."

They had had this discussion many times; each time, Boone coming a little closer to agreeing with Liam. "You're sure we can trust this Frenchman trader friend of yours, this Jimmy Two Birds?" asked Boone, not for the first time. This was the sticking point for Boone; the tendrils of doubt, however, were loosening their grip.

"We can trust him to give us a good price for the furs, we can trust him to keep our identities secret, and we can trust him to give us good information about the fort," countered Liam, not for the first time. "Of course, the price he gives us for our goods will be a little less than usual; after all, silence and information does have a price."

They spent the winter repairing what needed to be fixed, gathering and chopping firewood, and occasionally patrolling around their camp to assure no one else was around. They had dug a trench in the middle of their lean-to floor; each night, they filled it with hot stones from the fire pit. This made the coldest nights bearable, but it also meant they awoke very cold in the morning once the heat was gone. Liam woke up shivering, saw that it was barely daylight, grabbed his bow, and headed outside. "Gonna take a look around," he told Boone. "The walk will hopefully warm me up." Snow had fallen during the night, adding another five inches to what was already there, but the sky was clearing and Liam could see that the sun would indeed be out this day. He started down the hill, intending to follow the creek for a couple miles. He had travelled almost that distance when he heard the grunting of a herd of buffalo, and then felt the rumble of their movement in the direction of the salt lick. He climbed the creek bank, and then the hill that arose from it. He looked down on a herd of about thirty buffalo traversing the snow-covered meadow.

The entire herd had nearly cleared the meadow to enter the trees, except for one older animal, a cow with an early calf. They lagged behind, the newborn stopping to take a look behind and then trotting on a few more steps. Liam soon saw the reason for the animal's concern – a very determined looking and half-starved coyote came loping across the snow, looking for a chance to take down the defenseless calf. The mother headed away, calling the calf to her side, but the calf floundered on unsteady legs and sank into the snow. The coyote saw this as its chance, and picked up speed. Liam immediately rushed toward the coyote and calf, nocking an arrow to his bow as he ran. When he was close enough, he dropped to his knees. The coyote slowed, its attention diverted.

That was all the hesitation Liam needed; his arrow flew straight and true, catching the coyote behind its front shoulder slamming it sideways across the snow where it died. The mother walked over to her baby, and used her head and hooves to clear the snow around the calf. She then lay down to comfort her frightened baby. Liam retrieved his arrow from the dead coyote. He left the carcass, deeming the mangy hide of the poor beast to be not worth the trouble of skinning. After one last look at the buffalo cow and calf, he headed back to the camp, full of that sense of calm and peace that followed his encounters with his buffalo totem spirit.

At long last, a string of warm days melted enough snow so that Liam and Boone could pull the sleds, piled high with their booty. It took them a day to negotiate the sleds down the riverbanks to the water, having to pull them through mud in some places. They survived nights without fire, wary of attracting attention being this close to the river, and awoke shivering, often to a threatening sky. The next three days, they worked in an almost steady snow fall, fashioning a canoe from a birch log. This one didn't need to be as large as the other one – just big enough to carry what didn't fit in the larger canoe.

The larger canoe remained at the bottom of the icy river. Wanting to have dry clothes to put on after the retrieval, they both stripped down and waded to the spot where the canoe lay. Pulling on it didn't work too well, so Boone dove under and began removing the rocks from the canoe. He surfaced and dove three times before he had them all out. He went down one more time, and got behind it and pushed while Liam pulled. Finally, they had it out from under the overhanging branches, and were able to tie a rope to it and manhandle it up onto the beach.

There, they turned it first on its side and then completely over to empty out. Without waiting to catch their breath, they pulled on their dry buckskins and boots, vigorously rubbing their arms and legs and stomping around to get warm. Once they shook off the chill, they repaired the damage done to the canoe while it was under water.

Liam and Boone shoved off early the next morning, and rode the current down to the Ohio River. They beached the canoes about a quarter mile before they reached it. Caution led them to hike to a bluff overlooking the larger river, and scour the shorelines for any sign of trouble. No one was in sight.

Their trip up the Ohio took twelve hard-paddled days, but at long last they saw Fort Duquesne in the distance. Wanting to arrive in darkness, they pulled ashore before making the last bend in the river, and rested the few hours before sunset. They beached their canoes under the watchful eyes of a group of boys who were fishing from a short pier. Liam persuaded the boys to keep an eye on their goods, over the years having learned enough French from Pierre. The boys were more than happy when Liam gave each of them a few coins, with the promise of more once the furs were sold.

The weather cooperated, and it was soon drizzling through a mist as Liam and Boone approached the gate. They were both bundled up against the chill, their fur caps pulled down over their heads and the collars of their jackets pulled up over their chins, leaving just eyes and noses in view. Two farmers were leading a wagon of hay and firewood into the fort. Liam and Boone walked over behind the wagon and started pushing, giving the gate guards the impression that they were with the farmers. Without any challenge from the guards, they entered Fort Duquesne and headed over to the tavern of Jimmy Two Birds.

****

After a year in the woods with only one other human being, the tavern was like entering an unknown world. It was smoke filled, and smelled of stale ale, some kind of meat stew bubbling in a cauldron, and the tang of unwashed humans. Liam headed over to a vacant table in the corner, gesturing to the man behind the bar for two mugs of ale. Boone sat down across from Liam, and chanced a lingering look at the barmaid who had just set down their mugs. "Is Jimmy Two Birds around?" Liam asked.

"Oui, he is upstairs with one of the girls," she answered, "perhaps one of you would like to go upstairs with me?"

"Not just now, but thanks all the same," Liam replied. While they sipped their ale, Liam scanned the room, looking for any possible hints of danger. His attention was drawn to a table where a group of French soldiers were gambling on a dice game. One of them rose, knocking over his chair and a companion's tankard, screaming, "You been fucking cheating the whole night." He reached for his knife. The soldier accused of cheating reached across the table and grabbed his friend by the wrist, twisting it so the dagger fell to the floor. "Course I've been cheating, you daft bastard. You gave me these crooked dice last night." The table erupted into raucous laughter, while the gullible soldier sat down and said, "I knew you was cheating."

As Liam relaxed his grip on the hilt of his knife, he saw Jimmy Two Birds coming down the stairs, a beautiful woman on his arm. He gave the crowd a once over, until his eyes fell upon Liam. He made his way over, and in a hushed voice said, "Go down the hall. First door on the right, I'll be there shortly." He then whispered something to the girl, and walked away to mingle with his guests. Liam and Boone waited until they finished their ale, and then went down the hall. They entered what amounted to a combination storeroom and office. One corner was filled with wine and ale casks, another, a pile of deer hides. A large oak desk littered with paper and a large skunk-hide hat sat in front of a safe, and a French flag hung on the wall. A cot, a table, and two chairs completed the furnishings. They had just sat when they heard a knock. The door opened, and the same young woman entered with a tray of food and more ale. She left without a word, but gave them a lovely smile as she turned to close the door behind her.

Jimmy walked in a few minutes later. "Sorry for the delay, my friends," he said, "but one must tread delicately in my line of work. When the French Commander comes in for a glass of wine, I must play my part, and grant him more attention possibly than he deserves. Now, what in the name of all that is holy are you doing in this fort, in my tavern? There are, I hope you realize, plenty of people who would love to get their hands on you, Liam, especially among the Shawnee."

"Two reasons, my old friend," Liam said, "business and news. My partner and I... oh, may I introduce Daniel Boone?"

Two Birds took Boone's hand in a firm grip and shook it in an excited manner. "Boone, you say? We have heard of you, young sir. Seems there are also a few in this fort who would love to get to you because of poor Lieutenant LeFurge, though I wouldn't have thought the lieutenant had that many friends, being the surly whoreson that he was. Now you were saying, business and news?"

"We spent the last year below the Ohio in the Cantuckee land, and have two canoes full of hides and furs. We figured that the best way to unload them at a reasonable price was to bring them here. This is our business. As for news: what better place to catcht up on the news than to see the man who gathers that information?"

Two Birds walked over and sat at his desk. "As to the furs, I'll have my man take a look at them tomorrow with young Boone here. I'm afraid it is too dangerous for you, Liam, to venture outside during the daylight. That tick-ridden, mangy coyote, Huritt, returned from his home village a week ago, and is stirring up the younger braves hanging around the fort. That brings me to part of the news. It seems that Huritt was up near Albany about a year ago, and staged a raid on your sister and Henry's place, but was driven off. His hatred of you and your family grows by the day. Oh, yeah, the day that Huritt attacked was the same day that Liza gave birth to a son."

"Well I'll be damned," answered Liam, "I'm an uncle." He raised his mug in a toast "To my sister and Henry; not only do they have a child, but they have it while fighting off the pride of the Shawnee. I cannot wait to hear the full telling of this tale. We had sight of Huritt in Cantuckee, but thanks to Boone, here, I refrained from taking my revenge. Too many of them to take on, even for us, and especially since their war chief, Pucksinwah, was with them. I fear him more than I fear Huritt, though Huritt still haunts my dreams."

Two Birds poured himself a goblet of wine, cleared his throat, and said, "There is more news. London and Paris have formally declared war, and the way things are shaking up, it won't be long until this fort changes hands. The French are undermanned – not only here, but all over the frontier. Troops are being sent to Quebec to protect Canada from the British, and there isn't much hope that more troops will be coming here from France. The British and their German allies are keeping the French effectively tied up in Europe. I daresay that I will be replacing that French flag with a British one soon enough."

They talked long into the night, Two Birds occasionally leaving them to make appearances among his customers, until they could no longer ignore Boone's yawning. Jimmy directed them up the back stairs, to the room set up for them. They planned for Boone to meet Jimmy's right hand man down at the canoes just after dawn. Liam arranged, through one of Two Bird's barmaids, to enlist the young boys to watch them during the night. It may have been due to sleeping in a real bed for the first time in who knows how long, or maybe just ale-enhanced fatigue – but Liam slept soundly, without his usual nightmare.

****

Liam spent most of the next day alone. He wrote a letter to Liza, and one to Daniel, and now wanted nothing more than to be away. Knowing that what he had learned from Two Birds needed to be made known, Liam decided to make his way back to Colonel Washington in Cumberland, and rejoin the scouts. Not only was this information important strategically, but it also increased the chance that he and Huritt would meet again.

Chapter 10

Fort William Henry

These were long and trying days for Colonel John Parker, militia commander of three hundred fifty reconnaissance forces.

He'd arrived at Fort William Henry two days earlier, only to endure a most unsatisfying meeting with Colonels Munro and Doherty. The first, a more vacillating man he had never met — at one moment, Munro was positive about the need for a scouting mission; a heartbeat later, he dithered because of the risk involved. Doherty, a man of greater conviction, agreed with Parker about the need, but could not convince Munro to send some militia scouts along on the mission.

Parker beckoned three lead canoes to scout ahead. The remaining force would bed down for the night. He hoped that the men he sent were smart enough to stay out of trouble. Later that night, after those sixteen scouts had divulged Parker's plans before they perished – some from torture – Ensign de Cor-biere stood with an Abenaki warrior, promising him a bloody day tomorrow. The Abenaki grunted, while tying another scalp to his war lance.

The next morning, de Cor-biere used the three canoes as decoys, so Parker thought it safe for his regiment to land. As his canoes turned in to the beach, the French troops were joined by Abenaki, Huron, and Ottawa warriors – they rose from behind the shoreline bank and opened fire. At the same time, fifty war canoes came around the bend to surround Parker and his men. The unfortunate men thrashing about near their overturned canoes became easy targets for the Indians – some of whom jumped into the water and speared the men as if they were salmon. In the end, only Parker – and less than one hundred of his regiment – returned to Fort William Henry.

****

Colonel Gordon Doherty prided himself on being a good soldier, who never questioned his orders. It was easy, at least on the surface, for him to accept Colonel Munro as his superior officer, despite the facts that Munro had no battlefield command experience, and that what he did know was grounded in old style tactics. It seemed, Doherty mused to himself, that London must be so full of just such an officer that there was no choice but to elevate them beyond their abilities. Why, he often wondered to himself, did it appear that they were unable to see the benefits of using the colonial militias? These questions vexed Doherty, but he did not complain or voice his opinion to his superiors; that was Sergeant Mulhern's role.

"I tell you, Sergeant," Doherty said as they walked away from Munro's headquarters, "I don't know what is worse –that we lost almost everyone from Parker's command, or that Munro still doesn't understand how or why an ambush like that is possible. By God's own farting arse, he cannot even make the decision to repair the walls or to dig a bloody defensive trench around the militia camp without hesitating for days, when anyone with a speck of good sense could see these things needed doing right away."

"Aye, Colonel darling, but you know I'm just a lowly sergeant and am much too busy keeping this army functioning to be lost in such deep matters of the mind. Perhaps the colonel will feel better after a wee drop of comfort," grinned Sgt. Mulhern, reaching into his tunic and pulling out a flask of brandy.

Doherty took the flask. A large swig of the amber liquid burned its course through his weary limbs. He returned the flask to Mulhern, wiped his sleeve across his mouth, and said, "Have I ever told you, Sergeant, what excellent company you have been over the years? Aye, and for sure, an excellent one for an Irishman."

"Why, thankee, Colonel, and begging the Colonel's pardon, you ain't half bad yourself for a sheep-buggering Scottish bastard," replied Mulhern, continuing a conversation started many years earlier.

Cumberland

Sitting at his desk, Washington wished – for neither the first or last time – that he were in the field, instead of mired in the bureaucracy and endless paperwork of commanding a military camp. He was tired of the flood of complaints from tavern owners, and the constant bickering between his quartermaster and just about everyone in the camp. He finished his response to a colonial governor (arguing that the governor's militia must be kitted out before they were sent on), and reached for the next piece of paper. He was pleasantly surprised to see it was a letter from Colonel Doherty. He chuckled his way through the first few paragraphs of light-hearted banter, but his chuckle quickly turned into an audible sigh, and finally a growl, as he read further. Laying the letter aside, he called for his aide. "My regards to Daniel Mallory; have him report to me as soon as he is able." He soon picked it up to reread Doherty's less-than-complimentary assessment of his commander, Colonel Munro, and his plea for a few scouts to bolster and train his troops.

Daniel entered the office to find him pacing, and muttering about the sorry state of affairs in London.

"Ah, Mr. Mallory. Come in, come in, and have a seat. Read this while I conjure up some refreshment," said Washington, handing Daniel the letter from Doherty. At the door, Washington sent his aide for wine. Resuming his seat behind his desk, he looked at Daniel. "So, what do you think? Can we afford to send anyone?"

Daniel placed the letter on the desk, rubbed the two days' stubble on his chin, and replied, "Colonel, sir, I admit that we are short – what with Liam, Henry, and even Pierre elsewhere – but I am pleased with Winslow and Winningham's results in training the new blood in the unit. In fact, they have assigned the training to a new corporal, who is very well-schooled in our methods and tactics. Timothy has even started brewing a little on the side. I think we can spare both Timothy and Marcus for a while. Besides, Colonel Doherty must really need the help. I would volunteer for this, but as you know – and have already approved – I am going on furlough in a couple days. Since I will be heading up to see Liza, Henry, and the baby, I can accompany them as far as the farm."

"Very well, Mister Mallory. Send Timothy and Markus to our friend, and please give my regards to your sister and family," Washington said as he rose to shake Daniel's hand. Just as Daniel was about to close the door behind him, Washington added, "Oh, yes, please ask Mr. Winslow for a barrel of his finest before he leaves. I find things much more bearable with a pint or two in the evening."

Norman's Creek

Thomas Joseph Clarke, now eight months old, was the darling delight of Liza and Henry. He nuzzled at Liza's breast while she sat watching the setting sun, enjoying the warmth of a June evening. Henry turned a deer haunch on the spit. He shot the deer this morning practically from his cabin door, as it grazed in their newly-planted herb garden. He glanced up when he heard the sound of a wagon coming down the road. "Woman of the house," he cried out to Liza, "I think we have company coming." He grabbed his musket and walked over to get a better view of the occupants. When the wagon rounded the final bend before the road descended to the farm, Henry saw Daniel on horseback riding alongside the wagon. "Daniel, Timothy, Markus, well, if this ain't a pleasant surprise," exclaimed Henry as they entered the clearing surrounding the farm house, "come down off your perches. Glory be! I couldn't be more surprised if King George came a'callin'."

Daniel held his nephew through most of their meal, and later around the campfire as they talked —relinquishing the baby only when he needed to be changed or fed. Timothy had unloaded two casks of ale. "One for tonight, and one for whenever the need may arise," he declared while topping off his mug. Most of the conversation centered on the frontier, and what the future held in store as France and Britain readied themselves for the next stage of the war. Henry wasn't too concerned about his place. There had been no further sightings of hostile raiders in the area, but Wahta maintained a close watch nevertheless. As the evening progressed, and they emptied the cask, their talk turned to Liam. Daniel had not heard from him since he left with Boone, but Liza had just recently received a letter from him delivered by a trapper friend of Jimmy Two Birds on his way to Albany. Liza retrieved the letter from the cabin to read to the others:

Dear Liza and Henry,

I don't have much time before Two Birds needs this, as his associate is ready to leave for Albany. Boone and me spent almost a year in the Cantuckee land, and brought back many fine hides and furs. We sold them to Two Birds for a good profit. You would not believe the beauty and the bounty in Cantuckee. No one lives on this land, as the Shawnee and Cherokee aim to keep it as their private hunting ground. Sooner or later, there will be settlements there; the land is just too good for it not to be settled.

In other news, I learnt from Two Birds about war being declared and all, not that that surprised me. Control of the frontier and the unknown treasures down the Ohio are too important to leave to the French. I also heard from him about Huritt, and his raid on your place, and that I'm an uncle. I will be glad to rid us of Huritt, as it seems fated that we will meet again, and I will be glad to make the acquaintance of my nephew or niece. Look for me in the summer.

Liam

****

The next morning Timothy and Markus left for Fort William Henry, the parting words of Daniel still fresh on their minds. "Boys, you do what you have to do, and get the job done. Just don't take too many chances. If Colonel Doherty has doubts about the commanding officer, then you can be sure there is good reasoning behind those doubts. We all know how it is to be part of a battle gone badly, and I have the feeling that you two are heading into another one. If things go like the fight on the Monongahela, get yourselves out and make it back to Cumberland. You boys are too good to waste on another fiasco."

Daniel planned to spend his ten remaining days of leave with Liza, Henry, and his new best friend, his nephew Thomas. He hoped that Liam might appear while he was still there. The three of them decided that they would not yet mention the future of the trading post with Liam. On the eighth morning, Daniel sat on the creek bank, pole fishing. Thomas slept on a blanket next to him, cooing in his sleep and occasionally finding his thumb with his mouth. Daniel was so entranced by the sight and sound of his nephew that he didn't notice Liam standing on the other side of the creek. "Ho, there, brother," Liam called out, "is this the way you protect our niece or nephew, letting someone sneak up on you?"

"Oh, I reckon I would have noticed you by the time you stepped into the creek," replied Daniel, a huge grin on his face, "and it's a nephew. Come across and meet him, but don't you drip creek water all over him."

Liza was working in the garden when she saw Daniel emerge from the woods that bordered the creek. She was confused – he wasn't carrying Thomas, but rather had an extra musket, a bow, a quiver of arrows, and someone's pack. "Saints above, Daniel, where is my baby?" was all she could shout before she saw Liam carrying Thomas, talking to him as they approached the cabin. Dropping everything, she dashed out of the garden, ran to Liam, and threw her arms around his neck, careful not to disturb his hold on Thomas. "Oh, Liam, it is so good to see you," she cried, as she led him into the cabin yelling out to her husband, "Oh, Handsome Henry, Liam is here. Best be putting another haunch of that venison on the spit, and open up that cask of Timothy's ale."

The rest of the day and long into that night, Liam talked about his sojourn in Cantuckee, and his partnership with Daniel Boone, while he took turns with Daniel holding Thomas. "I suppose it's a good thing that you guys aren't staying here for a long time, otherwise my poor son would be spoiled beyond all good sense," said Henry as he took a long pull on his tankard.

Liam just smiled at Daniel, who wrinkled his nose at the smell now coming from Thomas and handed the baby to Henry. "Well, at least I have the good sense to hand over the child when his care is beyond my ability. Now, as to my stay here; I'm sorry to have to keep it short, but I must head up to Donehogawa's village to exchange news, and to see my other family. It might be a good idea if you came with me, Daniel, so you can report to Colonel Washington what he can expect from the Mohawk when the time comes. I reckon that I will go with you to Cumberland, but in an unofficial capacity only. I have a feeling that my participation in the future of this war will be one in which I may not want to be beholden to a set of orders."

Fort William Henry

Timothy and Markus settled in well with the group of scouts and skirmishers they were charged to train. Colonel Doherty hoped that they could get them ready, but feared that there wasn't enough time. If rumors were to be trusted, the French had amassed a sizeable force to throw at William Henry, not just in men but in cannon as well.

Sergeant Mulhern would ordinarily be in the militia camp, drilling the infantry portion of the militia, but today was out on a training mission with the scouts. He was keen to know how they operated, not with an eye or ambition to become a scout, but to understand the tactics so, as he put it, "my bunch of colonial bog trotters know not to shoot in their direction."

They headed east from camp, intending to skirt the southern edge of Lake George and head north for a few miles, while taking the time to point out anything that could be useful in locating the enemy. The scouts stood on a bluff overlooking the shore, when one of the men spotted a canoe being beached about 200 yards from their position. Out of the canoe stepped an Abenaki warrior, who hid the canoe and began heading down the beach toward the fort. Markus unshouldered his musket, one of the new ones with a rifled barrel and said, "No time like the present to see how far I can shoot this thing." He won the new model in a shooting contest back in camp; while he had yet to take a shot at a live target, he was impressed at how much farther away he could still hit a target. He took aim, adjusted for the slight cross breeze, and squeezed the trigger. The Abenaki saw movement and then a puff of smoke from the bluff above. He dove for cover, but the lead shot slammed into his torso, passing through his liver.

"Whoohee," screamed Timothy, "what a shot."

Markus shook his head, and replied, "A goodly distance to be sure, but I never try to gut shoot an enemy. I am sorry for the poor bastard; he'll be suffering for a while afore he dies."

****

As the weeks went by, the scouts noticed more and more signs of enemy activity; scouting parties of Ottawa, Abenaki, and Huron kept themselves hidden in the area. Finally, Doherty's persistent urging led Colonel Munro to send scouts to General Webb at Fort Edward, asking for immediate reinforcements. Of the three dispatched riders, two were caught and killed, their message forwarded onto the French commander at Fort Carillon. The third one managed to get through to Fort Edward, but the return reply was intercepted − that, too, fell into the hands of the French. General Webb, reacting to a report that he was about to be attacked by a large force of French and Indians, had declined the request for more men, feeling that he needed all the men he had to defend his own position.

Emboldened by this information, Major-General Louis Joseph de Montcalm-Gozon, Marquis de Montcalm (the French commander), understood that this was the time to attack Fort William Henry. According to his scouts, the fort walls were still in need of repairs. Knowing that there would be no reinforcements, he gave the order to proceed. He split his force, sending a combined two thousand Canadian militia and Ottawa to the south of the fort, sealing it off just in case Webb changed his mind. The six thousand remaining French regulars, Canadian militia, and Indian allies set off in 250 bateaux, some of which were lashed together to float the cannons. They met no opposition, and landed safely on the west shore of Lake George.

The combined forces began preparations for a siege. Montcalm surveyed the arrayed cannon and howitzers, nodded his approval, and remarked, "It is time to see if we let loose these beasts of war, or if Colonel Munro has a moment of clarity as to his chances of surviving their ravenous appetite for blood and death."

Colonel Munro, with only an aide and an honor guard of four, rode through the gate to parley with Major-General Montcalm, secure in the knowledge that he could withstand the French attack long enough for Webb to send help. Montcalm, on the other hand, did not intend to enlighten Munro with the truth of the matter, at least not yet. "Colonel Munro," began Montcalm after the preliminary pleasantries had been observed, "surely you must see the hopelessness of your situation. I sincerely hope to end this affair here and now, without the needless shedding of blood."

"Major-General Montcalm," replied Munro, his demeanor one of supreme confidence, "I would not be doing my duty to God and King if I surrender at this juncture, most especially since I have every confidence that we will withstand your siege and prevail."

"I urge you to reconsider, Colonel; once I give the order to fire my cannon, the terms of surrender will of necessity change. Plus, you must understand that while I will do all that I can possibly do, I cannot guarantee anyone's safety from those of my allies seeking war trophies or captives."

"We are resolved to hold this fort as ordered, and that is what we will do, but I thank you for your courtesy," answered Munro. There being nothing else to discuss, both parties returned to their respective armies. Montcalm gave the order to open fire as soon as Munro entered the fort.

Colonel Doherty watched the second day of exchanged artillery fire from his post in the militia encampment. The cannon and howitzers of Munro's force were giving back as much as they were taking from the French – but it was just a matter of time, he thought, before the walls were breeched, and the real slaughter began. Realizing that something had to turn the tide, he headed to the fort for yet another confrontation with Colonel Munro.

He entered headquarters to find Munro hunched over casualty reports. Before he could speak, a tremendous explosion rocked the building, knocking candles out of their sconces and shaking the windows. "That was not an enemy shell," exclaimed Doherty as he extinguished a burning candle that had fallen to the floor, "sounded more like an exploded cannon." He ran to the door and saw that one of their twelve pounders had indeed exploded while firing, killing three soldiers and wounding four others. "That's the fourth one plus one howitzer. We're killing our own more efficiently than the French are," he said, as he sat opposite Colonel Munro.

"Sir, this fort is going to fall, and sooner rather than later. The walls cannot take much more pounding, and our counter artillery is rapidly falling apart. We need to do something to save the men from being mercilessly slaughtered. The French can talk all they want about keeping their allies in check, but they won't have the will to do it."

"What do you propose, my dear Colonel Doherty," replied Munro, "that we attack the French?"

"Yes, but not the force besieging the fort, and not conventionally," said Doherty, his excitement mounting with every breath as he laid out his plan. "We attack the force guarding the road to Fort Edward. That is our objective, getting as many of these troops to General Webb as we can, rather than waiting on the General to send troops to us; troops that would have to fight their way in and for what, saving a doomed fort? We send in the militia just before dawn, catching them by surprise, and as the sun comes up, you lead the regulars in, and from the road deliver a few massed volleys. That should do the trick, and will buy us enough time to march the twenty miles to Fort Edward."

"An interesting thought, Colonel, but I have no intention on leading a doomed-to-fail attack. Your idea of having the irregulars execute a raid in semi-darkness is not only foolish, but is not the way I will prosecute this war. We are outnumbered. We will wait for the reinforcements that I'm sure will be here in two or three days. If they do not, I have full confidence in the French commander and his honorable word."

"We may not have two or three days, Colonel. We need to..."

"That is enough, Colonel Doherty. I will hear no more about it. You are dismissed."

Colonel Gordon Doherty prided himself on being a good soldier. It was only that pride that stayed his voice, and allowed him to give a rather slipshod salute just before he slammed the door. He was heading to his own tent when he heard an incoming bombardment thud into the wall. Up until now in their siege, the French ceased their artillery firing once the sun went down. "Not so tonight, it seems," Doherty thought, "the end is near." When he reached his tent, he sent his orderly to find Sergeant Mulhern, Timothy and Markus. He sat down at his camp desk, and began writing out their orders.

As they entered, he motioned them to sit. He looked at each of them intently before he read their new orders aloud. "The three of you are hereby ordered to vacate this camp in the event of surrender, and report at best possible speed to General Webb at Fort Edward. You are too valuable to be captured or killed. This order will nullify any chance of desertion or cowardice charges ever being discussed. That takes care of the legality of your disappearance; I would ask one more thing. If I am taken captive and appear certain to be tortured or burned, do what you can to end it."

Timothy and Markus shook Doherty's hand. "I really didn't want to give up my new musket anyway," said Markus. "Been getting pretty good with it too," he continued, looking the colonel in the eyes, "I can hit what I aim at."

Sergeant Glyn Mulhern reached inside his shirt and pulled out his flask. "A wee bit of comfort and fortifying, Colonel, darling." He handed the brandy to Doherty, who raised it and toasted: "To all the campaigns we fought, to all the glory we sought, to all the regiments we led, to all the privations we endured, to the friendship we forged. To you, my Irish bog trotting friend." After taking a drink, he handed it back to Mulhern, who could only manage to reply through his tears, "Colonel, darling." He took a drink, saluted, and followed Timothy and Markus back to camp.

The artillery barrage the following morning continued relentlessly for three hours, twenty pieces in a constant bombardment of the walls. After a tremendous double salvo, the firing ceased, and a French officer headed across the open meadow under a white flag. He was met by a company of grenadiers, blindfolded, and led to Colonel Munro. He handed the colonel two letters, one from Montcalm detailing surrender terms, and the other the message from General Webb stating he would not send reinforcements.

"Thank the Major-General for his generosity and concern. He will have our answer shortly," responded a noticeably shaken Munro.

The French aide returned to Montcalm and relayed Munro's answer, and then asked, "What about our allies? They are not going to like losing trophies and the like. You know that that damnable Shawnee Huritt will be stirring up trouble."

Montcalm paced back and forth. "I will speak with the chiefs in the morning, but not with Huritt. The other chiefs will have to keep him and the other hotheads in check. Once the British surrender, we will supply the normal honor guard; make sure they know that they are to keep the British safe as they leave the fort."

Huritt stormed into the Shawnee encampment, eyes spitting fire, hands clenched tightly on his war lance. He had been to the French camp, and heard the rumor that the British were going to surrender, and that they would have safe passage out of the fort. The chances for scalps, captives, and other prizes of war – not to mention the basic thrill of battle – were all to be taken away by these craven French. Huritt knew Montcalm would approach the chiefs and tell them to not make trouble, but he would not listen to the French or the chiefs. He would make his own plans; gather those of a like mind from across the tribes assembled, and then dare the French to stop him.

The next morning, Colonel Munro addressed his officers. "Gentlemen, we are faced with a hopeless situation. Our munitions and supplies are dangerously low, our morale is low, and we can expect no help from General Webb, an act of deplorable negligence on his part. Major-General Montcalm has offered us full honors; officers may keep their side arms, and we and our baggage will be safe. All other weapons will be stacked up in the fort. I will not wait any longer. I will walk out and surrender the fort. Colonel Doherty will accompany me."

An hour later, the sun just now cresting the hills to the east, Colonel Munro and Colonel Doherty, with an honor guard bearing a white flag, trotted out of the gate. Major-General Montcalm, expecting such a move, had already mounted when word came that the British were riding out. The two parties met in the meadow just west of the fort. As Doherty scanned the group of French cavalry attending the Major-General, his eyes were drawn to a lone Shawnee brave standing on a hilltop. "That bloody chap does not have the look of acquiescence about him," Doherty muttered under his breath. His attention returned in part to Colonel Munro, who was officially surrendering the fort, but he couldn't escape the look of that Shawnee. "I see my death in his expression," he whispered to himself.

"What was that?" asked Colonel Munro.

"It is nothing, sir, just a moment of private reflection." Montcalm saluted Munro, and headed back to his camp. Colonel Doherty finally turned away from Huritt's stare, and rode back to the fort, his gaze now falling upon the three men on horseback leaving the militia encampment.

Munro's troops spent the rest of the day stacking arms under the supervision of a troop of French Marines, and moving the troops from the fort to the larger militia camp. Timothy, Markus, and Sergeant Mulhern camped in a small valley, between the hills to the east of the camp. They agreed to take turns watching the militia camp. Markus had the first watch, but had seen nothing noteworthy; his ears perked up as he heard Timothy climbing the hill to relieve him. "Nothing's going on down there. I 'spect it'll be quiet until morning," Markus told Timothy as he headed to a well needed sleep. Timothy found it hard to stay awake through the long and quiet night; he was startled when Sergeant Mulhern tapped him on the shoulder.

"I'd kick you six shades of shite if you was regular army, napping on guard duty," chuckled Mulhern. "I presume all is quiet? Oh, well, now what have we here?" Mulhern pointed down to the foothills below them, where a large force of Shawnee, Ottawa, Huron, and Ojibway warriors were spreading out on either side of the road out of the camp, keeping to the depressions between the hills so to avoid detection. "Go and help Markus saddle our horses. I have a feeling down the back of my neck that we will need to follow the colonel very shortly."

Colonel Munro led the contingent of regulars out of the gate, followed by Colonel Doherty and the militia. The baggage and civilians made up the rear as they marched out to the fanfare of drums and military band of the French. They had barely cleared the gate when they heard the cries of Indians, who began killing the wounded that had been under French care in the fort. The already somber mood of the British became noticeably tenser, their eyes darting back and forth expecting to see a horde of bloodthirsty savages descending upon them.

On horseback, Colonel Doherty saw them first. The militia had travelled about 500 yards when they heard a loud war whoop. The hillside was suddenly alive with tomahawk-brandishing warriors. Some of them headed to the baggage train to loot it, finding among the valuables a sizable quantity of rum. Others went straight into the British ranks, indiscriminately killing and scalping, or grabbing men out of the line as captives. Soon, the 2500 unarmed men and women panicked, and began running, some trampling on the bodies of the fallen and the dead. The sight of brain matter, the coppery smell of blood, and the loosened bowels caused many to stop and bend over, retching. The French were quick to react, but were ineffective in quelling the slaughter. They did manage to put a protective cordon around Colonel Munro, but were too late to help Colonel Doherty. Doherty had pulled out his saber, using it to club and slash at the hands trying to pull him from his mount. He had just succeeded in repelling an Ojibway, by cutting off two of his fingers, when he locked eyes on Huritt as he leapt onto the back of the horse while bringing the pipe end of his tomahawk down on Doherty's skull, knocking him unconscious. Huritt grabbed him to keep him from falling, and took the reins. With a victory scream, he galloped away with his prize, heading north to a Shawnee village on the east shore of Lake George.

Colonel Doherty awoke to a sharp pain in his head, finding that he sat lashed to a tree trunk. His feet and hands were bound together. He grimaced through the pain, and tried to focus on his surroundings, but his eyes were blurry from the blow to his head. Soon Huritt came to him, set down a bowl of food, and untied his hands. "Eat, Colonel. You will need your strength to run a gauntlet in the morning." While eating, he reached his hand up to his head, and felt the stickiness of caked blood and an indentation in his skull. The touch had him almost screaming, but he had made up his mind that he was not going to give Huritt the satisfaction of hearing him suffer; he would go to his death silently. When he had finished the food, Huritt came over to re-tie his hands. Huritt said nothing while he stared into Doherty's eyes, thinking to intimidate Doherty. Doherty stared back, and was about to look away when the sound of a curlew reached his ears.

Timothy, Markus, and the sergeant had taken a position in the hills east of the lake, where they had a good view of the Shawnee camp and Colonel Doherty. The possibility of rescue, after much debate and with much sadness, was deemed impossible. The Shawnee camp grew larger as the night wore on, as more and more warriors came into the camp with their captives or with their many scalps. The constant activity – and the fact that the captives, including Doherty, were held in the middle of the camp – made any rescue attempt a suicide mission.

Sergeant Mulhern had learned to imitate the songs and cries of the birds of his homeland when he was a boy. Through his years with Colonel Doherty, they had always used the curlew as a means of communicating in the field. When Doherty heard Mulhern's bird call, his resolve strengthened. With a grin, he said to Huritt, "You think to gather my warrior spirit and courage by killing me; God's bollocks you will. You will get nothing from me but this advice; you are doomed, Snake Slayer will avenge his family and me. If I were you, I'd head west of the Father of Rivers, and perhaps sleep with your eyes open. He will find you, and you will die." Huritt snarled and rose, his slap to the back of Doherty's head causing him to spasm with fresh waves of pain. Still, he did not scream – but he did vomit most of his just-eaten dinner on Huritt's feet and lower legs.

The Shawnee camp, a temporary one used only during the siege and battle for Fort William Henry, did not contain many women or the older members of the tribe. This meant that both sides of the gauntlet was manned by young men and warriors, each holding some sort of club or a cluster of thorn-covered boughs.

Huritt led Colonel Doherty to the beginning of the line, and said, "Now we see if you live or die." He gave him a shove in the back to start him running.

Timothy watched as the colonel, stumbling in a slow jog, was met with a hail of blows to his back, buttocks, and legs. "Come on, Colonel. Make it to the end, and you might live through this," he exhorted.

"I don't reckon them Shawnee are gonna let him finish," replied Markus. "Do you see the size of the bastard at the end of the line? If the colonel makes it that far without falling or losing consciousness, that beast will stop him."

Doherty moved as quickly as he could, but did not avoid some of the more vicious hits. He was soon able to walk only slowly, almost shuffling his feet as he progressed down the line. His mind was now numb, as fresh bouts of pain took their toll. He was about three-quarters through the gauntlet, and only with great effort did he move one foot in front of the other. A glancing blow to his head sent him reeling, but he caught himself before he hit the ground. A young Shawnee boy then lashed at him with a thorn-laden branch, scraping it down his back and creating several rivulets of blood that streamed down his back and legs as he struggled to right himself. Somehow, the blow of the thorns digging into his back and sides triggered him into action. With a roar, he grabbed the boy and using him as a shield moved closer to the end, finally throwing him into the body of one of the last warriors in line. He glanced up at the only one left. With a cry of rage and his instinct for survival, he launched himself at the large warrior. Huritt, who was now standing behind the muscular brave, watched with an amused look on his face as the warrior raised one of his ham sized fists and brought it down on the back of Doherty's head right where the tomahawk had done its initial damage. The colonel went down, unconscious before he hit the ground.

When Colonel Doherty awoke, he found himself tethered to a pole by a noose around his neck. His hands were tied, but his legs were free from restraint, allowing him to move in a circle around the pole. He pushed back the throbbing pain in his head, and willed himself to focus his sight on his surroundings. A pile of brush and firewood was stacked around the pole, while a five foot radius had been cleared so that the condemned could shuffle about in a vain attempt to avoid the heat and flames. He looked out at the gathering warriors, and saw the many empty rum barrels scattered throughout the camp. He vaguely remembered hearing, while he was coming to consciousness, the whoops of drunken men and the beating of drums, but now it was eerily quiet as they all waited for Huritt to light the fire. To compose himself before his fiery death, Doherty thought back to his last conversation with Sergeant Mulhern, and fervently prayed that his friends were nearby. He looked up to the hills, and realized that the morning was without even a breath of wind. He managed a small smile. His smile grew when he heard the curlew's distinctive trilling.

Markus had used the pre-dawn darkness to creep down the hillside until he found a covered position behind some boulders. He estimated that he was about 225 yards from the execution site, and was pleased to note the absence of any wind. Timothy and Sergeant Mulhern remained at the top of the hill, their muskets loaded and horses saddled.

Growing impatient at the wait, one of the more inebriated Shawnee grabbed the unlit end of a smoldering piece of firewood from the camp fire and entered the ring, intending to inflict more pain on the prisoner. Doherty backed up as far as he could, until his back was against the pole and waited for his tormentor to get close. Reaching for a reserve of strength he was not sure that he had, he leaped up and delivered a two footed kick to the Shawnee. His kick caught him in the groin and sent him sprawling into the brush and logs, where he lay moaning in pain while his fellow warriors laughed. Huritt picked him up and shoved him out of the way, and lit the bonfire.

Huritt stood back from the growing conflagration as the brush ignited all around the condemned colonel. He looked for the fear, listened for the begging screams, but Colonel Doherty just stared at him, his face emotionless. When the heat grew too fierce, Huritt backed away, and joined his warriors who were screaming their approval and their hate. Doherty felt the hair on his legs begin to curl and singe; his feet began to throw off smoke as he retreated as far as he could. Then some of the Shawnee with long poles began pushing the burning wood closer to the cut-ta-ho-tha – the condemned one. No longer able to hold out, Doherty screamed out, "For God and Saint Andrew, for King and Britain. MULHERN!"

Markus knew it was time when he heard the Colonel cry out. He raised the musket, quickly prayed for accuracy, and squeezed the trigger.

Huritt was beginning to feel good about the proceedings, and had even allowed himself a long drink from a rum cask. His eyes, however, never veered away from his victim. Just when it appeared that the flames would engulf the pole and the man tied to it, Huritt watched the colonel's head recoil as if from a blow, while it erupted in a fresh spray of blood, skin, and hair. He threw down the rum, and looked back to the hillside just as a white man scrambled up from the boulders. Cheated of the victorious death of his enemy, and realizing that he would not be able to catch the shooter, Huritt bellowed with rage – too many empty rum barrels meant too many warriors unable to take up the chase.

Sergeant Glyn Mulhern saw Markus raise the musket to his shoulder, heard the shot, and watched his friend die – cheating the Shawnee of some of their barbaric notions of glory, honor, courage, and strength. "Farewell, Colonel, darling, you sheep shagging Scottish bastard. The Good Lord and Saint Andrew will take care of you now." He nodded to Markus as he joined him and Timothy, and handed him the reins to his horse. With unabashed tears and without looking back, the three rode away.

Chapter 11

The Forbes Expedition
Mohawk Village

Liam shook the water from his hair as he rose from the river. The sun was just beginning its climb in the Eastern sky; with its ascent, the woods came alive with the songs and cries of warblers, thrushes, and crows. Late August meant that the mornings were chillier. Soon, the women would harvest the squash and corn, and the men would begin to repair holes in walls and roofs in the village longhouses. Liam put on his linen shirt and buckskin trousers, and walked back to the shelter he shared with Daniel. Not for the first time, he thought about how much he liked the life here, and how much he missed Orenda.

It had been a busy few weeks for the village. Timothy, Sergeant Mulhern, and Markus arrived after reporting in at Fort Edward. They decided to stay until after the forthcoming council between the Mohawk and the British Agent for Indian Affairs, Colonel William Johnson. With all of the British losses to the French, the London command deemed it necessary for Johnson to do what he could to maintain the alliance with the Iroquois Confederacy, an alliance that now hung by a thread – and threatened to unravel.

Johnson, a great friend to the Iroquois – adopted by the Mohawk and given the name Warraghiyagey, he who takes on great things – often joined the tribes for festivals and dances. He was instrumental in gathering warriors to help the British. Now, however, the mood of the Iroquois had changed. Too many warriors lost; the refusal of the British commanders to let them make war in their own way; and the dawning realization that the whites would continue to expand their settlements, and drive out the tribes –these obstacles, would prove to be too much for Johnson to overcome, even with his considerable oratorical skills.

Late in the evening of the third and final day of the council, Liam joined Daniel and the others to discuss their plans. Markus, Sergeant Mulhern, Timothy, and Daniel were under orders to report to Fort Cumberland, but Liam remained unsure whether to follow them. While he was obviously interested in seeing the French driven out, he was more inclined to want to take the fight to one tribe, and in particular to one individual, Huritt of the Shawnee. His nightmares, which had subsided during his stay with Liza and Henry, returned with the news of Huritt's responsibility for the death of Colonel Doherty.

Donehogawa's influence allowed Liam to attend the council, but only as a guest. His presence was valuable; although he had no voice in the debate, he could pass firsthand knowledge of the council decisions. "The Iroquois will no longer supply the numbers of warriors to the British that they had in the past," he reported, as he sat down and stirred the embers of the campfire. "Colonel Johnson was only able to get the promise of a few hundred."

"Aye, that is a blow," replied Sergeant Mulhern, "saints preserve us if we are commanded by them that's not fit to hold a candle."

Daniel nodded his head, and added, "Aye, if they let the irregulars play a part, but we all know how the British command operates and looks down on us. My question is, what are you going to do, Liam?"

"I could tell the way the debate was going after the first day," Liam said, "so I've talked with Donehogawa and Wahta. They agreed that I should pursue Huritt, and Wahta and Deganawidah have volunteered to join me. We will start at the camp the Shawnee had on Lake George, and pick up the trail from there. My guess is that we will find that he has gone west again, though whether that means Fort Duquesne, Fort Frontenac, or if he has headed to the Ohio country, I do not know."

"We should be away at dawn," answered Mulhern, "Colonel Washington will be a wanting this information post-haste." Mulhern reached over and took Liam by the shoulders and with a rueful chuckle said; "Now lad I am sorry you will not be coming with us, but I understand. Don't be a fretting about Huritt; we'll probably meet him again. That Shawnee bastard seems to be everywhere we go. I'll try to restrain myself from sending him to Hell. I will leave that to you, Liam."

"If I might make a suggestion," said Liam, "the Fords live near Pharaoh Lake; they will have information about Fort Carillon; might come in handy later on."

Pharaoh Lake

Deborah Prescott, the daughter of Quaker parents, understood their belief in the goodness of humanity, and indeed shared this ideal as a child. They had hosted many Indians over the years on their farm twenty miles north of Albany, and were considered friends to most. But, the trust that they developed with Indians led to mistrust by other settlers. Frightened by the recent increase in Indians who marauded and murdered, some settlers began to find fault with those who befriended those 'demons of the woods'.

Taking out their rage and frustration, many white settlers used the Quakers as scapegoat examples and the result of this faulty logic was Deborah's parents being killed by a drunken group of Delaware, emboldened by the liquor given to them by the settlers. She had been away at the time of the attack, visiting Mary and Oliver Ford. She could not bear to live at home after the raid, and returned to the Fords, their farm tucked safely into a small valley between Pharaoh Lake and Wolf Pond. She was scattering feed for the chickens, when she heard the sound of horses coming down the track to the farm. As the death of her parents had diminished her faith in the goodness of humanity Deborah grabbed her nearby musket and awaited the visitors.

They rode in a single file. Daniel, in the lead, spied a young woman pointing a musket at him. He abruptly reined in, causing his horse to rear slightly as he brought her under control. Holding his hands out in a gesture of peace, he climbed down. "Good day to you, my good woman," Daniel said, "is this the Ford place?"

Deborah was a fairly good judge of character; seeing that these men were not a threat, she lowered her musket, and replied, "Yes, it is, though they are not here at present. I'm not really sure when they will be back. They're down to Albany, doing some trading."

"Ahh, I see," said Daniel. "We're on our way to rejoin our scout unit at Fort Cumberland, and were hoping to get some information on doings at Carillon." He reached into his saddle bag, produced the letter of introduction that Colonel Washington had given him, and handed it to her.

"I don't know how much help I can be along those lines," she said, as she read the letter, removing her wide brimmed hat and shaking out her raven black hair, "but the very least I can do is offer you gentlemen a meal and a place to bed down tonight."

"That would suit our needs," replied Daniel, who suddenly realized that she was beautiful. "I am Daniel Mallory, and my companions are Timothy Winslow, Markus Winningham, and Sergeant Glynnie Mulhern of His Majesty's 48th regiment."

"Pleased to make your acquaintance, gentlemen," she said with a slight curtsey, "I believe there is enough fodder for your horses over in the barn."

While Timothy and Markus cared for the horses, Daniel and Sergeant Mulhern lent a hand preparing the meal, hauling water and cutting venison up for the stew pot. Deborah entered the kitchen, carrying fresh carrots, onion, garlic, and basil from the garden to add to the stew. Daniel found that he could not take his eyes away from her as she chopped the vegetables, even to the point where he nicked his thumb with the knife he was using on the venison. "Mr. Mallory," Deborah implored with a grin on her face, "I think we have enough meat for the stew from the deer, you need not add your own flesh and blood to it."

Sergeant Mulhern burst out laughing at Daniel's embarrassed look. "You'll have to excuse the lad. You see, lass, he hasn't seen a pretty face in a long time, and for sure you are a beauty."

"I'm sorry you missed the Fords, but I can tell you what they talked about before they left," said Deborah as she watched the four hungry men devour her stew. "They have noticed increased activity around Fort Carillon; patrols are more frequent, and there are more Indians coming and going."

Daniel looked up from his meal and asked, "Did they mention any specific tribes?"

Deborah thought for a moment. "The usual local tribes, Huron, Lenape, and the like. They did seem a little concerned at the arrival of some western tribes as well. I think they said there were Ojibway and Ottawa warriors camped outside the fort."

Mulhern held his hand over his mouth as he tried to stifle a belch, "Ahh, excuse the poor manners, lass. Did the Fords mention anything about any Shawnee in the area? Ya see, we have a special place in our hearts for those bloody savages. Again, pardon my vulgar ways. Seems I'm more fit for the company of men than with a pretty lass like yourself. Ain't that right, Daniel me boy?"

"Huh? Umm... ahh... well, yes, she is." Daniel mumbled, embarrassed, his cheeks blushing red.

The next morning, after a breakfast of coffee, bacon, and freshly baked biscuits, the men saddled up and made ready to leave for Fort Cumberland. Deborah had risen before dawn in order to bake the biscuits. She came out of the cabin, carrying a hide pouch filled with more biscuits. She approached Daniel, and handed him the pouch. He started to tie the pouch to his saddle, but fumbled with the drawstring and almost dropped it. "Oh, Mr. Mallory," said a smiling Deborah, "I certainly hope you handle your musket better than this pouch, or your knife."

Daniel, once more blushing red, stammered out a reply, "We thank you, ma'am, for your hospitality, and for the extra biscuits."

Deborah helped him attach the pouch. Speaking so that only he could hear, she said, "You take care, I look forward to seeing you again." She reached up, touched his arm, and smiled.

He quietly replied, "I will." Looking back to his grinning friends, Daniel said, "Well, let's get going. It's a good two week ride to Cumberland." They rode through the gate and onto the track leading south. Daniel took a last glance back, and saw Deborah, who stood at the gate watching them depart. After her recent experiences with the settlers, she felt somehow comforted by the presence of these men, especially Daniel Mallory. As for Daniel, he could not remember having such intense feelings of want and desire about a woman. He decided that in order for him to be at his best, he needed to ignore them, if possible.

Carlisle

Brigadier General John Forbes studied the rather incomplete map, and sighed. He had received command of the next attempt to take Fort Duquesne. From his headquarters in the town of Carlisle, he had issued the orders for a new road to be constructed – further north than the one Braddock had used. This caused much debate and consternation among the officers who had been with Braddock, but Forbes would not change his mind.

Colonel Washington had arrived with the troops from Cumberland; since he was a Virginian, he was more interested in the southern route. There was a growing dispute between the colonies of Pennsylvania and Virginia over control of that frontier, and the Braddock Road gave easier access to the frontier from Virginia. However, no amount of talk would change Forbes' mind, and the construction continued.

"I am sure you gentlemen will appreciate the new route," said Forbes to his officer corps, "especially the fact that there are fewer rivers and creeks to cross than on the Braddock route. Another departure from Braddock's plan is that we will not move out until that road is just about complete. I will not struggle along at the pace of three or four miles a day.

"Now, to the next order of business. We will start moving troops and material to Fort Littleton, our new base of operations. Colonel Washington will be in command of the first move, and take half of the troops. You will depart here at dawn tomorrow. I know we won't be staying there long, but that fort was originally built to protect fleeing settlers from Indian raids. It is not designed to hold 7000 men, so you will need to clear some land for our encampment. Major Grant, you will take command of the remaining troops, and will be responsible for getting our supplies, artillery, and the like ready to go. That is all for now, gentlemen; unless there are questions, you are dismissed."

Washington swallowed the last of his ale, belched, and rose to leave the officer's mess. Daniel walked in, stretched out his aching back and shoulders, and noticed his commander. "Colonel Washington, I see that you're leaving, but if you have no pressing business, could you stay while I refresh myself? It has been a long stretch in the saddle, but I'm anxious to learn what's new here, as well as to pass on news from the Mohawk."

Washington sat down, and drank another pint while they exchanged news. "You know what the road Forbes is making runs through?" queried Daniel. "It is right in the middle of hostile Delaware camps." He drained the last of his ale, and chuckled, "I think I would prefer having more rivers to cross."

They left the mess hall, and headed to see Sergeant Mulhern. Washington wanted desperately to have him posted to his command. Given the confrontational possibilities lying ahead in the next few weeks, he wanted to have the best men he could get. "Ah, my good sergeant; first let me say how sorry I am about Colonel Doherty. He was a fine man and an excellent officer, and I shall miss him."

Mulhern saluted, and then shook Washington's hand. He replied, "Thank you, Colonel. He was indeed those things, and though his death was too early, he died brave like a true Scotsman. Now, I am having a feeling down the back of my neck that you want me on your staff. If that be true, Colonel, darling, then I graciously accepts."

"Thank you, Sergeant. Now, get rested up, we're heading to Fort Littleton at dawn tomorrow." He reached into his vest pocket, pulled out some coins, and handed them to Mulhern. "Here, take Mr. Winslow and Mr. Winningham for a couple pints. I know it won't be up to Winslow standards, but it will still refresh."

Shawnee camp north east of Duquesne

Liam, Wahta, and Deganawidah tracked the movement of Huritt and his warriors, following his trail with little trouble, but were not able to come into contact with them, due to Huritt's head start. Finally, today, they spotted his camp nestled along a small creek in an Allegheny Mountain valley, northeast of Fort Duquesne. The camp was fairly large, as there were contingents of Ojibway and Ottawa, along with Huritt and his Shawnee. "Definitely too many for us to take on," said Liam, looking down at the camp. He vented his frustration by snapping a tree branch over his knee.

"Snake Slayer, my brother, we need only wait," answered Wahta, pointing to movement in the camp below. "Huritt is most likely headed to the Duquesne fort, but the others are not. They will be heading to their homes in the land of the big lakes, after selling their captives to the French at Detroit."

"You are right, my brother," answered Liam, "let's go back farther in the trees to make camp."

Liam had trouble sleeping that night. He imagined the coming showdown with Huritt, and could not eliminate the images. A couple of hours before dawn, he finally rose and walked to the creek at the bottom of the hill. Bending down to scoop a handful of water, he saw the stars reflected in the ripples he'd made. He sat with his back up against the trunk of a pine, and stared up in the sky. Gradually, his mind emptied of the images keeping him awake. He dozed off, his head bowed over his chest.

Suddenly, a snort across the creek startled him, not enough to awaken him but enough so that the vision seemed real. It was dawn, a gray, eerie dawn. A swirling mist rose from the creek surface. Through the mist, Liam saw a buffalo watching him. It gave another snort, pawed the ground, and left. Liam felt as if he were still asleep, and that the scene unfolding before him was a dream. At first, he watched Huritt leaving the camp and heading south. He carried no weapons, but wore a buffalo head as a headpiece, its hide draped over him as a robe.

The scene then switched to a pleasant meadow, carpeted in wildflowers spreading out in all directions; it ended at the beach of a large lake. A settler's wagon entered the meadow; the wife and children frolicked in the flowers. The man driving the wagon looked at Liam; he appeared to be making a silent, pleading cry. A party of Delaware warriors rose up from the beach, and made for the helpless family of settlers. Nearby, a lone buffalo stood atop a mound of sand, pawing the ground and nodding his massive head. The dream ended; the buffalo reappeared in the creek mist. It looked at Liam, nodded once, and vanished once more. Liam awoke, knowing that he must abandon his pursuit of Huritt. Instead, he would find his way to the large lake that lay a day's march to the northwest.

Liam told the others of his changed plans, as a result of the visit from his spirit brother. The three took one last look at Huritt's camp, and started their march to the lake. The first day of the trek took them up and down heavily wooded hills. Wahta was in the lead; his speed was uncanny for a man his size, and his strides were long and graceful. Liam followed about five yards behind Wahta, his bow in his left hand, a musket strapped over his shoulder and hanging at an angle across his back. Deganawidah brought up the rear, pausing every so often to listen and watch for anyone who might have been following.

The second day, they emerged from the foothills to a flatter landscape, a mix of small open meadows, marshy creeks, and stands of maple and oak. They avoided most of the marshy areas until they came to one too large to skirt; splashing their way across, they scared up scores of turtles and frogs. Eventually, they reached dry ground. Liam stopped, and pointed ahead. "This is the place. That mound of sand there in the distance is where I saw my spirit brother." They slowed their pace to a more cautious one, and headed to the mound. From there, they could see out over the meadow of wildflowers; in the distance, a wagon approached them. It was still a mile or so away, and the occupants were unaware of the three men standing on the mound, or of the converging band of Delaware coming at them from the woods that edged the beach.

Liam sprang from the mound, leaping the distance to the bottom. He raced at top speed, pulling an arrow from his quiver, Wahta and Deganawidah right behind with their muskets at the ready.

The raiders, seeing the three pursuers, split their group, sending three to attack the wagon and the five remaining warriors to face the new threat. Liam shot one of the five attacking them in the hip, his arrow let loose while he was on the run. He continued toward the wagon while he nocked another arrow. Wahta and Deganawidah each fired their muskets, wounding one of the attackers in the shoulder and killing the other. With no time to reload, Deganawidah pulled out his tomahawk and Wahta his war club. They charged the two Delaware facing them.

Wahta barreled over his foe, and then clubbed him on the side of his head caving in his skull. Deganawidah had been knocked to the ground, his opponent on top of him. The Delaware brought his tomahawk down, striking Deganawidah in the temple, the blade cracking through his skull and into his brain. Deganawidah was dead. So, too, the Delaware – his momentum had carried him onto the blade of Deganawidah's tomahawk, which tore open his throat. The two dead warriors clasped in a grim death embrace, their blood saturating the ground around them.

At the wagon, Albert Jameson — a baker built like a blacksmith – climbed down from the wagon seat while he grabbed his two muskets, ammo pouch, and powder horn, and knelt by the front wheel. He handed the extra gun and ammo to his wife, Margaret, who along with their fifteen-year-old daughter Rebecca had crawled under the wagon. When the three charging Delaware were in range, Albert fired, striking the closest one in the chest, the musket ball breaking through his ribcage, puncturing a lung and exiting out of his back. Margaret quickly handed him the second musket; with no time to spare, Albert shot the next brave point blank in the face. He had just enough time to parry a tomahawk strike from the last raider with the barrel of the musket, but the force of the charge knocked him flat on his back.

The Delaware raider made ready to strike a killing blow. As he raised his arm, he was knocked sideways, an arrow shaft protruding from under his arm. The arrow head ripped through his heart, and he fell to the ground, dead. Albert, his face streaked with the blood of his second victim, heaved the body of the third one off of him, and stood. Liam and Wahta approached him.

Fort Littleton

After allocating work details to build a camp for 7,000 troops and assorted baggage, wagons and artillery, one of the first things Washington did was to temporarily reassign Timothy to his personal staff, his sole duty to make beer. Sergeant Mulhern was ordered to train regulars on the art of wilderness fighting.

Daniel and Markus resumed leading the scouts on patrol, aware that Delaware raiding parties were scattered throughout the area. As days and weeks rolled by, it became increasingly clear how dangerous the area had become. Not only did Daniel's scouts come across small parties of Delaware on their patrols; forage parties from the camp were harassed, and the occasional soldier killed or wounded. Washington soon ordered Mulhern to take four platoons on an extended reconnaissance to accompany Daniel. They began to systematically push the Delaware back along the intended line of the coming march.

Major Grant arrived with the rest of the troops, leaving only General Forbes and his staff still in Carlisle. The General was suffering from an intestinal disorder, and found it difficult to eat. He was in such a state that he was barely able to stay on his horse, and rode the last few miles to Fort Littleton in a supply wagon a week later. It was now late August; if this army wanted to conquer Duquesne before the winter snows, it needed to move more quickly. Accordingly, Major Grant and Colonel Bouquet were sent on ahead to prepare Fort Ligonier, the final outpost before Fort Duquesne.

A somewhat tense staff meeting preceded the move to Ligonier, as Bouquet and Grant firmly declined any help from the scouts and guides. "I appreciate your concern, Colonel Washington," said Major Grant, "but Colonel Bouquet and I both feel we can supply our own scouting parties. After all, my dear Colonel, your scouts have done a top notch job clearing the Delaware out of the area, so we should have no problems on the march."

Washington sighed, and replied, "Thank you, Major, but we have only pushed them back. They are not destroyed, and can still be a nuisance, at the very least. If you won't take some scouts with you, then please take Sergeant Mulhern along. He is familiar with the area, and has taken some of your troops out on patrols."

At this point General Forbes excused himself. Heading for the latrine, again, he said on his way out of his command tent, "Take this Sergeant Mulhern, as Mr. Washington suggests. That is all for now."

Fort Frontenac

"It's settled then," Liam said to Albert and Wahta, "we will lead you to Colonel Bradstreet at Fort Oswego." As two wounded warriors had escaped, they buried Deganawidah and six dead Delaware warriors, and then set up camp.

During the evening meal, Albert explained why his family was where they were. "I was wounded when I was with Braddock's army. A musket ball to my knee rendered me a bit lame, making it necessary for me to leave the army; I went back to my old trade as a baker. I hired on with Bradstreet and was part of the march to Frontenac, but had to pull out when one of my mules went lame. Took a couple days to find a replacement, by which time Bradstreet was already getting to Oswego."

Liam excused himself, and walked down to the small creek that fed into the lake. He splashed the cool water on his face; the weariness of the last three days washed over him, and he let out a loud yawn. "I can understand how tired you must be," said Rebecca, startling Liam, "it must be very tiresome rescuing people. I can't thank you enough for what you did, and I'm very sorry about your friend dying."

"I must be tired if a girl can sneak up on me like that," replied Liam a little grumpily. He stood up and started back to the camp, but for a second their eyes met. In that brief glance, Rebecca could see his sadness, but despite that, and his terse manner, she could also feel the goodness hidden behind the sorrow.

****

The next morning, they started off, following the lake's shoreline east. Wahta scouted a little ahead, and Liam followed behind, for – as Liam pointed out at breakfast – "the two Delaware we wounded could be gathering some friends." After a few miles of walking next to the wagon, Rebecca fell back to walk with Liam.

"What are you doing back here?" he asked.

"I hope you don't mind, but I'd like someone to talk to besides my ma and pa, and your Mohawk friend kind of scares me," she replied with a big smile.

"You're kinda brash for a youngster, wanting to keep company with a brute like me."

"I am not a youngster, Mr. Mallory, as I'm sure you're aware. Oh, yes, I've seen you watching me. I don't mind. In fact, I kind of like the attention. As for you being a brute – why, Mr. Mallory, I know you are much more than that."

"What do you know about what's inside a man like me? "

"Well, I do know that on the outside you are a gruff warrior, but that is only a part of you. My pa told how being in a battle changes a man; that he becomes an animal bent on destruction. He says most men learn how to control the rage, and to put it behind them, but some don't. Are you one of those, Mr. Mallory?"

"Your pa is a right smart man. I saw him become that animal yesterday, and I see him now as if it didn't happen. He's a lucky man. For me, it is harder to let it go." He stopped for a moment, wondering why he was telling all this to a young girl he barely knows. "I'm not sure you'd understand, so let's just drop it."

"My pa says he knows you from General Braddock's army; not that he ever met you, but you were often the subject of soldierly camp fire talk. He told me of that awful day at the trading post. So, you see, Mr. Mallory, I may understand you more than you think I do. After the battle, my pa had to leave the army. We moved to Schenectady, and opened a bakery shop. One day, a group of Mohawk came into the village, and with them was one white man. Mr. Baptist came into pa's shop to see him; you see it was Mr. Baptist what doctored his leg, and they spent the rest of the day talking. Mr. Baptist didn't seem to mind my presence; he is such a kind man, anyway, he got on talking about you, how you were when you were young, and how different you are now. They are both worried for you, afraid that the goodness you have inside will stay hidden, but my pa thinks you will conquer this."

"Like I said, your pa is a smart man, but I also said to drop the subject. Since you seem to learn a lot from your pa, what else has he taught you?"

"He taught me to shoot and to hunt."

"Did he really, and what have you hunted and shot, my fair young maid?"

"Many things, Mr. Mallory, do you doubt my prowess with a musket? In our wagon is the hide of a large black bear. It was killed by me. Does that make me rise in your estimation, Mr. Mallory? I surely hope so," she said, her mouth shifting into a mischievous pout.

Liam, in what seemed like the first time in months, burst out laughing. He grabbed Rebecca by the shoulders, and said, "You are a wonder, make no mistake about that. You cheer me, but it is time for you to go back to the wagon. Maybe your pa will learn you some more things. We should be getting to Oswego in a couple hours, and I need to backtrack a little now. We can talk some more later on. Now, go."

****

As the sun set over the western end of the lake, the caravan entered what remained of Fort Oswego. The French destroyed the fort when they took it in 1756, but never occupied the site. Colonel Bradstreet had taken 3600 troops across the lake; besiege Fort Frontenac, leaving a small garrison at the fort. The duty officer directed Liam to the bateau he hired to ferry them across.

The next morning, they rolled the wagon onto the bateau and shoved off. The sky was threatening, and soon thunder rumbled. Lightning flashes approached from the west. The wind picked up, and the lake started rolling the bateau. Albert went forward to steady the mules, shortly joined by Liam. The others held onto the wagon, but soon Wahta was vomiting over the side. Rain came down in sheets, and the waves grew larger – but the boatmen, after a brief struggle, had the vessel headed in the right direction. The storm fled further east, and the approaching shoreline soon came into view. As they drew near, one of the boatmen dropped into the shallow water and guided the bateau to the beach. Wahta still held on to the wagon after it was offloaded; his legs were unsteady, though his color was improving. The others were soaked clear through, and shivered in the cool morning air.

They found their way to the place where they would set up camp. Rebecca and Margaret changed into dry clothes in the wagon, while the men crouched around the newly-kindled fire. When they were dry, the three men left to find Colonel Bradstreet. The rumble of thunder was now that of Bradstreet's cannon, as they battered the limestone walls of the French fort. This was the third day of the siege; Bradstreet shared the feeling around the camp that the French would surrender within a day or two. Their provisions were low, as were their numbers and their morale.

The Colonel's adjutant took Albert to the other bakers' camp. Colonel Bradstreet invited Liam and Wahta into his tent, and beckoned them to sit. After a few minutes of light banter – including describing Wahta's bout of seasickness – Bradstreet said, "When we have taken this fort, the French communications and the supply line between Montreal and the western forts will be cut. I need to get the news of our victory to General Forbes; this could have a bearing on how he proceeds with his plan to take Fort Duquesne. I was wondering if I could persuade you two to deliver that news. I could send a courier from my ranks, but none would have the detailed knowledge of the area that you two possess."

Liam looked at Wahta, who nodded his head, and said, "I will go with my brother."

"Fine, Colonel, we'll deliver your message. We will need horses and provisions," replied Liam.

"Thank you, gentlemen," answered a smiling Bradstreet, "I'll see to the mounts and food. Where can I find you once the surrender is agreed?"

"As you won't be needing us for any fighting," Liam said, "we'll be over with the Jameson family."

The next morning, the French opened the gate and surrendered. Bradstreet took the fort without casualties, and was more than generous with the French, allowing them the honors of war and permitting the commander to leave for Montreal. Having already written the dispatch for General Forbes, he instructed his adjutant to take it, and the horses, to the bakery portion of the camp. Liam groaned, and said to Wahta, "Damnation, but Bradstreet is sure in a hurry. I was hoping to rest for another day."

Wahta grinned, slapped Liam on the shoulder, and replied, "You speak only part of the truth, my brother; you would like to spend more time with young Rebecca." Liam saw her looking at him from a table where she was kneading dough. She had worked steadily since they arrived; little time remained to relax other than at supper last night, after which she was just too tired to talk. She knew that she might never see Liam again; at the very least, it would be months or maybe years. Wiping her hands on her apron, she walked over to where Liam and Wahta were readying their mounts. Her nervousness concealed, Rebecca reached up, took Liam's head in her hands, and pulled him gently down to kiss him. "You take care," she said, looking up into his surprised eyes, "I want to talk more with you, Mr. Mallory." She gave a slight curtsey and walked away, the tears now beginning to well up and run down her cheeks.

Fort Ligonier – Fort Duquesne

"These incursions, these harassments by the enemy – they have to stop," Colonel Bouquet said to Major Grant. Since beginning the construction on Fort Ligonier, they had been under almost constant attack, especially the timber and foraging parties.

"I have a plan," answered Major Grant. "Give me five hundred men, and I will lead a reconnaissance in force. If we can coax the French into attacking what they think is a forage detail, we can deal them a crushing blow."

"I like it, but take seven hundred fifty men," replied Bouquet, "and be sure to take Sergeant Mulhern. He's regular army, and I know you dislike the colonial troops. He at least has their measure, and can be relied on to give good counsel."

"Very well, Colonel," answered Grant, "I consider Sergeant Mulhern as more colonial than regular, but will look to him for advice."

"Fine," said Bouquet, "leave at dawn tomorrow. If you do not draw the French out by the time you get within five miles of their fort, leave some lookouts, and return here."

The next morning, at dawn, seven hundred fifty troops left the nearly complete fort, unaware that two Ojibway warriors watched.

Sergeant Mulhern drank from his water skin, and wiped his face with some cool water. The march had proceeded with surprising speed, causing the hair on the back of Mulhern's neck to stand up. They were only a couple miles from Duquesne, and so far had met no resistance, but no amount of talking could convince Major Grant that there could be trouble ahead. His latest attempt drew nothing but scorn from the Major, and now the Major overstepped his orders by continuing the advance far beyond Colonel Bouquet's stipulation.

Grant split his force into three wings, putting the sergeant in charge of one. Grant was on the right, approaching Fort Duquesne from the Allegheny River side; Lieutenant Collins, a new arrival with no wilderness fighting experience, led the left. He was to follow the course of the Monongahela River, to the fort. Mulhern had the center, and spread his men out to take advantage of the woods' cover.

The reflection of the sun on moving bayonets caught Mulhern's attention; he barely had time to shout a warning before the first arrows arrived, one catching the corporal standing next to Mulhern in the right shoulder. "Down! Take cover! Be sure of a target before you shoot," shouted Mulhern as he dragged the corporal over behind a tree. "Be a good lad, and hand me your musket after I shoot mine, and reload mine. We'll take a look at your arm shortly." The woods were now alive with the war cries of Ojibway, Ottawa, and Shawnee, the sound of musket fire, and the screams of the wounded. Mulhern surveyed the situation, and decided they could hold long enough to retreat in an organized fashion.

After about half of an hour, the French and allies backed off and retreated, and started back to the fort. Mulhern gathered up his men and his wounded and headed back to the site where all three wings started. Survivors of the other two groups began to return to the defensive position Mulhern had established. Most of those arrived in chaos. Many were without their muskets, thrown down in fear in the face of the enemy.

Lieutenant Collins died in the first rush. Many of his group was killed while attempting to escape in the river. Major Grant's group fared no better; only a hundred of the two hundred and fifty men made it back to Mulhern. The Major, and eighteen of his men, were captured by the French. Mulhern arrived at Fort Ligonier with four hundred men alive from the original seven hundred and fifty. One Mohawk also accompanied him, as Wahta had appeared, carrying a message from Liam.

Liam and Wahta watched the ambush of Major Grant's group, unable to render any aid. They saw him captured, and taken to Fort Duquesne. They could also see the battle with Mulhern's command, and understood that he would withstand the attack. Liam told Wahta to find Sergeant Mulhern, while he headed to Fort Duquesne. "There are a couple things I need to do," Liam told Wahta. "Jimmy Two Birds needs to know about Frontenac falling, and what's coming his way. I know he's French, but I owe him, and he's a good contact to have. I'm also going to take a look at the French garrison; see what kind of shape they're in, the mood of the troops, can they hold out in a prolonged siege. Tell Mulhern to tell Washington that I'll be along in two days."

Fort Duquesne

Liam gave his horse to Wahta, poured water over his face and streaked it with dirt, and ran to catch up with the French. He fell in next to a wounded Marine and helped him limp into the fort, all the time keeping an eye out for Huritt. Fortunately, Huritt had led the attack on Lieutenant Collins' group; he was a mile away, returning to the fort with Collins' scalp a new trophy hanging from his war lance. Leaving the wounded Marine in the care of a surgeon, Liam made his way to Jimmy Two Birds' tavern.

Entering through the back door, he went into the kitchen area and gave a coin to the cook. After sending her to get Jimmy, Liam waited for him down a hallway. A few minutes later, Two Birds walked in. "Liam, my boy, why am I not surprised, seems like things are coming to a head around here."

"Quicker than you may think, my friend," Liam replied, "Frontenac has been taken from the French, and General Forbes has assembled more than enough men to take this place."

"Frontenac taken? Mon Dieu! That cuts the supply line rather effectively. Well, I knew this day was coming. A word of warning, however; the French commander, Lignery, is an aggressive sort, as you can tell from today's little action. He may not just roll over and play dead for General Forbes."

Liam stood and walked around the room, gesturing toward the hides and the wine and ale casks. "What are you going to do? Things could get ugly once the British overrun the garrison here."

"No need to worry about me. I can cope with most circumstances. In addition, our friend Mr. Trent has allowed me to use his trading post land. I've built a few storehouses, so the bulk of my goods will be safe. Once the British rebuild this fort, I will simply open a new tavern, with a British name, of course."

"Rebuild? Why would the fort need to be rebuilt? Some sections, perhaps, because of the artillery bombardment – but surely not the whole place."

"You underestimate Ligerny. He will blow this place to kingdom come, rather than surrender it. He may be running out of provisions, but he has plenty of ammunition and he's not the type who leaves things for his enemies."

Liam spent the night at the tavern. He awoke to the news that the Ojibway, Ottawa, and Shawnee had packed up their new trophies and headed back to their homes, leaving defense of the fort strictly to the French garrison of less than fifteen hundred men. With a hearty handshake, Liam left Jimmy Two Birds with the promise to return at war's end. Liam was able to slip out of the fort with Jimmy's help, using a gate in the outer defense perimeter that only Jimmy knew about, having it built for just such emergencies.

Fort Ligonier

After hearing Liam's report, Washington took him to see General Forbes, who had finally arrived at Ligonier – having to make the journey by litter, too ill to sit a horse or ride in a wagon. They entered the General's tent, to find him in bed, dictating notes to his secretary about troop dispositions for defense and construction. "Ah, Colonel Washington, I presume this young man is the famous Mr. Mallory. Come, sit down. Please pardon my appearance, Mr. Mallory, dying of the bloody flux, you see; damned nuisance to say the least. So, tell me, Mr. Mallory, how are things in Fort Duquesne?"

General Forbes put the fort on full alert after hearing Liam's assessment of the conditions at Duquesne, and the probable attack from the ever audacious Ligerny – an attack shadowed by Mulhern, Liam and Wahta. Colonel Washington ordered Sergeant Mulhern to step up the patrols. Mulhern was pleased to have Liam and Wahta as companions. They sent the rest of their patrol back to warn the fort, while they followed and planned a small ambush for the inevitable retreating French force. Soon, they heard the booming of two French cannon, and headed over to see about eliminating that threat.

The advancing twelve hundred French were met with a withering musket volley, followed by an artillery barrage of grape and canister shot. The French were overcome and demoralized in the face of the blistering attack and dozens of attackers fell. Liam took aim, and let an arrow fly, hitting the artilleryman in the hand as he was about to light the fuse. Mulhern and Wahta raised their muskets, and with Liam advanced on the six French soldiers manning the cannon. None of them were armed other than with ramrods, and six pairs of arms were soon raised in surrender.

Encouraged by the results of the French attack, Forbes decided it was time for an all-out assault on Duquesne. Despite the misery of his illness, Forbes insisted on being in command, and accompanied his twenty-five hundred men – though he sent Washington to the front of the march, to take charge of the actual fighting. They were still a few miles away when night came, so they made camp, sent out a patrol, and set a line of double sentries around the perimeter.

At the fort, Ligerny – under orders to avoid surrender – supervised the setting of demolition charges, and the preparations for his garrison to leave in the middle of the night. They would head for Fort Le Boeuf, fifty miles north on the Lake Erie shore. If he could not defend the position, then he would at least deny the British not only the use of the fort, but also the use of his store of cannon and ammunition. Jimmy Two Birds also made his plans for evacuation; soon, his wagonload of goods and his whores were headed to Trent's old place, though he remained behind to say farewell to Ligerny and to prepare for the British.

Liam, Wahta, Daniel, Markus, and Sergeant Mulhern, having led the patrol in a wide circuit around Fort Duquesne, were camped by the Allegheny River ford, which the army would use in the morning. The explosion shook the ground where they lay sleeping. At once, the night sky was aflame with fire, and the smoke rose so thick that it concealed the stars.

The patrol members were startled awake. Liam and Mulhern stood together, as more explosions ripped through the now blazing fort. "Aye now," exclaimed Sergeant Mulhern, "sure that'll make taking the fort a mite easier, but what a bloody waste of ammunition."

Liam nodded and pointed. "There go the last of the French troops, most likely the demolition team, and there – on horseback – that must be the commander. Not much chance we'll catch them now."

General Forbes, unable to sleep, was drinking a concoction of ground hartshorn mixed in beer, a mixture his surgeon suggested. While unsure how much good the drink was doing him, it was certainly better than being bled, or purged. He had the mug to his lips when the first explosion surprised him, the mug falling from his grasp and spilling on his blanket. "God's bollocks, the French bastard blew the fort," he said to the doctor, "go find Colonel Washington. I need to know the extent of the damage, and the whereabouts of the French."

Washington and a platoon of infantry crossed the Allegheny, and met up with Liam's patrol. He saw Liam conferring with Wahta and Markus, who then ran in the direction taken by the French away from the fort. "Well, Colonel, that surely was a rude way to wake up. Two Birds told me this might happen, but I thought the French would at least put up a fight."

"From what I can see," replied Washington, "most of the fort itself is burning, though there are some buildings outside the walls that are still standing. I hope your friend Two Birds made it out of there."

"Climb on down from your horse, Colonel, sir," said Sergeant Mulhern, "I have the boys making coffee, and it will be a while before Wahta and Markus return with news of the French."

Liam held the halter while the Colonel clambered out of the saddle. "I wouldn't be worrying too much about old Two Birds. I'm guessing the rascal will be there to greet us in the morning, probably draped in a Union Jack."

This elicited a chuckle from Washington. "I look forward to making his acquaintance."

Wahta returned two hours later, bearing the bloody body of Markus in his arms. He laid him gently down, and said only, "Huritt." Daniel and Liam looked at the scalped and mutilated form of their friend. Tears streamed down Daniel's face, but Liam stood like a stone, his face a mask of hatred.

"What happened?" growled Liam.

Wahta met Liam's eyes. "We split up when we reached the trees. I went ahead, to see if I could find the beginning of the French soldiers. Markus stayed behind, to see if others were lagging. I was on my way back when I heard him scream. Huritt had followed us, and taken Markus by surprise. When I saw Huritt, he was scalping Markus. He saw me, but disappeared into the shadows, waving the scalp in triumph before I could take a shot at him. I am sorry, brother."

Washington came over, knelt, and covered the body with a blanket. He looked at Wahta, and asked, "What about the French?"

"They are too far away for pursuit. They are moving quickly toward Fort Machault."

General Forbes arrived at the ruins of the fort in the morning, the dysentery having kept him up most of the night. "Gentlemen, we will need to rebuild this fort. It is the key to controlling the Ohio, but it is too late in the season for the entire army to stay here. Therefore, I will return to Ligonier with most of the troops. Those who stay will start building Fort Pitt.

Colonel Washington, I must ask you to make all possible speed, and take the news of our victory to Philadelphia. Please take what men you need. Now, if you will excuse me, gentlemen, I feel my strength ebbing, and desire to sleep."

Washington looked at Liam and Daniel, and said, "I would have you, along with Sergeant Mulhern and Wahta, accompany me back East." Liam made to protest – his desire was to follow Huritt – but Washington forestalled his response with a hand on Liam's shoulder, "I know how badly you want to catch up with that Shawnee, but I need your skills with me. The war is not over yet; there are still battles to be fought."

Liam grasped Washington's hand, and with one last look at his friend's body, replied, "I will go with you."

Chapter 12

Fort Carillon

Spring 1759 - Ford's cabin

Liam, Daniel, and Wahta gazed down upon a small homestead, noting the smoke rising from the chimney. "Looks like we're in luck," said Daniel. "From what I heard, the Fords are more likely to be out rather than in."

Oliver and Mary Ford managed a comfortable life out of a rugged environment. Oliver was known for his hunting ability and his all-around woodcraft, while Mary was not the typical 'stay home and tend the crops' type of woman. An excellent shot, and an expert trap setter, she accompanied Oliver most of the time. Together, they always had furs and meat, to trade with their Mohawk neighbors for corn, beans, and medicinal herbs. They were also part of William Trent's network of watchers, and as such were keeping an eye on the comings and goings at Fort Carillon. Also living with the Fords was Deborah Prescott, the eighteen year old raven-haired daughter of the Fords' friends, who lived with them after her family died in an Indian raid. She tended the cabin and garden in their absence.

Colonel Washington sent Liam and company to find out what the Fords had learned, if anything. As they walked down to the cabin, Oliver came out from around its corner, where he was butchering a deer. "Ahh, let me see," exclaimed Oliver as he greeted the trio, "you've come from Trent or Washington; else I'm the King of England. I 'spect you're hungry as well. Fresh venison, do ya?" Patting them all on the back as they walked by, he chuckled and yelled, "Mary, darling! We've company for supper."

Deborah emerged from the cabin. When she saw Daniel, her eyes lit, and a smile coursed across her face. Daniel nodded to her as he dismounted; with blushing cheeks, he smiled back.

After a refreshing meal of venison, boiled potatoes, bean stew, and the finest quality ale, Oliver pulled out a map of Fort Carillon. While he unrolled it, Deborah circled the table to refill everyone's mug. She reached for Daniel's at the same time he did, and their hands met. Daniel looked up at her, the piercing gaze of her sparkling green eyes startling him. Deborah smiled as she withdrew her trembling hand, and finished filling the mug.

"Thank you, Miss Prescott," said Daniel, hoping no one heard the slight crack in his voice.

"You're very welcome, Mr. Mallory," replied an equally flustered Deborah, and left the room.

Wiping his mouth with his hand after a satisfying drink, Oliver remarked, "Yeah, that's just about the last of it. I picked up this ale on a trip to Albany some time back; bought it off a fella name of T. E. Winslow. Best brewer I ever met, though I heard tell he joined the militia, and sent down to join Braddock. I hope he survived that fiasco, waste of a good brewer if he didn't." He took another swallow and exclaimed, "Mother's milk! Oh, excuse me for my crude remark, gentlemen. Now, I suppose you want to know about Fort Carillon?"

"Yes sir," replied Daniel, "but first let me set your mind at ease about our acquaintance, the good brewer, Timothy Edward Winslow. He is indeed still alive; in fact, he is part of Liam's scout troop. He even saved Liam's life during that battle. He shot and killed a Shawnee brave , who had Liam in the sights of his musket. Ordinarily, he would have been with us on this trip, but Colonel Washington decided he needed Timothy's skill as a brewer for the time being."

While everyone else smiled and chuckled to hear Daniel's story, Liam slunk back further into his chair, with an angry scowl on his face. Oliver noticed the change in demeanor, but decided to hold his tongue, for now.

"Wonderful news, and that's a fact," continued Oliver. "This, too, is a fact. Fort Carillon was real quiet for a while – just the normal routines of drill and patrols – until a couple of weeks ago, when a band of Shawnee set up camp just outside the fort. At first, there were only ten or twelve braves, but as the days went by, more and more trickled in. Then, yesterday, a band of thirty warriors arrived, led by the Shawnee, Huritt."

At the mention of Huritt, Liam flinched, and banged his knee on the table. Daniel reached over, grabbed Liam by the shoulders, and eased him back into the chair. When Liam appeared calm, Daniel let go. Liam, before Daniel could react, sprung to his feet and hastened toward the door. Turning around as he was about to cross the threshold, he stammered, "Thank you for the meal, ma'am," and then continued out into the night. Mary rose to go after him, but Wahta, his quickness and gentleness belied by his size, reached out and picked her up as she opened the door. He carried her back into the cabin, saying, "Let my brother go. He has a rage burning inside, and is best alone while he seeks to control it. He will be back soon."

Mary sat down, and asked, "What is this burning rage? Has it to do with Huritt? And, more importantly, husband, are you going to let this savage carry me about like a sack of flour?"

"It has everything to do with Huritt," responded Oliver, stroking his beard as he thought, "or I miss my guess. I think I've pieced it together. A while back, we heard of a massacre at Trent's post near Fort Duquesne. A Mohawk woman was brutally murdered by a Shawnee named Chogan, who if I'm not mistaken was killed later by Thomas Mallory, who was in turn killed by Huritt, Chogan's closest friend – some say they were brothers. Further, the woman was Liam's wife. When you add all that together, you can understand the bad blood between them. "

"He's had a bad time of it, we both have," said Daniel, "but with him, it's as if the rage has taken over, and he's convinced nothing will help but revenge."

"It is a dreadful thing to have to overcome, this grief and its need for revenge," replied Oliver, "but we mustn't let that deter us from our task. Perhaps Liam's destiny is at Carillon, but first we need to see if we can get you in there. Now, as to this savage," Oliver smirked with a wink, "I'm sure, dear wife, that you would prefer me to be in one piece and breathing, so we'll ignore his crude behavior this one time."

Later that night, Liam returned, still sullen but less angry. He sat next to Daniel by the campfire; they would sleep near it for the night. "You feeling better?" asked Daniel, as he poked at the embers absentmindedly.

"As well as can be expected, I suppose," replied Liam, "but I cannot shake the hatred and the fear. I have dreams, nightmares actually, where I confront Huritt. The dream is always the same. We see each other across a large meadow. With tremendous roars, we run at each other, tomahawks ready to strike. Neither of us can land a blow when we meet, but the force of the collision knocks us both to the ground. My tomahawk flies from of my hand; before I can reach it, Huritt is up and leaping at me with his tomahawk poised for the kill. That's where the dream ends. I always awake then, shaking and in a cold sweat. I tell you, brother. I am afraid of this confrontation, but at the same time I know it's inevitable. Down deep, I look forward to it, whatever the outcome."

"Brother," replied Daniel chuckling, "I don't need any dream to tell me that you and Huritt will someday meet. Hell fire, seems like the bastard shows up everywhere we go. As to the outcome, no one can say for certain, but as sure as I'm standing here, I believe what Pa used to say: 'you weren't born in the woods to be scared by an owl', nor by the brother of one who called himself Blackbird."

Liam stood up and said something that caught Daniel by surprise. He smiled, and said, "You comfort me, Daniel. I swear that between you and Pierre, I may make it out of this with all my wits intact; yet, those feelings of hate and fear are still within me, and perhaps always will be."

Daniel reached out his hand to Liam. "Help me up, brother," he said, "at least I got to see you smile, if only for a moment. Come; let's go back in the cabin. I believe I am still hungry, and Deborah said something about a berry pie."

"You fool me not," chortled Liam, "it's not the pie that beckons you."

****

The next morning, after a quick breakfast of bacon and biscuits, Oliver and Mary led the trio down the trail toward Carillon. Oliver had explained to them that he had a contact at the fort – a blacksmith, Angus McGee – who may have a way for them to enter the fort unobserved. He had been living in the town just outside the fort since before it was taken by the French almost a year ago, and had given the French no cause to think he was a spy. Indeed, he was a fine craftsman making such beautiful swords – both ornamental and for battle – that he was in high demand by French officers and foot soldiers alike. While they made their way through the forest, following a game trail, Daniel asked, "Say, Oliver, I remember Major Trent saying you and Mary had children. Where are they now, if I may be so bold to inquire?"

"Yes, we have two children, both grown now and years away from their leaving kith and kin so to speak," replied Oliver, "and while their paths are not the same as ours, we couldn't be prouder of them."

Mary beamed, her smile wide, and added, "Charlotte always had a hankering for the stage. She would read Shakespeare until all hours of the night if we let her. She went off and joined a traveling troupe of performers. It turns out she could act well enough; she spent the last year or so entertaining, from Massachusetts to the Carolinas. The last letter we received was from Philadelphia. She quit the Shakespeare group, and is now madly in love with a poor-as-a-church-mouse poet; Jacob Bennett is his name. They are both teaching and tutoring, in order to make ends meet, but they are happy, that's what's important.

"Our son, Ross, also developed an artistic bent, and is a painter, living in Richmond and painting portraits of wealthy plantation owners and their families."

The game trail led them through a mixed forest of beech, elm, oak, maple and pine, each a different shade of green, which formed a canopy above the forest floor. They climbed to the heights northwest of the fort, and the village just beyond. "Well, I'll be," remarked Oliver, "the Shawnee have flown the coop. Their camp was down in that meadow just yonder. You know what that means, don't you? The French are all alone." Daniel looked at Liam, and thought he saw a sigh of relief in Liam's eyes, but it was fleeting, and soon the hatred returned.

"General Amherst was due to start his way here first part of May. It's June, and he still hasn't gotten on the road," said Daniel.

"Let's head down to the village, and talk to Angus – see what he knows about the doings with the French. Maybe we'll learn something that'll speed old Amherst up a mite," replied

Oliver, "though I think my savage friend here should stay behind. Mohawk warriors built like the maple tree he's named for would be a bit noticeable. Oh, Liam, leave your bow as well, not too many white men toting Mohawk weaponry."

****

Angus McGee was a slightly built man, his solid frame muscled from years of forging metal into instruments of farming and of war. He sat on a bench outside his workshop – mopping his brow of the sweat of the day and the furnace – when he saw Mary, Oliver, and two strangers heading his way. When they arrived, he stood and enveloped Mary in a big hug. "When you gonna leave that vagabond hunter husband of yours?" he said with a mischievous grin. "Oliver, always good to see you. Who are the serious looking young'uns?"

As Oliver removed Angus' arms from Mary, and shook his hand, Mary said, "Husband, another man lifting me like a sack of flour. You know, a woman could get used to this. I rather like it myself."

"To answer your question, you would be thief of other men's wives," replied Oliver, "these are the Mallory brothers, Daniel and Liam. Working for Colonel Washington and General Amherst, come to have a look around. One thing we noticed was the number of bateaux crowding the harbor. Another was the lack of a guard on the village gate."

"The Mallory brothers. Well, now, is that a fact? You boys have picked up quite a reputation. The French are most eager to meet you," he said, with an initially menacing look. Then, he burst out laughing, "Come into the cabin. We'll quench our thirsts and plan a siege."

"Make yourselves to home. There's ale in that jug. You may have to share mugs; not used to so much company." Angus went back into the smithy, opened up a chest, and retrieved a rolled up piece of parchment. He also picked up four old discarded horseshoes. "Mary, would you be so kind as to weigh down the corners of this map," he said as he handed her the horseshoes, "this is as detailed as you're gonna find. The French were kind enough to let me wander at will, always with an armed escort of course. Ahh, my young friends look a little puzzled. Why would they let me roam around their fortress? Well not only am I the finest blacksmith in all the colonies, and a craftsman of the finest swords, I am also an accomplished actor and liar, and have them convinced I'm a Frenchman at heart. So, as a result, I have put together this map."

Oliver and Daniel pored over the map, while Angus talked to Liam about the Shawnee who had camped outside the fort. "They showed up all ready to spill British blood. When that

154

character Huritt got here, their insistence on battle reached a boiling point, but the French Commander, Bourlarmaque, refused to leave the fort with his troops, in order to surprise Amherst. That caused Huritt to take his warriors away from the 'woman-hearted French', and he headed out – where to, I do not know."

Liam allowed himself a slight grin, and replied, "Another time and place, then, I reckon."

Oliver looked up from the map, and said, "What about the troops? How many are left in the fort? It certainly doesn't appear like the whole garrison is here."

Angus drained the last of the mug Liam had handed to him, walked over to the map, and said, "Bourlarmaque left with almost two thousand men a week ago. They headed up the lake to Fort St. Frederic. Captain d'Hébécourt commands about four hundred men. I had a talk the other night with one of the sergeants, over a few cups of wine. While the good captain is under orders to put up a short yet spirited defense, the intention is to destroy as much of the fort as possible, by blowing the two munitions supply barns here at the back of the fort, and escaping the ensuing chaos in the bateaux you saw in the harbor. I know this captain, did a job for him reattaching the hilt of his sword, and he's not one to shy away from overstepping his orders, so I expect there will be some surprises in store for any who try to stop the blast."

The Battle

The word brought back by Daniel and Liam had the desired effect; 11,000 troops were now marching at a quicker pace, an easy victory seemingly within their grasps. Amherst, a veteran of many battles - both in North America and Europe – rode at the head of the column. He had expected to have to fight for the French redoubts. When he found them abandoned, he turned in his saddle and crisply ordered his adjutant racing to the rear, to have the cannon brought up quickly. "Orderly," said Amherst pointing down the formation to where Colonel Alun Williams was sharing a laugh with Sergeant Mulhern, "please give my compliments to Colonel Williams, and ask him and his head scouts to join me after the camp is set. Have the chief engineer report to me immediately. No time like the present to let the French know our intentions. Let's get to work, gentlemen."

It was a warm July evening, so the General set his camp desk outside under the boughs of an old oak tree – where there was at least a slight breeze – rather than in the stifling heat of the tent. He sipped wine from a crystal goblet while he reviewed tomorrow's troop assignments. He watched Williams and the scouts approaching, the dapper Colonel Williams in stark contrast to the three buckskinned colonial backwoodsmen and one very large Mohawk brave.

Colonel Williams had undergone a change of heart concerning the irregular troops, at least regarding the scouts. Having read the command reports of the battles at Fort William Henry and Fort Duquesne, he gained a new respect for Daniel and those in his charge. He even pulled strings to get Mulhern permanently assigned to what was now called Mallory's Militia. Williams was so impressed that he volunteered to take command of the irregulars, once it became known that Colonel Washington, having come down with a fever last winter and only now resuming military duties, was not going to be part of this expedition.

General Amherst stood when they reached his desk. "Ah, gentlemen, please, be seated. I'll try to keep this short; there's much to do, and I want to make sure we make every effort to save that fort from being destroyed." Looking at Daniel, Liam, Mulhern, and Wahta, he continued: "Colonel Williams told me of your plan for getting into the fort prior to the powder magazine blowing, and I approve. If this works, it will save us a lot of time and effort. Now, is there anything else that you need from me?"

Daniel cleared his throat, pulled out the map, and pointed to a section of the wall. "General, we did some more talking about it, and it came to us that if you concentrate some artillery fire at this point in the fort wall it could, if effective, make our climb that much easier."

"Consider the order given," replied Amherst, "the artillery should be ready to commence firing in just a short while. I take it you have men posted, so that we'll know when the French begin their flight to the harbor?"

"Yes, sir, General," answered Daniel, "We're maintaining a constant watch. We will get plenty of advance notice, though I don't think anything will happen for a couple of days. In three nights, there will be no moon – the perfect time for the French to abandon the fort, and the perfect time for us to go in."

"Excellent," said Amherst, "we should be able to soften up that portion of the defenses for you over two days. God go with you, gentlemen." At this dismissal, they stood and headed back to their tent for what would be an interrupted sleep, as the first of the cannons belched forth in fire and iron, the first shot falling just short of the wall.

Over the course of the next two days, both sides exchanged artillery fire, neither side causing much damage to the other. The French did manage to knock out one battery, killing four British soldiers, while the British cannon did little to damage the formidable stone walls, except in one spot where there was now a fairly good sized gap surrounded by piles of stone rubble. The French commander anticipated the British; to counter the expected move by the British, he stationed shooters on the roofs of the two barrack buildings. Taking one last look at the powder trails that led to the munitions barns, he saluted his chief engineer and headed to the gate to lead the rest of the remaining garrison to the waiting boats.

Daniel and the others were preparing their gear for the assault, when the message came from their lookouts that the French were boarding the bateaux. They trotted the short distance from the redoubt, clambered down the defensive ditch outside the wall, and headed to the rubble-strewn opening in the wall. Picking their way through the scree, they took a position behind one of the barns. They could see the two powder trails, and the men with torches getting ready to set fire to the powder.

Liam pulled an arrow from his quiver, and in one swift motion shot down the nearest torch bearer, knocking him back such that his torch flew harmlessly to the ground. Sergeant Mulhern took aim on the one farthest away and shot. The lead ball struck the French soldier in the chest, but his forward motion continued and his torch set the powder trail sizzling toward the other munition-filled barn. Without hesitation, Daniel handed his musket to Wahta and raced between the two barns to stop the trail of sputtering powder from reaching the waiting barrels of powder inside. The sniper on the far barracks roof fired, striking a boulder in front of Daniel, a shard of stone striking him a glancing blow on the cheek. The closest sniper now took aim on Daniel, firing and hitting him in the leg. Daniel reeled from the blow to his leg, and fell to the ground. He knew he had no chance to reach the powder fuse, and began to crawl away from the coming blast.

Wahta had seen the flash of the muzzle. He ran toward the barrack, the sniper now in a crouched run to the ladder on the other side. He reached the ground, and took two steps before the blade of a tomahawk cracked into his back severing his spine. Liam and Mulhern stayed behind the second barn, but made their way to where Daniel struggled toward the interior wall.

Colonel Williams, and the follow up assault team, were poised outside the defensive ditch, waiting for the signal from inside. The blast had them all hitting the ground, as the flames rose up into the night sky. Williams had had the foresight to equip the men with as many buckets as they could scrounge from the camp; some were filled with water, some with sand. The colonel looked to his aide, and said, "That wasn't the signal I expected, but it'll do. Get the men moving; put out that fire." Another blast shook the night, slowing their advance, but soon the men had formed a bucket brigade from the barn to the two wells in front of the barracks; some doused the flames, while the others threw water on the walls and roof of the second munitions barn.

Colonel Williams wandered over to where Liam, Mulhern, and Wahta huddled over the still form of Daniel. The first blast had thrown him into a pile of rubble, the back of his head striking a boulder and a large splinter of wood was protruding from his side. Liam had wrapped a bandage around his brother's head. Daniel was alive but unconscious, as they gently picked him up and carried him outside the walls to await the surgeon.

General Amherst stood in the entrance to his tent – now a makeshift hospital tent – and watched the surgeon cleanse and bandage the wounds to Daniel's head and leg. That he had given over his living quarters to a lowly colonial irregular was astonishing by itself, but the General found that he was genuinely fond of the lad. Colonel Washington had sent him an effusive letter of praise regarding the scout troop, and the Mallory brothers in particular. Some of that letter came to him now: "there is no one braver of spirit or one truer of heart." No, he did not fully understand his action, but he was not going to be bothered by the fact that he would now be bunking with Colonel Williams for a few days.

When he glanced over, he caught Liam looking down at his injured brother, tears evident on his usually stern countenance. "Ahh," thought the General, "his mask of hatred has slipped a bit," – another trait hinted by Washington – "matters weigh heavily on this young man." The doctor was now preparing to examine the gaping hole in Daniel's side from where he had extracted a seven by two inch piece of wood.

As he began to probe for smaller splinters, Daniel awoke. "Mr. Mallory, I imagine your head is pounding like a drummer calling a change in formation," said Dr. Martin Locke, personal physician to General Amherst. "That is quite a bump you have; most certainly a concussion. Your leg wound will heal fine, no bones were hit, and the bleeding was minimal. Now, about the wound here in your side – again, nothing vital was hit, but I need to be certain that all of the bits of wood are removed, or a nasty infection could set in. It would be best if you were not squirming around while I am probing, so you would please drink this. It will relax you, and make my job easier and you more comfortable." Daniel tried to nod his head yes, but the throbbing pain seemed to him to be oozing out of his eyes and ears; even the pressure of closing his eyes sent yet another wave of pain. Dr. Locke put a cup to Daniel's lips, and said, "This is a mixture of opium and an extract from the leaves of the hemp plant mixed in elderberry tea. You'll be asleep in a few minutes; then, I will continue with the procedure."

Later when he finished, Dr. Locke placed a loose bandage on the wound, deciding to leave it open for a few days to make sure that the bit of wood he just dug out was the last. "He will sleep for a while. When he awakes, have him drink some broth, and another draught of the tea. He needs rest more for his head wound than the other ones. The hole in his side looks good, but I will check it again in the morning." The doctor packed up his kit, and headed for the entrance.

General Amherst backed away to let the doctor through. "Thank you, Dr. Locke." Dr. Locke took in the nighttime sky, shrugged off the tension and fatigue in his shoulders, and nodded a greeting to Colonel Williams and Sergeant Mulhern as they arrived. They smelled of smoke, and were soot-stained from the firefighting efforts, but the situation was now mostly under control. Wahta had gone down to the harbor, checking to see if the French had any more surprises waiting.

Liam came out of the tent, the adrenaline from the night's actions finally bleeding away. He bent at the waist, and retched. After a moment, he stood and gasped in lungsful of air, his head gradually clearing. Walking over to Williams and Mulhern, he said, "Quite the night, eh? Daniel looks a sight right now, but the doc says he should be fine after a bit of rest. Sergeant, once you are cleaned up, can you sit with Daniel? I'll be back shortly, I want to find Wahta; I still have a job to do, you know."

****

It was two weeks before the doctor agreed that Daniel could be moved. During that time, General Amherst saw to the rebuilding of Fort Carillon, and made preparations to follow the French up the lake – though he thought the chase to be futile, as the French had already abandoned and destroyed Fort Frederic, and were now on their way to Canada. Liam and Wahta had just returned from leading a party of engineers to the ruined site of Fort Frederic, and left them there to begin the construction of Fort Crown Point. When Liam learned that Daniel was beseeching anyone who would listen that he was fine, and needed to do something other than lie around on his arse, he approached General Amherst and received permission for Sergeant Mulhern, Wahta, and himself to accompany Daniel to the Ford place, and the gentle ministrations of Deborah Prescott for his continuing convalescence. While he was improving, Daniel was still feeling the effects of the blow to his head; any sustained activity brought on a throbbing pulse of pain.

Daniel Boone had arrived with a wagon train load of material, to be shipped up the lake to Crown Point. He joined them, and drove the wagon. It was only twenty miles or so to the well-hidden valley the Fords called home, but to Daniel Mallory, every mile was painful. Even after a reluctant draught of the opium-laced tea, an occasional jarring bump would bring him to a foggy state of wakefulness – but the vision of Deborah kissing and soothing his brow lulled him back to sleep. It was with great relief that Daniel finally clambered out of the wagon and, with some help from Wahta, made it to a nice soft bed – and to more dreams of Deborah kissing and soothing his brow.

Chapter 13

Return to the Trading Post

The Fords Autumn 1759

Daniel stopped for a moment, and leaned against a tree to catch his breath. "God's bollocks, I am tired," he said to Liam, "but at least my head isn't pounding. I suppose I should be grateful." The brothers had begun taking longer and longer hikes – in part because Daniel started feeling stronger, but also after a comment by Sergeant Mulhern. He'd spoken a little too loudly outside the window where Daniel was being looked after by the lovely Miss Prescott. "Aye, and for sure I would be wanting to get out of that bed, to prove to the young lass that I'm capable of more than being mollycoddled." The jest had its effect; he was hiking every other day with Liam, and helping Oliver with chores, or chasing after his four-year-old nephew on the other days. There were days, however, when mollycoddling was just what Daniel needed, especially after once stretching to reach for Thomas – the hole in his side tore open some of the new healing.

As Deborah cleaned his wound, Daniel reached out to take her hands in his. He looked into her eyes, and asked, "Deborah, will you marry me?"

Deborah pulled away, and frowned at Daniel. "Not quite the romantic moment I envisioned, with me sitting here holding a blood soaked bandage."

"Oh, I am sorry. I didn't mean to upset you. I'll take it back..."

"Yes, I will marry you," Deborah interrupted, bending down and kissing Daniel softly. She threw down the bandage, and sighed as Daniel took her in his arms, and stroked her back while kissing her, wincing when the kiss became too passionate.

Mary Ford walked into the room, and came to an abrupt halt. "Oh, dear me, I seem to have interrupted something. Well, I just wanted to see if you needed anything, but I can see things are well in hand here." She turned away, a huge smile on her face as she walked out.

****

"Winter is coming soon," said Liam, handing a water skin to Daniel, "time enough to sit idle. You need to be ready for spring; some General or Colonel will be wanting your services again."

Daniel took a long drink. He looked at Liam. "Brother, I am not so sure I will be able to take part in any more of this war. I haven't told anyone else, but Deborah and I plan to marry. We want to settle down somewhere, and raise a family. I've had enough of tracking all over this land, sleeping on the ground in all types of weather. Besides, since winning at Carillon and the taking of Quebec by General Wolfe, the fight here is over. It is time I became a farmer again."

"Ahh, that's just the wounds and being out of shape talking," Liam replied with a dismissive wave of his hand, "and I have a feeling we're not done yet. The British may have won, but that might not sit well with many of the tribes. There'll still be work for us, of that I am certain."

Daniel shook his head, and took Liam by the shoulders. "No, Liam, I am done. Deborah and I are getting married in the spring, and we've talked to Liza and Henry about going back to re-open the trading post."

Liam reeled as if he were shot; the thought of the trading post open again set off a wave of anger. He found it hard at first to accept that Two Birds was using the spot, but this was much more. This was family; how could they think to settle on land that was drenched in the blood of loved ones and friends? Not trusting himself to speak, Liam turned and walked away.

"Liam!" shouted Daniel. "Come back. Let's talk about this." Seeing that Liam did not stop, Daniel began his walk back to the cabin, muttering to himself, "I should have known he would react like that. Good thing Wahta is around, Liam would be a misery to be around otherwise."

****

Henry and Liza had already arrived for an extended stay when they heard Daniel was hurt. "I want go huntin' wif Uncle Lim," pouted young Thomas, "you pwomised I go huntin' wif him."

Liza saw the tears forming, and reached out to hold her son. "I'm sorry, Thomas, but Uncle Liam left early this morning with Wahta." She looked over to Henry and Daniel with a questioning glance. "I'm sure he will take you when he comes back. Now dry those beautiful eyes. I saw Uncle Pierre heading to the stables; maybe you could help him for a while with the horses."

Thomas screwed up his face in thought, and said, "I go wif Pear and help with horsies. I like horsies, don't I, Momma?"

"Yes, you do; now, run off and be good," she said, then turned to the others. "What if he doesn't come back this time? We all know how he's been since the raid, but this is the angriest I've seen him. I imagine he feels betrayed by us, and he still has all that hate for Huritt. Are we doing the right thing?"

Henry stood behind his wife, and put his hands on her shoulders. "We just need to give him time. Daniel and I had a talk with Wahta. You know how much Liam relies on him. Wahta is taking our unknowing brother to see that young girl, Rebecca. Her family has settled down in Schenectady. Let's hope she can bring him out of this. In the meantime, we have a wedding to plan, eh, Daniel?"

Daniel nodded at the question, but had stopped listening to the conversation. He pondered what Liza said. Are we doing the right thing? Have we betrayed our brother? After a moment's reflection, he answered: yes and no. If Liam did not want to be part of their plan, that was his choice.

Schenectady

When the Jameson family returned to Schenectady after the battle at Fort Frontenac, they reopened the bakery – much to the delight of the village, not only for the quality of the bread and cakes, but also for the vibrant young woman who cheered everyone she met.

Rebecca, her apron covered in flour, kneaded dough while her father checked the loaves in the bake oven. Even with her auburn hair tied back in a bun, and a fine mist of flour on her cheeks, she was more beautiful than ever. Her voice nearly angelic, she sang an Irish ballad. "I swear, child, you make me feel as if I'm in the finest church in all of Ireland with that voice of yours. Why, it makes one want to believe in the Almighty, if only for the creation of such a voice as this," said Albert Jameson.

Margaret Jameson – packing up an order of bread, her mind focused on her daughter's song – was startled by the appearance of a very fierce-looking Mohawk warrior standing in the doorway.

She put her hand to her heart, exclaiming, "Wahta, you oughtn't sneak up on people like that! Don't just stand there like a big tree, come on in. Oh! Mr. Mallory, I didn't see you behind this scowling savage." At that, Wahta burst into a big grin, and gave Margaret one of his bear hugs. "Oh, put me down, what will my husband think?"

"He'll think some good friends have come by," said Albert, wiping his hands on his apron and reaching out to shake Liam's hand. "By the blessed saints, it is good to see you, and that's a fact. Rebecca, get your hands out of the dough, and come on out here, we got company."

When Rebecca came into the front room, busily wiping her hands, Liam lost sight of all else. She became the only thing or person in the room. Looking up from her apron, she shrieked gleefully and ran to him. Throwing her arms around him, she exclaimed, "Oh, Mr. Mallory, you don't know how happy and surprised I am! Of course, we all heard about that fight at Carillon, and that you were there along with your brother. We were so sorry to hear he had been hurt. How is he doing, we've not had any news about that? But, where are my manners? Ma, Pa, they will be staying for dinner, I'll not take no for an answer. Did you two fine hunters bring anything, or shall I go bargain with the butcher?"

After a long pause, Liam finally found his voice. He stammered, "Umm... we have a deer and a turkey."

Ford's Place – Spring 1760

Deborah rose from the blanket where she and Daniel sat. It was a glorious early spring afternoon - the first blossoms of the year were coming to life, and the trees were in bud, a good day for a picnic away from the busyness and the crowd at the cabin. The Ford family was hosting Daniel, Liza, Henry, Sergeant Mulhern, Thomas, Pierre, and Joseph Clarke. Much to everyone's surprise, Timothy had arrived with Colonel Washington. Donehogawa, his wife Onatah, and a few others from his village were expected any day, but no one was sure about Liam.

"We can't wait much longer," said Deborah, "we don't even know if Liam wants to come to the wedding."

"I can't wait much longer, either," growled Daniel as he pulled Deborah close, "but let's give him a few more days; just until Donehogawa arrives, then we'll have the wedding."

****

Colonel Washington learned of Daniel's injuries, and his upcoming wedding, from Colonel Williams' letter. When he read that the wedding was to be at the Ford's place, he asked Major Trent for details on the layout of the 'battlefield', as Oliver so colorfully described it. When Daniel and Deborah returned to the cabin, they found Oliver Ford and Colonel

Washington – each with a tankard of ale – supervising Henry, Sergeant Mulhern, and Timothy as they erected three large field tents that Washington requisitioned from the Philadelphia Quartermaster. "Good thing we have those youngsters to do the hard work," smiled Oliver, taking another pull from his mug.

"I wouldn't say that Sergeant Mulhern is a youngster, but he is a fine leader of men," replied Washington after a raucous belch. "Notice that Henry and Timothy are doing most of the work, while the good Sergeant urges them on."

"I was thinking the same thing. We should save him from all that agony," answered Oliver. "Say, Sergeant," he called over to Mulhern, "looks as though you have them headed in the right direction. Could I tempt you with a mug of the mother's milk of ales?"

"Saints bless you," Mulhern smiled and replied, "'Tis thirsty work a watchin' these youngsters work."

Timothy looked over at Henry, as they pounded in the last tent stake. "Aye, not only am I putting up the bloody tents, I made the bloody ale. What say we stage a little mutiny, I'm thirsty."

Schenectady

Liam and Wahta stayed with the Jamesons for two weeks, doing the odd chore. Liam took long walks with Rebecca. Wahta took to scowling at the village children, and then surprising them by swooping them up for piggyback rides. The astonished townsfolk could talk of nothing else. For Wahta, it was like being home with his own children.

Liam's anger at his family slowly subsided. Rebecca's gentle coaxing – and, at times, just the sound of her voice – relaxed him, as had been hoped. Liam even had the notion to steal a kiss from this wondrous lass, this beautiful maiden of the woods – but he restrained himself, thinking, 'She's too young!' And, then – surprising himself again – thinking that she wouldn't be too young in a couple of years.

When the sun moved lower in the sky, they began their return to the village. From the top of the hill just outside of town, they could see Wahta playing with the children. One six-year-old boy looked up at the tall Indian and said, "Wahta, you are the most famousest Indian in the whole village."

Wahta laughed and picked him up, replying, "Wahta is the only Indian in the village."

A voice startled him from behind. "Wahta not the only Indian in the village." Huritt's hands were held away from his weapons. Wahta let the boy down. He instinctively reached for

165

his tomahawk, but remembered he never carried his weapons while playing with the children. He shooed the boy away and turned to face his enemy.

As Liam and Rebecca descended the hill, they lost sight of the village street. Now, rounding the last curve, they saw Huritt.

Liam halted, pulled Rebecca behind him, and yelled, "Huritt!"

Huritt, without taking his eyes off Wahta, and keeping his hands held high, replied, "Snake Slayer today is not the day for killing. I come from the Shawnee chiefs Pucksinwah, Corn Stalk, and Black Snake, with news – and a warning."

Rebecca whispered, "Be calm."

Liam said, "Let us not speak of these things out in the open. Come to my friend's shop. We will talk there." Their eyes locked for an instant, the hatred in evidence, as they walked to the Jameson's bakery. Before entering, in another gesture of his peaceful intentions, Huritt removed his war belt and handed it to Rebecca.

The three men sat at a table kept out for customers. An old checkerboard's pieces remained as they were when Rebecca last beat Wahta, a regular occurrence. "What message has my mortal enemy to say?" Liam said, somewhat menacingly.

Huritt's sneer faded as he began to speak. "My chiefs tell you that the British – who have driven away our French brothers – must be wary and wise. Many, who live near the fort called Detroit, and near the fort where the big waters meet at Michilimackinac, will not remain quiet if the British do not treat them well. The Ottawa, Potawatomi, Ojibway and others will take up the hatchet against the British. The Shawnee wish only one thing: that the whites stay out of all Shawnee land above the river Ohio. Only that, and there will be peace with our British fathers. We do not wish to take up the hatchet, but we will against those we find on our land. The Shawnee are not a conquered people, and should not be treated as such. So say Pucksinwah, Corn Stalk, and Black Snake."

His message complete, Huritt stood and headed to the door, stopping only to retrieve his war belt from Rebecca. He trotted down the path – curious onlookers flinched if he looked their way – and then he was gone, swallowed by the underbrush, the woods, and the evening shadows.

Albert came bounding over from the kitchen doorway from where he observed the meeting. "Well, now, that was something, and make no mistake. I 'spect you'll be leaving us now, to pass on this news. Yes, sir, what a tale for the grandchildren, if we are ever so blessed," he said with a wink of his eye at Liam. As he walked away, he cackled, "Imagine that, Huritt and Snake Slayer set face to face in my bakery over a checker board."

Liam and Wahta were stunned beyond speech at Huritt's appearance, and the news he brought. Any thoughts of a peaceful frontier suddenly disappeared. Rebecca stood behind Liam. Her hands reaching up to rest on his shoulders, she said, "Well, Wahta, looks like I'll be handing over to you the care and well-being of Mr. Mallory again. Look after him well, as a she-bear over her cub."

"Hah," Wahta laughed, "you hear that, Snake Slayer, my brother? I am your momma bear! Come along, my cub; we need to prepare for our journey tomorrow."

Rebecca looked at Liam. "I don't think that my love, Snake Slayer, has heard a word we said."

While he had heard the conversation, Liam had focused solely on the spot where Huritt had been sitting – but the words 'my love' caught him short. 'Is this what is happening?' he thought, 'am I falling in love? Is this what I felt with Orenda?'

At the thought of Orenda, his mind suddenly filled with the thought that she hung disemboweled from a tree, reached out and called his name. He shivered, and – shutting his eyes – softly moaned as he forced that horror from his mind. He looked at Wahta, and finally said, "Yes, let us go prepare, she-bear."

Ford's Place

The three huge army tents, and Donehogawa chasing young Thomas, were the first things Liam and Wahta saw as they emerged from the deep woods guarding the entrance to this hidden valley. Liza was the first in the camp to see them. She ran toward Liam, but stopped abruptly, uncertain of the reception she would meet. Liam walked to Liza, and said, "I'm back." Deborah reached them. He turned to her and placed his hands on the sides of her face, kissed her on the forehead, and asked, "When's the wedding?"

They continued into the camp, Liam's arms around both of the women – their faces tear stained – while Wahta sought Mulhern and Colonel Washington. Henry and Daniel awaited them in front of the cabin. Liam turned to them all, and said, "You have my blessing on reopening the trading post. Not that you need it – but I just wanted to let you know that I am happy that you are doing it. Furthermore, as a peace offering and a wedding gift, I will go with you and help you get started. Things may get serious again in the near future, and I want to make sure the old place is well defended. I'll tell you all more after I have talked to the Colonel."

****

That night, everyone met in one of the large tents. A table laden with platters of meat and bread, and a cask of Timothy's ale, sat to the side. Everything that could be a seat formed a semi-circle; Liam stood to face them and repeat Huritt's message.

Oliver rose from his seat on a log, and using it to perch one foot as he gestured with his mug-filled hand, said, "It all comes down to how the bloody British respond. Personally, I'm not holding out much hope. Amherst may be a fine battle commander, but now that he's in charge, I don't see him as the type to be reasonable, and there's bound to be some discontented Indians."

Donehogawa then strode to the middle. Turning as he spoke, he said, "My brother – the hunter – speaks with wisdom and a true heart. It is with sadness that I say that there are many in the Seneca part of the Iroquois who speak of taking up the hatchet against the British. Not even our brother Colonel Johnson can sway them from that view. If such talk can exist among my brothers the Seneca, then it is certain that others are talking this way, as well."

Colonel Washington cleared his throat, interrupting those discussing Liam's message in muted tones. "I know we are all taken somewhat aback by this news, but it is not a complete surprise. I know that there is no imminent danger — but what if the tribes do rise up? Even worse, what if they rise up behind one banner, one tribe, one man?" Washington looked around; seeing that he had their rapt attention, he continued. "If history teaches us anything, it is that it will repeat. Imagine the tribes – and I intend to include dozens of different tribes – banding together, and rallying behind one man of vision, one man of power. I was speaking with Pierre some weeks ago about the leader of the Gauls, Vercingetorix, and how he almost succeeded in defeating Julius Caesar. If the tribes have their version of Vercingetorix, ready to throw off the yoke of British usurpation and oppression, will we be the equal of Caesar's mighty legions? Indeed, do we have a Caesar to save us from ruin?"

Grinning widely, he suddenly stopped. "Apologies, my dear friends. It seems like I rambled on a bit there. I think the point I was trying to make before waxing eloquent is that we need to be vigilant. I have to give this more thought, but I will be sending Liam's information to General Amherst, and pray it is acted on in a fitting manner."

****

The sky threatened ominously. Daniel and Deborah were marrying today; everyone busied themselves moving the arrangements to inside an already-cluttered tent. Henry and two Mohawk boys hastily erected shelters to cover three fire pits, already spitting as juice from the venison, pork and beef hit the coals. Oliver, sweat beading on his bald head, paused his labors to look at the foreboding gray and declare, "All this extra work gonna be for naught. Sky will be clear by noontime. Mark my words. Now I'm going to have a seat, and a pint, and wait for the sun to start shining off my head." That did the trick; soon everyone smiled and laughed while they worked, though keeping an eye to the sky.

Washington, Mulhern, Liam, Wahta, and Donehogawa sat in the cabin. They had decided that this was the best time to meet, as Washington and Donehogawa were leaving the next day. Washington spoke first. "Gentlemen, I think; I hope we can all agree that we need more information about the various tribes in question. What I would like is to have some of the scouts from Mallory's Militia ..."

He was interrupted by Sergeant Mulhern, who chuckled loudly and said, "A fine bunch, no doubt."

Washington smiled, and continued. "As I was saying, to scout the lands of the Ojibway and Ottawa. Those tribes are the greatest threat, in my estimation." He paused for a moment. Fixing his eyes on Liam, he said, "Liam, what say you? I would rather have you than any other for this mission."

Liam sat back in his chair, rubbed his hands through his hair, and replied, "Colonel, sir, you are the man I most respect in the military, and am hopeful to be thought of as your friend. So, to answer your request, I say: 'yes, you have me' to the military man – but I ask of my friend that you allow a delay. I have pledged my help in the rebuilding of the trading post. Once we have made it safe, then I will travel to the Michigan territory.

"However, we won't be totally in the dark before then. Two Birds will have had his feelers out, I'm sure. I wouldn't be surprised to find that he has already started building block houses at the post. Now, I can't really speak for the others, but I know that Daniel and Henry are not available, and neither is Timothy – I would rather have him remain with the others at the post. He's a good man under fire."

Sergeant Mulhern cleared his throat. "Ahem. Thankee, Liam, for allowing me to speak for meself. Now, Colonel, Sir, my enlistment runs out in three months, and I'd be pleased not to have to travel back east for the joyous occasion. So, if you would do me the kindness of taking the paperwork and forwarding it to the appropriate clerk, I will stay here and go with the laddie. You see, I don't trust that tree sized she-bear to keep the lad out of trouble."

With an ear-to-ear smile, Wahta clapped Mulhern on the shoulder, nearly knocking him off his chair. Wahta exclaimed, "Snake Slayer has no fears with momma bear nearby."

So, it was decided that Liam, Mulhern, and Wahta would embark on a mission to Detroit and Michilimackinac, two forts which were deep in the suspect areas. They would first see to the defense of the new trading post, a task that they estimate would take more than a year, including the time to get there. Donehogawa cautioned them again about the Seneca, and said he would ask his Oneida brothers for some warriors to scout for the trading post, an idea that pleased Liam as that would free him to work on the stockade and block houses he planned to build.

They turned when the door opened; Oliver stuck his head in. "Well, lads, as I predicted, the sun is out, the sky is an azure delight to the eyes, the birds are chirping away like a church choir, and the bride and groom want to get this party going. So, if you please, rise up, and bring that table and those chairs with you."

****

They joined the flurry of activity, as everyone returned tables and chairs to the outdoors. Mary directed the placement of the furnishings, foodstuffs, and drink. The guests' chairs and benches formed a semi-circle around a campfire, with access to tables laden with food and drink arranged behind them. The wedding couple sat at a table across the fire, at the top of the semi-circle.

The wedding itself was a relaxed affair. After Pierre – in his role as Justice of the Peace, duly licensed in both colonies of New York and Pennsylvania – led Daniel and Deborah through the Christian vows, Donehogawa – in his role as Mohawk spiritual leader– invoked the blessings of the Great Spirit.

The ceremony concluded with the newlyweds entwined in a long kiss, accompanied by the encouragement of enthusiastic onlookers. Pierre announced, "Anyone who wishes to raise a toast should do so now, in the hope that – since we have just begun the drinking portion of the ceremony – the toasts will be pure in thought and sentiment."

"Fat chance of that," laughed Oliver. "I happen to know that the good sergeant has been drinking all morning."

"Aye, been with you, my bald-pated friend, a true heart to never pass up the opportunity to cheer on the hardworking around him. Now, since me blood is up and me mug is full, allow me to begin." Mulhern turned to Daniel and Deborah, raised his tankard, and said, "Health and a long life to you. Land without rent to you. A child every year to you. And if you can't go to heaven, may you at least die in Ireland. 'Course, that last part is up to you. Bear with me, as I have one more word of wisdom from the old country. Go mairir is go gathair. May you live, and may you wear it out. Starting tonight, if you catch me meaning," finishing with a wink.

Amid the sounds of mirth all around, Mary stood. Pointing at Mulhern, she asked, "Would you listen to the talk of that man? You should be ashamed, Sergeant Glyn Mulhern. I say should be, because as sure as the sun is shining on me husband's head, I had the same thought." Pierre now knew he had lost that battle, and soon found himself joining in the ribald festivities.

As the afternoon wore on, and the shadows began to lengthen, they moved the chairs to make a larger circle, and the musicians began to play. Pierre and Timothy had fiddles, Henry a banjo, and Oliver a squeezebox. Jigs, reels, and waltzes kept everyone busy, dancing or clapping along. Mulhern, in a voice worn down through long years of yelling at dense recruits and fueled by many pints of Timothy's finest, sang *The Star of the County Down*. Wahta took over for a while, and had everyone dancing to the sound of Mohawk drums.

During the merrymaking, Liam gradually withdrew to a bench set against one of the tents. The feelings of joy he felt for his brother and Deborah were slowly replaced by feelings of pain and longing, and by thoughts of Orenda and Rebecca. In the end, the image of Orenda remained. Unaware of her approach, he soon found himself crying into the shoulder of Onatah – rousing only when he heard the bawdy comments heralding the departure of the bride and groom to their nuptial tent down by Wolf Pond. He nodded his thanks to Onatah. When he stood and turned to go to his tent, he found he was under the concerned gazes of Donehogawa and Wahta.

The next morning, Liam woke to the sounds of birdsong, and of Sergeant Mulhern snoring where he lay by the campfire. Liza, drawing well water from the front of the cabin, beckoned him to join her. She went inside to get the coffeepot and two mugs. Henry shook off her efforts to awaken him, claiming his head was going to explode. Returning to Liam outside, she sat down at the table and poured them both a cup of coffee.

Liam took a sip of the bitter brew, and exclaimed, "Aye, this stuff would raise the dead."

Liza smiled, and said, "Remember, Pa used to say that his coffee needed to be strong enough to grow hair on a rock."

"Well, dear sister, I think you may have followed his advice, and from the sounds of Henry and Mulhern, you're going to need a lot of it," Liam replied, holding out his mug out for more.

"That was a fine party, "said Liza. "Now, it's time to start planning. We've been talking about the trading post, and we're of a mind to expand it – eventually building it into a village.

171

The obvious problem with that is finding others to come settle with us." Liza looked at her brother, waiting for the argument.

Liam sipped his coffee. Grinning at his sister, he surprised her by saying, "A wonderful idea, one that I had myself weeks ago when I came around to the thought of the place being rebuilt. I was waiting for the right time, and I guess now is a good time. I invited the Jameson family to join us, and they agreed. Albert is a fine baker, and I've seen him in a fight; he'll be right handy in that regard."

Liza threw her arms around a startled Liam, "Oh, Liam! I cannot wait to meet the Jamesons, especially Rebecca."

She felt him tighten up when she mentioned Rebecca, but he soon relaxed and said, "We will pick them up in Schenectady. I also made arrangements with the newspaper in Albany to advertise for settlers to come, and Colonel Washington agreed to post this at his headquarters as well." Liza was so taken aback, and excited at Liam's comments, that she didn't know whether to laugh or cry.

Then, giggling madly, she went back into the cabin. "Sore head or no, handsome Henry needs to hear this."

Schenectady – early summer, 1760

Albert paused for a moment to rest his damaged leg. He had worked all morning, sorting through the items he needed to load onto the wagon; his shattered knee now reminded him of his limitations. He sat on the bench outside the shop, his hands rubbing his leg to ease the discomfort. Rebecca came out of the bakery, handing him a mug of ale as she said, "Sure is a lot of work getting ready to move. Hope that this is the last time for a while."

Albert turned to his daughter and replied, "Nothing is certain in this life. If I had my druthers, I would still be in the army. I wanted to be a soldier more than anything when I was growing up, but my Ma and Pa insisted I learn their trade; 'you need something to fall back on', they kept telling me. Well, they were right, and that's another important thing to learn and remember; always listen to your Ma and Pa."

Rebecca giggled, and gave Albert a hug. "And what is it you would have me learn today, Father?"

Albert grinned. "For one thing, how to load this dang blasted wagon. Liam and the others will be here any day now, and we should be ready to go when they do."

****

"You know, brother," began Daniel, "it seems like we're forever heading west to the same area. First, the move to the trading post, twice with the army, and now the second trading post move."

"If all goes well, you should be set for life this time around," answered Liam. "As for me, my future lies even further west. When not troubled by with nightmares, I dream of buffalo – a vast herd, grazing in an endless sea of grass. I'm going to find that herd one day. For now, though, I will be content with the trading post, and the mission for Washington."

They stopped at the top of a hill, and waited for the three wagons to make the climb. "We'll be at the Jameson's place in less than an hour, only one more hill to climb," said Liam. "It'll just be getting dark." Looking at the overcast sky, he continued, "Hope the rain holds off until we get there."

Daniel chuckled and said, "If Oliver were here, he could tell us when it's going to start."

Margaret was drawing water from the village well when she saw the party of wagons descending the slope. She hurried back to the shop. "Husband, daughter, Liam and his family are on the edge of the village," she said excitedly. "I hope we have enough to feed them."

Rebecca shrugged off her apron after giving the stew pot another stir. She headed for the street, saying, "Oh, I'm sure they will have provisions to share. There are some mighty hunters in that group." She smiled at her mother, and then sighed. "What I hope is that Liam is well."

Chapter 14

Vercingetorix
La Grand Traverse – Summer 1760

Nearing forty years of age, Ottawa war chief Pontiac was on the verge of accomplishing his lifelong dream, since living on the banks of the Detroit River. Raised with his mother's Ottawa people – although his father was an Ojibway warrior – he learned early that their reliance on the French was essential to the wellbeing of not only the Ottawa people, but the other tribes in the region as well.

Pontiac led the combined force of Ojibway, Potawatomi, and Shawnee to defeat General Braddock's British troops in the Fort Duquesne battle. He felt then the first surge of glory that followed commanding a war band of differing tribes to a stunning victory over a vastly superior force. And, he learned an even more important lesson. He became convinced that creating war parties of unified tribal warriors was the best way to defeat and drive the British from the tribal lands. Fighting together, under a strong leader, was the way to ensure victory – and he was convinced he was that leader.

Many of the tribes agreed to meet near La Grand Traverse, the great bay reaching inland from Lake Michigan. It was a place of spiritual power, a place blessed by Manitou. According to Ojibway folklore, the dune had once been a she bear, and the two islands in the bay her cubs. They swam across Lake Michigan from the west to escape a terrible forest fire, but the cubs did not make it to the shore. The mother lay down on the bluff, waiting for her cubs, and died there. Here, Pontiac would convince the Ojibway, Potawatomi, Huron, Miami, Delaware, Seneca, and many other tribes that the time was coming to throw off the oppression of the British; that the time was now to accept his leadership; that the time was now to begin preparations for war.

****

Pontiac sat atop a sand dune that stretched for miles along the lakeshore, and watched the sun sink into the watery horizon. He was tired, and not a little sore from the multi-tribe game of baaga`adowe (a game of stickball that his people had played for centuries).

The game started at dawn, and just concluded a short while earlier, when Pontiac scored the deciding points by striking the top of the goal post with the hide-covered ball after carrying the ball from one end of the field to the other. The young men of his tribe, who formed his bodyguard, shouldered or otherwise knocked his opponents out of his way. Pontiac himself brought down the last of the defenders with a sly spinning move, using his hip and elbow to clear the way to the goal. As a gesture of goodwill after scoring the goal, Pontiac went back and helped the bloody-nosed Piankashaw chief to his feet; in return, the wounded chief lifted Pontiac's arm in a victory salute. After watching the final play and the ending token of peace, the on looking crowd cheered for what felt like hours. Pontiac knew then that he had created the mood for success.

Trading Post
Autumn 1760

Jimmy Two Birds sat on the tree he had just labored to fell, and watched his hired men stripping the branches from the other logs to be used in the second blockhouse. Colonel Washington, writing from Fort Carillon, used General Amherst's military dispatch to send a note to Two Birds through the Fort Pitt commander, advising Two Birds of the plan to rebuild the trading post. Aware of the unrest among some of the tribes, he knew that Liam would want to set up defenses, and decided to get the project started. The first blockhouse sat along the banks of the Allegheny River; the second one would be built on the Kiskiminetas. The physical labor reminded Two Birds of his poor physical condition; he was sweating profusely, and his arms and shoulders ached from wielding the axe. He rolled his shoulders, and stood to begin stripping branches, when one of his workmen shouted that there was a wagon train coming down the road along the river.

Liam kicked his horse into a trot when he saw the party of workmen, and raced on ahead of the others. Two Birds was waiting for him as Liam dismounted, smiling . "Liam, old friend, as you can see, we began preparing for your arrival. I hope you approve of where I have built the blockhouses, though I'm sure that you will want a couple others – as well as a stockade wall – to connect them."

Liam grasped his friend's arms and replied, "Two Birds, I knew you would be busy, and you have given us a fine head start."

"Indeed we have," Two Birds said. "The main cabin has also been rebuilt, and now that you are here with the others, we will get this place up in no time. Though, for tonight, I think we should feast, and share news. I have the spits turning the elk your Oneida friends brought in this morning. There is plenty of wine, and I presume, since I see our esteemed brewer Timothy is with you, that you can supply the ale. By the saints above and the spirits of this land, I am glad you are here. We do have much to talk about."

La Grand Traverse

Early autumn 1760

Pontiac stood at the top of the dune in the moonlight, facing the large gathering of tribes who had come to hear this imposing and captivating Ottawa warrior and chief. The wind from the lake blowing his unbraided hair, he waited until everyone settled before beginning to speak in what he hoped would be the right words to unite the tribes behind him.

The tribes had camped together for two months. During this time, Pontiac and his followers visited each of the tribes. They talked of rebellion against the British and the ways of the white man. Tonight, he would learn whether they supported his leadership.

Since there were many tribes and many languages and dialects, he placed those who could translate among the people, so that all would understand exactly what he said. He raised his eyes and his hands to the star-filled night sky, and softly uttered, "Manitou, be with me and speak through me." His chosen bodyguard joined him, after seeing that everything was in readiness for their chief.

"The Great Spirit in his wisdom made this land for us," Pontiac began, pausing frequently for the translators. "He made it for us to dwell in for as many years as there are specks of sand on this hill, or stars in the sky. He gave us everything we needed from the forest, from the lakes, from the fields we plant, from the streams and rivers. Then, the evil spirit came to us, and we became dependent on white men – first the French, and now the British – to supply us with things we did not need before they arrived. Now, the whites hold those supplies back, and we cry to them because we feel betrayed, because we have become dependent on them. This is not what the Great Spirit intended for his people.

"The whites also brought us new ways to worship, claiming they knew more about the Great Spirit than our fathers did, that their Christ was more important than the lessons of our fathers. This also is not what the Great Spirit intended for his children.

"The white man also brought us sickness and death, with his smallpox, and with his whisky and rum.

"Our time with the French is now over. It is true that they started this attempted elimination of our culture, our religion, our identity. But, they did not steal our land, or dishonor treaties when we allowed them the land they desired for their forts and trading posts.

"The British whites are not like the French. They have stolen the land from us, and they continue to do so, as they push us farther and farther into the setting sun – even when they have said they would not. Time and time again, they have ignored their treaties with us, ignored their promises.

"Now, the British have driven the French away. How long will it be before they drive us from our land, here and in the Ohio country? How long will it be before the whites enter our sacred hunting lands below the Ohio, the Cantuckee lands? The Great Spirit has appeared, and spoken with many of his children of these evils. He tells us to throw off the yoke put around our necks, and to return to the time of our fathers, to return to the time before the evil one brought the whites to our land. The Great Spirit tells us to resist them, to fight them, to halt our reliance on the evils they bring.

"The time to do this is now, but we cannot succeed against the British if we take up the hatchet as individual tribes. The Ojibway, the Potawatomi, the Delaware, the Shawnee, and the Ottawa – we cannot bring victory if we fight alone. If we take up the war hatchet, we must be as one, we must fight together. We must throw aside old arguments and differences. Just as we allow the wind to blow away the chaff from our crops, we must let the problems between us blow away. Instead, let us use the wind to fan the flames of war.

"The Great Spirit calls us to unite; only by being as one people can we return to the ways of our fathers. I know we can do this, but it will take time to form alliances, to gather the warriors to rid the land of this evil. I ask that the war chiefs of all who gather here to speak to their people and to prepare for when the time becomes ripe for war. I ask all of the chiefs to give me some of their young braves, that I may use them to spread the word of our plans and our purpose. I ask the chiefs to give me the power to lead our people to the victory that the Great Spirit intends for us."

****

Pontiac awoke the next morning to the sound of waves breaking along the shore. A brisk wind from the northwest promised to bring rain, as it whipped the previously placid surface of the lake into four foot, white-capped waves. He followed a trail down the dune, and plunged into the lake, the water refreshing him and helping to ease the aches from yesterday's game. He stood in the water as the waves broke upon him, remembering the thundering roar of the people – his people, after he spoke last night. On the beach, Eluwilussit – the wizened with age, white-haired Ottawa holy one – watched his chief, and spoke. "Just as these waves strike and fall away from you, so shall the British disappear as droplets of water into the air."

Pontiac shook the water from his hair as he approached his spiritual advisor. "Manitou will lead us to great victories, but we must do the fighting," he said, taking Eluwilussit by the shoulders. "Come, old friend, let us begin."

****

The delegation from the Seneca waited for Pontiac to emerge from his tent. With them were Pontiac's most trusted warrior, Machk, and a few Delaware and Ojibway braves sent by their chiefs. They sat around the campfire, the Seneca cloistered in conversation, when Pontiac – preceded by Eluwilussit – emerged, resplendent in his finest buckskin leggings and war vest. A headdress, adorned with two eagle feathers, covered his long hair, braided and finished with the downy breast feather of a wild turkey hanging from the end. They stood as Pontiac made his way around the circle, greeting each by name. "Sit, my friends," he said, recognizing the positive effect his appearance and manner had. "The time has come for us to begin striking fear into the hearts of those who would take our land, who would destroy our way of life. It will be many moons before we are ready to strike Fort Detroit or Michilimackinac, but we have an opportunity in the land of our brothers, the Seneca. I have talked with the chiefs of many tribes and I speak now their words to you." He then described the plans he and the others agreed upon for the coming spring. The Seneca, along with warriors from the Delaware and Ojibway, and led by Machk, would destroy the many white settlements along the Allegheny River, working their way south toward Fort Pitt.

Trading Post
Spring 1761

Winter came early. The heavy snowfall impeded the building efforts of the settlers, but they continued to work on the stockade wall. The four blockhouses were completed before the harsh weather set in, and were now manned day and night. The population of the post grew with the arrival of three more families.

Two of the families – the Lapleys and the Webbs – planned to farm the land just across the Allegheny, so plans were made to build a bridge large enough to handle the coming and going. The third family brought needed skills; Richard Crane was a blacksmith, and of his six children, James was a carpenter. The total complement of permanent residents was now fourteen men, ten women, and six children under eleven. This meant that two of the blockhouses could easily be manned at all times, and all four if needed.

Four of the women took occasional duty, while Rebecca insisted that she be part of the regular rotation, partly because she was an excellent shot – but also because her father couldn't take part. A group of Oneida also scouted the area on a daily basis.

****

Two Birds and his workmen had waited too long to leave. Snowed in by the early blizzards, they returned to Fort Pitt when the weather finally broke. Work on the stockade was complete; it encircled most of the settlement. Only the livestock paddock remained outside the log wall.

Newly-arrived Richard and James Crane aided tremendously with building the bridge over the Allegheny, and the four gates of the stockade. Both were keenly interested in how things worked, and Richard – during his time with the militia – had come into possession of a British Army engineer's manual.

The two farming families began to plow the large meadow. They and their families continued to live in tents within the walls, until work could begin on the two farmhouses and barns. Every few days, Liam left to hunt and to have a look around – not that he doubted the reports from the Oneida, but he felt it his duty to be sure of the situation, guilt still persistently gnawing at his heart.

With all of the work in progress and yet to do, there was little time to relax. Only on Saturday nights did everyone meet for a meal and music. Despite the daily rigors and the back breaking labors they all faced, the residents' feelings remained buoyant. The bitter cold was also partially responsible for the future growth of the town, as Liza became pregnant with her second child, and Deborah with her first.

Liam, unfortunately, had little time to spend with Rebecca, but he found that he cherished the time he did get to spend with her. Her calming effect on him was a welcome relief from his cares and worries for the safety of the entire settlement, as well as the turmoil in his heart.

Seneca Camp
Late winter 1762

Machk watched as the group of mixed Delaware and Ojibway warriors headed west with the frightened white women and children captured over the course of the last few weeks. He was sending them to Pontiac, now camped just south of Detroit. These prisoners would be valuable bargaining items with his growing number of allies – and in some cases with the British – as Pontiac intended to be seen as a friend right up until the time he struck. Even with their departure, Machk still had a mixed coalition of forty warriors from the Seneca, Delaware, and Ojibway tribes, and five newly arrived Potawatomi. So far, they had taken fourteen scalps and eleven captives, with only one brave wounded while raiding farms unprepared for an attack. Machk knew that the next target would not be taken as easily. Machk would have to use cunning and strategy.

Trading Post
April 1762

Two Birds slowed his horse to a walk as he rode over the last hill, and saw the welcome sights of blockhouses and the log wall surrounding the settlement. He had left Fort Pitt shortly after dawn, and it was now about two hours before sunset. His backside ached from the pounding it had taken in the saddle, and he knew that he would be worse off after a night's sleep – but the news couldn't wait, and he didn't want to entrust the delivery to anyone but himself. He waved up at Daniel, who descended the blockhouse ladder as Two Birds rode through the gate. "Ho, there, Two Birds," said Daniel, "I have a feeling this isn't a social visit. Climb on down and we'll head over to the store. Henry and Liza are in there. I'll have someone fetch Liam, he's across the bridge helping the Lapleys and Webbs pull up stumps and rocks from our future cropland." Daniel saw the Crane's youngest son, Robert, and called to him, "Son, please take Two Birds' horse to the paddock, and then go tell Liam that Two Birds is here with news. I'll square it with your folks so they won't think you're just off fooling around."

They entered the store, where Henry was going through some of the furs that were just brought in. Liza, now seven months along in her pregnancy, was sighting down the barrel of one of the new rifled muskets when she saw Two Birds.

"Mr. Ouellette," she said, putting the musket down on the counter, "I was just telling Handsome Henry about the quality of these new muskets," and with a slight chuckle continued, "perhaps you could convince the gunsmith to move here."

Two Birds took her left hand and kissed it and bade her to sit down. "You should be taking it easy. From the looks of you, I would say seven more weeks and it is a girl," he said smiling. "As to the gunsmith – well, he lives in Philadelphia, but I will let him know of your invitation."

Daniel emerged from the kitchen with a pitcher of ale and mugs, and sat at the table. The others joined him, and conversation resumed, mostly about the defensive improvements made since Two Birds last visit. Soon Liam entered through the back door of the cabin, still sweating from his exertions across the river.

He grabbed a mug from Daniel. After slaking his thirst, he turned to Two Birds. "While I am always glad to see you, I can't help but wonder what it was that made you leave your women and ride in haste to see us."

Two Birds reached into his saddle bag, and handed Liam a military dispatch from Washington. "That's part of the reason; the other is just rumor, but one that carries the ring of truth to it. My contacts in the various tribes are telling me of an Ottawa war chief who is agitating against the British. Yes, yes, I see the look on your face, there is always someone doing that, but this Pontiac fellow is doing a bit more than that. He has gathered at least a dozen tribes together who acknowledge him as the sole leader in the coming conflict. He has surrounded himself with the like-minded of the tribes and with a spiritual guide, and they are encouraging other tribes to join them."

Liam looked at Daniel, shook his head, and asked, "What tribes are following Pontiac?"

"Among others, the Ojibway, Potawatomi, Delaware, Huron, Shawnee, and – even more interesting – the Seneca," replied Two Birds, "and that's the real reason I am here. The Seneca were to bring war to all the settlers along the Allegheny, and are doing so in a most brutal and efficient manner. A young boy escaped his captors after the raid on his family's farm and made his way to Fort Pitt. He was barely alive when one of the British patrols found him, but has recovered enough to tell a very sad tale indeed. From what we could gather from the boy, at least six farmsteads have been hit so far, and the next in line is right here."

"A bit sooner than I expected," Daniel said, "but I think we're as ready as can be. I'll make sure that all of our water buckets are filled and placed where they need to be. Henry will double check that we have extra muskets and ammunition placed in the blockhouses and around the wall."

Liam stood, and stretched his shoulders to relieve the tightness and the tension. "You appear to have everything under control here. I'm in need of sleep. In the morning, I'll join Wahta and Mulhern with our Oneida scouts, and find the war party. If we can surprise them with a few tricks of our own, then their numbers will be of no advantage."

"If I may venture a thought," called Liza from the other room, "if Liam finds them, he can let us know when to expect the attack. They need to think that we are caught off guard, so I suggest that everyone go about their normal activities. Now, that includes Jonas and Seth being across the river working in the field, but they won't be alone. The Seneca will probably be coming down the Allegheny by canoe, and will land on our side of the river – so they won't notice Liam and the others hiding in the woods by the bridge on the other side."

"Two Birds, my friend," said Liam as he headed for the door, "you are welcome to bunk in my tent tonight. I will be gone early. I agree with Liza's plan. I'll get word back as quickly as I can, and will have our little surprise ready by the time our attackers arrive."

He stopped at the Jameson's to grab bread for the morning. Rebecca was adding logs to the bake oven, to be ready for tomorrow's baking. He approached her and bent down to raise her up. He kissed her softly. Startled, she pulled back to look at him, and then just as quickly pulled him to her and returned his kiss. Albert's clearing his throat broke the embrace. "I am sorry to interrupt," he said with a grin, "but the girl's mother and I would like to know your intentions regarding our daughter. Hah! Listen to me prattling on about something I know very well, and have neither the will nor the ability to do anything about."

Liam drew back from Rebecca with a smile on his face, and turned toward Albert. "Actually, I'm glad you're here," he said, his face now furrowed in worry. He relayed the news to them. "I must leave in the morning. Please take care of yourselves." He took Rebecca in his arms and kissed her again, saying, "Please, take care of yourself."

****

After shrugging off his buckskin shirt, Liam lit a candle and sat at the desk to read the dispatch from Washington. The lingering thoughts of Rebecca soon vanished as he read:

> Liam,
>
> Forgive me for asking this of you so soon but I need your invaluable skills. Matters are proceeding faster than we anticipated. There have been reports from Detroit, Michilimackinac, and some of the smaller garrisons scattered throughout the Ohio territory of growing unrest among most tribes. There is word of a large concentration of Ojibway, Ottawa, Miami, Huron, Potawatomi, and others in the La Grand Traverse region of Michigan all gathered to hear an Ottawa by the name of Pontiac. I need to know if all this activity and unrest is his doing. If it is, then I fear we may indeed have a Vercingetorix to contend with. I implore you to go there at the

soonest opportunity. I've enclosed a letter, authorizing you to make use of our fastest couriers and as an introduction to the various fort commanders.

Yours Most Truly,

Washington

P.S. I have found five new families who will join you within the year – GW

Liam blew out the candle and climbed into his cot, muttering, "I hope, dear Colonel that we are still here to receive them."

****

Daniel stepped out of the cabin and into the pale light of the almost full moon as it shone through the thin clouds blowing across its face. The breeze, coming from the northwest, still had that tinge of winter to it. Deborah was finally asleep; her pregnancy made it difficult to be comfortable, and the process of finding the right position made it hard for Daniel to fall asleep as well. Tonight, though, it was his troubled mind that forced him from his bed and into the cool night air. When he had made the vow to rekindle his parent's dream, he knew it would be hard but he hadn't imagined it would be threatened again so soon.

He gazed up at a clear patch of sky and not for the first time wondered about God's role in men's lives; if indeed God was involved at all. While his mother had held on to the Catholic beliefs she brought with her from Ireland, there hadn't been much in the way of religious teaching when the children were young (other than her frequent imploring cries to the many saints she revered). Christmas and Easter were the exception, as she insisted on reading aloud from the Bible on those occasions.. Sometimes, Daniel mused to himself that the names of St. Patrick and Mary were heard in the house more often than the names of her children.

His eyes were drawn to movement in Liam's tent as his brother closed the flap and blew out his candle. Did God have a hand in changing Liam's mind about the resettling, or was it the calming effect of Rebecca or were the two entwined? He returned his gaze toward heaven. "I'm just a simple farmer," he spoke quietly to the sky, "matters of God I do not understand. I may just be talking to myself, but by the spirit of my parents, I beseech you, God, give us the strength. We cannot, will not lose this place again."

Along the Allegheny

Machk stepped out of his canoe, and joined the rest of his warriors for a final war council before they began their attack on the trading post. They met on an island about two miles upstream from the post. Twenty of his warriors split into three canoes; two would carry five each as the first wave of the assault. The third canoe of ten would follow a few minutes later, to deliver a crushing blow to the gate and wall along the river front.

Last night, Machk further split his force by sending 25 warriors five miles south to where the Kiskiminetas River was fordable. They hid among the heavily wooded hills south of the post, waiting to hear the first shots before they assaulted the main gate. Machk knew it was important for him to lead the attack, as it would add to his prestige and to that of his chief, Pontiac. If this coalition were successful, there would be ample reward for those who faithfully followed and carried out the commands of this compelling and dynamic Ottawa leader, and Machk intended to collect. He already had five new scalps on his war lance, and was poised to add more to his collection.

Liam watched Wahta and Mulhern head down the back of the ridge, where they had been observing the Seneca war party on the island across the river. Mulhern observed, "That ain't all of them." The ensuing discussion ended with Wahta heading to gather up Jonas and Seth while Mulhern crossed the bridge and warned the rest of them of an imminent attack probably from more than one place. When Liam was sure of the Seneca plan of attack, he and the others mounted their horses and raced back to the ambush point along the bridge.

Trading Post

Deborah awoke to the movement of their child within her; she nudged Daniel, and placed his hand on her belly. He was, as always the last couple weeks, amazed at the baby's strength. As he reached over to kiss Deborah, Mulhern's cry of "To arms!" rang out as he raced into the compound, running from building to building to wake the occupants. Daniel and Deborah threw off the blanket and hurriedly dressed.

He saw her safely to the main building, where she, Liza, and Lily and Susan – the two older Crane daughters – would load muskets and tend to the wounded. Fourteen-year-old Robert Crane, and eleven-year-old Josiah Webb, would run weapons as needed. The rest of the women and children ran to the barn in the middle of the compound, Margaret Jameson and Hilda Crane both carrying muskets and ammo pouches.

The blockhouses were now all manned, as Daniel climbed into the tower in the southeast corner of the stockade. Timothy had the northeast tower; Henry, the northwest; the southwest tower held Richard and his son William, a former member of the Virginia Militia. Pierre, Albert, and Rebecca manned the stations along the stockade on platforms, as slots were built into the wall to allow musket fire.

Mulhern had taken command of the situation, and placed Pierre by the trading post riverfront gate. He thought to put Albert there as well, but in light of Albert's limited mobility, he decided to leave him by the southwest gate near his cabin.

The look that Rebecca gave Mulhern said, I am fighting, and I am staying by my father. She took the wall slot next to Albert. Mulhern looked at the young girl and thought to himself, no, young woman, I'll not move ye. He said to her, "Aye, lass, you keep your eyes peeled over yonder. I've a feeling down my neck that they will hit this spot hard in the next few minutes. I will be back with help if you need it, but I need to get to the north gate. That's where they're going to hit first."

Wahta reached the ambush point in the woods at the end of the bridge, and told Jonas and Seth to lie on the ground. Liam and four Oneida scouts clambered down from their mounts, to hobble them deeper in the woods. They reached Wahta just as Pierre and Mulhern opened fire on the two canoes that were beaching below the gate. Two of the enemy went down; the eight remaining charged the gate. A second volley from Pierre and Mulhern, this time joined by Henry from the tower, wounded two more, but Machk succeeded in opening the gate.

Richard and William Crane saw the fight occurring across the compound. Without a word of command from his father, William – his service as a former militiaman ingrained in him – raced down the tower and to the north gate.

Liam maintained his focus upstream, and ordered that no one fire until he gave the command. The ten-man canoe made its way around the last bend in the river. Every Seneca and Delaware warrior trained his eyes on the gate just a quarter mile ahead. Just as they beached the canoe, Liam ordered his men to shoot. The effect of the resulting volley was devastating. Five warriors died from the volley; two more were hit by subsequent shots from Liam and the two Oneida equipped with bows.

Pierre raised his musket to ward off the blow from Machk's war club, but he was struck above the right temple as the club slid down the barrel of the musket. He crumpled to the ground. Machk's cry of victory was cut short by the sound of the volley from the ambushers. He turned to see his warriors being massacred, his rage now out of control.

He lifted his tomahawk, and bent to scalp Pierre when two musket balls hit him. The shot from the musket of William Crane hit his leg; the second one killed him, as Liza, from the window in the main building, hit him square in the back of his head, the ball, bone, and brain matter exploding out of the front of his head and onto the still unconscious form of Pierre. The remaining five assailants, having lost their leader, ran back to their canoe and pushed off into the Allegheny.

Liam, Wahta, and the four Oneida raced across the bridge, Wahta and two of the Oneida giving chase to the escaping canoe. Liam and the other two Oneida paused at the trading post to check on Pierre when they heard Rebecca scream, "Thomas!" The ever-inquisitive Thomas had snuck away from the barn, by climbing out the window that faced the corral. He was standing in the open, watching the three Seneca warriors breach the gate and enter the compound. An initial volley from Daniel, Rebecca, Albert, and Timothy had slowed the advance, but the greater numbers soon told and the gate was flung open.

Daniel and Timothy grabbed their spare muskets, climbed down from their towers, and ran to the gate. One of the Seneca raced toward Thomas, ready to strike him down. As Rebecca screamed, Albert turned and shot the brave, which left him open to a thrown war lance that entered his back and pierced his heart. Rebecca screamed again to her father, and shot the brave as he advanced to claim his prize.

Mulhern grabbed Robert and Josiah, and headed to the corral to an empty wagon. They pushed and pulled it to the gate, and blocked the entrance, while Timothy and Daniel fought hand to hand with tomahawk and knife. Liam – having already taken care of the third Seneca in the compound – arrived at the gate with his two Oneida companions, and began firing arrow after arrow into the crowd at the gate. The others now had a chance to reload, but not before a war lance snaked out under the wheel of the wagon barricade, and gashed Timothy across the back of his calf. Mulhern covered him, while Timothy took his bandanna and bound his bleeding leg.

Soon, Richard Crane joined William and Henry to defend the main gate. Half of the assailants now lie dead, and another six were wounded. Recognizing that a continued attack was now fruitless, the Seneca retreated to the hills, taking their wounded with them.

The defenders let out a deafening huzzah, and smiles and congratulatory claps on the back were passed around. Liam grasped Mulhern by the forearm in the manner of two Roman legionnaires, but released his grip immediately upon seeing Rebecca cradling her father's head in her lap. He went to her, knelt behind her, and held her tight as her tears fell onto his hands.

Margaret's position in the barn doorway allowed her to see Albert fall.   As she approached Liam and Rebecca, her voice quaking, she said, "Come, Rebecca, let's get your father inside, so we may clean him up." Richard Crane helped Liam get Rebecca to her feet, and then the burly blacksmith carried Albert's lifeless body to the trading post, where Hilda and Deborah prepared him for burial.

At the same time, Liza tended the now-conscious Pierre, who had diagnosed himself as having a slight concussion, and asked for a cup of blackberry tea with some poppy extract to slow down the galloping herd of horses in his head. Lily Crane cleaned and bandaged the gash in Timothy's calf, under the jealous gaze of her younger sister, Marsha.

****

Margaret and Rebecca brought Albert's militia uniform for his burial. Jonas, Seth, and William dug a grave in the cemetery from the original settlement, right between Stump Nose and Rob Carter. The burial took place in mid-afternoon; Liam said a few words, but it was young Thomas simply saying, "Thank you, Mr. Jameson," that brought forth fresh outpourings of tears. Finally, Rebecca began to sing *The Parting Glass*. When she stumbled over the words, Mulhern took over until she joined him for the ending chorus.

The group spent the rest of the afternoon in preparation for a victory feast, and a "proper Irish send off for Albert," as Mulhern quipped. To that end, Timothy rolled a couple barrels of his finest ale to a table set aside for them, with help from the youngsters Robert and Josiah, who Timothy promised a pint of their own for their bravery during the fight.

Wahta returned to report that they pursued the Seneca canoe as far as the island, but it was apparent that the retreating warriors would not slow down. Liam, not leaving anything to chance, left to patrol the perimeter with two Oneida, and missed the beginning of the festivities. Mulhern, tankard in hand, took a seat next to Wahta. He asked, "So, what was the big idea of momma bear taking off after them Seneca, when you're supposed to be watchin' after Liam?"

"Ahh, Snake Slayer looks all right to me," replied Wahta, grinning.

"Aye, no thanks to you," Mulhern said, wiping ale foam from his mouth.

"Momma bear has no worry about Snake Slayer. Momma bear has faith in the little Irishman," answered Wahta as he slapped Mulhern on the back, promptly spilling ale all over the front of his shirt – causing a loud bout of laughter from everyone in earshot.

"You ignorant savage," said Mulhern laughingly, while he walked over to refill his tankard, "didn't no one teach you not to spill an Irishman's beer?"

When Margaret and Rebecca joined the festivities, the atmosphere immediately became more subdued. Margaret quickly announced, "We're supposed to be celebrating our victory. Please, don't stop because a good man died, protecting a defenseless child. I am proud of my Albert, and we should be celebrating him, too. I am going to miss him so, but I am proud of him. Now, go on, and be merry; he would want it so."

Their recognition that Albert would join have joined in the celebration helped to change the mood, and soon the laughter returned. When Liam returned from his patrol, he heard the sound of music, and saw Mulhern dancing with seven-year-old Ruth Lapley.

After speaking with Daniel and sending him off on his patrol, Liam sat next to Rebecca. She handed her half-full mug of ale to Liam, and placed his arm around her shoulders so that she could rest her head on his chest. She looked up at him with a smile, but hers eyes still glistened with sorrow..

As days and weeks went by, and summer arrived with warm mornings and stormy afternoons, the small village returned to a normal daily routine. Liam and Daniel continued to patrol the perimeter every day. Mulhern, Wahta, and two Oneida were on an extended patrol, following the Allegheny north to the settlements that were hit. The Jamesons welcomed help from Marsha Crane, who had the makings of a good baker. Hilda or Lily helped fix their evening meal.

Liam and Rebecca spent as much time together during the day as duty allowed. They began to visit the graves of Albert and Orenda as part of their daily ritual; it seemed to both that every visit brought a greater sense of peace. While Liam could still feel anger and hatred within, he could also sense his love for this mesmerizing young woman growing. As for Rebecca, her bouts of grief occurred less frequently, and her zest and charm were back on display. Her only doubt was about her future with Liam. He would be leaving on his mission for Washington soon; he would always be leaving for some mission or other.

One evening, Rebecca thought about their future once again, and realized that she would have his heart, but he would always be leaving to follow a dream. She rose from her bed, put on her robe, and left the cabin to head for Liam's tent.

Margaret heard the door open, and left her bed to investigate. She opened the front door and peered out into the darkness; she saw light from a candle coming from Liam's tent. As she was only a few yards away, she heard their voices. "Are you sure?" asked Liam. Rebecca took his hands in hers and replied, "I've never been surer about anything else before. I love you, Liam

Mallory, and I want you. You'll be gone soon, and we may never see each other again." Liam kissed her, took her by the hand, and closed the flap of his tent. Margaret smiled, and said to herself, 'Aye, and it's about time, Liam Mallory.'

Indian Coalition camp south of Detroit
November 1762

The night's snowfall weighed down the evergreen boughs; a slight gust of wind gave off plumes of snow smoke to sparkle in the early morning sun. Pontiac had just returned from a trek that included visits to tribes from Michilimackinac (in the north) to Forts St Joseph and Miami (in the south). As was his daily habit, he dove into the icy cold water of the Detroit River. Emerging, he stood to face the rising sun, and prayed to Manitou for guidance for the coming day.

His position among the tribes was never stronger, despite the news about the defeated Seneca. He downplayed the loss, and instead praised their efforts, and the successes they did have. He privately lamented to his staff the loss of Machk, and bemoaned his impetuous nature.

"We must have patience, and choose our time wisely," he said to the crowd around him that night. "We must continue to be peaceable with the whites. I am heartened that we continue to play stickball daily by the soldier fort. This makes our combined presence appear less threatening; they are used to seeing us in a large group. During my travels, I arranged with our brother tribes an all-tribe stickball tournament in the spring, outside of Fort Detroit. Then, we shall see what happens. Be patient and be strong; soon, we shall fight." As with every speech he had given over the past months, his words were greeted with a thunderous roar of approval. He had to fight back premature thoughts of what he could become.

Fort Detroit
April 1763

Not counting the fact that they still had to make their way back to what was now Mallory Town, Mulhern figured they had traveled close to a thousand miles since they left there last June. They had visited Forts Sandusky, Miami, Saint Joseph, and Michilimackinac, and were now closing in on Fort Detroit.

Each visit had a similar pattern. Liam first presented himself to the post commander, carrying Washington's letter of introduction. He and Wahta would then spend a few days sizing up the mood of the tribes in the fort's vicinity. In the meantime, Mulhern spent most of his time in the always-present tavern, buying rounds for the garrison soldiers, merchants, and settlers, while getting a sense of the morale and expectations of military and civilians alike.

The mood at Fort Sandusky was such that one soldier, after a few pints, confessed to Mulhern that he was planning to desert before the savages tore the fort apart. Mulhern, knowing it wasn't any of his business, did however offer some advice. "Before you go off and do something you'll regret, remember this: if you're caught, you're dead for sure. If you stay, you're only probably dead. Not much of a consolation, I'll admit, but something to think about when you sober up."

After the visit to Fort St. Joseph, Liam wrote his assessment to send via military courier to Washington in Philadelphia (by way of Fort Detroit and Fort Pitt).

Colonel Washington,

We are heading to Michilimackinac in the morning; it will be weeks before I can send another report, but I feel it's imperative that you have the latest information. Have visited three garrisons, and every tribe we came across. The situation is peaceable at present, but the mood among the whites is one of dread and anticipation. The tribes show no outward animosity or any sign of aggression. Indeed, they go out of their way to feign friendship. However, our belief is that they are just biding their time until word comes down from the chief they now follow, the Ottawa warrior Pontiac. He is bringing a message of hope to his people; that hope resides on the destruction of the whites.

Pontiac is traveling throughout the Michigan territory and the Ohio, attempting to bring around some of the fence sitters, and is doing quite well. There was a French trapper, hired by Major Gladwin to report on Pontiac, who was witness to many of these meetings. The number of allied tribes is, at best guess, fourteen, which does not include the Shawnee – but who knows how long they will stay out of the coming fight.

Make no mistake, Colonel, there will be war – probably by next spring. The forts here are ill equipped, undermanned, and have poor morale. It will not take long for them to fall, and the settlers and traders are, for all intents and purposes, defenseless. The British command needs to act now.

Yours,

Liam

PS It seems I may have the chance to see and perhaps meet this Ottawa Vercingetorix when we arrive at Michilimackinac. Pontiac sent an Ojibway to invite the tribes near Fort St. Joseph to some sort of stickball competition at Detroit in the springtime. Wahta heard from the messenger that Pontiac was going to spend the winter at Michilimackinac. I will report from there as soon as I can.

The maples, oak, and birch displayed full red, orange, and yellow colors, in distinct contrast to the deep greens of the eighty-foot tall white pines that rose in magnificent groves throughout the northern woods. Mulhern and the other travelers felt that this would be a nice place to explore, once the threat of war was gone.

They had followed, for the most part, a native hunting trail that veered a few miles inland from Lake Michigan, through stands of white pine and open meadows. Deer was in abundance, as was pheasant and wild turkey, and they came upon a herd of elk spooked by an earlier group of Ojibway hunters. They were camped for the night near La Grand Traverse, just a few days from Michilimackinac.

" 'Tis a fine place for sure," voiced Mulhern, "I can see why them that are already here wanna keep other folks out."

"Those Ojibway didn't seem too pleased to find us in their hunting ground," replied Liam, "though once their chief silenced them, they became almost too friendly."

"Aye, but I am grateful for that elk haunch they left with us," said Mulhern, "wouldn't you agree there, momma bear?" Wahta could only grin and nod his head, the drippings from the large morsel of elk in his mouth running down his chin and chest.

****

The fort at Michilimackinac was originally a major French trading post, linking the St. Lawrence waterway to the Mississippi. Although the French maintained good relations with the native population with periodic generous gifts, this practice had been severely curtailed by the British under the governing edicts of General Amherst.

Two days later, Liam and Mulhern entered the lightly guarded front gate, as most of the garrison watched a stickball match from the wall. They were directed to the headquarters and cabin of the garrison commander, Captain Terence Justice. He stood in his doorway as the two strangers approached; his quick assessment told him that these were two formidable woodsmen, one carrying a military dispatch pouch. He hurried back inside to retrieve his red outer jacket and his sword.

As they entered the cabin, Mulhern started to salute the smartly turned out captain, but caught himself while Liam chuckled at his side. "Please excuse the former Sergeant," said Liam while he offered the introduction letter. "He sometimes forgets he is no longer under the King's command."

"Quite alright, uh, Mr. Mallory", said Justice as he read the letter. "Well, now, welcome to this outpost on the edge of the world. Ha, ha, just my little joke on being posted so far from the finer things. I'll have my adjutant show you where you can bunk while you are here, if I can draw him away from that native game. Once you are settled, come back here, and we'll dine together and talk about your mission. Um, I see by the letter you have a third companion, a Mohawk, no less. Well, I would like to meet this Iroquoian. Pray tell me where is he?"

"Captain, laddie, you'll have to wait on that," replied Mulhern with a smile. "Seems our good companion discovered some Huron in the camp. He used to fight against them; he's talking over old times, I expect."

After settling in the cabin, Liam and Mulhern wandered around the fort for the couple of hours until dinner with Captain Justice. The ball game had ended, and the fort was alive with activity – most of which was occurring outside the barracks where an argument broke out over a lost bet. Along with the soldiers, quite a few braves also entered the fort; it appeared to Liam that they were looking things over as they milled about as a group, stopping from time to time to point at something. "That's interesting," said Liam, "I wonder if that is a regular occurrence. It will bear watching. That'll be my job. Yours, my fine little Irishman, will be to learn all you can from that motley crew of the King's finest."

Conversation over dinner mostly centered on war experiences; Captain Justice was with General Wolfe at the Plains of Abraham, and took part in the victorious battle at Montreal. He was most interested in the recent trouble at Mallory Town, especially after Liam mentioned that it may have been backed by Pontiac.

"I find it to be improbable that Pontiac would have been involved," said Justice, "he has been most gracious in my many meetings with him. I assured him that I had written General Amherst, and expect a reply any time now. I'm sure the general will relax his policy on giving gifts to the tribes. I am scheduled to meet with Pontiac again day after tomorrow. I think it would be appropriate for you to meet him as well. Perhaps he will quell any notion you may have about his intentions."

Captain Justice rose from the table and made to refill the wine glasses of Liam and Mulhern. "Shall we take our glasses out to the yard? It is a pleasant night; not many of those left, soon we'll be hip deep in snow."

"Begging your pardon, Captain, darling," inquired Mulhern. "Now, I have enjoyed the wine, and that's a fact – but, I was wondering if you had any ale about?"

Captain Justice laughed, and answered, "Why yes, of course, a proper drink for a soldier, eh, Sergeant?"

****

Pontiac rode into the fort on a magnificent white stallion, surrounded by his bodyguard mounted on matching black ponies – each bore a symbol of a stickball bat painted across the right front shoulder. He wore his finest buckskin leggings, and his chest was bare, except for the bear claw necklace hanging down on his well-muscled torso. A single eagle feather was tied to his hair, and he wore gold bands on each arm.

Liam stood with Captain Justice outside of the headquarters, and watched this warrior chief of the Ottawa with great interest. He also noticed that a group of warriors - different from the last two days – had entered by the back gate, and were taking the same tour of the fort.

Pontiac gracefully dismounted, and handed his staff to one of his bodyguard. He could not take his eyes away from Liam; bypassing the proffered hand of Captain Justice, he strode directly to Liam, and said, "I see in you a brother spirit. You are one of Manitou's people."

"I am Otetiani, adopted son of the great Mohawk chief, Donehogawa," Liam replied, bowing his head in respect to Pontiac's spiritual awareness.

"It is an honor to meet such a glorious warrior," Pontiac said as he grasped Liam by the shoulders, "and that explains that giant of a Mohawk wandering among my people. He must be Wahta; he who named Snake Slayer, and his constant companion."

Captain Justice interjected, "Perhaps we would be more comfortable inside. I'll have a fire lit; there's a definite chill in the air today. I wouldn't be surprised to see snow by nightfall."

****

It did indeed snow that night, but the few inches became a slushy, muddy mess by mid-morning. Liam stayed awake most of the night, thinking about his encounter with Pontiac. At first, he was impressed with the dignity and almost regal nature of this obviously charismatic leader, but something rang false about him; a smirk, a rolling of the eyes, shrugging of shoulders. Liam, expert hunter that he was, noticed those signs, while Pontiac spoke about his hope and desire for peace.

Captain Justice was firmly under Pontiac's spell. This does not bode well for the future of the fort, thought Liam. After a few hours of sleep, Liam wrote another letter to Washington.

> Colonel Washington,
>
> Having been here at Michilimackinac for about a week, and with the weather already showing signs of changing to winter, I thought it best to get a report off before the route becomes impassable. It is much the same here as at the other garrisons in the south. The fort is surrounded by many tribes, all professing peace under the guidance and direction of Pontiac. I am convinced he is your Vercingetorix. I have met him, and though he hides it well from Captain Justice and many other garrison commanders, his true purpose is war – against not only the British military, but also against any whites who are found in their territory. I have formed this opinion from my observations of the man, and by reports from Wahta, who has been actively engaged with many of the different warriors camped around the fort. They never say anything directly to him about their goals, but he overhears enough at the nightly camp fires.
>
> I think it is important that I remain wherever Pontiac is, and it appears he may winter here and head for Detroit in the spring, so that is when I expect to be there. I hope this sounds alarming enough, because the three of us feel that springtime will bring war. I hope you can explain to your superiors the dire situation they will find when all of those tribes take up the hatchet.
>
> Your Obedient Servant,
> Liam

Chapter 15

Siege of Fort Detroit

Of the officers Liam met on this mission, the fort commander, Major Gladwin, was one of the very few who did not harbor any illusions about Pontiac and his plans. While Gladwin was cordial and attentive to Pontiac's overtures of peace, he did not trust him. He prepared his soldiers; Liam was relieved to find an alert and ready garrison in Detroit. Word of the stickball competition, and the chance to hear Pontiac speak, had drawn close to 2500 warriors, plus women and children. The twelve tribes encamped around Fort Detroit was the largest assemblage of natives that Liam had ever seen.

Liam also found a letter waiting for him, from his brother. He opened it as soon as they were settled in their quarters, and he beamed with a wide smile as he read the opening sentence:

Liam,

You're an uncle, twice more. On July 28[th.] Deborah gave birth to Bowie Rhys Mallory, and four days later Liza brought forth Meagan Jane Clarke. All are doing well; indeed, the babies are thriving among a throng of female admirers.

As to other matters, we continue to patrol as far up the Allegheny as the island, and up to the ford on the Kiskiminetas. The Oneida have gone home to participate in an Iroquoian council meeting with Colonel Johnson; with things having quieted down here, I didn't see any harm in letting them go. Our loss of their numbers is offset by the arrival of the five families introduced by Colonel Washington in his letter to you. All of the men have military experience; one was even a scout with Roger's Rangers, up in Quebec with General Wolfe. He has already proven to be a good addition to our patrols. Another is a former quartermaster's clerk, who has taken over the running of the trading post itself – freeing Henry for other duties, and allowing Liza to take care of Meagan.

We get news now and then from Two Birds – mostly rumors, but a name keeps coming up: Pontiac. The general opinion around the fort is that he'll soon be turning his sights on Fort Pitt. All we can do is keep alert and ready.

Liam awoke in a cold sweat. He had not been haunted by the nightly dreams for quite a while, but last night the vision of Huritt returned. This time, the fight between them was on a snow-covered plain, amid a herd of grazing buffalo.

He sat on his cot, still trembling from the disturbing dream, when Wahta entered the cabin to describe the plot he learned a few hours earlier. An excited Potawatomi warrior, who thought Wahta was a Huron, told him that Pontiac would lead a large group of warriors into the fort while the garrison watched the daily ballgame. They would remove the weapons hidden under their robes, and massacre the soldiers.

Liam shook Mulhern awake, who – like the old campaigner that he was – slept through both Liam's moaning and the arrival of Wahta. Once hurriedly dressed, they headed to Major Gladwin, whose breakfast was interrupted by their unannounced entry. Liam relayed the plot to Gladwin; although he turned to Wahta and questioned him for greater detail, the Major had already decided to act.

Calling in his duty sergeant, Gladwin ordered a call to arms, and for all three of the gates to be shut and barred. "How are you fixed for a siege?" asked Mulhern. "That will likely be one of Pontiac's responses when he is not allowed entry. The other response will be rather bloody; the settlers, soldiers, and traders outside the walls will be targeted."

"I thought the same, and will send out a patrol shortly to gather in as many of those folks as possible," replied Gladwin. "In the meantime, gentlemen, I would ask that you take places at the front wall and gate. We are vastly outnumbered, but we have something Pontiac does not have: mortars and cannon."

****

Pontiac knew that something was wrong when he saw the closed gate – a gate that was usually guarded, but open. There were many more uniformed and armed soldiers lining the palisade than usual, and Major Gladwin – in full dress uniform – stood near Snake Slayer in the blockhouse atop the front gate.

The retinue of warriors behind him stopped, as Pontiac raised his hand and approached the gate. "Major Gladwin," he called to the blockhouse, "I wish to enter and talk. Why this display of British might?"

"If you want to enter the fort, then let you and your warriors undo the robes and blankets you are all wearing this fine, warm morning," replied Gladwin, "otherwise I must refuse your request to enter the fort."

Pontiac threw an angry look at Gladwin, turned, and returned to his followers. On his signal, they dropped their robes and blankets to raise their bows and sawed-off muskets. They fired once at the fort before retreating. Gladwin responded by signaling one of the mortar teams, whose round landed just beyond the armed group to strike a group of onlookers and kill three warriors.

Over the course of the next two hours, Pontiac's warriors surrounded the fort; they killed all of the British settlers, and three unfortunate traders. He also captured four soldiers; they were loaded onto a canoe and floated by the fort. The stunned soldiers on the riverfront wall watched, unable to respond, while their four comrades were scalped alive and thrown into the river.

Mulhern looked over the landscape facing the front gate and wall – a landscape now filled with Ojibway, Ottawa, Potawatomi, Huron, and Wyandotte warriors. The warriors took cover behind anything they could find, especially the fallen trees and stumps that .ted the killing ground. Occasionally, they fired at the fort to little effect, which prompted some verbal taunts from a couple of soldiers standing near Mulhern. One of them even stood and bared his arse, inviting the Indians to take a shot at him.

On seeing this, Mulhern turned toward the soldiers. "Laddies, the next one who speaks out or otherwise pulls a stunt like that will find my musket shoved up their nether region. Do I make myself clear?"

Major Gladwin heard the reprimand as he climbed up to the blockhouse. "My apologies, Major, for reverting back to my old self," Mulhern said.

"No apology necessary, Mr. Mulhern," replied Gladwin, "as far as I'm concerned, you still hold rank when we are together."

They were interrupted by cries of 'Fire!' from the blockhouse over the south gate. Pontiac had ordered fire arrows shot at that gate and wall, attempting to cause a breach in the defenses. The barrage had taken effect, and soon a section of the gate was a blazing inferno. At once, Liam organized a bucket brigade to quell the fire. Gladwin, in anticipation of a rush to the gate, ordered one each of the six-pound and the three-pound cannon positioned just inside the gate, loaded with canister shot.

"You know, Major," began Liam, "we should let them make the charge. That cannon will certainly dissuade them from trying this again."

"An excellent idea," said Gladwin. He ordered his men to stand back from the gate, leaving it hanging half open to give the impression that the fire had indeed had its desired effect.

In a matter of minutes, a screaming horde of warriors advanced on the gate at a run, Pontiac leading the charge. As he neared the gate, Pontiac saw the barrel of the cannon through an opening, and yelled for his men to fall back – but it was too late, as first the six pound and then the three pound cannon fired into the tightly bunched group of warriors. The effect was devastating; at least a dozen warriors went down, their bodies riddled with shrapnel. Pontiac escaped, covered in the blood and debris of the unfortunate warriors.

While not prepared to end the siege because of this setback, Pontiac knew he needed a victory in order to maintain his position. After cleaning off the residue of battle, his war council meeting resulted in a large group of warriors heading south to Fort Sandusky, Fort St. Joseph, and Fort Miami. Pontiac also realized that he needed help to defeat the besieged fort, and sent a request to the French commander at Fort de Chartres for men and cannon.

****

The siege was in its sixth week when a sentry on the riverfront wall spotted a flotilla of bateaux, approaching from the Canadian side of the river. Major Gladwin raced to the wall when the cry went out. When he reached the blockhouse, he saw ten bateaux filled with British soldiers held prisoner by a band of Ojibway warriors. A supply detail had been dispatched from Niagara; ambushed by the Ojibway, all but thirty of the ninety-seven men had been killed or captured. Of those survivors, a company of eight red-coated Marines were the only ones who eventually reached Fort Detroit; the others returned to Fort Niagara.

Liam joined Gladwin in the tower, and watched as Pontiac killed the force commander and scalped him, shaking the bloody scalp while giving his fiercest war cry. That cry was taken up by the warriors surrounding the fort and by those in the bateaux, as they continued to float the fort to Hog Island, where the remaining prisoners were killed and scalped.

"Major," said Liam, "it seems to me that Pontiac isn't likely to abandon his plans for this siege anytime soon. It also seems to me that any relief needs to be aware of what they're likely to run into before they get here. With your permission, I'd like to take Mulhern and Wahta, and make our way to Fort Niagara or Fort Pitt. We'll bring back the force needed to break this siege."

"I think we need to wait a while longer before we resort to that," replied Gladwin. "I prefer to wait until we hear what is going on with the forts to the south of us. If those garrisons are holding out, then we only need wait until the tribes tire of the siege tactics of our friend Pontiac, and start suing for peace."

"If those garrisons are still alive, I will be very surprised," said Liam, "but I understand your logic. Well, the offer stands, and we'll be ready to go when you give the word."

****

Pontiac and Gladwin received the news on the same day; Pontiac from a delegation from the groups he had sent south and Gladwin from Marine Sergeant Tiny Castle. The Major was inspecting a mortar position when a blockhouse sentry shouted that a group of British Marines were approaching the fort, pursued by a band of Indian warriors. Mulhern yelled down from his spot on the wall to Major Gladwin, "Major, we need to cover those boys, or they won't make it."

Gladwin put his hands to his mouth and replied, "When they are in range of a volley, say the word, Sergeant."

Sergeant Tiny Castle gathered his men together in the cover of the trees. They had been in a running fight for the better part of three hours, and Castle knew they needed a breather before the last sprint for the gate of the fort, a sprint that would see them leave the trees and into the clearing before the walls. The sergeant pulled a kerchief out of his sleeve and wiped the sweat from his well-weathered, craggy face.

"Right, then, boys. We're gonna give 'em one volley, and then run like our arses are on fire and pray that whoever's in charge of that bloody fort has his wits about him."

Major Gladwin raced to the gate. He ordered it opened, and for a company of muskets to be ready to fire a volley from just outside of the gate. He could see the Marines raise their muskets, and saw one man lift his arm, bringing it down with a yell.

Sergeant Castle gave the order to fire and then retreat. He took one last look at the warriors coming for him, and ran like his arse was on fire. First seeing soldiers lining the wall, their muskets aimed and ready to fire, he then saw a company of muskets come through the newly opened gate. "Straight to the gate, lads. Anyone gets shot buys the whiskey."

As soon as the last of the Marines was past the kneeling soldiers, Gladwin gave the order to fire. Sergeant Mulhern followed suit, and the muskets on the wall belched out fire, smoke, and death. The pursuing warriors met a concentrated wall of lead, and five of them went down as the volleyed fire tore through their ranks. They stopped their pursuit, and retreated back to the trees.

One brave took a last shot before joining the others. Sergeant Tiny Castle stopped by the front of the gate; as he turned around, he flinched from the sting of a musket ball gliding across his shoulder, leaving a furrow of torn skin and muscle before sinking into the wooden gate. His blood seeping through his fingers as he held the wound, he faced his squad. With a scowl on his face, Castle snarled, "Bloody hell. Looks like I'm buying the feckin' whiskey." His scowl quickly became a grin.

Sergeant Castle reported to Major Gladwin that the forts at Sandusky, St. Joseph, and Miami had all fallen to the tribal coalition within two weeks. Sandusky and St. Joseph were simply overrun, and the fifteen-man garrisons of each were slaughtered, along with any British traders and settlers in the area. At Fort Miami, the commander was lured out of the fort by his Miami mistress and killed. The garrison surrendered, but five of them were taken for burning; the other nine were allowed to leave and made their way to Fort Pitt.

Further east, Fort Venango, Fort LeBoeuf, and Fort Presque Isle became the victims of the warring tribes. In the north, the fort at Michilimackinac was taken by trickery as the Ojibway, while playing a game of stickball, entered the fort in force to retrieve their ball. Fifteen of the thirty-five soldiers were killed, and five more were tortured and burned. Captain Justice was one of those captured, but was taken by an Ojibway chief (and later adopted into the tribe).

The noise from over a thousand warriors celebrating throughout the night kept most of the garrison awake, the exception being Mulhern. Liam looked over to his snoring friend and smiled to himself. At least I won't trouble him tonight with my nightmare, he thought. He went outside, and climbed up into the blockhouse to Wahta and Major Gladwin.

"They sure are a lively bunch," said Liam.

"Ah, Mr. Mallory, couldn't sleep either, I see. They do seem rather pleased," replied Gladwin. "Wahta? What is this word – Obwandiyag – I keep hearing them shout?"

"That is Pontiac's Ottawa name. It is a sign of their devotion," answered Wahta.

"If he wins here, or at Fort Pitt, he'll have the rest of the fence sitters calling out his name sure as I'm standing here," said Liam.

Gladwin nodded his head. "Yes, but what he doesn't know is that there is a two-hundred man relief force on its way here. That was the only good news that Marine sergeant reported. The relief column should arrive in a couple of days. I know the captain in command; he's a no-nonsense sort of man. So, it seems, my friend that we won't need to send you and your friends out amongst the enemy, except maybe in the forefront of a sortie to break this damn siege."

Pontiac sat at the campfire, talking with Eluwilussit about the teachings of the Delaware prophet Neolin, and how best to use them to gather even more control of the tribes. It was hard for Pontiac to completely ignore the adulation, but he knew that he would lose the ever-fickle crowd, unless Detroit fell.

His chief advisor, Megegagik, arrived, and sat next to Eluwilussit. He reported to Pontiac: "I bring news. A large force of British soldiers is on the way. I do not think we can stop them from entering the fort."

Pontiac nodded, and smilingly said, "We do not need to stop them. They will come out for us, and we will be waiting."

****

Major Gladwin knew that Captain Dalyell did not like to be on the defensive, so it was not a great surprise when two days after arriving with the relief force, Dalyell suggested rather heatedly that the time to strike was at dawn the following day. What did surprise the Major was that Liam and Mulhern both agreed with him.

"Pontiac knows we're going to hit him, but he doesn't know when. The sooner we strike, the less chance he will find out, and the less time he has to prepare," said Liam.

"All right, gentlemen," responded Gladwin, "we attack at dawn. Captain Dalyell will be in command. I suggest using the river gate, as it is less visible than the front."

Sergeant Castle cleared his throat. "Major, Sir. Me and me boys would like to take part. We haven't had a chance at a proper fight, and we are a mite riled at what happened to our mates. Sir."

"Very well, Sergeant. Your squad will form the rear," said Major Gladwin. "Anything else, gentlemen?"

Liam pointed to Wahta, and smilingly said to Tiny, "Now, don't let any of your men take a shot at my friend here. Wahta gets a mite riled when someone shoots at him." The ensuing laughter broke the somber mood of the gathered officers – although aware of the risks of a pre-dawn raid, they were determined to break this siege and cripple Pontiac's confederation of tribes.

****

Pontiac knew that his change in plan would violate a main point of his strategy for the tribes' independence from the white man – but he was learning that it was sometimes necessary for those in power to bend, or even discard, the rules. His spyglass, a gift from the captain of a French trading vessel, was one example of the white man's ingenuity that he was not ready to give up. He carried it as he climbed up into the oak tree, which gave him a vantage point to keep an eye on the British. As the eastern sky horizon heralded the new day's first light, Pontiac focused on the fort's far wall. There was little activity at the front gate, but he noticed the many soldiers forming up near the river gate. 'So, I was correct in thinking you would make your move tonight,' he said to himself while clambering down from his perch. He walked to Megegagik and told him, "Ready your men, and make sure they remain hidden. I will join you shortly, to lead the charge."

****

Liam, Wahta, and Mulhern left the fort through a small opening in the north wall, behind the kitchen building, intending to scout the area between the open killing ground and the main encampment of the tribes. They hid behind a large fallen log to watch the early morning activity of the camp.

"Something's not right," said Mulhern, "I don't see many warriors; only women and children."

"No sentries either," answered Liam. "What is Pontiac up to now? Let's go back to the river, I've a feeling we're in trouble." They moved as quickly and quietly as possible, as they made their way toward the approaching troops. They saw Captain Dalyell in the lead, when the terrifying screams of attacking Indians shattered the quiet of the morning.

As Pontiac watched the soldiers cross the small creek, he waited for the last of them to enter the knee deep water. Shouting his war cry, he led 300 Ottawa, Ojibway, Potawatomi, and Huron braves in a charge that caught the British by complete surprise along their right flank and rear. The result of the first volley killed eight soldiers, and sent the rest into a panicked flight back across the creek.

The Marines had just reached the creek when the attack came. At Tiny's command, they hurriedly got into formation and fired a volley into the group attacking the rear. Seeing the confusion, Captain Dalyell ran to the rear so to halt the retreat and to re-form the line. A musket ball tore through his chest and killed him instantly, the victorious Huron racing to scalp his victim. Wahta reached the fallen captain just as Liam shot the Huron. While Liam fought with a madman's fury, his quiver now empty, his tomahawk a blur of motion, Wahta carried the body out of the battle and back to the fort.

Sergeant Castle sent his men to cover the retreat, while he ran to cover Wahta's retreat to the fort. He fatally shot one attacker. His next kill required hand-to-hand combat, grabbing the warriors tomahawk-wielding hand and snapping his wrist to force him to release the weapon into Tiny's other hand. One plunge upward and the warrior spouted blood from his ruined throat.

The attackers pressed their assault; the creek was soon full of the dead and wounded, the water now reflecting blood red by the rising sun. Having taken down three warriors, Mulhern was now battling with his tomahawk as he issued orders for the retreating troops to re-form and make for the fort. With no foes to his front, he turned to see how the retreat was progressing. Megegagik saw his chance, and charged. A shout from Liam alerted Mulhern, who he spun around in time to block the descending war club, but the force knocked him to his knees. Megegagik struck again with the club, hitting Mulhern in the back of the shoulder, but could not land the killing blow, as Mulhern kicked his foot out and tripped the attacker.

Liam ran to them, and with one hand helped Mulhern to his feet. With the other, he invited Megegagik to attack. Megegagik took one look at the gore-spattered face and arms of Snake Slayer, and backed away.

Watching the rout and retreat from the river front blockhouse, Major Gladwin ordered the men on the wall to fire a volley. He also ordered the three mortars to fire, landing their shots just beyond the creek. The last to reach the gate was Liam, who stood looking out over the horde of attackers. Pontiac ordered a halt to the pursuit, as the mortar and musket fire was too intense. He caught Liam's eye, raised his hand in salute, and made his way back to the encampment and another victory dance.

When Major Gladwin determined that Pontiac had withdrawn, he sent out a party to retrieve the wounded and dead under the protection of the three-pound cannon. The number of casualties was twenty dead and thirty-four wounded – these were over twenty per cent of the force sent out.

"Pontiac knows for sure he has us bottled up, now that he has foiled this attempt," Mulhern told Gladwin.

Major Gladwin, his face showing both stress and weeks-long food rationing, replied, "Yes, Sergeant, that would seem to be the case, but we have one more play to make. Please ask Liam and Wahta to join us in my quarters after they've cleaned up. How is your shoulder?"

"Naught but a bruise, though I imagine it'll hurt like blazes tomorrow," answered Mulhern.

****

"Gentlemen, please be seated," began Major Gladwin, as Liam, Wahta, and Mulhern entered his quarters. "Captain Dalyell carried a dispatch from the commander at Fort Niagara. A new schooner, HMS Huron, will soon be sailing Lake Erie and will be heading our way with supplies in a few weeks. I think we can hold out that long, but it will mean cutting the rations again –though the addition of what Dalyell brought will certainly help."

Liam ran his hands through his still wet hair and said, "Being a little ignorant about boats and such, I need to ask, does the Huron have a chance to get through? Pontiac is sure to try and stop it, and he's been damned good at spoiling our plans."

"A very good chance," answered Gladwin. "Dalyell saw the ship from a distance; from what he could tell, she has eight to ten cannon, plus there will be a party of Marines aboard as well. That should be enough to repel whatever Pontiac sends against her."

****

The next few weeks saw increased dissent among Pontiac's allies, as the siege wore on and the thrills of the past victories waned. If he didn't achieve a victory here soon, there was real danger that the coalition would dissolve. He had already heard rumblings of seeking peace with the British, a possibility he would contemplate on his terms – not the terms of the British, or of these cowardly malcontents.

He had planned a surprise assault, but the best time for it never presented itself. He observed Snake Slayer and Wahta patrol the fort's perimeter in the early morning, so there was little good chance to deploy his forces. When he did make an attempt, it was discovered, and soon the mortars from the fort would fire. Now, he learned of the approach of a British ship, and how it had fended off an attack of ten war canoes, with a blistering round of canister shot from eight cannon, and well-timed volleys from the Marines.

If the arrival of additional British supplies was not enough to convince Pontiac to abandon the siege, then the message he just received from the French commander at Fort de Chartres certainly was. While the French fervently hoped for Pontiac to win, they could not send any aid or help.

****

Liam smiled at his friends, as Mulhern helped Wahta away from the railing of the schooner. "Good thing this is gonna be a short trip," he said, "else our poor momma bear would be nothing but hide and bones."

Wahta had continued to lose his enormous breakfast, his discomfort with the large ship's motion having begun soon after HMS Huron left the dock at Fort Detroit. Once it was determined that Pontiac had indeed abandoned the siege, Liam and his companions boarded the schooner for a trip to the eastern shore of Lake Erie. Sergeant Tiny Castle and his Marines joined them, as they began the trek back to their Fort Niagara unit.

The plan was to land somewhere south of Fort Presque Isle, as the fort itself had fallen to Pontiac's allies. From there, they would ride to Fort Pitt, and then continue to Mallory Town.

During one of their early morning patrols, they discovered the abandoned main encampment; some of the tribes were heading back to their villages. The majority still followed Pontiac, as he headed to a new center of operations on the Maumee River. From there, he planned to solidify his hold on the lands his people had recovered from the British. Pontiac also intended to send a large force to join up with the Seneca chief, Guyasuta, and the tribes now surrounding Fort Pitt.

The captain of the Huron took a long look through his spyglass, and ordered the ship to dock at Fort Presque Isle. It appeared that the victors had abandoned the fort, after defeating the garrison there. This was a definite plus, as this meant they would be able to disembark their horses more easily than if they had to swim them ashore. Wahta fell to the ground as he stepped off the gangplank, and swore to the Great Spirit that he would never board another watercraft larger than a war canoe.

Liam shook Tiny's hand. "You and your men are welcome to join us. We could use fighting men with us when we get to Fort Pitt."

Tiny smiled, the deep lines in his face rolling up like a small wave across his face. "Ah, laddie, as tempting as that is, me an' me boys have had enough of tromping through the woods. That's fer infantry sloggers and donkey wallopers. Marines belong on the deck of a ship, where we can see the bastards trying to kill us."

Even though there were still six hours of daylight, they set up camp for the night, so that the horses could calm after their time aboard ship, and for Wahta to recover a little strength.

Liam grabbed his bow and said, "Gonna see if I can find us some supper, otherwise we're stuck with Mulhern's cooking. I must say that it feels good to be back on our own land again."

"Aye," replied Mulhern, "though I've a hankering to see those big pines again. Now, as to supper, you better find something big, our momma bear hasn't eaten in three days. Now that his feet is gracing God's green earth again, I'm thinking he may be a bit peckish." Wahta could only look at them and groan as he laid back down, still too weak from his ordeal to reply.

Chapter 16

Fort Pitt – Mallory Town
Fort Pitt – October 1763

While the siege of Fort Pitt had little effect on Jimmy Two Birds, the same could not be said for the garrison. Half rations for three weeks made for a rise in surliness and a fall in morale, so the fort welcomed the news that British relief was coming. The mood was worse among the gathered tribes; the lack of success – or even activity – led to increasing restlessness. When a Delaware brave reported to Guyasuta that a large British relief column approached, he leapt at the opportunity; nearly the entire besieging force left camp to intercept them. The ensuing battle saw Guyasuta's warriors inflict severe casualties. Nonetheless, the British reached Fort Pitt, where Guyasuta's siege ended.

****

Liam, Mulhern, and Wahta were unaware of these developments as they made their way south. While crossed an open meadow, Wahta reined in his horse and signaled for quiet – but the band of ten Delaware braves had already seen them, and were even now rushing forward. With little time to react, but having the advantage on horseback, the three pulled their tomahawks from their belts, kicked their mounts, and charged the oncoming Delaware. Wahta swung down and struck the brave reaching up to pull him from the saddle, knocking him to the ground under the charging hooves of Liam's horse. One brave grabbed Liam's arm so that he lost his grasp of his tomahawk. Reaching back to his quiver, he drew an arrow and stabbed his attacker in the eye. In a matter of seconds, they passed the Delaware – but before they were out of range, a thrown tomahawk hit Mulhern in the back of his shoulder, the blade embedding through the fabric of his coat and in his back. The force of the impact threw him forward in the saddle; he lost his grip on the reins, but hung on by the horse's mane. Liam slowed to ride next to Mulhern; he and Wahta kept Mulhern upright as they rode away, not daring to stop until they had outraced their foes (though it appeared that the Delaware were not keen to pursue). When they reached a safe distance from their attackers, they stopped and gently helped Mulhern dismount.

"Now, laddies," he said through gritted teeth, "would you please be a-getting this thing out of my back?" They rigged up a travois for Mulhern, whose shoulder was certainly broken in addition to the deep wound that required stitching. They were only a day away from Fort Pitt, so Liam rode ahead. Not knowing that the siege was over, he was pleasantly surprised to find the gate open and the bustle of everyday activity. Turning his mount around, he galloped back to Wahta and Mulhern to tell them the news. Mulhern immediately responded, "Then, why are we dawdling around talking? I need a drink, stitches, and a sling; in that order, if you please."

****

Two Birds gave Mulhern the backroom of the tavern to convalesce. Liam left to report to the garrison commander, while Wahta stayed with Mulhern to "make sure the little Irishman doesn't roll out of bed."

The post surgeon set his scalpel and probe aside; having readied the needle, he was ready to stitch the wound closed. As he opened the wound to properly clean it, Mulhern endured the process with nary a whimper – he had toasted the health of Two Birds with each of five glasses of Irish whiskey.

When Liam returned to the tavern, Two Birds handed him the letter that had arrived almost a year ago; with all the trouble stirred up by Pontiac, it hadn't been possible to forward it along to any of the western forts. Carrying a mug of ale, Liam bade Two Birds good night and went to the room he shared with Mulhern and Wahta. He set a lantern on the table next to his cot, and opened the letter.

Daniel's letter told Liam of the state of affairs at Mallory Town and of the occasional exchange of gunfire with Seneca or Delaware. Then, the handwriting changed. Rebecca wrote just a few words: *I am with child. Hurry home, my love.* Liam sputtered, and coughed out a mouthful of ale. "I'm gonna be a father. Wait, this was sent a year ago. I *am* a father!"

Mallory Town – October 1763

Albert Jackson Mallory busily suckled at Rebecca's breast, while his twin Liam Caleb slept at her side to await his turn; they'd had grown too big for her to hold and feed at the same time. Jack took Rebecca's finger as she waggled it in front of his eyes and smiled as the nipple popped out of his mouth, his mother's milk dripping down his chin. Rebecca mused to herself that, at eighteen months, their personalities were becoming more apparent. Jack smiled a lot, cried very little, and was usually content to stay wherever he was placed. Caleb, on the other hand, smiled rarely, but twisted and turned toward everyone or everything he could see or hear. Now that they were more mobile, Caleb would try to sneak away from their blanket on the floor, but Jack's whimpering would alert Rebecca. Sometimes, however, even Jack would fail to notice that Caleb had gone off. Rebecca recalled to herself a morning just last week, when she found Caleb bumping his head against the door trying to get outside. She really felt Liam's absence during these quiet times in the evening and morning; it was when she most resented George Washington. "I know it's not Mr. Washington's fault that your father is so good at what he does," Rebecca said to Jack as she laid him down. "As for you, Caleb," Rebecca whispered as she picked him up, "I almost feel sorry for the woman who falls in love with you. You're going to be just like your father."

During the day, Rebecca was far too busy for private thoughts; the children and the bakery consumed her attention. Marsha Crane was more involved now with the day-to-day business of the bakery, which left Margaret more time to be a doting grandmother. She did what she could to comfort Rebecca; Margaret understood how Rebecca felt, having been through the same thing with her Albert before he was wounded. Both he and Liam had wandering spirits; it had taken Albert a while to adjust. They knew Liam was not ready yet to settle down.

At mid-morning, most of the day's baking was either in or freshly out of the ovens. Liza took Meagan outside, while Marsha and Margaret finished up in the shop. Rebecca and Deborah brought their children over; the cousins would play together while the grownups talked. Thomas, the oldest at seven, had gathered a pile of sticks and was attempting to fashion a log cabin, with help from Caleb. Jack, Meaghan, and Bowie were more interested in the fallen leaves tossed by the breeze. The sounds of sawing and hammering came across the common, as the new church neared completion.

Rebecca looked up from the children as Reverend Shields approached the bakery. "Ahh, the aroma from here is just heavenly," said Shields as he took in a long breath, "certainly much more bearable than the smell of sawdust and sweat. As the Good Lord provided loaves and fishes for the masses, I hope to do the same, at least the loaves part. I have a hungry crew to feed today."

Rebecca smiled and replied, "Certainly, Mr. Shields, my mother is inside and will see that your crew is well fed."

"Thank you," he said as he entered the shop.

"It will be nice when the church is finished," said Deborah, "though I do not find the good preacher's Puritan-tinged sermons very beneficial."

A shout from Thomas at Bowie, as the one year old was about to crawl into his cabin under construction, drew the women's attention. The crisis was averted by Thomas, who scooped up a happily shrieking Bowie. Coming out of the bakery with a basket filled with fresh baked bread, Reverend Shields exclaimed, "Ladies, your children are just delightful, and are the images of health itself."

"Why, thank you," replied Liza, "we are blessed in that regard."

"All by God's good grace, of course," said Shields, who then turned his attention to Rebecca. "Miss Rebecca? When shall we expect Liam to return? I would very much like to see you two properly wed, in the eyes of God and of these good people."

Momentarily taken aback, Rebecca calmed herself before answering, "Liam and I are already properly wed, in the eyes of God and of these good people. But thank you for your very considerate offer, Mr. Shields."

"I am sorry you feel that way and I assure you that you have not heard the last of this immorality," Shields snarled and walked away.

"I really detest that man," said Rebecca as she reached down and gently plucked a leaf out of Jack's hand as he began to put it in his mouth.

"From what Daniel tells me, the good reverend and Micah Townsend have been little by little swinging the townsfolk to their ideas of how to run this village," said Deborah, "and Daniel doesn't like much of what they propose; especially the notion that the church should have more say in how we run our lives."

Liza nodded her head and added, "Henry and I think it's more for power than any religious belief. He's also a little concerned with how the tribes are being treated by the British, and is talking about stepping up patrols in the area again."

"We've each of us lost parents and family in the war," said Rebecca, "I surely hope we have some peace for a while."

Fort Pitt – early November 1763

Liam found it hard to wait, but knew it was for the best. Even so, in a moment of frustration, he yelled to no one in particular, "Pierre can take care of him as well or better than any army doc!"

"Aye, that may be so," said Mulhern, "and I know how you feel – but, laddie, it's only a couple more days. If truth be told, I'm starting to feel my age. These old bones can use the extra rest before venturing out again. And, if I know you, Liam, darling, it won't be long before you're dragging me and momma bear out on another adventure."

Liam looked down at his old friend, and smiled. His frustration soothed, he responded, "Sergeant, take all the time you need. Since we're on the subject, I am feeling that pull to go back to Cantuckee. Not right away of course, but the buffalo dreams have returned. Huritt is still out there."

Three days later, Two Birds filled the wagon with goods for Mallory Town; it would return with a load of Timothy's finest. Upon leaving, Mulhern rode in the wagon, his horse tethered and following behind him. As his left arm was in a sling, every bounce sent a jolt of pain to his very tender shoulder. Liam rode ahead, his excitement building with each passing mile.

As he exited the forest edge and entered the open ground surrounding the settlement, he was surprised by the new buildings, and newly-cleared farmland outside the walls of the post. Ignoring the stares of some newly-arrived settlers, he trotted through the gate and headed straight to the bakery. As Liam entered the cabin, Rebecca, holding Albert, squealed with delight, which in turn started the baby crying. Rushing over to her, Liam hugged them both, and took the baby in his arms and kissed him. "Liam, this is your son, Albert Jackson," said Rebecca, "and if you would care to come to our room, you will find his brother, Liam Caleb, asleep in his crib."

Pontiac's Camp, near Fort Ontario
July 1766

In 1764, the British entered an agreement with most of the tribes in the Ohio-Michigan territory; while there were still sporadic fighting and raids, the frontier was as peaceful as it had ever been. The following two years took their toll on Pontiac, who aged considerably. He lost most of his allies along the way. Understanding that he would not create his empire, Pontiac nonetheless was content that, at the very least, he had forced the British to recall Amherst. The new governor had begun a relationship with many of the tribes that was closer to the French approach.

Pontiac came to Fort Ontario to meet with the British Commissioner of Native Affairs, Colonel William Johnson, and to sign a formal treaty of peace. Liam came for the ceremony with Daniel, Mulhern, and Wahta. Of the many dignitaries who were on hand for the ceremony, Pontiac was most anxious to see Liam. The day before the conference was due to end, his opportunity finally came. He arrived at Liam's tent just as Liam and Mulhern were saying goodbye to Wahta, who was heading back to his family in Donehogawa's village on the Mohawk River.

"Snake Slayer," said Wahta, "our journeys are not yet finished. I have had a vision of us walking through a vast grassland, heading toward mountains that touch the sky." Turning to Mulhern, he quipped, "So, it is up to you, little Irishman, to keep Snake Slayer safe until momma bear returns."

Pontiac watched the Mohawk warrior walk away, motioned for his bodyguard to leave him, and approached Liam. "Snake Slayer, my brother, and my foe," he said, "for a little while we have peace once more. I wonder how long it will last. You whites never seem satisfied with things the way they are. How many times have we signed treaties with our British fathers, only to have them ignored soon after?"

"Pontiac, honored chief," replied Liam, "it is good to see you other than in battle. I am glad that peace is here again. I am tired of fighting, but, like you, I have my doubts as to how long it will continue. It will be impossible to keep settlers from moving farther and farther west as time passes, despite the treaty. What will you do, now that the hatchet has been buried?"

"My position among the tribes is now gone, thanks in some part to you and your valiant companions," Pontiac said, grinning, "but it is as Manitou wills it – though I do not understand why. I am reluctant to return home. There are many among the tribes who blame me for our failure, and would see me dead. I will go to the Illinois country, and rest for a while. If Manitou allows, I will cross the Mother of Rivers and visit my brothers, the Lakota."

Liam reached out; setting aside any lingering enmity, he grasped Pontiac by the forearms, warrior to warrior. "Farewell, my brother. I hope Manitou grants health and peace to you. Perhaps we will meet again."

Mallory Town 1766

Ten year old Thomas Joseph Clarke was used to his sister Meagan (now four years of age), and his toddler cousins — Bowie, Abigail, Jack, and Caleb, (ages four, two and three respectively) – following him around every day while he patrolled the interior walls of the town. Today would be different, however, as Thomas was going on his first patrol outside the village walls with Timothy, William Crane, and his best friend, Samuel Webb. He received his own musket shortly after the raid – when he was saved by Albert Jameson – and became a better shot every day.

Now that the village was growing, Daniel and Henry rarely went out to patrol, and became more involved with the planning and governance of the community. Every month saw more people arrive; some elected to stay, while others opted to venture further west. It had even become necessary to remove the southern wall to accommodate the growing population. With the arrival and settling of a preacher, construction began on a church, and a schoolhouse planned. A large garden – filled with flowers, shrubs, and a variety of herbs for everyone's use – filled the central courtyard.

****

"My word, Mary," said Oliver as they entered through the western gate, "would you look at this place? I feel like a barbarian Gaul on his first sight of Rome."

"I'll take that as a compliment," said Liza as she ran to hug Mary. "What a surprise! I am so happy to see you two. What in the world would have you leave Wolf Pond?"

"Progress, I guess you could call it," replied Mary. "Hunting and trapping get a little harder when the settlers start pouring in. Now that the Indian threat is over, the countryside is filling with plows, milk cows, and barns."

"Looks like the same thing is happening here," added Oliver. "Now, Liza, my dear, do you have room for a couple of travel weary nomads? I 'spect we'll be staying for a month or so before moving on."

"Of course we do," said Liza. "Now, come on over to the store. Henry and Daniel will be thrilled to see you two again."

The arrival of the Fords set off a frenzied rush to set up a welcome feast. The warm August night allowed tables and chairs to be arranged outside to accommodate everyone – including Liam and Mulhern, who had just recently returned from Fort Ontario. Talk at dinner turned to the Mohawk, and how much was changing now that settlers were beginning to flood the Albany area.

Daniel asked about the chances of survival. Oliver's response was animated. "Not good. Not good at all. This migration of whites changes everything; the forests will be plowed under, and the rivers and creeks will be harnessed for mills. Turkeys and other game are already disappearing." He paused for a few seconds, and added, "The Iroquois League is already coming apart, what with the Seneca trouble. I believe this will be the final straw. The tribes – all of them, not only the Mohawk – will be forced to either move further west or north, or become what the Black Robes started, a people stripped of their way of life."

The Fords also brought one other piece of news: Donehogawa was dying. The aged chief and spiritual guide had barely survived an outbreak of cholera a year ago, and was now a frail shell of the man he once was. So it was that Pierre decided to return to the Mohawk River village. Pierre wanted to live the rest of his life among the people he had come to love so many years ago. He felt bound to the life and success of Mallory Town, but with the arrival of a real doctor, his medical skills were no longer needed. It was painful for him to leave, and there were many tears shed – especially between Liza and Pierre. Soon, his canoe disappeared around the bend, and the village returned to its normal activity – except for Mulhern, who stood by the river for a long time, tears running down his weathered face. With a final sigh, he pulled out his flask. Extending his arm to the sky, he drank and toasted, "To one of the finest humans on God's green earth."

****

Liam returned to his cabin. He stood in the doorway, watching Jack and Caleb playing on the floor. Their antics and attendant giggles were infectious, and Liam soon found himself on the floor, the two boys climbing over him and begging to be tickled. Rebecca sat in her chair and smiled at her family, knowing that soon Liam would be off again with Mulhern to spend the winter trapping and hunting down in Cantuckee. The sight of him frolicking with his sons triggered a feeling that she wanted to present Liam with another child when he returned in the spring. Well, she thought, we have maybe three months before he leaves. Plenty of time, and there is no time like the present.

Liam looked up at her smiling face. "What are you grinning about?"

"Oh, I was just enjoying seeing the three of you having so much fun," she replied while getting to her feet, "but I think it is nap time for the little ones." She winked at Liam, and added, "I think we could use a nap as well."

Epilogue

Mallory Town – December 1766

Ethan Daniel Mallory cried for all his eight pound body was worth as the midwife handed him to Deborah. Sweat soaked, tired but happy, Deborah looked over her baby boy and placed him on her breast. His crying ceased as he began to suckle. Daniel walked to the bed, having finally been allowed to enter the room by the midwife he deemed overly officious. He bent down, kissed his wife on the forehead, and gently placed his left hand on his nursing son. Liza entered a few minutes later, carrying Daniel's two year old daughter, Abigail; his eldest son, four year old Bowie trailed behind. Daniel took Ethan from Deborah, eliciting a cry of protest from the newborn and held him out to introduce him to his siblings. Abigail climbed on Daniel's lap for a closer look. Feeling a little left out. Bowie pulled himself onto his father's other knee. Daniel handed the baby to Liza and hugged his other children, his tears falling onto their heads. "He's a fine looking boy," Liza said to Deborah as she placed Ethan into her hands, "such a beautiful family. Mother and Father would be very pleased, I think, with our brood and with our efforts to build for the future." Still holding the children, Daniel stood and took a deep breath to regain his composure. "Aye, sister, we have made a good beginning; a good beginning, indeed."

Cantuckee – Late February 1767

Fresh snowfall covered the grassland, burying the needed forage under six new inches of white powder. Many in the herd used their sturdy foreheads to sweep the snow away, while some pawed their way to the brown grass below. Needing some time alone, Otetiani had left Sergeant Mulhern back at the base camp this morning. The nightmares had returned each night for the last week or so, and were becoming more disturbing. Last night's baleful dream was the worst yet, Otetiani waking screaming and in a cold sweat, shaking with fear. The last image of a body, he couldn't tell who it was, impaled on a set of buffalo horns; the look on the victim's face, extreme anguish in its eyes – and then a wave of dark emotions seemed to roll over him, a sinuous apparition rising from his body. That image stayed with him even after being awake, lurking on the edges of his thoughts.

As he walked along the edge of the prairie, Otetiani spied grazing buffalo up ahead. One large bull, however, was not grazing. He watched the approach of a Shawnee hunter, dressed in the hide and head of a buffalo and armed with a lance and a musket, crawling on all fours toward the herd. The bull then swung his head toward Otetiani, who emerged from his haunted thoughts. Otetiani reached for his tomahawk, but realized he was armed only with his knife.

The Shawnee hunter caught the movement in the corner of his eye, and saw Otetiani trudging through the snow heading toward the bull buffalo he stalked. When Huritt recognized Otetiani, he let out a yell. "Snake Slayer! It is time for me to kill you." At first, Otetiani froze in his tracks on hearing that voice. Abruptly, and just in time, he dove to the side as Huritt rose up and fired his musket. The lead ball hit Otetiani in the back portion of his upper left arm. Fortunately, it went through his arm without hitting any bones or large blood vessels. He grabbed into the pouch around his waist, and hurriedly stuffed some goose down in the hole while he pondered his next move.

Huritt looked at the buffalo. A flicker of recognition, and he understood: this animal was special to Snake Slayer, this was his spirit brother. He picked up his lance and headed toward the bull, racing as fast as he could while shedding the buffalo robe to lighten his steps. Otetiani, too, ran to the bull, holding his left arm. The buffalo watched Huritt advancing to him, and remained still, seemingly offering itself to the plunging blade of the lance. He remained standing as he bellowed in agony, the lance entering his upper front shoulder, the force of the thrust sending it past the ribs and into the heart.

Otetiani screamed and threw himself at Huritt, who drew his tomahawk and swung it at Otetiani's undefended chest. It scraped across, gouging a long shallow cut from left breast to almost his right hip. Otetiani crashed into Huritt, picking him up slightly and pushing him back. Huritt tried to regain his balance, but fell back toward the buffalo – until the force of buffalo horns impaled him, ripping through his groin and chest. The dying buffalo collapsed, his legs folding beneath him. The force of the buffalo hitting the ground drove the horns even further through Huritt's mangled body. Huritt looked over at Otetiani and with his last remaining strength pulled a necklace over his head and in a quivering voice said, "Give this to my uncle, Pucksinwah." He gasped as a wave of pain coursed through his body, "tell him it is over." He mouthed a silent agonized scream, as his body twitched twice and then was still.

Otetiani lay on his stomach, the blood from his wounds staining the ground around him a light crimson, the cold of the snow slowing the flow. He looked eye to eye with the buffalo, their farewells wordless. When the buffalo's eyes closed at last, Otetiani sobbed – until finally, he surrendered to mental and physical exhaustion, and fell asleep.

As he lay in the snow, Otetiani drifted in and out of consciousness; he wasn't sure if he was awake or asleep when he had another visit from his brother, the buffalo. This time there was also a woman; Orenda stood beside the buffalo, holding a baby in her arms and smiling at

Otetiani. In a lilting, ethereal voice, she said, "Otetiani, my love, do not grieve for us any longer. Remember us, yes, but do so in the happiness that we shared together. Let go of the rage that eats at your heart, and turns you into a man you are not. Cherish *us* in your heart, not the hatred." A mist rose around them; from what seemed like a great distance, Otetiani heard Orenda say, "Farewell, my love, we are always with you."

Otetiani found that he was now sitting, tears streaming down his face. He raised his left arm to wipe his eyes, forgetting for a moment the wound in his shoulder. The pain brought him back to reality. He saw through his tears a buffalo calf standing where Orenda and the old bull had been in the dream. In a playful gallop, it came over to Otetiani, licked his hand and then scampered back to the herd. The pain from his wounds increased when he stood up; it took a moment before he was able to start walking. He stood over the body of the buffalo and with his arms upraised committed his brother's spirit to his creator. He then turned to Huritt's gored body and as gently as he could lifted it off of the horns and placed him on the ground. Not having the means to bury Huritt, he left him lying next to the buffalo taking the necklace saying, "Farewell, I will do as you ask." While Otetiani continued looking at the body of the enemy he had pursued for so long and for so many miles, the rage and the hatred he carried in his mind – those twin qualities of destruction that ate away at his soul, which had become the driving force of his life – seemed to melt from his heart.

The bleating sound of the calf drew Otetiani's attention. He watched as it moved away, occasionally leaping into a zig-zagging trot. He hadn't a care in the world. Then, Otetiani noticed a splash of white fur on the right shoulder of the calf. It was the size and shape of the lance wound Huritt inflicted on the old bull. Otetiani smiled broadly. "Farewell for now, my brother," he called out, and began the hike back to the camp.

"Glyn," Liam called as he stumbled into camp, "had a bit of trouble, be a good soul and help me take care of this wound. May need to sew it in a couple spots – before you start sticking me, let me have a mug of Tim's ale."

"Been meaning to talk to you about that," said Glyn as he helped Liam to lie down, "we're almost out. Cracked open the last barrel yesterday. My, that is a nasty looking cut there, kinda messes up your good looks. I take it that Huritt is dead?"

"How did you know this happened with Huritt?" asked Liam.

"You think I could sleep through that dream you had last night? I had a feeling that today was gonna be it, and then you barely make it back to camp all carved up like a side of pork. To top it off, you have not stopped smiling since you got here," Glyn answered, handing a full mug to Liam.

"It is hard to explain, but since I woke after the fight, I have felt unburdened in my mind. I can think of Orenda without falling into remorse, and what is more puzzling is that I keep thinking about Rebecca," Liam replied and then chuckled. "As to our supply of life-giving elixir, I think it's time we head back to civilization. Give me a couple days to recover, and then we'll be off. I think the time has come for me to finally settle down."

Illinois Territory –1769

Near the village of Cahokia, Pontiac is assassinated by a warrior of the Peoria tribe.

Boston – 1770

The mood in the colonies slowly but relentlessly turned against the British, and the high-handed manner of the Crown and Parliament. Many felt the tax and tariff policies now foisted upon them were unjust. Of course, the British felt perfectly justified in demanding that the colonies help pay for the war against the French. Sam Adams' favorite tavern was a breeding ground for strong talk against the British. It wasn't long before talk of rebellion dominated the conversation.

The End

Cast of Characters   (Historical figures in **bold**)

Mallory family

Thomas born 1709 – family patriarch
Abigail born 1712 – family matriarch
Daniel born 1730 – eldest son of Thomas/Abigail
Liam born 1732 – youngest son of Thomas/Abigail
Elizabeth (Liza) born 1734 – eldest daughter of Thomas/Abigail
Grace born 1754 – youngest daughter of Thomas/ Abigail

Relatives and friends of the Mallory family

Joseph Clarke – family friend
Henry Clarke born 1731 – son of Joseph – marries Liza
Thomas Joseph Clarke born 1756 – son of Henry/Liza
Meagan Jane Clarke born 1762 – daughter of Henry/Liza

Deborah Prescott born 1738 – wife of Daniel
Bowie Rhys Mallory born 1762 – son of Daniel/Deborah
Ethan Daniel Mallory born 1766 – son of Daniel/Deborah

Albert Jameson – friend of Liam
Margaret Jameson – wife of Albert
Rebecca Jameson born 1743 – daughter of Albert/Margaret – Liam's wife
Albert Jackson Mallory born 1762 - son of Liam/Rebecca
Liam Caleb Mallory born 1762 – son of Liam/Rebecca

Personnel at Trent's Trading Post

William Trent – militia Captain, serves as Washington's spy master
Pierre Baptist – former Black Robe, mentor to Liam
Phil Burke – businessman from Philadelphia
Timothy Winslow – brewer, scout in militia
Rob Carter – fur trader
Rafe Stump Nose Emerson – fur trader
Jack Tomlinson – teamster

Military

George Washington – Colonel, Virginia Militia
Edward Braddock – General, British Army – leader of first expedition to take Fort Duquesne
John Forbes – General British Army – leader of second expedition to take Fort Duquesne
Jeffrey Amherst – General British Army – leader of expedition to take Fort Ticonderoga

Gordon Doherty – British officer under Braddock and Munro
Glyn Mulhern – sergeant in British army
Marcus Octavius Winningham – scout in militia
George Munro – Commandant Fort William Henry
Alun Williams – Colonel British army
Charles LeFurge – lieutenant French army
Henry Gladwin – commandant Fort Detroit
Terrance Justice – commandant Fort Michilimackinac

Native Americans

Donehogawa - Mohawk chief
Onatah – wife of Donehogawa
Orenda – daughter of Donehogawa/Onatah – wife of Otetiani
Otetiani – Liam's Mohawk name
Wahta – Mohawk warrior
Teeyeehogrow – Mohawk name of adopted runaway slave Rufus
Chogan – Shawnee warrior
Huritt – Shawnee warrior
Pontiac – Ottawa war chief – leader of tribal confederation

Various others

Daniel Boone – teamster with Braddock expedition
Jimmy Two Birds Ouellette – French proprietor of tavern/brothel Fort Duquesne
Simon James Atkinson Turney – plantation owner in Virginia
Rufus Atkinson Turney – slave (later freed) of SJA Turney
Oliver & Mary Ford – hunters and part of Trent's team of information gatherers
Crane/Lapley/Webb families – early settlers of Mallory Town

Historical Note

The French and Indian War has been called (quite correctly, I think) the First World War; it was fought on the North American Continent, and on various battlefields in Europe, the West Indies, and on the Atlantic Ocean. The battles portrayed on the colonial American frontier are largely historically accurate; since this is a book of fiction, I exercised some poetic license in describing some details... after all; I needed to find things for my fictional characters to do. ☺ For those interested in the history of that war, I recommend *Empires at War* by William M. Fowler, Jr.

I included the conflict known as Pontiac's Rebellion (which technically occurred following the French and Indian War) for a couple of reasons. First, the rebellion was a direct result of British treatment of the native tribes after the French were defeated. Secondly, Pontiac's coalition was a harbinger of things to come under the Shawnee leader Tecumseh.

Concerning my renderings of the historical personages in the book; I tried to remain true to their personalities, as far as I could determine during my research. George Washington presented with the chance to show him as a young man; somewhat naïve and certainly idealistic, but who was learning how to lead an army in battle – traits that would serve him well in the future.

I hope you have enjoyed reading book one of The Mallory Saga. Their story continues in book two, Sundering of Empire, occurring during the American Revolutionary War. Any and all errors are the fault of the author, though he may flog his staff mercilessly in the mistaken belief that it was their fault. (Note: there is no staff besides my editor, and I'm scared of her.) ☺

If the mood strikes, or your Muse inspires you, please leave a review on Amazon, Goodreads, etc, etc. A short note of ecstatic praise will do. ☺

About the Author

Paul's education was of the public variety and when he reached Junior High he discovered that his future did not include the fields of mathematics or science. This was generally the case throughout his years in school as he focused more on his interest in history; not just the rote version of names and dates but the causes.

Paul studied Classical Civilization at Wayne State University with a smattering of Physical Anthropology thrown in for good measure. Logically, of course, Paul spent the next four decades drawing upon that vast store of knowledge working in large, multi-platform data centers, and is considered in the industry as a bona fide IBM Mainframe dinosaur heading for extinction.

Paul currently resides in the quaint New England town of Salem, Massachusetts with his wife, Daryl. The three children have all grown, in the process turning Paul's beard gray, and have now provided four grandchildren; the author is now going bald.

You can find Paul:

His Facebook page: https://www.facebook.com/Clash-of-Empires-1115407281808508/

On Twitter: @hooverbkreview

Email: mallorysaga@gmail.com

20871146R00127

Printed in Great Britain
by Amazon